Straker's Island

Also by Steve Harris

ADVENTURELAND

WULF

THE HOODOO MAN

ANGELS

BLACK ROCK

THE DEVIL ON MAY STREET

Straker's Island

STEVE HARRIS

VICTOR GOLLANCZ

LONDON

First published in Great Britain 1998
by Victor Gollancz
An imprint of the Cassell Group
Wellington House, 125 Strand, London WC2R 0BB

© Steve Harris 1998

The right of Steve Harris to be identified as author of
this work has been asserted by him in accordance with
the Copyright, Designs and Patents Act, 1988.

A catalogue record for this book is
available from the British Library.

ISBN 0 575 06582 6

Typeset by SetSystems Ltd, Saffron Walden, Essex
Printed in Great Britain by
St Edmundsbury Press Ltd, Bury St Edmunds, Suffolk

98 99 5 4 3 2 1

This One's For You
My Little Star
(You Mon-Star!)

Acknowledgements

As ever, a lot of people (some of them unwittingly) helped along the way, some with the support I needed so badly ('97 sure wasn't *my* best year!), some with practical matters and some with knowledge I didn't have but needed. So, thanks to: Elaine Cummings (the psychic with the power); Caroline 'I know I'm bootiful' Vaughan (she is, she is!); Joey 'I hate you Harse' Rattigan (for his insults); Charlene 'let me at 'em' DeVito (we'll be rich!); Phil and Anthony Lockley and Geoff 'let's do bombs' & Sarah 'I'm reading' Barrs (who all seem to like me for some unknown reason); Elizabeth Sites (for being the fount of all knowledge and a better writer than me!); Simon Wady (for his boundless enthusiasm and endless support); George Harding (we must have a drink!); Steve Crisp (for being a great artist and a great guy, too!); Jo Fletcher (for publishing this); Hazel Orme (for a neat edit); Lucy Ramsey (for publicity); Schelley L. Gallimore (for lots of support and enthusiasm); Elsie 'it's too hot' Rotenberg; the staff of the Hampton Inn, Sanford, FL; the staff of the Holiday Inn, Key West, FL; Tony Wheeler and his mad dog Bracken (for a fun day); Florence 'chilly mortal' Edmundo-Ross (for too much to list); the undernet psychics (for interesting readings); Ant Barker & Tanjen (we'll see what we can do!); all those I forgot to mention here (you know who you are!) and especially you, my readers, whoever and wherever you are. Thanks for everything!

Errors and inconsistencies in time, place, hair colour or weaponry are undoubtedly mine. I've screwed around a little with the geography of Florida: there is no Seaford. Everything else, however, is true! So let's go for a walk in the *very* black forest . . .

Chapter One

The Master of Disaster

1

'You won't come back this *time!'*

The six words, spat out as if they were poison, echoed up through the big, empty warehouse to where Jim Green hid, watching the action. Jim mouthed the words, tasting them as Hillsborough spoke them. He grinned and thought: *What do you know about anything, Bobby?*

Down on the warehouse floor, Bobby Hillsborough pumped a shell into the sawn-off. The noise of the slide being worked seemed much too loud – as if for a moment reality had pulled it into extreme close-up.

Hillsborough's back might have been turned to Jim Green, but Jim could see the expression on his face as plainly as the man to whom the remark was addressed must have seen it. Hillsborough's brow was sheened with sweat, and his face was contorted with rage and loathing – and something that just might have been fear.

You bet it's fear, Jim told himself distantly as he fought to record the action. *Walt Creasey might not look like anything special but he* is *a mutant, after all.*

The three men backing up Hillsborough – two brandishing handguns that looked big enough to drop elephants and the other clutching a Luger – all looked scared enough to puke.

Which wasn't so surprising, Jim supposed. Walt Creasey, the man in the dusty, torn business suit, who now had four guns pointing at him, mightn't have looked much, but there was something *wrong* with him. Something *very* wrong. Which was why the slightly built Creasey, who under normal circumstances looked about as frightening as the average

9

soft-furnishings salesman, had been so badly beaten. And why he was now tied to a wooden chair with thick rope.

Whatever you did to him, Creasey kept coming back.

And now something new was happening to him.

'What's going on, Bobby?' Merv Dodd asked hoarsely.

Mervyn Dodd was twenty-seven, Jim knew. He'd killed his first man at the age of seventeen in Palms, Los Angeles. He'd netted an expired Mastercard, twenty-seven dollars, three quarters and a handful of pennies. The jacket he'd had to throw away – because the guy's blood had spattered it – had been worth ninety-five bucks. Mervyn reckoned he was three years away from being a made man. Jim knew that Merv was going to die before all this was over. They were *all* going to die.

Jim Green would see to that.

'What's he doing? He's ... *vibrating!*' the guy with the Luger cried, taking a backward pace. This was Timmy Jones, aged twenty. He was going to die in an explosion. A very violent explosion.

You deserve it, too! Jim thought, putting Timmy out of his mind and concentrating on Walt Creasey, who was struggling ineffectually against his bonds. Until a month ago poor Walt had been an office manager at Winn-Dixie in Sanford, Florida. And then something had happened. Something terrible. Something that had brought him – in a series of stolen cars – all the way to Los Angeles. As yet Jim wasn't sure quite what that thing was. But he would find out before all this was done. He always did. Jim Green trusted himself implicitly.

Creasey wasn't just perspiring, he was drenched in sweat. His eyes were dark with fear, his cut and bruised face contorted with panic.

And he was shimmering slightly.

Jim frowned down at him. He looked very slightly blurred, as if Jim was seeing him through the lens of an out-of-focus camera.

'He's gonna do something!' Timmy yelled, backing off another pace.

Hillsborough glanced over at him and sneered at his apparent cowardice. 'He's trussed up like a fuckin' chicken, man. What th' fuck you think he's gonna do?' Hillsborough wasn't a man who possessed much of an imagination.

'You gotta let me go! You don't understand what you're doing to me! Let me go!' Creasey piped in a cracked voice.

Hillsborough thrust the barrel of the shotgun against his chest. 'Y'r goin' nowhere, Creasey, 'cept direc'ly to hell.'

Jim grinned, anticipating what was to come. It would end badly. Messily. It always did where he was involved. But Jim didn't care; he wasn't going to lose sleep over this kind of low-life pond-scum. Creasey, however, he felt sorry for and a distant part of him wondered if he should *do* something on Creasey's behalf. After all, he'd stood by taking notes as Creasey watched his daughter die. And then his wife. And three members of his staff at the supermarket.

You're getting soft! he admonished himself.

Down on the warehouse floor, Creasey's rate of vibration had increased. He was very blurred now. Not only did his face shimmer like the tines of a tuning fork that had just been struck but the vibration was giving off a clear tone, which may have been middle C. He was twisting his head back and forth, as if to escape what was happening to him.

'Bobby?' Timmy asked, in a faltering voice. 'What's happening?'

From somewhere outside the warehouse, Jim could hear the soft trilling of a telephone.

Bobby glanced over his shoulder at Timmy. He looked supremely confident. His face lit in a big grin. 'He's gettin' ready to die. That's all.' He turned back to Creasey. 'Ready, mutant?'

The sound that Creasey's body was emitting increased, drawing harmonics out of walls and pipes in the warehouse. Suddenly the entire building seemed to be wailing in sympathy with him.

Jim frowned as the tone of the telephone grew more strident. It didn't fit at all with the rising sound of Creasey and the warehouse as they built to a crescendo.

Who the fuck is calling now? he asked himself. *How the hell am I supposed to get any work done like this?*

Creasey now looked like half-solidified smoke. He was

11

writing in agony. Jim shook his head sadly. This monkey was going to heaven.

'Ohhhh! I can't stop it!' Creasey wailed, his voice taking its tone from the long, singing note his body was issuing. *It's too late! Too late!*'

Mervyn Dodd raised a hand to his head, glanced back over his shoulder as if the movement would lessen the noise of Creasey's shrieking. He saw Jim, way up at the back of the warehouse, and their eyes locked. Jim felt the accusation in that brief, hard stare and a long deep shudder ran down the length of his spine. *It's not* my *fault*, he wanted to yell to Dodd. *None of this is* my *fault!* But Dodd would have known that for the lie it was. The fact was, *everything* was Jim's fault. It always was. They didn't call him the Master of Disaster for nothing.

Dodd's nose gouted blood. He wiped his top lip, gazed at his hand for a moment as if he'd never seen blood before, then turned back to Creasey as if he'd forgotten Jim ever existed.

I did that, too, Jim told him mentally. *I made the rate of Creasey's vibration rise enough to bust those vessels in your nose.*

'F'r Crissakes, shoot 'im, Bobby!' Dodd yelled over the shriek. 'Quick, before he does something!'

Too late! Jim told him, and the demon inside him, the nasty little being who powered all this, capered around joyously, grinning fiercely.

Why wasn't someone answering that fucking phone?

Jim tried to ignore the ever-increasing urgency of the ringing.

Down below him, Walt Creasey stopped shimmering. He looked utterly relieved, as if he couldn't believe it was all over. His face lit with a big sappy smile. 'Phew!' he said, drawing a deep breath and releasing it with a shudder. 'It's okay,' he assured his captors. 'It's finished. It's all over!'

And his head exploded.

12

2

Jim Green, Master of Disaster, felt himself tear away from the warehouse. The bleating of the telephone did it to him every time – reached in a long electronic hand, got him by the scruff of his neck and yanked him back from wherever he was, whether it was Florida or Florence, Iceland or the Ice Age.

For a few seconds he was in two places at once: his mind back in his workroom (or the slaughter-house, as Sooty called it) and his subconscious in the warehouse. It was disconcerting, and Jim watched as his fingers typed a few more words before they realized he'd left without them, then joined him in the real world.

He continued to ignore the phone, reliving the explosion of Walt's head. Then he clenched his fist, punched the air and said, 'Yuk!'

At the bottom of the computer monitor, beyond which lay the warehouse where Creasey had just died, were the couple of extra lines his fingers had typed. He glared at the phone, muttered, 'Just a mo',' and read them.

'What the fuck happened, Bobby?' Dodd screamed. He turned to Bobby who was dripping with brain and blood. 'What the fuck *happened*?'

Jim smiled and said, 'No good asking him, you asshole. Only one who knows is *me*!'

He still felt as if a good part of him was in the warehouse, watching the dripping mess as Creasey's body sagged and his four murderers reacted. Leaving a story always felt like this when he was burning along and it was a good thing. There hadn't been much of it happening lately. Which was why he'd left orders that he wasn't to be disturbed. He glared at the phone again, then picked it up, thinking, *It just better not be Spreadbury, that's all!*

'Hello?' he snapped, already sure it *would* be the lunatic 'psychic' who'd been calling just recently and frightening Sooty.

'Sorry to disturb you, Jim, but—'

'There's been a death in the family?' Jim finished, already

13

feeling guilty for his peeved tone. It wasn't Spreadbury, of course, it was Rosie, his assistant. It couldn't have been anyone else, he remembered, because while he was working (or, lately, just sitting here curling up at the edges with frustration because he was blocked as solidly as a four-inch drainpipe full of dead rats) all calls were routed through Rosie's office. No one could reach him but Rosie. Not even Spreadbury could get through directly. Not since the new switchboard had been installed.

I'm a man who needs *a secretary and a switchboard*, he thought distantly, still unable to believe it. *Not* wants, *but* needs.

If he faced the bald truth, he'd needed a secretary for much longer than the year he'd had one: Sooty hadn't been able to deal with all the other incoming shit for something like three years. The incoming *still* weighed down the two of them – *and* his agent. Like it or not (and Jim *did* like it) the no-hoper kid from Onich in the wilds of Scotland had made good. He was Big in America.

'A death?' Rosie sounded bewildered.

He ignored the fact that while he was in here no one was supposed to disturb him for a reason short of death. Rosie didn't deserve it. 'Walt Creasey just died,' Jim said. 'A character in *Shimmer*. My muse finally got over its constipation and shat gold. I'm back in business.'

'Oh, Jim, I'm sorry to disturb you. I really am. I thought . . .'

Jim nodded. 'You thought I was still sitting chain-smoking Virginia Slims, tearing out my hair over games of computer solitaire and wondering about sucking the barrel of this Colt .45 I have here, right?' Jim said.

'No, I—'

Jim chuckled. 'Just joking, sweetheart. The fact is, I've done a lot of that in the past two months or so.' It was more like three and a half months, but for six weeks he'd had what he liked to call 'other business'. Things that took his mind off not being able to write. The new movie had been released. He'd had several speaking engagements. It may have only amounted to half a dozen days' travelling but, he claimed, you had to *think* about these things. They distracted

14

you. 'Not contemplating doing a Hemingway, but just sitting here stewing in my own juices, wondering. Wondering what the hell was stopping me doing what I'm best at.'

'I know,' Rosie said. 'And I'm glad you've passed through it.' Her tone hinted that she'd been more than worried – as had poor Sooty – that she thought he really might have considered sucking the barrel of that Colt. His wife kept up the pretence that she hadn't known just how close he'd been, but sometimes he could see traces of the pain in her eyes.

And anyway, Jim noted, as he lit a cigarette to replace the one that had burned away in the ashtray while he'd been writing, *Sooty hid the bullets*.

Jim still hadn't let on that he knew about *that* little safety measure. If he mentioned the missing slugs to his wife it would prove that he'd handled the gun during his dry spell, which would tell Sooty that he really *had* been contemplating the big one.

As if! Jim thought, trying not to remember that hot night-time rummage through the desk one desperate Sunday. He shrugged. He hadn't been thinking about suicide at all: he'd just wanted to feel the weight of the gun in his hand, take comfort from knowing it was there.

'Anyway,' Jim said, trying to keep the excitement out of his voice and failing miserably, 'I'm in the saddle and driving the tale along with a whip! It feels good to be back. Now, what's the problem? Just don't tell me it's Spreadbury on the line.'

'Relax, it's not Spreadbury.' Rosie paused. 'If I'd known, Jim, I really wouldn't have disturbed you. I'm sorry. Look, if you want to get back to it, I'll tell him to call back later, okay?'

'Tell who, Rosie?'

'It's Davey Smith. He says it's urgent.'

Jim chuckled. Seaford's one and only grease-monkey and seller of second-hand cars didn't have an urgent bone in his body. 'Okay, Rosie, put him on,' he said, wondering what Davey wanted.

'I'll try,' Rosie said doubtfully. 'If I can figure out this damned switchboard.'

Rosie vanished with a click. And the receiver emitted an

ear-splitting screech so loud that, for a moment, Jim thought he'd undergone an ultrasound lobotomy. He held the phone away from his ear, wincing.

A while back, when Jim had first dried up, Sooty had bought a book on *feng shui*, hoping to clear any bad atmosphere/vibrations/spirits the house might have gathered. There were now wind-chimes over the front door, and Jim had strict instructions always to leave the toilet seat down and to keep the lid and the bathroom door closed. This stopped luck being flushed away, apparently. Either that, or it was a ruse on his wife's part to get him to put the seat down. According to the book, Jim's workroom was out of balance and needed a mirror to set things right. Which was why, when he looked up to his left, as he did now, he caught sight of himself in it.

The writer sits at a desk in a big, light room, Jim thought. Now he'd started fictionalizing, he found he was having trouble stopping. This was another good omen. *It's a busy, untidy room. Posters on the white walls advertise his previous novels – all horror. The bookshelves are full of James Green screenplays and manuscripts and first editions and translations of his novels. Green is dishevelled, his hair tousled, his shirt half unbuttoned. There is a cigarette dangling from the side of his mouth and an overflowing ashtray beside his keyboard. He is holding a phone a good distance from his ear. There is an expression of distaste on his face . . .*

The phone screeched again and Jim wondered if the new system was already in trouble. In spite of the *feng shui*, electrical and electronics things didn't seem to live long in The House That Jim Built. The computer had been shuttling back and forth between here and Skate and Chips in Miami over the past two months and practically every part of its guts had been transplanted. Henry Skate reckoned he'd never seen anything like it and complained, 'Top-name components never go belly-up like this, man! It's just one thing after another. You sure you're not really Static Man in disguise?'

Jim listened to the phone howl and let his gaze stray away from himself (*yes*, the crow's feet *were* worsening and, *yes*, those single-figure grey hairs were now in tens, at least) to the big picture window and the huge landscaped backyard that lay beyond. In here the chiller kept the temperature down to the mid-seventies but, by the look of it, outside it was a perfect southern Florida summer afternoon. Hot enough to melt granite and humid enough to grab a handful of air and wring out the moisture. An intermittent breeze ruffled the leaves on the trees and the flower borders. Sea birds wheeled high in the clear blue sky.

Down beyond the pool, which sparkled invitingly in the sun, in the middle of the huge, neatly clipped lawn, Sooty sat in a shaded swing chair with Gloria, the apple of this man's eye. *Seven already*, Jim thought in wonderment. *Where the hell does the time go?* He could remember her birth as if it were yesterday. It *felt* like yesterday, for God's sake! For a few moments, Jim ached to be out there with his family. But he was late and there was work to be done. Money was riding on *Shimmer*. A great deal of money. And it had to be earned.

A voice squeaked from the phone.

'Well?' Davey Smith asked.

'Sorry, Davey, I wasn't listening,' Jim said. 'What did you say?'

Davey chortled. 'When your mom and pop moved down here back in 'sixty-nine when you was just a whippersnapper, I said to your mom, "That kid'll never amount to anything 'cause he's got a severe attention deficit!" Looks like I was right, don't it? You listening, Jimbo? Now pay attention! I said, "Hiya, Jimbo. Hot enough for you?"'

Davey would never let him forget the year in which he'd celebrated his fifth birthday. Jim had been whisked away from cool, rainy Scotland where his father had gone bankrupt and set down in what had felt like a blast-furnace. First he'd got such bad sunburn that he'd been whisked off to hospital in Miami, then, like his mother, he'd merely wilted under the heat. The family had only stayed six months before they went home.

But those first six months in Seaford had done something awful to Jim: turned up his internal thermostat or something. After those months in the furnace, Scotland had always been too cold and, for ever onwards, he'd wanted to be back in

17

Florida. Jim Green was a Snowbird whose dreams had come true.

'It's fine in here,' he replied. 'I've got the air-conditioning set to "Freeze".'

Davey made a sound of disgust. 'Air-conditioning's for pussies!' he scoffed.

Jim laughed. *Davey Smith sits in his grubby office in a garage workshop*, Jim's 'working voice' extemporized without any prompting. Sometimes it was like having someone else live inside your head with you. Sometimes it was fun and sometimes it was spooky. Jim liked it either way. He was just glad to have it back. *On the other side of the glass, grease-monkeys are working beneath cars on ramps, or are bent over the engines of Camaros and Thunderbirds. Davey sits in a tube-frame chair, which he's tilted back; his legs are out straight, his feet on the desk. The heels of his dirty, ancient work-boots are pinning down paperwork – invoices and bills – and printing greasy crescents among the prices. Davey is fat – he's put on a few extra pounds in the past few months since his old mutt Charlie died and he quit doing a daily walk. He's dressed in a stained white undershirt and jeans so greasy they've probably never been washed since Maude passed away in '87. Tilted way back on his head, partially covering his grey hair, is the Caterpillar cap he's worn since he helped resurface Highway 1 down as far as Conch Key during the lean years. Davey is wet with sweat and the smouldering stub of a Marlboro is fixed in the corner of his mouth; if you listen carefully you can hear him trying to breathe around it and not burn his throat with the smoke. His great lined face bears an expression of surprise, but he's grinning like there's never been a happier man born in the history of humanity. He makes a point of calling James Jimbo, Pussy, or kid to let him know that no matter if Collis and Anstey Books has recently offered to advance him twenty-six million on his next four novels, no matter if Paramount is pleading with him to write the screenplay of Shimmer, he will always be just plain Betty Green's boy to Davey.*

'Okay, so I'm a pussy,' Jim said, smiling. 'Now, what do you want, you old fart? You're keeping the maestro from working, y'know.'

18

'Work? You call that key-clacking *work*? An honest day's work would kill you, Jimbo. And, besides, the day you write a book worth reading'll be the day hell freezes over! So, kid, is it true they offered you twenty-six million bucks for ... *books*?'

Jim pulled a face. He didn't think he'd ever get used to talking about money in telephone numbers. His own dad had said of professional footballers: 'They don't *earn* that money. They might *get* it, but they surely don't *earn* it.' And Jim had had to agree with him. It wasn't just embarrassing thinking of people giving you huge amounts of money: the responsibility that came with it was frightening.

'So my agent says,' Jim said, trying to lessen the enormity of the question. He was half certain that the big payoffs had been responsible for his block. 'I'll believe it when I get the contract,' he added.

Davey chortled. 'Well, I just called to tell you my price went up. So, kid, gonna have any pictures in that there book you're writing? Cause I ain't buyin' it unless there are.' He feigned disbelief. 'Goddammit! Twenty-six million and they don't even want *pictures*. I can't believe it!'

'You get the Critic of the Year Award. Now what do you want?'

'You got that Oldtimers' Disease?' Davey asked. 'Or did you just forget to pay your brain bill? You sure can't remember much of anything. When you was still a whipper-snapper I said to your mother, I said—'

'Davey!'

Davey rolled to a halt. Jim heard his rasping breath. Eventually he said, 'Tonight.'

'Tonight?' Jim took a quick inventory of his memory and felt as if he were teetering on the edge of a precipice: nothing was there. Then it came. 'Oh, *shit*!' he said. 'Straker's Island.'

'You're quick, kid,' Davey said. 'That's where we always go.'

Straker's Island wasn't where they *always* went, but it had proven to be the most popular, and the last four trips had indeed all been there.

Davey sounded concerned. 'Did someone cancel and not

tell me? It's still on, right? We gonna scare the shit out of 'em, or what?'

'I'm sorry, I forgot,' Jim said, surprised at himself. He felt as if his face had been slapped by a stranger. Inside his head, his writing voice had fallen silent. *You've been under a little stress, that's all*, he assured himself. *It's nothing to worry about.*

'But it's still on?'

'Oh, yeah! Sure, Davey. My mind was elsewhere.'

'That's what they pay for you,' Davey said, coughing. 'Anyway, I got us some big mischief lined up.'

'What have we got this time?' Jim asked. He checked his watch, scowling. It was three fifteen. That gave him about an hour more writing time. It probably wouldn't matter now anyway, he realized. He'd been well and truly pulled out of the story and didn't think he'd be able to get back in again, not now he'd remembered he had a hot date on his favourite island with half a dozen of his biggest fans. He just couldn't believe how he'd managed to forget it.

I was sure it was next week, he told himself. *I was positive.*

'We got plenty bells and whistles,' Davey said, sounding like a kid looking forward to opening his presents. 'Standard weird noises, 'ceptin' I've added to 'em. Stuff to crash through the trees, new and improved. Ghostly figures, also more convincing that those old sticks and sheets we've been fighting with recently. Laughing boxes. And there there's the piss-yourself de resistance . . .'

'And what might that be?' Jim asked, suddenly concerned for reasons he didn't quite understand. For a sixty-five-year-old garage mechanic, Davey had a terrific imagination: each trip had held weirder and more violent surprises. His star turn on the last outing was a realistic disembowelment that he'd kept secret even from Jim. How he was going to top this, Jim didn't like to imagine.

'Jimbo, you won't *believe* it! I've been working hard over this. You're gonna love it. This time we're gonna kick ass *seriously!*'

Jim frowned. 'Go on,' he said.

Davey cackled like a crone. 'Blood-bags!' he wheezed delightedly.

20

'Blood-bags?' Jim repeated, picturing one of his greatest fans dying of a heart-attack and the relatives suing him. *Still, if they can take a few yards of guts hanging out, they can probably live with blood*, he reassured himself. 'What are you planning to *do* with these?' he asked, but he thought he already knew. Straker's Island was forested. They'd be up in the trees, waiting for people to walk by on the ground.

'I won't tell you where they'll be,' Davey chuckled, 'but you're gonna need a raincoat.'

'Sounds like a lot of laughs,' Jim said, doubtfully. He wasn't altogether sure he wanted to be sprayed with anything remotely resembling blood. In spite of his fearsome track record of literary tortures and maimings he was starting to get quite squeamish. He'd first noticed it a couple of years back. They said it had to do with having children, but Jim suspected it had more to do with getting older. 'You sure this'll be okay?'

'Stop worrying, pussy, it'll be lots of fun!' Davey said cheerfully.

Yeah, but it won't be you that the blood-bags are bursting over. It'll be you setting them off, Jim thought, as a shudder cruised down his spine. There seemed to be something fundamentally wrong with using blood-bags. 'What's it made of?' he asked.

'Huh?'

'The blood. The red stuff you'll be raining down on us. What's it made of?'

Davey chortled. 'Blood, of course,' he replied. 'Sheesh, Jim, do you think I'd short-change you? I have a pal who works in a mortuary in Miami. You know how they drain the blood outa you when you're dead and put in embalming fluid to stop you going rotten in front of your visiting relatives? Well, they just dump the blood. Except this time . . .' He tailed off, giggling.

Jim smiled. Davey liked to keep his trade secrets to himself. Add to that that ever since they'd started running these trips he'd made it his business to best the Master of Disaster, and what you had was a line of bullshit. It didn't matter if Davey didn't intend to tell him. The blood would be water – distilled if Jim knew anything about Davey's

21

mind – with some thickening added and some food-grade red dye in it. Nothing to worry about.

'Fireworks to end it all,' Davey told him. 'I got better stuff fixed up this time, too. I have a talent for it. We'll have real snappy stuff! They'll have a real good time. How many are we tonight?'

Jim shook off his shivers and doubts. He may have written a bunch of novels that sold in the millions in paperback, he may have scripted three of the decade's biggest grossing films and directed the last two, but he was a writer, not a public figure. Speaking live terrified him. And tonight he wasn't just going to have to entertain half a dozen strangers, or however many there were, he was going to have to do a bit of amateur dramatics in front of them, too. It wasn't surprising he felt a little jittery.

'I'm not sure,' Jim said. 'Hold on, I've got one of the competition ads here somewhere.' He groped through the mounds of paperwork on his desk and eventually found a dog-eared copy of *Cosmopolitan*. Collis and Anstey Books insisted that nearly seventy per cent of the people who bought his books were women and had placed ads in several of the bigger women's magazines. His male readership were targeted through film magazines and the fan club. The magazine fell open at the advert.

Win An Evening On A Haunted Island
With Master of Disaster James Green!
Take a tour of terror with the man who brought you
the bestsellers **Deathless, Miriam, The Third Coming,**
Damnation, Miami Five Fifteen *and* **Dark Heat**
and the films
Switchers, Killing Spree *and* **Miami Five Fifteen**
Celebrate the publication of the latest
James Green novel

Black River

with Collis and Anstey Books
and James Green himself
Five lucky people can win! All you have to do
is answer three simple questions . . .

Jim shut the magazine. 'Five,' he said, 'or thereabouts. Although they've said five before and we've had more turn up. We'll manage.' He frowned again as the butterflies made themselves known to his stomach in a big way.

He didn't know who the lucky competition winners were, or what they looked like (probably much the same as last year's batch), but he could already see the expressions on their eager faces and it made his heart sink. They certainly wouldn't go home disappointed, but Jim knew he'd go home thinking that he'd let them down. They'd be expecting some kind of minor god, as sharp-witted as a chat-show host; a raconteur whose every word sparkled and who could charm birds from trees. What they'd get, as far as he was concerned, was an ordinary human being. Sure, he could write a bit, and he'd been lucky enough to become popular for it, but it was a job, just something he did on a business-as-usual basis. That didn't make him an extra special being. He wasn't *different*.

But they'd be in awe of him. It wasn't something he thought he'd ever be comfortable with.

'Mugs,' Davey said, and laughed. 'Let's just hope they bring clean underwear! They're gonna need it! And so are you, Jimmy boy!'

'Thanks for everything. See you later, Davey,' Jim said.

'Oh, you won't see *me*. You'll see what I do and where I've been, but you won't see me. I've been over already today, setting up, and I'm going over again at five. You'll be coming at six, won't you?'

Jim thought about it. There was a note here, he was sure. Hadn't Rosie left it pinned up somewhere this morning when she brought him coffee? It wasn't on the cork-board.

What's wrong with you, man? he asked himself and instantly replied: *I've been working. You'd better believe it!*

He brightened a little – Sooty would have been happy to testify that when her husband was writing he forgot about everything except smoking. Shit, and why should this year's promo trip be any different from last year's?

'I guess I'll do what I always do,' he told Davey. 'Go down to the harbour and meet them about five, or whenever someone calls to say they've arrived. We'll have a few beers

23

or something and then we'll come over on the launch. Sure, six it is. So,' he said, finally getting this little shock under control, 'how much are you shafting us for this time, Davey?'

'Two eight seventy-five and fifty-cents, including my cut. You wouldn't get better cheaper. You wouldn't get better for twice the price, come to think of it. Wait till you see the results! Be haunting you!' Davey hung up.

Jim lit a fresh Virginia Slim and drew on it, gazing out of the window. Rosie was now down in the swing with Sooty and Gloria. Sooty was pointing at a little card she held in her hand and shaking her head and grinning. Whatever it was, Rosie found it amusing, too. Gloria was bent over her latest project. She'd recently dug Jim's ancient Sega Game Gear out from under the junk in a closet and was fighting her way through a game. *Probably* Sonic the Hedgehog, Jim thought, blowing a perfect smoke ring and letting his mind drift back.

A publicity/promotions guy called Marc Versy at Collis and Anstey had come up with the original promotional idea: *Spend an Evening of Terror with Master of Horror James Green in a Genuine Haunted House!* way back when Dookie was a pup. Marc was gone now, someone big at Saatchi and Saatchi the last Jim heard, but he was the one Jim had to thank, he supposed.

Marc had timed the first competition to coincide with the launch of Jim's third book *Deathless*. Originally the idea had been to gain media exposure for what Collis and Anstey – and more especially, his editor Liz – had seen as an up-and-coming writer. It had worked, too. *Deathless* had sold nearly a million in hardcover and had done another seven million worldwide in paperback, dragging the sales of the first two books up into the millions along with it. Whether the national television coverage of that first horror trip had boosted the sales or not was arguable. James thought his break-out would have happened anyway, but the outing had certainly started the ball rolling.

Since that time (and the first trip had been a disaster in terms of scaring people – the special effects had been non-existent and who could frighten fifteen people with a camera

24

crew and movie lights and an ABC news team present?) the field trips had become something of an institution.

But who wants to live in an institution? Jim thought, as his butterflies began to flutter again. He didn't enjoy these trips. Never had. And since Spreadbury, the lunatic 'psychic', had begun to bother him, although he didn't take it to heart as much as Sooty did, he'd been doing some thinking. God knew, he'd had plenty of time for that while he was dammed up.

It wasn't just that he didn't enjoy performing for his fans – he could handle that, he supposed, and at one time, he'd been so desperate for publicity he'd have gone anywhere and done anything – it was that all the recent trips were to Straker's Island.

And the island was a *special* place.

Taking a gaggle of fans over there had always seemed like profaning sacred ground, but since good old Aaron Spreadbury had appeared out of nowhere, full of portents and omens, Jim had realized that he didn't want to do another trip after this one. And if he *did* do one, it wouldn't be on his island. This was the last time.

He ground the cigarette stub into the ashtray and checked his watch. The ancient Casio Janus (this was his writing watch, the one he'd worn from the start) now read three forty-five and it looked pretty much like work was over. He needed a shot of strong black Colombian coffee and he needed to check out the details of the trip and then get showered, shaved and changed.

He had taken two paces towards the door when something on the computer screen made him stop and go back. He sat down heavily in the chair and looked at it, his scalp prickling. His last sentence ended with the words: *but nothing moved except the dripping contents of Walt Creasey's head.* There was a paragraph break code after this.

To my knowledge, I didn't break it there. No, goddamm it, I didn't!

And under this, typed in block capitals and neatly centred were the words:

YOU WON'T COME BACK THIS *TIME!*

25

Bobby Hillsborough's words repeated. The words with which he had opened this chapter. The words, in fact, with which he had opened the novel, page one, line one.

Jim looked at the words, his flesh creeping like cockroaches. His fingers *had* typed on for a few words after he'd been whisked back from the warehouse to answer the phone, he knew that, but he'd since read what he'd typed and it had ended with the line about Walt Creasey's dripping brains.

I didn't type that! he protested. *Not when I was talking to Davey, nor when I was talking to Rosie. Those words typed themselves!*

That this wasn't merely unlikely but actually impossible didn't make him feel any better. Over the past fifteen years of writing fantastic stories his impossibility quotient had lessened. Impossible no longer meant what it once had. A little of the essence of his writing had rubbed off on him. Impossible used to mean something that *couldn't* happen, but to Jim now it meant something that *shouldn't* happen but might, given the right opportunity. Far from working out all his innermost fears, writing horror stories had increased them.

You wrote it. God knows why, he told himself and deleted it, smiling grimly. 'And *you* won't come back this time, either!' he snarled, getting up. It was time to stop entertaining those little demonoid thoughts that'd made him so wealthy and (a) get himself a cup of Colombian coffee then, (b) find out what he was supposed to be doing tonight. He picked up his cigarettes and his lighter and strode from the room.

As the door closed behind him the flashing cursor began to move silently across the screen, leaving characters in its wake:

Yooooomm,ΦδωπϑΩΩΩξΨΞnmnmnmn, tktktkta.

Chapter Two

The Cast

1

Walking from the air-conditioned cool of the house into the garden felt pretty much the way Jim thought it would if you walked from an industrial freezer into an industrial oven. The instant you got outside you could feel the sun biting your skin right through your clothes. The humidity was high, too: Jim briefly entertained the notion that if he were to swipe his arm through the air, when it came to rest it would be beaded with condensation. An experiment was out of the question, however – he was carrying a tray bearing three cups of coffee and an icy bottle of Pepsi for Gloria.

Clouds were gathering inland, in the direction that Jim was wont to describe as 'Over Will's mother's', a catch-all phrase used to describe the place where whatever was happening overhead was happening, and he expected a short, sharp summer-afternoon cloudburst inside the next hour. It'd dry up and the sky would clear right after, though, and there was no wind, so with a little luck he wouldn't have to deal with any cases of sea-sickness on the boat trip to the island.

Down on the swing, Rosie said something to Sooty and Sooty looked up. When she saw him her face lit in that sunny grin that, even after all these years, *still* made him go weak at the knees – or in the heart, or wherever it was. Jim wasn't certain of the location, only of the effect. Something inside him responded to that smile and ran through him like warm honey. Jim found himself grinning back like a fool and wanting to wave.

'The butler approaches!' Sooty called. Gloria glanced up

from the Game Gear then looked back at it. Jim could hear the damned thing bleeping right back here.

'Thanks, Jim,' Sooty said, as she took her coffee from the tray. She puckered up and blew him a kiss.

Jim sighed theatrically. 'I don't know,' he said. 'I pay a secretary top dollar to do nothing but make me coffee and when I buzz for her, she's never there. I guess she's hiding somewhere, sitting in the sun and goofing off.'

'She's right here, Daddy,' Gloria said, without looking up. Her thumbs danced on the Sega's buttons and her mouth contorted from one grimace to another. Judging by the sound effects, she was playing *Razor Gang*. It was a tough one, Jim knew. When he'd played it he hadn't only grimaced, he'd sworn a great deal. So much that Gloria – who, back then, had just been starting to speak – had taken to saying, 'Fuckit!' with a slight Scottish accent. She wasn't saying it now, Jim was pleased to note.

'This woman here?' Jim said, holding the tray out to Rosie and feigning surprise. 'This woman is my *secretary*? I thought she was my mother. She's always telling me what to do ... when she's not sitting in the garden.'

'Yes, and sometimes I wonder what I've done to deserve it,' Rosie said. 'You do make a fine cup of coffee, though,' she added, sipping.

'So,' Jim said, squeezing into the gap between his wife and his daughter. 'How come no one told me today was the big day?'

'I reminded you this morning,' Sooty said, reaching out and gently squeezing his thigh. 'It's not my fault your short-term memory isn't what it was.'

'And I posted a note on your cork-board,' Rosie added, moving her mobile phone out of range of her coffee. This little Ericsson was her fifth phone this year. One she'd dropped down the toilet, one she'd run over in the 4X4 that was five sizes too big for one small middle-aged widowed grandmother, and three had succumbed to the weird anti-electronics atmosphere of the house.

Jim smiled. 'I worked,' he said. 'I *wrote*. You can't expect me to remember things when I'm writing.'

'You can't remember anything *ever*!' Gloria said, glancing up.

'So shoot me!' Jim said happily. 'What's the set-up for this evening, then? Davey's doing his bit, he tells me. Other than that . . .'

Sooty took his hand. Jim glanced at her and saw the concern beneath her smile. He winked at her and grinned an *I'm okay!* look her way.

'It'll be the same as last year,' Rosie said. 'We've been through it already.'

Jim nodded. Now he thought about it, they had. He simply hadn't been listening because his mind had been lost in the middle of that desert they called writer's block and nothing else had mattered.

When the phone rang Rosie jumped. Coffee slopped into the saucer and Jim just *knew* he could wave goodbye to the Ericsson: the chances of Rosie answering it without filling it with the best Colombian were minimal.

'Phone,' Gloria said, without looking up. Her thumbs hammered the Sega's controls and her feet danced in the grass.

Rosie set down her coffee before picking up the phone.

The mobile lives to fight another day! Jim thought.

'Hello?' she said. 'Oh! Good. Yes, he's right here! Hold a moment, please.'

She put her hand over the mouthpiece and held out the phone for Jim. 'It's Elaine from your publisher's. She's at the Radisson in Miami. The fans all turned up yesterday as planned.'

Jim took the phone. 'Hiya, Elaine! What have you got for me, half a dozen monsters?'

Elaine gave a short snort. 'Near enough,' she said. 'Got the pictures? I'll talk you through, then you can impress them with your in-depth knowledge of them.'

Elaine might have been a shit-hot publicist, but it had been Jim's idea to ask for photographs of the contest winners and personal details. People liked to think you were interested enough to find out a little about them. It got things off on the right foot if you could go up to someone who, after all, regarded *you* as an old friend and say, 'So,

29

how're things? That ankle you broke last year is completely recovered, is it?'

Jim covered the mouthpiece and turned to Rosie. 'Do we have pictures of the lucky competition winners?'

'You're sitting on some of 'em,' Rosie replied.

Jim got up. 'Hold on, Elaine. Just getting them,' he said into the phone.

Between them, Jim, Sooty and Rosie retrieved the strewn – and somewhat creased – photos of the five competition winners. Jim now realized what the thing was he'd seen Sooty holding and giggling about earlier: a picture of one of the fans. He wondered which one had caused the mirth.

'Ready,' he said, into the phone. 'I'm looking at a grey-haired guy in his late thirties or early forties. Thin face. Big nose.' He caught Sooty's eye and mouthed, Light me a ciggie, sweetheart!

'That'll be Frank,' Elaine said. 'He's an English teacher from a high-school in Boston. He's got a little notebook and he's writing down everything as it happens. He's already filled three pages. He has a manner about him—'

'Like a teacher? Stern?'

'Let's just say I don't care much for him,' Elaine said. 'He looks like trouble about to happen. He isn't going to be easy to deal with, is my opinion. Looks like a complainer. Course, *you* could probably charm him, Jim,' she added.

'Okay, Frank the teacher from Boston. Next I've got is a young guy. Kinda hollow-eyed and hungry-looking.'

'Jon Short,' Elaine said, tailing off with what felt to Jim like a grin.

'Let me guess,' Jim said, sighing. 'There's always one, isn't there? And this is him, right?'

'Yep,' Elaine said. 'Jon is the wannabe writer. That's the bad news. Want the *worse* news?'

'I already know it,' Jim replied. 'He's carrying a manuscript and he's gonna want me to read it.'

'Well, he's carrying what looks supsiciously like a selection. I have a feeling he may have a couple of screenplays there as well as a novel. At the very least. I haven't yet found out if he's a wannabe screenwriter or a novelist. Or both, like his hero.'

'Okay, here's what you do,' Jim said. 'Send him to the shops to get you a pack of Marlboro. Then get everyone else on the bus and drive off without him.'

'I wish!' Elaine said. 'You should have photos of a fat woman and a thin one there somewhere.'

Jim put the picture of Jon Short at the bottom of the pack. The next photo wasn't of someone he would have described as fat *or* thin.

Pneumatic would be a better word, he thought, gazing at the three-quarter length colour shot of the young blonde girl. The white bikini she wore was almost non-existent. This photo was signed 'Candy' and two kisses were scrawled along the bottom. Jim wondered why she wasn't too busy working on *Baywatch* or posing for *Playboy* to come here. He waved the photograph at Sooty, grinning. Sooty snatched it from him, pulling a face and looked at it, shaking her head.

The next picture was of a thin woman. The following one of the fat one. Jim fanned them out so he could see the faces. 'I've got them,' he told Elaine.

'The fat one's Martha. She says she's your *greatest* fan.'

'If we're talking about mass, she could well be right.' Jim chuckled.

'The thin one is June,' Elaine continued. 'They're both divorced and both forty-three years old. Martha eats, June knits. They seem to have teamed up. Neither seems terribly bright, I'm afraid, but . . .'

'Yeah, I know. I get the readers I deserve.' Jim finished the tired old joke for her. 'And talking of deserving, I think that this time we'll make it an all-nighter rather than just an evening.' He reached for the photo of Candy. Sooty held it out to him, then snatched it back as he was about to grab it.

'Ah, you have the picture of Candy,' Elaine said, just as Sooty poked him in the ribs with an extended knuckle. Jim yelped.

'Don't get too excited, Jim,' Elaine said. 'Nature isn't so fond of what's inside Candy's head.'

'Excuse me?' he said, trying to whip the snapshot from Sooty's fingers and failing again.

'Nature abhors a vacuum, Jim,' Elaine said tiredly. 'But, seriously, you want to watch out for her. I only spoke to her for about ten seconds but she clearly conveyed the impression she wants to get in your pants.'

Jim laughed. 'Did I say all-nighter? How about we make it a week? Everyone else leaves at midnight but Candy and I stay over at the island.'

Elaine didn't even chuckle. 'Just go steady, Jim, is all I'm saying. She's trouble.'

'Are you feeling okay?' Jim asked, suddenly worried about his publicist. She was usually a good deal more bright and chatty than this.

There was a long pause. Then Elaine said, 'Yeah, I'm fine.'

'Really?' Jim said.

'No, not really,' Elaine admitted. 'What's the opposite of rose-tinted?'

Jim thought about it. 'No idea,' he said. 'Gloom-tinted?'

'I'm just seeing the world through gloom-tinted glasses today, that's all.'

'Mark?' Jim asked. Elaine had been living with Mark Chambers, or as Jim liked to call him Mr Ego-on-Legs or Mr Slimeball, for five years. Mark, the owner of Typhoon, a successful advertising agency in New York, was a control-freak of the nastiest kind. Elaine deserved better.

'Who else?' Elaine replied. 'He's history now. Or at least I *hope* he is.'

'Meaning?'

'Dumped but he won't disappear. You know the score. It's the old *if-I-can't-have-you-no-one-else-will* routine. He's coming after me, he says. He's just trying to frighten me, I know that. He's never hit me and he's only ever abused me verbally and I doubt he'd *do* anything, but the threat scares me.'

'I'm sorry to hear it,' Jim said.

'Yeah and I know what you're thinking. That I'm better off without him. You're just too diplomatic to say it. Unlike everyone else I know. Including me. I know I'm better off but, Christ, Jim, I *loved* that man . . .'

'I know.'

'Oh, forget about me. I'll be back to normal in half an hour or so. You know how I am – these little bouts of depression don't last long. Anyway, tell Sooty I'm looking forward to seeing her tonight. I'll cry on her shoulder if I need to. Or we'll just sit around and bitch about everyone and get drunk. It'll be good to see her again. I'll meet you down at the dock at five, then?'

'Okay, sweetheart,' Jim said. 'And I'll tell Sooty. 'Bye!' He hit the button on the phone to cut off the call and handed the Ericsson back to Rosie.

'You'll tell me what?' Sooty asked.

'I'm not saying unless you give me back my photograph!' Jim challenged.

Smiling, Sooty held it out for him, then snatched it away again the moment he reached for it. 'You're a lecher!' She laughed.

'It's part of my writerly charm,' Jim said. 'Anyway, Elaine says Candy wants my body!'

Without looking up from her game, Gloria said, 'What does she want your body for, Daddy?'

Sooty, Jim and Rosie all glanced at Gloria for a moment then looked at one another.

'She wants to sell it to a hospital,' Jim said. 'For medical science.'

Gloria stabbed at the buttons on the Sega, her gaze focused intently on the tiny screen. 'They'll cut you up into little pieces like in the film of *Miami Five Fifteen*. Gross!'

'You've seen *Miami Five Fifteen*?' Jim asked, astonished. The film had had to be cut before it even got certification at the 18 rating. It was still widely held to be *the* most violent film of the decade. There had been no question of letting Gloria see it, even the version that came out on video with the extra cuts.

'Yeah, at Sally's when I slept over,' Gloria said. 'Everyone said the F word a lot. It was pretty boring except the bit where they cut that man up into little pieces.'

Jim looked at his wife and shrugged. 'Course, she could

33

be a body-snatcher who wants to take me over,' Jim suggested.

'She probably just wants to take you to bed,' Gloria said, still concentrating, and while Jim and Sooty were staring, open-mouthed at one another, she snapped, 'Donner and stinking *Blitzen*! They got me *again*!'

The Sega blew a long discordant raspberry, signifying, if Jim recalled correctly, that it was start-all-over-again time. The main reason he'd fallen out of love with the Game Gear was the simple fact that you had to complete an entire game in one go. There was no 'save game' feature.

Gloria thrust the Sega into Jim's hands, leaped off the swing, snatched up her bottle of Pepsi and fought with the screw cap. Jim glanced at the screen.

'I got further than I've ever been before, too!' Gloria said. 'Right into the spin-dryer!'

But Jim wasn't listening. He was looking at the Game Over screen on the Sega while the blood rushed away from his face and a sickening chilly feeling rose through his guts. Over a graphic of two crossed bread-knives were the words:

GAME OVER
YOU WON'T COME BACK THIS TIME!

It doesn't matter, Jim told himself, not believing it for a moment. *It has no significance. This game* is *mine, after all. I must have seen this screen a hundred times or more in the past. It's probably where I got that little motif I've been using in* Shimmer. *I simply forgot where I'd snatched it from.*

This was possible, Jim supposed. Or would have been if the words had seemed familiar. *But bells should have rung,* he thought. Whenever his subconscious mind coughed up something he'd stolen and he was later exposed to the source material, he remembered. Not that he'd decided to steal it to use – it didn't work that way – but the memory of having seen it would be triggered. He should now be clearly recalling the last time he'd seen the line, where he'd been, what he'd been doing. That was the way it worked. Except this time the bells hadn't rung.

Which means? Jim didn't know *what* it meant. The word *trouble* came to his mind and he thrust it away again.

34

'Don't you dare!' Sooty said.

Jim looked up. For a second he felt as if he'd been dragged out of a dimly lit icehouse into a bright, warm world. It was a good feeling. 'Dare what?' he said.

'Start playing that damned game,' Sooty said. 'I know what you're like. You'll say, "I'll only have a quick go. Five minutes, that's all," and you'll still be there when the sun goes down.'

Jim smiled. 'The batteries wouldn't last that long,' he said, and switched off the Sega.

'You don't have time,' Sooty continued. 'If you're gonna be at the dock by five you'd better hurry yourself up. We all know how long it takes you to shower and shave.'

'Nag, nag, nag!' Jim said. He leaned over and dotted a kiss on Sooty's nose. 'Your wish is my command, O Mistress. I'll go get ready. I think tonight will be fine.'

Sooty raised an eyebrow, which plainly stated: *And tonight will be the last time you take strangers to Straker's Island, too. You promised!*

Jim nodded and winked. The tension in Sooty's face eased.

'I wish *I* was going,' Rose said wistfully.

Both Jim and Sooty looked at her in disbelief. Rosie seemed embarrassed.

'To the island?' Jim asked. 'Why?'

'Yes, I know,' Rosie said. 'I'm a fifty-five-year-old grand-mother living a grandmotherly life when I'm not here being a surrogate mother to a lunatic writer. I sit indoors and knit and watch *Dr Quinn, Medicine Woman* and *The Price is Right* and on Tuesdays I play bridge with a bunch of other old women and on Sundays I go to church. God, I even *look* like a little old lady.'

'No, you don't,' Sooty protested. 'You look like a sharp senior secretary.'

'In her forties,' Jim added.

Rosie waved a dismissive hand. 'I know what impression I give,' she said. 'But inside this elderly body, there's a young girl craving excitement.'

'You can go,' Jim said. 'I'd love it!'

'You mean that?' Rosie sounded shocked.

'Sure! Why not? It'd be fun to have you along.'

'I'm glad,' Rosie said. 'Only I heard a rumour, y'see.' She glanced at Sooty. 'A little bird told me that this would be the last time anyone outside the family went to Straker's Island and I didn't want to miss out. I've heard so much about the place that I want to go there.'

'Hey, you *are* family, as far as we're concerned,' Jim said. 'All you had to do was ask. And If you'd rather have a private guided tour, I'll take you there personally and without a bunch of fans tagging along.'

Rosie shook her head. 'Oh, no! I want the full works. Sure, I want to see the old house where, I understand, you and Sooty used to go ...' She tailed off, glancing at Sooty again.

Sooty took Jim's hand. 'I told her,' she said. 'Do you mind?'

Jim felt himself heat up. The blush wouldn't show on his face, he was sure of that – they never did, these days – but that didn't mean he didn't get embarrassed. 'Er, you told her *what* exactly?'

'All of it.' Sooty smiled.

Rosie said, 'Like how you two used to go out there when you were courting and lie naked on the porch of the old Straker house. Like how Gloria was conceived there, even though the doctors told Sooty she couldn't have babies. And I already know about the way the place inspires my favourite writer and fills him with ideas for his stories. I'd just love to see the place.'

'You don't *have* to go tonight, y'know,' Jim said.

'Oh, but I do!' Rosie said. 'That young girl inside me wants to visit a haunted island with the Master of Disaster in charge. I want you to scare me half to death. I want to experience what the fans experience!'

'Okay. You *shall* go to the ball,' Jim said. 'I'll introduce you as a fan from nearby. That'll explain why you didn't overnight with the others. But, remember, you give me any trouble when I'm telling tall tales and it'll be over the side of the boat for you.'

'It's a deal,' Rosie said. 'And I won't poke holes in your lies, I promise.' She leaned over and kissed his cheek. 'Thank you,' she said. 'You don't know how much this means to me.'

36

'Just make sure you wear your old clothes,' Jim warned her. 'It's gonna be messy!'

2

When he was writing, Jim's workroom became something akin to a gravitational singularity to him. It didn't sing to him like a siren and draw him in, half enchanted, it merely took him by the lapels, *dragged* him in, sat him down and forced him to write.

It wasn't impossible for him to pass by his room without entering but it was difficult. Which was undoubtedly the reason he now found himself inside it when he'd intended to go upstairs to the bathroom.

It certainly wasn't anything to do with those chilling words, *You won't come back* this *time!* that had begun to pop up everywhere. Jim knew that, because he'd spent the last five minutes convincing himself of it.

At least the fresh gobbledygook that had appeared on the screen since he was last in here didn't constitute a warning that might easily be applied to the forthcoming trip to Straker's Island. This crap just looked like the kind of computer-garbage you got when something went wrong. It read:

Yooooomm,Φδωπϑ$\Omega\Omega\Omega$ξΨΞnmnmnmn, tktktkta.
≈®$\sqrt{\,}\sqrt{\,}$γΩε.χ ΣψΞΓ mmmmmm,
tktktktktktktktktktktktk

And there was no way even Jim could interpret this as a warning. *Unless it's in some ancient language,* he told himself, and managed a grin. This language was about as ancient as the first home-computer crash if he wasn't very much mistaken. It looked like the machine would soon be winging its way back to Skate and Chips for the nth time.

Unless there's just a loose cable somewhere, Jim thought. It had happened before. Jim was no techno-whiz but he could find a cable connector falling out of a socket as well as the next computer nerd. He took hold of the wire that connected the keyboard to the back of the computer and wiggled it, watching to see if anything happened on the screen.

tktktktktktktktktktktktktktktkkktktktkktktktktktktkktktktk
....

Jim had no idea why the fresh line he'd just brought into being by moving the cable had begun a new paragraph, but that wasn't terribly important. He now knew that the cable was loose. Or faulty. He wiggled it again. Nothing happened. Frowning, he twisted it a little, then pulled the curly cable taut.

mmmmmmmmmmmnmnmnmnmnmnmmmmststststrstrstr

'Thank Christ for that! You had me going, there,' he told the computer. He tracked the lead to its socket at the back of the computer's tower and wiggled it. It seemed tightly fixed and no fresh lines appeared on the screen. Evidently there was a frayed wire inside the lead. He'd get Rosie to call Henry Skate in the morning and have him send over a new keyboard. This one was packed full of cigarette ash and specks of tobacco anyway. And the quote key had been sticking a little for ages.

'Looks like it's back to the olden days tomorrow. Again,' Jim announced, turning. His old Smith Corona sat in the centre of a smaller desk on the other side of the room. This was what Jim jokingly called his auxiliary workstation. The desk was amazingly clean and neat. 'That won't last long once the ashtrays and the paperwork get moved over there,' he said aloud. He turned back to the computer, deleted the unwanted lines, saved his chapter, copied it to a floppy disk and shut down the machine.

'Goodbye, Jim!' the recorded voice of Leonard Nimoy said, as the machine went through its shutting-down routine. Henry Skate had set that one up, thinking it would amuse Jim. It had for the first couple of days. An unidentified sexy female voice would follow this with the words, 'See you *soon*!' and the machine would be ready to shut off.

Jim waited, his finger on the power button. The computer's drive made a series of rapid clicking noises, but the female voice didn't come. Jim waited, certain that when it did, it wasn't going to make that sexy promise, it was going to say, 'You won't come back *this* time!'

When the tension got too much, Jim quit waiting and shut off the power, hoping he wasn't damaging anything. It didn't much matter – today's work was on a floppy disk anyway. He locked the floppy in the top drawer then turned back to the table on the far side of the room.

And when Jim looks, his mind fictionalized for him, *he sees that there is now a sheet of paper inserted into the platen of the typewriter.*

Suddenly Jim was back in the icehouse. Over on the other desk, the sheet of paper issued a silent challenge: Come and see what's written on me!

That wasn't there when I last looked. It damned well wasn't!

'I just didn't spot it, that's all,' he reassured himself as he moved towards the typewriter. 'It was there all the time, but I didn't notice it.'

Neatly centred on the white page, half-way down the sheet were the words:

DEEAD MANNNN, THIEFfff

Which weren't, if Jim recalled correctly, the proper words to the end of *Tinker, Tailor, Soldier, Sailor.*

He backed away slowly from the typewriter in much the same way as he had the alligator with which he'd once come face to face on his back lawn. His heart squeezed painfully in his chest and his mind chittered like a bug.

'Spreadbury,' he whispered, suddenly understanding. And the fear left him. He might have been trembling like a jelly on a plate and his heart might have begun to hammer and feel like it had been let out of an iron-tight clamp, but he was no longer frightened. He strode back to his desk, lit a Virginia Slim and stabbed at the button on the intercom.

'Jim?' Rosie sounded surprised. 'I thought you were upstairs in the shower.'

'Who's been in here?' he demanded.

'In where?'

'My workroom. Who's been in here? Today and yesterday?'

'What's wrong?'

'Rosie, just answer the question. It's important.'

39

'No one, to my knowledge,' Rosie said. 'What on earth has happened?'

'That cleaning girl you hired. The short girl from San Juan. Anita? She been in here?'

'Her boyfriend took her to·Vegas last week. She's probably going to come back married.'

'Anyone from Henry Skate's gang?'

'No! What—?'

'Spreadbury? He called again?'

'No, Jim—'

'And he couldn't possibly have gotten in here?' Distantly he cursed himself for saying 'gotten'. He was turning into a Yank at long last.

'It's possible, but unlikely. You know how good your damned security system is.'

'So, who's been in here?'

'You've been in there all day, Jim. No one else. No one but you went in there yesterday, either. Not while I was here, anyway.'

'So, I must have done, it, right?' Jim said angrily.

'Jim, *what's wrong*?'

Jim caught himself. 'Sorry, Rosie. I didn't mean to yell,' he said tightly. 'I have a bit of a mystery here. But I think I know exactly what's happened. I'm sorry. The computer's playing up again. I thought someone might have been at it.'

'Listen, Jim, Spreadbury is just a harmless crank,' Rosie said. 'God, he's almost as old as me and he's as rich as Croesus. He's not the type to break and enter. Trust me, some of my friends know him.'

'Yeah, I know,' Jim said. 'It's just that he spooked the shit out of Sooty and she spooked me. I know what the problem is now. I know what happened.'

He cut off the intercom, still angry and still shaking with the remains of the fear, but now he knew exactly what had happened and where the typing had appeared from.

Other than Jim there was only one person who entered and left his workroom as was her wont. She didn't do it often – usually her mother sent her in the hope of dragging her dad out for meals – and until now she'd kept her solemn promise not to touch anything. Jim found a smile at last. *Gloria!*

Gloria who had been playing *Razor Gang*, a game that blinked up all sorts of messages as you played it. Jim didn't remember the words 'dead man' or 'thief' ever appearing while he'd played it, but that didn't mean much. It'd been a long time since he'd touched that Sega and he hadn't even remembered the words, 'You won't come back *this* time', had he? And he'd *used* those.

He went back to the Smith Corona, tore the sheet out of it, ripped it up and put it in the bin.

He felt better after a long, cool shower.

Chapter Three

Elaine

1

'No, not really,' Elaine heard herself admit to Jim, in response to his probing as to whether or not she was *really* okay. She cursed inwardly, wishing she'd managed to keep her emotions to herself, and asked, 'What's the opposite of rose-tinted?' in what she hoped was a more cheerful voice.

At the other end of the line, or the ether, she supposed, since they were both using mobile phones, Jim paused, thinking about it. Elaine loved Jim dearly but he was a tad *too* perceptive at times. It sometimes felt a little eerie – as if you were talking to God or something. As if you could hide nothing from him. And Jim was the kind of person you automatically trusted. If you didn't watch yourself, you'd be telling him all your deepest, darkest secrets without even realizing you were doing it. It was probably what made him such a good writer, she thought.

'No idea,' Jim said finally. 'Gloom-tinted?'

Elaine scanned the street outside the hotel. It was busy with traffic and thick with exhaust fumes, but there were no pedestrians in sight. Which was a good thing.

'I'm just seeing the world through gloom-tinted glasses today, that's all,' Elaine said, taking a Camel from the pack in her pocket with her free hand. She needed the nicotine more than she needed the glassed-in safety of the hotel lobby where smoking wasn't allowed. She was surprised to find she felt a good deal more exposed than she'd anticipated.

Mark is in New York, she told herself. *He's still up there. Sitting in his office fielding calls between bawling out his secretarial team and trying to think up a hook for the campaign for the new Gaultier perfume's launch. What he's* not *doing is heading towards you on foot carrying a deadly weapon.*

'Mark?' Jim asked, as if he'd read her mind. Elaine jumped and caught herself before she could gasp, '*Where?*' Mark was in New York, that was where he was, and he might have been many things but he wasn't a stalker.

'Who else?' Elaine replied, still scanning the street in spite of herself. 'He's history now. Or at least I *hope* he is.'

'Meaning?'

Meaning he solemnly promised that he'd kill me if I hadn't gone back to him in two weeks, she thought, but didn't say it. Neither did she tell herself that today was the sixteenth day; that the two-week period had expired two days ago.

'Dumped but he won't disappear,' she told Jim. 'You know the score. It's the old *if-I-can't-have-you-no-one-else-will* routine. He's coming after me, he says. He's just trying to frighten me, I know that.' She held the cigarette in her lips and sucked on it furiously while her fingers stole to her ribs. There was still a tender spot there. More than one in fact.

'He's never hit me and he's only ever abused me verbally and I doubt he'd *do* anything, but the threat scares me,' she continued, wondering if Jim could hear the lie as it left her lips. The fact was that when push had come to shove, Mark had been the one doing the pushing and shoving. What she should have told Jim, what she wanted to tell him, was that Mark had only ever abused her verbally until sixteen days ago when she'd dumped him and his penthouse with its splendid view of Central Park. Then, somehow, verbal had become physical.

'I'm sorry to hear it,' Jim said, and Elaine could almost hear the flicker of his thoughts as they passed through his head. They were the same ones her friends and colleagues thought – and told her.

'Yeah, and I know what you're thinking. That I'm better off without him. You're just too diplomatic to say it. Unlike everyone else I know. Including me. I know I'm better off but, Christ, Jim, I *loved* that man . . .'

Even though he berated me so often and for so long that

43

my confidence deserted me. Even though the stress was so great that my Camel intake rose to two and half packs a day and my weight dropped right down to one hundred and twelve pounds. What fools us women are. What poor choices we make.

She finished with Jim, shut off the call, took one last deep inhalation from the Camel, threw down the butt, ground it out with her heel and strode back into the hotel foyer, forcing herself not to check the street again.

2

Elaine's gang of five stood in a little knot around their luggage in the air-conditioned cool of the hotel lobby, exactly where Elaine had left them.

Frank, the English teacher, was scowling and scribbling on his notepad. All Martha's concentration was focused on eating something she'd evidently dragged out of her bottom-less bag of supplies. June was staring at the receptionist, a large, cheerful black man, with an expression that looked like a combination of distaste and lust. Jon Short, his package of manuscripts clutched to his chest with both hands, was alternately staring at his feet and stealing glances at Candy, who was wearing a pair of cut-off Levi's – so cut off that seen from behind she showed a good expanse of pert, tanned backside – and a halter top. Candy was pretending that she hadn't noticed Jon Short noticing her; pretending just enough so that Jon knew she *had* noticed.

You'll hit your late thirties one fine day, Miss, Elaine thought. *And you'll probably be overweight and pasty-looking and worrying about cellulite. And then what?*

The truth was, Elaine supposed, that *then* Candy's rock-star or film-star husband would divorce her and pay her a few million bucks. Life was a bitch and no mistake.

'Okay, folks,' Elaine said. 'We have a stretch limo coming for us in . . .' she checked her watch '. . . about three minutes. There's room enough inside to hold a party, so you'll be very comfortable during the journey, which is about an hour from here.'

'Where the hell does this man *live*?' Candy whined.

'Seaford,' Elaine said. 'The town that time forgot. It's one of the oldest fishing towns in the US. Rumour has it that Ponce de Leon used the bay as a base for his exploration of Florida, as far back as fifteen thirteen. Although James Green looks younger every year, he insists that his house was *not* built on the site of the Fountain of Eternal Youth.'

Martha and June tittered. Frank scowled and wrote it down. Jon Short gnawed his lower lip and looked worried and Candy looked as if she was about to ask (a) who the hell was Ponce de Leon and who cared anyway? and (b) if the Fountain of Eternal Youth wasn't in Jim's backyard, then where the hell was it?

Elaine continued before Candy's mind had the chance to process the questions she wanted to ask. 'Highway One passed by Seaford and the townsfolk didn't care. Until the Second World War, all that led from the highway to Seaford was a dirt road, so the town stayed small and old-fashioned. It's a pretty little place. What you'd most likely call "quaint".

'Most of Seaford's trading was carried out on the water because the access to other local ports was easier that way. But in recent years the fishing trade has died down and a lot of people have left for the bright lights of Miami where there's work. Nowadays Seaford is a low-key tourist resort. It's where people go to get away from it all. And because James Green likes peace and quiet when he's working, he's stayed there rather than move to California or New York.'

'He was born in Seaford?' Frank asked, suspiciously.

Elaine wondered whether Frank had ever read a James Green book. The back flap of every one of them clearly stated that Jim had been born in Scotland. 'No, he's a Scot,' she said. 'From a small town called Onich, I believe. He now has dual nationality, so he's also an American.'

Candy opened her mouth to speak. And Elaine's phone began to ring. Elaine said, 'Excuse me,' and walked away from the group, pulling the mobile from her pocket as her heart sank and her chest tightened. She knew exactly who would be calling and what he was going to say.

She took a deep breath and pressed the button to take the call while she told herself, *It's only Mark and he's far away and he can't hurt me. Not again. Not ever.*

45

'Hello?' she said.

'Who is this?' a male voice asked.

Elaine glanced at the tinted glass by the hotel's entrance. For a moment she was certain that Mark wasn't coming for her at all, but in his place he'd sent a hired gun. A man who was on the other side of that glass where she couldn't see him, peering in at her, rifle already aimed. As soon as she identified herself, the glass would break and a high-velocity bullet would pierce her heart.

'Who is *this*?' she responded.

'It's okay,' the man said. 'Everything's okay. You're safe. No one's going to hurt you.'

What is this – mind-reading day? Elaine screeched inwardly. She dragged the phone away from her ear and hit the cut-off button. She took several deep breaths then turned back to her gang of five.

The phone rang again.

Elaine reached into her pocket and turned it off completely. Then she realized that her knot of fans were all staring at the revolving doors looking surprised. She felt her muscles tense and automatically ducked, her arms tucked in at her sides.

No one shot her.

'Ms Elaine Palmer?' a voice boomed from behind her.

Candy pointed.

'No!' Elaine squeaked.

Candy giggled. 'That's her!' she said, inadvertently playing Judas.

'Ma'am?' the voice said. It was closer now, and sounded concerned.

Elaine stood up and turned, cringing inwardly and waiting to die.

'Your carriage awaits,' said the tall, uniformed black man with the gold-toothed smile.

3

The video in the back of the limo had a choice of three films: *Miami Five Fifteen, Killing Spree* and *The Best of Mr Bean*. No one seemed to want to watch the films Jim had scripted

46

and three of the five were now chortling at the antics of Rowan Atkinson's creation. Frank continued to scowl and take notes, and June had fallen asleep, her knitting in her lap.

Elaine sat thinking and sipping cool mineral water. She was being paranoid, she knew. In spite of his having pushed her around a little and digging his fingers hard into her ribs, Mark wasn't a physically violent man. He wasn't even a *big* man. If she'd fought back, she could probably have trashed him, but the truth was, she half thought she'd deserved those few bruises she'd collected last week. After all, it had been her who'd been running out on him, not the other way round. And she'd felt guilty about it. She *still* felt guilty about it.

Don't be so damned ridiculous! she told herself. *You've suffered years of abuse, even if it wasn't* physical. *Just ask yourself why you wanted to leave him.*

It was all true, of course. The relationship had been beyond redemption. But she still felt that damned guilt at having walked out.

And she still felt that someone was out to harm her. Sitting in the back of the limousine, sipping Perrier and smoking a fresh Camel she began to realize that she might perhaps be pointing her finger in the wrong direction. She hadn't felt threatened while she was still in New York, not in the office and not while she'd been staying at her sister's place. And Mark had known exactly where to find her there.

Now she thought about it, the feeling of being threatened hadn't begun until she'd stepped off the plane at the airport in Miami, which was where . . .

I spiralled, she thought.

She had never been a good flyer. Her nerves got the better of her every time, even though she'd safely flown half a million miles or more. And her sinuses weren't suited for rapid changes of air-pressure either: a descent invariably led to shocking headaches, earaches and sinus pain. Except that on this flight there had been none of that.

Elaine had stepped off the Boeing 737 thinking, *I can't believe I got away with it this time!* when she'd spiralled.

At first she thought she'd fainted. The sensation was

strange: as if something inside her had become detached and had slid rapidly downwards in a corkscrew motion. It seemed to go on long enough for that loose part of her to have spiralled down into the centre of the earth. She'd been so dizzy she could see nothing but a blur of colour around her.

And then it had stopped and not only had she not fainted, she was still upright, still walking along with the other passengers as though nothing had happened.

All that had changed was her feeling of security. She'd been feeling pretty good all week, as a matter of fact. She was proud of having dumped Mark. Her downtrodden ego had begun to reinflate and she'd started to wake up in the mornings looking forward to the forthcoming day.

And in Miami yesterday, as soon as she stepped out of the plane, that feeling had vanished. Perhaps because her deadline had expired . . . or perhaps because of something else.

A premonition? Elaine smiled. Premonitions and portents were Jim's territory. Then the smile clouded. A stranger had called her mobile phone and said: *It's okay. Everything's okay. You're safe. No one's going to hurt you.*

Elaine ground out her cigarette in the arm-rest ashtray and wondered about it. In spite of the feeling of doom that still wouldn't go away, it was pretty unlikely that the caller had been a hit-man, hired by her ex-lover. It was pretty unlikely that Mark's threats were anything other than empty. Which left what?

She didn't know. Coincidence. Synchronicity or something.

But I know what I can do about it, she told herself, taking her mobile from her pocket. *I can call Mark.*

The question was, did she have the nerve to dial his direct line?

Elaine lit another cigarette and thought about it for a while. She suddenly wanted to pee, her heart was doing a free-fall descent and her stomach felt like it was filled with lead.

Snap out of it! she told herself. *You're a thirty-five-year-old grown-up woman and once upon a time people used to admire your firmness and steely self-sufficiency. You used to be nobody's fool. And now that it's all over with Mark there's*

*no reason why you shouldn't start standing on your own two
feet again.*

The trouble was, when you'd relinquished control to
someone else for three years it was difficult to adjust to
looking after yourself again. And, deep down inside, Elaine
wasn't even sure she didn't love Mark any more – in spite of
everything.

*Which is exactly what he trained you to think in those three
long years!* she thought angrily. *It's over and done. And you
will* not *let him sweet-talk you into coming back to him.*

But she didn't really trust herself to make the call until
she had reviewed a long list of the nasty things to which
Mark had subjected her recently. This raised her level of
righteous anger to a point where Elaine could feel her old
self slipping back into her cells. She lit a fresh Camel from
the butt of one she had just viciously smoked, pulled her
mobile from her jacket pocket and stabbed at the ON button.

PHONE LOCK, the display warned. And then ENTER CODE.

Elaine jabbed a number and hit the send button. Almost
instantly, the phone rang. She pressed the send button again.

'This is your recall service,' the network's pre-recorded
voice told her. 'You have one new message.'

And a familiar voice began to talk to her. Not the voice of
Mark, but the voice of the person who'd called her back at
the Radisson hotel. 'I know you've turned off the phone
because I frightened you on my first call and I know why
you're frightened. But you have no need to be scared of me.
I'm on your side. My name is Aaron and I badly need to get
in contact with James Green. I called his publishing house in
New York and they gave me your number. I understand Mr
Green is going on a trip this evening and is out of contact
because of this. I'm told you may be able to get in touch
with him. I know this is going to sound very odd, but I need
to speak to him because it's possible something very bad is
going to happen tonight. I have information which I need to
pass on. Please call me back on the following number . . .'

Elaine listened. The guy – whoever he was – didn't sound
like a total loon, but then again they often didn't. Until you
came face to face with them, that was. A lot of people read
Jim's books. And amongst those millions a few were bound

49

to have kinked Slinkys. He'd had death threats, letters signed in blood, you name it. This dipstick was just another in a long line.

And yet the name Aaron sounded familiar. Elaine shrugged it off. It was mere coincidence that the nutcase had seemed to know about her worries during his first call. Nothing more. She had been irrational, that was all. No hitman was coming after her.

She cancelled the playback and speed-dialled Mark's direct line in his New York office. The call was answered immediately.

But not by Mark.

'Hello?' a female voice with a French accent asked. 'Typhoon. Mark Chambers' office. Beatrice Raddice, executive vice president, speaking. How may I help you?'

'Beatty, it's Elaine,' she said. 'Mark's not there? I need to speak to him. You have a contact number? Where's he gone?' she blurted, both relieved and horrified that Mark wasn't glued in place in his big leather chair. If he wasn't there, he might be here, or on his way in Typhoon's Lear.

'Oh, Elaine,' Beatrice said, with what sounded like dismay. 'Of course, you wouldn't know. He ceased calling you on Tuesday. He was sure you wouldn't come back. So you couldn't know, could you? I'm *so* sorry.'

'Sorry? What are you talking about, Beatty?'

'Elaine, *Elaine* . . .' Beatrice's voice hitched. 'I don't know how to tell you, my darling. Poor Mark is gone.'

'Gone?' For a moment Elaine had no idea what Mark's second in command was talking about, or why she sounded so distraught. 'Gone *where*?'

'Mark died on Wednesday evening,' Beatrice said. 'I'm sorry.'

'Died? He's *dead*? *How*?'

'You've been away from New York? It's been on the television.'

'I spent some time with my sister after we split. She has no television and doesn't take a newspaper. She likes not knowing what's going on,' Elaine said. 'Then I visited some friends in Albuquerque, then I flew to Miami. No, I don't know what happened.'

50

'You'd like me to tell you?' Beatrice asked.

'Yes,' Elaine said, finding that long-lost tone of command. Inside she felt icy. 'I want to know everything.'

Beatrice sighed. 'You won't like it. He was shot dead outside a restaurant named the Blue Moon.'

Elaine nodded. She'd been there with Mark on more than one occasion. It was small and exclusive. The kind of place a man like Mark would take a woman for a romantic meal. A place where he could entrance her with those deep brown eyes of his and charm her until she was gasping for him. 'A woman shot him, right?' she asked.

'Yes,' Beatrice replied. 'A woman called Kristine Danvers. She shot him three times. She claims it was in self-defence. Mark was apparently carrying a loaded revolver. A Police Special, I believe. The woman says he'd threatened to kill her several times previously. She had finished with him, you see.'

'Yes,' Elaine whispered numbly. 'I understand now. He was evidently seeing her as well as me. We both dumped him. Probably in quick succession. Poor girl. I know exactly how she feels.'

'I'm sorry,' Beatrice said.

'I'm not,' Elaine rasped harshly. 'You know what, Beatty?'

'What?'

'Kristine Danvers saved me the trouble.'

4

I wonder if I should be grieving? Elaine asked herself, as she emptied a large slug of Jack Daniel's into the remaining Perrier in her glass. Mr Bean had stopped fooling about now and the five fans were arguing about which episode they would watch next and whether or not they would have time to see it all through.

Elaine didn't feel anything in response to the news that her long-term lover was dead. Not sadness, shock, or relief. She wasn't even numb now. The truth was, the bastard had deserved what he'd got. Not only that he had been shafting his 'one and only sex kitten' Elaine, in all senses of the word, but he'd been doing it to the poor cow who was going to go down for having shot him. Elaine couldn't even be bothered to be surprised that he'd been cheating on her. She felt absolutely nothing at all towards him. He was over. Gone. Past. History.

The odd thing was that the sense of foreboding was still with her. *Why?* she asked. *Evidently, Mark was the kind of man who wanted to do his own killing, so it's unlikely he's sent someone after me.*

She didn't know. What she *did* know was that she was going to feel a great deal better about things when she finally discharged this bunch of fans into Jim's hands and could talk to Sooty in peace and quiet.

Sooty was probably the most well-balanced woman Elaine had ever met. You only had to sit down in the same room as her to start feeling calm and happy, no matter how bad you'd felt when you arrived. She had an odd way of clearing your mind, just by her proximity. And whatever it was she (*and* Jim – they reflected one another like mirrors) radiated, good luck or goodwill, it was Good with a capital G.

Elaine sipped her whisky and wondered about falling spirals and cheating lovers and feelings of foreboding while *Miami Five Fifteen* played on the video and the fans murmured and gasped at the action. Eventually her eyelids grew too heavy for her to support.

She dreamed of dolphins.

Chapter Four

The Man in Black

1

Rosie wore an old pair of jeans, a yellow shirt and a pair of Timberland boots she'd forgotten she owned until now. According to Jim, old clothes were advisable because there was going to be 'blood' flying about. Rosie thought the idea sounded charming, but Jim hadn't sounded keen. She guessed this was, in part, due to his worries about his island. The flying 'blood' would be one more desecration in what was getting to be a long list. But this would be the last time. She'd reminded Jim of this and, surprisingly, he'd grimaced and said, 'Let's just hope nothing goes wrong.'

Rosie didn't see how anything *could* go wrong, but she was keenly aware of Jim's recent block and the fall-out from it. He'd only just managed to get back to work, so the odd mood here and there was only to be expected, she supposed.

After she'd showered and changed, she had driven down to what the locals still referred to as the docks, although all that now remained was a concrete apron and a long wooden jetty along which the occasional yacht and the odd cruiser docked. She parked her 4X4 on the apron and slipped into Spider Murphy's bar before the fans arrived.

The bar was empty but for Spider himself, old Carl Collins, who was smoking his pipe and reading the *Gazette*, and a couple of wealthy-looking tourists, a man and a woman whom Spider was already calling by their first names, Jack and Sophie. Over in the corner, several tables had been pushed together and covered in white linen, and Millie Lime was busy laying out a mouth-watering buffet.

Rosie ordered a beer and instructed Spider, Carl and Millie to pretend they'd never seen her before when the gang arrived. When Elaine came in, the lucky winners following her like ducklings paddling after their mother, Rosie grabbed her and explained.

Moments later, Elaine introduced her to the rest of the gang. 'Everyone! Meet Rose Baker. She's the sixth winner. Rose is from Marathon Key and made her own way up here. Make her feel welcome and then get yourselves a drink from the bar – it's all paid for – and if anyone's hungry,' she added, looking directly at Martha, 'there's a table of food set up in the corner.'

Rosie set about introducing herself, enjoying her own fiction as she created it. Inside ten minutes half the fans knew she was a divorcée who, fifty-five years ago, had been born to wealthy parents in Boston. She'd fallen out with her parents and left home at fifteen. She'd made for Cuba, where she'd worked in several casinos and had had a string of torrid affairs before marrying mad Davis Baker, who'd made her life a misery and who was now languishing in jail serving out a sentence of one hundred and fifty-five years.

'What did he do?'

Rosie shook her head sadly at Frank's question. 'It'd be quicker to list what he *didn't* do. Really, it doesn't bear thinking about. I can't even *force* myself to tell you. If only I'd *known* . . .'

This looked like it was going to be a fun evening. Not only was she going to get to see Jim's island, but she was discovering things about herself that she'd never known. Not only could she tell lies, she was good at telling them. And she could act, too.

'Excuse me, Frank,' she said, wondering why he was scribbling so frantically in his notepad – he'd filled three pages with shorthand squiggles while she'd been talking to him, 'but I want to go and meet that little blonde girl over there.' She wandered over to Candy, took the girl's hand and pumped it and said, 'Hi, I'm Rosie. I'm pleased to meet you. What do *you* do for a living?'

Now, fed, watered and feeling mellow, the five winners and the impostor stood in the sunshine on the dock's apron, gathered in a semi-circle around their guide. Elaine stood on the edge of the concrete, her back to the stern of the only large boat moored there. Behind her, the forty-foot power-cruiser, named the *Mary Celeste*, rocked gently in the water, looking powerful and luxurious.

'As you'll be aware, the annual competition to spend an evening of terror with James Green has become something of an institution. This year's trip is to celebrate the launch of his new book, *Black River*. To commemorate this trip we've had ten copies made of a deluxe edition of *Black River*. They're traditionally bound in quality hide, embossed in gold leaf, printed on quality paper, numbered, and they include illustrations by the renowned artist David Letts. James gets to keep number one, of course,' she smiled, 'but during the trip you'll be presented with your very own copy and James will sign each one and add a personalized message for you.'

The fans seemed thrilled by the prospect. Martha gave a little yelp of delight. Candy said, 'Cool!' Jon Short grinned and punched the air. Frank, however, Rosie noticed, didn't seem so impressed. He scowled a private little scowl and gave a curt nod, as if to say: *No more than I'd expected.*

The deluxe edition had been another of Jim's ideas. A good one, in Rosie's opinion. The books would be *very* valuable – although she doubted anyone would want to sell theirs.

'We thought you'd like that,' Elaine said, glancing round nervously, as if she were expecting trouble. 'They're actually very beautiful books. Now I'm sure you're all aware of the format for this evening, but just in case you're not, this is what'll be happening. James will welcome you aboard his cruiser and you'll make the short crossing to Straker's Island, which is deserted and reputed to be haunted. You'll build a camp-fire and James will cook food for you and then you'll sit in the dark and swap spooky stories. There may well be a surprise or two in store for you. Jim usually thinks of something. You'll be brought back when it's all over and, as you know, it's only a short walk back to the Seaford Hotel. Does anyone have any questions?'

Candy thrust her hand in air.

'Candy?' Elaine asked.

'Is Jim still with his wife?' the girl asked.

3

'Yes, he is,' Elaine said distractedly. 'Any more questions?' she added, watching the black car cruise slowly down the row of vehicles parked on the apron. She didn't recognize the car, which wasn't surprising, she realized, since she didn't live here, but she didn't like the look of it.

'I have a question!' Frank challenged.

Elaine barely heard him. The car was a sleek, black convertible Porsche, its hood up. The windows were tinted so she couldn't see who was driving. Whoever it was had already passed several parking places, so the driver was looking for one particular place to stop. Somewhere close to Elaine.

It isn't possible! she thought. *Mark is dead!*

But Elaine knew that didn't preclude the driver of that car being a hit-man sent by her dear departed Mark. No professional killer in his right mind would carry out a hit after the person who'd hired him had died. He would either pocket the money and forget about the hit, or if he hadn't been paid he would know he wouldn't be able to collect.

Unless whoever he hired doesn't know he's dead.

'Ms Palmer?' Frank insisted.

Elaine glanced away from the Porsche, which rolled slowly behind the fans, its turbochargers hissing like snakes.

'Yes, Frank?' Elaine said, peering past the man's head. The car was now backing into a space slightly to the right of the fans.

'Where the hell *is* James Green?' Frank demanded.

Elaine glanced at her watch, then back at the car. Nothing was happening there. 'He should be here by now,' she said. And mentally added, *But he isn't in that Porsche. Doesn't Jim only ever drive a Mercedes?* Then she thought that perhaps Jim *was* here. He had what he liked to call a warped sense of humour, so it was possible he was on board his boat already, waiting for the tension to build so he could pop up out of nowhere, shout, 'Boo!' and give everyone a scare.

But his Mercedes was nowhere to be seen.

Come on, Jim! she pleaded. *For God's sake, hurry up!*

'He may be on the boat,' she said, and wished she hadn't because now she was going to have to turn her back on the black car to call into the *Mary Celeste*.

'*Hiding?*' Frank asked, in a tone of astonishment and disapproval. 'Is there something *wrong* with the man?'

Elaine ignored him and turned to face the boat. 'Jim?' she called. 'Are you on board?' Her voice bore a distinct tremor.

'That's *Jim*'s boat?' she heard Martha say, around a mouthful of her latest sub – one which leaked red sauce each time she bit into it. 'My, that's a *big* boat!'

'Jim?' Elaine called again. She was certain she could hear the Porsche's door opening behind her, even though the car was a good fifty yards away.

'Look what the boat's called,' Jon Short said, as Elaine turned back. He had hold of June's arm and was pointing at the name emblazoned on the stern.

'The Mary Cellesty,' June carefully enunciated.

'That name explains everything,' Jon continued. 'James isn't here because he's slipped through into the Twilight Zone.'

'The *what?*' Candy asked.

Christ, do these people actually read *Jim's books?* Elaine heard herself think.

'I don't get it,' June said. 'Why does the boat's name mean he's vanished?'

The Porsche's door was closed. Elaine didn't know whether that meant that the driver was still inside or that he'd got out. She didn't know *anything* any more, except that she expected to die. She scanned the dock but couldn't see anyone. If it was a hit, the guy was probably crouched behind his car screwing his rifle together, or whatever they did.

Jon Short was rolling his eyes. 'The *Mary Celeste* was the

ship they found adrift with no one on board. The table places were laid for a meal. Wine had been poured into goblets. There was no sign of what had happened to the crew.'

But there *was* a sign of what had happened to the man who'd driven up in the black Porsche, Elaine noticed, through the gap in the knot of fans that Jon provided as he moved a step to one side.

The man was out of the car and coming this way. He was a tall, lean man dressed in black jeans, black shirt and shoes and was wearing one of those awful black balaclavas which covered his entire face but for two small holes where his eyes were. In his left hand the man was carrying something that looked like a short, squat bundle of sticks of dynamite, complete with a long dangling fuse.

Elaine froze.

'Can't we just get on the boat?' Candy asked.

'Go aboard, you mean,' Frank corrected.

Candy shrugged. 'Whatever. Elaine?'

Elaine couldn't reply. The man in black was less than thirty feet from them now and his right hand was dipping into the pocket of his jeans. She was going to die. The man was going to blow her up. Blow them all up, by the look of it. And there wasn't a damned thing anyone could do about it. She opened her mouth to shout a warning, but her larynx was as paralysed as the rest of her.

'Are you okay?' Jon Short asked.

Elaine wasn't okay. She would dearly have loved to have been able to tell Jon Short this. She wasn't okay, he wasn't okay and neither was anyone else in this party, but she couldn't act like a good friend and protector and warn them because she had turned into cold, smooth marble.

The man in black brought something metallic out of his jeans pocket. It glinted in the late-afternoon sun. For a moment Elaine saw a small gun – perhaps a Derringer – and then realized what it was. A Zippo lighter.

It won't matter if the wind blows then, will it? That's a wind-proof lighter.

It seemed ironic that she'd spent the last six years or so running round telling everyone how damned good Jim's books were and now she was going to die pretty much like a minor character in one of those books. One of what Jim liked to call his 'shreddies'.

Help me, someone! she pleaded inwardly as, through the gap between Jon Short and June, she watched the assassin set down the explosive device on the ground.

'Elaine?' Candy asked, stepping forward. 'Is there anything I can do?'

The girl looked genuinely concerned and Elaine suddenly forgave her for being a cypher of a Californian blonde bimbo.

I'm sorry, Candy, Elaine thought, her eyes still fixed on the trailing fuse that led to the explosives. The man was crouched behind the little clump of dynamite now, feeding the fuse through his hand, trying to find the end of it. *There's nothing anyone can do.*

As if she were standing only inches from him, Elaine watched the man in black flip up the lid of the Zippo and thumb the wheel. She could *feel* the grin on his face beneath the mask as the lighter ignited. In what seemed to be extreme close-up she watched the fuse begin to fizzle.

The man snapped the lighter shut, stood up and walked backwards towards his car. Now, all Elaine could see was the fuse burning rapidly down its length, marking off the last moments of her life.

I guess we should all duck or something, she thought stupidly, as the fizzling flame climbed the side of the stack and reached the top of the bundle.

And the flame gave a last tiny flash and went out, leaving a wisp of blue smoke behind.

Elaine began to laugh.

'What? What's wrong?' Candy asked.

And, as one, the lucky fans finally turned to see what Elaine was staring at.

'Jeez, what the hell is *that*?' Jon Short yelled in dismay.

'It went out,' Elaine chortled. 'It went out!'

Which was when the device detonated.

The world dissolved in a blinding flash, a devastating shockwave and thunderous noise.

Chapter Five

The Liar's Almanac

1

Elaine was surprised to find herself still alive. The only damage she seemed to have suffered was a ringing in her ears and a terrible weight on her back. One of her knees stung a little from where she'd hit the ground as she flung herself down.

She tried to move and couldn't, then realized she was trapped by the weight on her back. The weight that was clinging to her and *crying* on her back, making her neck damp. The frightened kitten mewling must be Candy.

Two of us got away, Elaine thought. *We survived!*

She tried to roll out from under Candy, suddenly aware as her ears began to clear that others were alive too and perhaps in need of help. Frank was cussing and Jon was repeating the words, 'I'm deaf,' over and over, and a couple of the women were making shocked noises. Someone was giggling.

'Shocks you want, shocks you got!' a voice announced.

Elaine twisted her head round.

And saw, wreathed in smoke, James Green. He was dressed in black, holding a balaclava in his left hand, and grinning from ear to ear.

'*You*—' Elaine snapped her mouth shut before 'mother-fucker!' could come out. Jim couldn't have known about Mark or her worries that she would be killed.

'I'm sorry,' Jim said, waving smoke away. He bent down and hoisted Jon Short to his feet. 'I wanted to start the evening with a bang. Unfortunately I hadn't planned on it being as big a bang as that. My friend Davey Smith built the firework for me and I guess he got a little carried away.'

'It wasn't very funny,' Frank pointed out, as Jim helped him up and pumped his hand.

'I know,' Jim said, and shrugged. 'I'm sorry. I'll make it up to you.'

'We came here to be frightened,' Jon Short observed, collecting his bag of manuscripts from the boardwalk, 'frightened we were. I can't see a damned thing wrong with that.'

'Me neither,' Martha said, dusting herself off. 'In fact I thought it was a wonderful introduction.'

'Snap!' June added.

Jim took Candy's hand and helped her up. She was tear-stained and her face was smeared with dirt. He took a tissue from his pocket and gently cleaned her up. 'I'm sorry. It was only meant to make you jump. I didn't want to blow bits off anyone.'

Candy reached up and took hold of his hand with both of hers. She smiled at him, doe-eyed. 'It's okay,' she said, squeezing his hand. 'I kinda *like* being frightened.'

'I'm glad,' Jim said, aware that Candy didn't intend to let go of his hand – or his gaze – unless he forced it. Elaine was right: Candy *was* trouble waiting to happen. Her eyes promised untold pleasures.

Candy licked her lips and lowered her voice. 'Being frightened makes me go ... *tingly*. Y'know, right down deep *inside*.'

Jim grinned. 'Well, er, I'd better go introduce myself to the others,' he said, pulling his hand free.

Candy chuckled. 'I've embarrassed you,' she said.

'Now we're quits,' Jim responded.

'Not quite,' Candy said quietly, as he turned away.

And his hand was grabbed again. By Jon Short this time. '*Nice* entrance, big guy!' he said enthusiastically as he pumped Jim's hand up and down. 'Scared the shit out of me! What a way to start the evening! My name's Jon Short. God, I'm *so* pleased to meet you. You've been my hero since I was a kid!'

Jim gave a wry smile. 'I'm not *that* old. I've only been publishing books for seven years,' he said, trying to ignore the bag of paperwork the man had in his other hand.

61

Jon was crestfallen. '*No!* No! When I say *kid* I mean *teenager*,' he explained quickly. 'I didn't mean to imply you were *old*. I'm sorry. You were my inspiration. The reason I began to write.'

'Oh, good,' Jim said, trying to summon up some enthusiasm and almost making it. 'And it looks as though you've brought some of your writing with you, too.'

Jon went from crestfallen to devastated. 'Damn it,' he said. 'What a fool I am. I'm sorry. I guess people do this to you all the time.' He mimicked a pathetic voice. '"*Read my book, Jim, you'll think it's brilliant. Take a look at this and tell me if I have what it takes.*" That kind of thing, right?'

Jim gave him a warm smile. 'Yeah, that's about the size of it. But I'd be pleased to take a look at your work.' *And I might even read some of it if it looks any good.* 'But if you want me to look, you have to sign the standard disclaimer.'

Jon Short looked shocked. 'Disclaimer?'

'Oh, yes,' Jim said. Jon was here to be made uncomfortable, if not downright frightened, and Jim intended to do his best. 'I'm a word-thief. Everyone knows that. Even some of the literary supplements have accused me of plagiarism. And quite rightly, too. If I see a good idea, I'll steal it without hesitation. The promise you have to give me is that you won't ever sue me for ripping off your stuff.'

An expression of pure agony passed across Jon's face. He shook his head. '*Me?* Sue *James Green*?' he said, as if the idea was akin to murdering his own mother. Nevertheless he tightened his grip on the bag of manuscripts, hugging them to him as if to prevent Jim stealing his ideas by osmosis.

Then a strong hand took his arm and whirled him round. And James Green came face to face with his *greatest* fan.

'Hi, Martha!' Jim said, finding it practically impossible to take her all in in one sweeping gaze. There was just too much of her, billowing beneath the thin floral – *wigwam?* – dress. Martha wasn't just big, she was mountainous, the kind that Sooty's friends on the airlines would call a two-seat special. And she was tall too – nearly six foot, Jim thought.

'Oh, *Jim*! You even know who I am!' she said in delight.

'Yep. I know *all* about you, Martha,' Jim said. 'You're forty-three, but you only look thirty,' he continued, watching

Martha's face light up at his deduction of ten years from her true age. 'You're from Tulsa, where you work for a computer company coding in C, and you have a Yorkshire terrier called Murder.'

Martha shook her head in admiration and appreciation. She took a deep breath and said, 'Wow! I've died and gone to heaven!'

Martha might have had rolls of dimpled fat that hung down on her feet from her ankles, arms like hocks of ham and a girth that the man with the world's longest arms wouldn't have been able to reach round, but she also had perfect skin, gorgeous long black hair and the clearest, most honest green eyes Jim had ever seen. Beneath her dumb-bunny rock-band hysteria, he could see the heart of a *good* person beating.

Jim reached out to shake her bear-like paw, then saw there was an unzipped banana clutched in it. Martha noticed, grinned inanely, switched the banana to her left hand, wiped her right on her dress then did a pretty good job of crushing Jim's hand.

'I also know all your other dark little secrets!' he said with a knowing wink.

Martha blushed bright red and tittered. 'You *do*? Oh, my! *James*, you *are* a naughty boy, aren't you?' And without warning she hugged him tightly and kissed his cheek.

'Put him down, Martha!' someone said, chuckling. 'I haven't met him yet!'

Jim was released and found himself looking at June, the knitter. She was trim and tiny, neatly dressed, with shoulder-length dark hair. She must have been a foot shorter than Martha, and when she smiled she showed those perfect American teeth of which Jim was so jealous. She offered him a small hand, which Jim took and kissed.

'I'm June Rivers,' June said smiling. 'That's June, *not* Joan. And you can forget Martha because *I'm* your biggest fan!'

'Pah!' Martha said happily.

'I've read everything you ever published,' June claimed. 'Some of them ten times or more.'

'I've read 'em all *twenty* times,' Martha scoffed, giggling. '*And* all the interviews, too!'

June smiled at Jim. 'It's lovely to meet you,' she said.

'You, too,' Jim said. 'And I hope you'll have a great time this evening. Now, let's all jump on the boat and get going!'

2

The sea was millpond flat and the wind had dropped to around two knots. The *Mary Celeste*, her big engines throbbing smoothly, surged out to sea leaving an ever spreading wake of white foam behind her. The sky above was deepening in colour now as evening approached. A few puffy clouds were dotted about, but there was no sign of the storm that Jim had expected. The sky back in the direction of Seaford was clear, the radar didn't show anything and the coastal weather reports for the night were good.

When they were half-way to Straker's Island and they'd cleared the shipping lanes and passed Old Rhodes Key, Jim eased off the power, gently slowing the vessel, then shut off the engines and let her coast to a standstill. He dropped the anchor, made her secure and went back to check on the fans. They hadn't been at sea for very long and the water was flat, but Jim knew that some folks got seasick just *thinking* about being on a boat. And during the last couple of trips he'd had a few who had puked. Last year, one girl had become so sick that he'd had to turn back and drop her off. It *had* been pretty choppy that day, however, Jim was forced to admit.

It looked pretty much as if today was going to be vomit-free, though, he realized, as he started down to where his little gang were lounging in the sun on the rear deck. He mightn't have been keen on blood these days, but he *hated* vomit.

Today's fans all looked pretty relaxed. Frank was on his own, leaning on the stern's guard rail, gazing back towards Seaford and smoking something in his pipe that smelt like camel shit. For once he wasn't taking notes. Rosie had changed into a swimsuit and was lying back on a lounger sipping a can of beer. Martha and June were sitting on the starboard side of the built-in bench that ran round the boat's stern. They were talking animatedly; June's small hands fluttered through the air like butterflies and Martha's alternately chopped like axes and delicately fed tidbits of food into her mouth.

The thing that *really* hooked Jim's eye was the sight of Candy in a white bikini so tiny it barely existed at all. She was posing on a lounger, gazing at Jon Short, who knelt beside her, through what looked like a very expensive pair of sunglasses.

Looks like Jon's in luck, Jim thought. The girl didn't just have a good body, she had a damned near perfect one. She wasn't top heavy or short-legged or wide-hipped or any of the other things that beach babes generally were when you saw them up close. Everything was in perfect proportion.

I could, Jim thought as he walked down the steps. But *could* wasn't *would*. He'd been with Sooty for so long it sometimes seemed like he'd never had a life without her, and he'd had plenty of offers come his way during signing tours and television appearances. On one notable occasion he'd even had an offer he could barely refuse from a world-famous actress and sex-symbol on the set of *Miami Five Fifteen*. But, in spite of all this, Jim had never been unfaithful to Sooty.

Yet, he told himself, tearing his eyes away from Candy.

Frank spotted him and hurried over, meeting him at the bottom of the steps. 'We've stopped,' he pointed out unnecessarily.

Jim made an apologetic face. 'Sorry, Frank, we're out of gas. And the radio's gone down so I can't call for help.'

Frank opened his mouth to speak, but Jim continued, 'You probably heard the noise as I tried to drop the anchor, too. Unfortunately ... damn it, I should have let them do that refit when they said the boat needed it.'

'Unfortunately *what*?' Frank demanded.

'The anchor capstan jammed. We're adrift. That'd be okay if it wasn't for ...'

Frank raised an accusing eyebrow.

Jim shrugged. 'There's a storm blowing up,' he said. 'A big one. I was hoping to get to the island before it hit, but now ...' He shrugged again. 'I just hope they put the flares back.'

'Who?' Frank demanded. 'What?'

65

Jim grinned. 'Be patient with me. I'm a professional liar.'

Frank looked as if he badly needed to scream and fling a punch but he merely sighed and fished his red notebook out of his back pocket.

Smiling, Jim left him and sat down on a spare chair where everyone could see him.

Martha grinned knowingly at him and said, 'We've broken down, haven't we? You old devil!'

Jim glanced at Frank who was now busy filling more pages with shorthand. 'No, we haven't broken down. We're about half-way there, so I thought it was about time I came down to ask if you were all feeling okay. The sea's flat but I've known people who can throw up just looking at the ocean. Everyone's okay, are they?'

The chorus of affirmatives that followed was gratifying. 'You know where the beer and stuff is, so help yourselves,' he said. 'And now I have things to tell you. Serious things. Everyone comfortable?'

Candy nodded and sat up attentively, which included thrusting her breasts towards Jim. Martha found a bag of potato crisps and popped it open. Frank scribbled, then looked up from his pad, pencil poised.

This guy is taking too many notes for my liking, Jim thought. *I bet he's going to try to sell an article to a glossy magazine when this is all over.* He thrust the thought away and did a quick head-count. He counted seven not including himself, which didn't tally, but surely meant everyone was here.

'Now,' he began, ignoring his stage-fright butterflies, 'I know you're from all parts of the States, but has anyone been around this area before?'

Frank said, 'I've been to Seaford once before when I was touring Florida. I just drove all the way down the road to see what was at the other end. It seemed like such a god-forsaken hole to me that I turned the car around and went back again.'

Everyone laughed at this sideswipe, including Jim. Frank was upset, and while he couldn't bring himself to take a direct poke at a world-famous writer, he could take one at that writer's place of residence.

66

'Yes, well as you've seen, it's pretty quiet. And that's one of the reasons I like it. It's good for working. And being a god-forsaken hole stops it getting too crowded and too big. And, as some of you know, I spent time here when I was a kid. And I guess I fell in love with the place. I came back as soon as I could.' Jim paused. 'So, does anyone know anything about Straker's Island? Rosie? You're from the Keys, just down the road a-ways. You ever heard anything?'

Rosie cleared her throat. 'Well, all the rumours I've heard are about a certain writer and his wife who used to run around there naked all day. I'm given to understand that this certain writer's daughter was conceived on the porch of the Straker house. Is there any truth in that rumour?'

'A neat curve-ball from Rosie there,' Jim said, suddenly embarrassed. Inwardly he felt as if he were blushing furiously. He threw Rosie a *you're-going-to-pay-for-this* look, but she merely smiled sweetly back at him. 'I haven't heard those rumours,' he said, fishing his pack of Virginia Slims from his shirt pocket and lighting up.

The fans all thought this was highly amusing. The laughter took a long time to die down, and when it did, June was waving her hand in the air like the only girl in the class who knew the answer to a particularly tricky question.

Jim exhaled plumes of smoke through his nostrils. 'Yes, June,' he said, bracing himself for more personal questions.

'It's deserted and it's supposed to be haunted. That's all I know,' she said.

It took a moment for Jim to realize that she was referring to his original question 'Does anyone know anything about Straker's Island?' rather than to his sex life (which had indeed been deserted while he'd been blocked and haunted by his angst).

'*That* was in the advertisement for the competition.' Frank snorted in derision. 'We *all* know *that*.'

June shot him a look that should have killed him.

Frank suddenly stood, a look of total shock on his face, Jim's working voice cut in. *He staggered forward clumsily, like a man walking in increased gravity. His hands snatched at his chest while he glanced around at the others, mutely*

67

appealing for help. No one moved. A tiny rivulet of blood crept down from his left nostril . . .

Jim smiled. *Wishful thinking!* he told himself, and said, 'Thanks, June. Straker's Island is indeed deserted. And it *is* haunted. You've probably heard the standard introduction from Elaine. But bear in mind that Elaine is the publicity director from the publisher and that she doesn't know everything. She'll have told you that we're going to land over there and cook food over a camp-fire and swap spooky stories and so on. The rest – the haunting stuff – will all have sounded like standard Orlando Attraction hype, added because of the kind of subjects I favour in my work. Well, I'm here to tell you that the *reality* isn't quite how you're picturing it.'

'There's no food?' Martha asked, in a pained tone.

'Oh, there's food. Whether or not you'll feel like eating it after you've been on the island for an hour or two is another matter.' Jim smiled. 'It's not a nice place. There are some things I've been meaning to tell you.'

He lit another cigarette. He could feel himself entering the story-telling groove.

'And now it's time I told you those things. Some of you may want to turn back when you hear what I have to say, but I won't listen to appeals. You've made your choices and you're going to the island, whether you want to or not.' He grinned evilly. 'I just want you to be prepared for what might happen.'

Five rapt faces stared at him, waiting for him to start. The sixth – Frank Blaine – was scowling down at his red notebook, while he scribbled. It was good enough as far as Jim was concerned. The story he would tell started with the known facts and was then open to whatever fiction he chose to weave around the island and the unknown person or persons who'd once inhabited it. Jim liked to do it in this way rather than have a set routine, because it prevented boredom and it tested his skills of improvisation. When this tale was done, he would take it home and add it to the others he'd told during boat trips like this one, in what he liked to call his *Liar's Almanac*. It made pretty interesting reading a couple of years later and Jim had drawn from it for several of his money-making enterprises.

He took a breath. 'Okay. Straker's Island is sixteen nautical miles off the coast of Seaford. Its one square mile rises to the staggering distance of twenty-two feet above sea-level. The body of the island consists of forest, filled mainly with plane trees and pines although there are plenty of palms around the beaches. There's a small swamp in the centre of the island, but you'll be pleased to hear there are no alligators in it.'

'You're sure?' Frank asked, during the pause Jim took for breath.

'He said so, didn't he?' Jon Short replied, irritated.

'I'm sure,' Jim said. 'Be patient and you'll find out why I'm sure.'

Without looking away from Jim, Martha pulled a banana from her bottomless bag and unzipped it. Beside her, June, her gaze also fixed on her hero, was knitting rapidly.

'No one lives on Straker's Island and there's no fauna on the island. No one's seen anything larger than the odd earthworm there for a hundred years. Birds do not go to Straker's Island to nest. In fact, birds don't go there, period. You won't even hear the cry of a seagull.'

This was was God's honest truth and one of the peculiarities that had first drawn Jim to the island. He suspected that the reason was magnetism, although he'd never bothered having the gauss readings metered. It didn't do to fuck around with the kind of magic that Straker's Island worked on him, which was the main reason this trip would be the last one that came to this special place.

While his audience made sounds of disbelief, Jim wondered what spooky tale he was going to come up with this time. And was delighted to discover that his subconscious had apprehended a fresh one, whole and seamless. His working voice cut in and took over his vocal cords. Jim marvelled inwardly at the strange and delightful sensation as his mouth began to utter words that didn't seem to belong to him.

'Now, I don't know *why* the place has no wildlife, but some folk have a theory. Many of the mainland locals say

69

the place is haunted by the ghost of Straker Dauphin and his family. I don't know about that, but I can tell you that none of the locals ever visit the place.'

Which was one reason why he'd been able to buy Straker's Island so cheaply. That and blind luck – by rights, the island should have been part of Biscayne National Park, wildlife or not.

Jim continued, 'Maybe if I tell you all about what happened on Straker's Island about a hundred and twenty-five years ago, you'll make up your own minds why that should be.'

Martha gasped, 'Oh, *Jimmy*! What *are* you getting us into?' popped the ring on a can of Tab and downed half its contents in one gulp.

Frank stopped scribbling, glared at Martha, then turned back to Jim. 'So what happened?' he asked.

Gotcha! Jim thought. '*This* is what happened. Straker Dauphin arrived in Seaford in eighteen seventy-four. He'd come to America from France in seventy-one and had gone to New York where he hoped to make it in the literary world.'

Jon Short asked, 'He was a writer? Like you?'

'He was a writer, yes,' Jim replied, 'but he didn't have my luck. He'd written several books, but none of them ever saw print. No one knows why. Perhaps he was out of tune with the times.' He shrugged.

In an almost perfect imitation of Martha, Rosie said, 'Oh, *Jimmy*! You're making this up! You're *such* a story-teller!'

Jim shot her a warning look and purposefully moved his eyes to the side of the boat, reminding her of his promise to throw her overboard if she caused him any trouble. Rosie grinned at him and winked. She looked as if she was having the time of her life.

Jim shook his head. 'As much as you might like to believe so, this is *not* made up. It's all documented. In 'seventy-four, half starved and in despair at his failed career, Straker Dauphin moved down to Seaford. We're not sure whether he did because he already knew the rich French girl who'd moved there the previous year, but it's generally assumed they'd known one another years before in Paris and that

70

they'd previously been romantically linked. The girl, Majesty Dios, was exceptionally wealthy. In early 'seventy-four the couple married and bought the deserted island from the town for seven hundred and fifty dollars. They had a house built on it and moved out there late the same year. Majesty was pregnant with a little girl they named Gloria.'

Candy indicated the empty ocean with her hand, and said, 'Why did they wanna move right out here? It's miles from anything.'

'Once a writer, always a writer, I guess,' Jim said. 'Straker couldn't find a publisher, but that didn't stop him wanting to write. Once it's in the blood, it's like malaria. It breaks out uncontrollably. According to the *Seaford Gazette*, Straker had been suffering from a particularly bad bout of writer's block and, after a fishing trip to the island, his block went away. He decided, I guess, that the island was a good place to be. It had its own freshwater spring and, in spite of the lack of animals, vegetables grow well and there are plenty of fish in the sea.'

Frank asked, 'Did he write anything while he was there?'

'Depends what you call writing, I guess. He kept a kind of combination almanac and diary. It's currently under glass in the Seaford museum.'

'What did it *say*?' Jon Short was suddenly alert and on the edge of his seat.

Jim smiled. These moments were what he lived for and so seldom got to see: the moments when his audience were sucked into a story, their disbelief suspended, their entire concentration focused on the need to know *what happened next*. He glanced over at Rose, who was nodding in what looked like appreciation of his spellbinding talent. She winked at him.

'It didn't say anything remarkable. At first. Along with the daily reports of the weather conditions there were details of the family's day-to-day exploits. It painted a picture of an idyllic lifestyle. The Dauphins farmed. Grew vegetables, kept chickens and pigs. Straker's writing is mentioned, but only in passing. According to the journal he'd switched track from his old style and was writing stories of a fantastical nature. Strangely enough, later, when it was all over, there were no manuscripts to be found. They may be there still, hidden somewhere. If they ever existed.'

'All over?' Frank asked, his notebook temporarily forgotten. 'What d'you mean, "later when it was all over"? What went wrong?' His fingers tamped dark tobacco into the bowl of his pipe, but the action was automatic: he was evidently entirely gripped now by Jim's story. Jim found his dislike of the man fading a little.

'The first inkling we have of anything amiss is in the entry in the diary dated July fifth eighteen seventy-five. There's no weather report on that day, no details of anything the family did. The page is empty except for the words: *Today the devil came.*'

'Oh, Lord. *Really?*' Martha asked round a mouthful of a new sandwich.

Jim nodded. 'Really. And on July eighth another page, blank but for the words: *The chickens have all died. No longer edible. Burned them.* Then the diary is blank for three weeks. The entry for July thirtieth reads: *Pigs all dead now. Majesty ill. It's boiling over.*'

'Boiling over . . .' Martha breathed.

Frank looked as if he'd suddenly been plunged into a genuine emergency. 'Why didn't they leave?' he demanded. 'Why didn't they go back to Seaford?'

'The answer to *that* question also lies in the *Seaford Gazette,*' Jim said. 'If you read the records for that year you'll find that the area had a terrible summer. Gales, tornadoes, high seas and the heaviest rainfall on record. The Dauphins couldn't have left even if they'd wanted to. And they probably *did* want to. Very badly.'

'What did he mean, "It's boiling over"?' Candy asked.

'Straker's Island was thought to be haunted even before the Dauphin family moved out there. Perhaps Straker inadvertently woke a sleeping demon. Or did it on purpose to help with his writing. It's my guess that when he said, "It's boiling over," he meant the demon was running out of control.'

June's knitting now lay forgotten in her lap. Her mouth was agape, her expression shocked. 'What happened next?'

Jim smiled. For a writer, hearing those three little words

72

spoken were as important as the other famous combination of three little words.

'Nothing,' he said. 'Not till August seventeenth. On that page the entry simply says: PAIN – in capital letters. After that the diary is empty.'

'Wow,' Jon Short said. 'And then what? They vanished?'

'Oh, no,' Jim said. 'They didn't *vanish*. The weather calmed eventually and on August thirty-first the guy that sailed the supply boat managed to get all the way out to Straker's Island with his delivery. He was very late, but he knew the family would have survived. They had fresh water and animals and vegetables. It was a routine trip for him. Until he arrived and walked up the beach to the house.'

'And found them all dead,' Martha said, awed.

'How did they die? What happened to them?' Frank asked.

Jim shrugged. 'Well, the report in the *Gazette* conjectured that they'd been attacked by seafaring thieves. There were still plenty of pirates in the Caribbean at that time and they often travelled up the Keys. The newsmen supposed that a vessel had been riding high seas and had gotten blown off course for Key Largo and had pulled into the bay of Straker's Island for safety.'

'Jeez,' June said, shaking her head.

'It had to have been pirates, the newspaper reckoned. What other kind of being would take little Gloria and do those things to her?'

'What things?' three of the audience said in unison.

Jim pulled a pained face, while inside his demon grinned and giggled. 'Gloria had been quartered and decapitated on the kitchen table.'

'*Ohhhh, my God!*' Martha moaned.

'But there's more,' Jim continued. 'Majesty had been violated in ways I can't bring myself to say. And her body had been disembowelled. Whoever had done it had hung her entrails from the porch roof and nailed them up around the door and window frames.'

'Straker did it,' Jon Short breathed. 'I know it!'

'Possibly,' Jim said. 'But Straker Dauphin's throat had been cut. He was sitting on a chair on the porch in a pool of

73

dried blood, clutching one of his daughter's severed hands. Rumour has it that when the seaman approached he thought Straker was still alive. What made him think so was that from a distance all he could see was movement on that chair. The movement, he discovered, as he drew closer, was due to the thousands of black flies swarming around Straker's body and the coating of maggots that were busily eating him.'

'Yeeech, *gross*!' Candy said, still managing to look lovely while screwing up her face in disgust and miming vomiting.

Jim paused just long enough for the audience to summon up a mental image of what it must have looked like, then continued, 'The knife with which he'd been killed was at his feet. The house was in order – nothing damaged or missing. Which suggests . . .' He trailed off, darkly.

'He killed 'em,' Jon Short said. 'He *killed* his wife and kid and then cut his own throat!'

'But *why*?' June asked. 'What would have made him do such a thing?'

Jim shrugged. 'Appeasement, perhaps. Maybe he was trying to lay whatever it was he'd woken up. Make it go back to where it came from.'

Frank had been scribbling furiously throughout the last part of Jim's tale. Now he glanced up again and asked, 'And their ghosts haunt the island?' Not only *asked*, but sounded as if he'd found the tale plausible, as if there really *might* be ghosts on the island.

A flood of warmth ran through Jim. Frank was his Doubting Thomas and even he was beginning to play along. *You still have it, Jim! It might have gone away for a while but it's back and it's cooking!* He looked Frank right in the eye with all the sincerity he could muster.

'Their ghosts still haunt the island. Oh, yes, *indeedy*!'

Chapter Six

Tricks and Traps 1

1

As he crested the rock that marked the far boundary of Straker's Bay, Davey Smith caught a glimpse of Charlie out of the corner of his eye and reached down to pat the old mutt who followed him to heel, whether he was going uphill or down dale. Or climbing over a rock-face like this one.

'Damn!' Davey said, realizing that what he'd taken for his dog was a shadow cast on his right side by an outcrop of rock. The feeling of disappointment came back to him, just as it had every time he'd done this since March when poor old Charlie curled up and went to sleep one night, and just didn't wake up again. That Tuesday night, Davey had been robbed of the best friend he'd ever had, barring Maude. The feeling of loss when he thought of either of them was as powerful now as it had ever been. In Davey Smith's book, what they said about time being a great healer was crap.

Davey just wished Charlie was back again. The dog – it had a beagle's soulful eyes, it had ears like a beagle, it *howled* like a beagle but, judging from its size, it was half moose – had taken care of him. Not only had Charlie dragged him round the two-mile walk daily, come rain, come shine, come hurricane, to keep him fit, but the old mutt had nursed him through the bad times after Maude's heart had finally quit on her back in '87.

Still, seventeen and a half was a good age for any dog, especially one that was clumsier than a bull in a china shop and had absolutely no road sense.

'About time I got me another muttley,' Davey told himself, as he picked his way down through the sharp rocks to the tiny hidden cove where he'd moored his speed-boat out of sight of Jim's trippers.

The fact was, Davey wasn't sure if getting another dog was such a great idea. This wasn't because he doubted that a new hound could live up to what Charlie had been to him – he'd had one dog or another since he was old enough to walk and knew that, although their personalities were all different, you loved them all just the same – but because for years now he'd been fifty-eight. For seven years, in fact. And for five of those years his heart had been gently reminding him each time he over-exerted himself that it wasn't as young as it used to be. If at sixty-five he got a pup, there was a good chance it would outlive him and he wasn't sure that was fair.

One thing he *was* sure of was that he wouldn't be running off to Sammy James up at the surgery. Once they found out the odd twinge in your chest was due to your arteries narrowing, like as not they'd want you up in that hospital in Miami to give you a triple by-pass, just like they had with poor Maude. And from there on in, it was downhill all the way.

Davey finally reached the tiny semi-circle of beach where he'd moored the speed-boat. It was nestled inside the craggy rock and barely big enough to stand in. If the wind got up, *Canary* would be banging on the rock-face either side of her. He waded into the shallow water, climbed into the boat and opened the waterproof stowage compartment, just knowing the detonators wouldn't be there – he'd have left them on the desk in his office back at the workshop.

But the little red box was there, wrapped in oiled rag. Davey grinned, said, 'Come to Papa!' and popped a kiss on the box lid. 'We live to fight another day!' he said and, ignoring the triangular *Danger! Explosive!* warnings on the lid, lit up a Marlboro.

2

The weird thing about Straker's Island, Davey thought, as he clung to the trunk of a tall tree and sawed off a branch to make room for one of his blood-bags, wasn't the silence, although the island was quite possibly the quietest place he'd ever been, but the feeling that you were never alone.

It was different, he mused, feeling his shoulder muscles tighten as he sawed, from the idea that Charlie was beside him when he wasn't, or the closeness he still felt to Maude when he spoke to her, which was often. It was as if the place itself had you under close scrutiny. Straker's Island, a place where no wildlife existed except insects – and there weren't even many of those – seemed alive, as if it were a sentient thing rather than a desolate square mile of woodland and swamp.

The branch creaked in what sounded like agony, then fell to the forest floor with a crash that was quickly swallowed by the undergrowth. Too quickly in his opinion.

'Weird,' Davey muttered around his cigarette, and groped for the blood-bag he'd hooked to his belt.

This trip was going to be something special, he knew. The bags were heavy – each contained a messy pint – but no one was going to get whopped on the head with one. His original idea was to have the bags burst when they hit the fans, but a pint of liquid was heavy and the idea was to scare the punters, not kill them. Davey had spent his entire working life telling folks he was ingenious and he'd lived up to his claims again with the blood-bag problem. Instead of having them on one line, he'd fixed up two. The bag would swing down from a height of twenty feet or so, to finish at a height of six foot three, about ten inches to the side of the path where the trip-wire was laid. Then the second line would pull taut and rip the bag apart. And a pint of his finest blood would cascade out over the poor saps below. Harmlessly.

Probably, he added to himself. There was always the chance that someone would have a heart-attack or something. Specially when they saw the stuff they'd been covered with.

Davey was proud of his blood-bags. He'd tested out a couple of early versions on the guys back at the workshop – these had been filled with red-coloured water and although they splattered well, the stuff looked just about as far off real blood as it was possible to get. He had tried various concoctions: wallpaper paste was *way* too thick and loosely mixed Jell-O just didn't work because he couldn't stop it setting in the bag. Combination oils ate through the thin latex and flour and water changed to glue.

And then Davey had had a brainwave. What he'd told Jim about collecting blood from drained bodies at mortuaries wasn't so far from the truth. The stuff in the bags had been bought from a pal and client of his up in Cutler Ridge. But Donald Edwardson wasn't a mortician, he was the owner of an abattoir. The filling in the bags was eighty per cent pig's blood, nineteen per cent water and one per cent anti-coagulant so the blood stayed nice and messy.

Davey grinned. It was so horrible, it was perfect.

He tied off the wires, tested the bag's security and began to climb down the tree, feeling pretty damned pleased with himself. There was one bag left, but he didn't think it would be necessary to rig it up. He'd already done a dozen and, as everyone knew, thirteen was an unlucky number. And if you didn't believe that, you could ask Maude whose by-pass had worked fine until the thirteenth of the following month.

3

He'd noticed it earlier, he realized, as he lugged a pile of cool-boxes up the beach, on to the porch of the old Straker house and down the hall towards the back room. He'd been aware of it when he'd reached down to pat Charlie, and again when the branch he'd sawn off the tree had fallen to the ground, but he'd shrugged it off. It wasn't the feeling that the island was watching him – that was so familiar he was barely aware of it – this was different.

It was a sense of anticipation.

It could merely have been his own anticipation at getting to play chief spook this evening, he supposed, but it didn't feel like it. Davey wasn't a man gifted in the sensitivity department, he would gladly admit. His wife, had she been alive to testify, would have gladly backed him up on this. What he *was* was a fine, gifted and cunning engineer. A happy man with an iron hide who could fix almost anything that broke, but who wasn't good at judging the moods of others. At times it had driven poor Maude to the edge of despair; at others, she'd leaned on it, desperately trying to charge herself with it. You couldn't be great at *everything*, Davey knew, and left the sensitive arty stuff to guys like Jim.

Which, presumably, was why it had taken him so long to realize that what he was feeling was not his own anticipation but something that oozed from the very air on the island. The island, he finally understood, as he put down the cool-boxes for the barbecue in the back room of the old Straker house, knew what was coming and was looking forward to it.

That was fine by Davey. He couldn't see any reason why a piece of land shouldn't possess a kind of life of its own; why it shouldn't be lonely when no one came here much. After all, he believed that automobiles and machinery had a weird kind of life of their own and the land had been there longer, hadn't it? The land had given up all the metal that things like cars were made of and it had grown all the wood for all the tables and chairs and pencils and what-have-you.

'Christ, I'm sixty-five and I'm turning into an Indian or something,' he muttered absently, as he checked that everything was present and correct. He was just about ready for the invasion now; the tricks and traps were set, the food and drink was all stowed and ready, and his home-made fireworks were all set up for the display later on. He'd have time for a beer and a smoke, and then he'd change into his black suit and hood and do the old vanishing act.

'And if you're listening, island,' he said, 'if you're looking forward to this evening, let me assure you you're gonna have the time of your life!'

He listened to the silence for a few moments, fancying he could feel the atmosphere of anticipation heighten, then he bent down and took a cold can of beer from one of the ice-buckets. He popped the tab, took a welcoming mouthful, swallowed and smacked his lips. The beer was so cold it hurt his throat. 'Lovely!' he said.

And out in the forest something crashed to the ground. Before the sound was dampened into nothing, Davey had time to tell himself it was the first time he'd ever heard a tree fall out here.

'Shit!' he said, wondering suddenly if his rigging had been

too much for one of the trees he'd fixed it to. The tree in question might have fallen across the path down which Jim was going to lead his party.

Davey took another swallow of beer and hurried out through the back door and across the overgrown clearing that had once been the Straker's vegetable garden. He was two paces from the path into the woods when he turned his ankle. It hurt. Badly.

He tottered a couple of paces, losing his can of beer as his arms cartwheeled with the effort to keep his balance. He steadied himself, cursing and hopping on his good leg. Certain his ankle was broken, he sat down at the edge of the vegetable patch to take off his high boot and examine it. As his behind touched the overgrown ground, something beneath him moved – something that felt very much like a snake. Davey's fear of reptiles was undoubtedly built in genetically from generations back when his ancestors had settled in Florida. Unable to get to his feet and run, he yelped like a kicked dog and shimmied away.

The thing he'd sat on, he realized, even as his movement made it rise from the dead grass, wasn't a snake but the handle of a rip-hook. The curved blade, orange with rust, rose close to his right hip as he moved and snagged the last remaining blood-bag that dangled from his belt.

The blunt tip of the blade had made a deep indentation into the latex. Relaxing now that he could see he wasn't about to become a snakebite-death statistic, Davey held himself still. He was wearing his working clothes so it didn't matter if the bag burst and got pig's blood all over him, but that wasn't the point. The point *was* that he didn't want to see one of his creations wasted, even if he had no good use for it.

Davey leaned towards the left, drawing the weight of the bag away from the point of the rip-hook.

'Damn!' he said, reaching carefully beneath the bag and lifting it. He was going to get away with this one. He knew it.

And if it hadn't been for his unconsciously moving his hurt leg, he would have. As he leaned and lifted, he shifted his foot for balance. It hurt. And he recoiled.

The bag jolted and burst. One moment he had hold of a

80

weighty, flexible bag of blood and the next the bag was gone and the blood was over his jeans, his shirt and pooled in the palm of his hand. Most of the pint of pig's blood, however, soaked the rip-hook and the vegetable patch.

'Fuck it!' Davey spat, more angry for having lost the bag than for getting covered in the blood.

Deep in the forest a tree creaked.

Swearing, Davey yanked the rip-hook free of the dead grass and flung it aside. He wiped his bloody hands on his jeans, shimmied over to a dry spot and undid his boot to examine his ankle.

Beneath his sock, his ankle was dirty – this wasn't surprising, the elastic had gone in the socks and they gaped at their tops – but it wasn't swollen. Davey felt up and down it, moving his fingers gingerly. He didn't think it was broken and, now he came to think of it, it wasn't hurting as much as it had.

Just twisted it a little, he told himself, pulling his sock back on. *It'll be fine if I keep working it.*

It hurt a little when he began to pull his boot back on, but he thought he'd live. He'd be favouring it for a while, no doubt, but he'd worked on with worse. He'd once spent two days wrestling with the innards of a rush gearbox job while his thumb was broken, so he wasn't going to let a little leg pain spoil his day.

Then Davey frowned, stopped trying to force his heel down into his boot and began to sniff as a faint whiff of perfume drifted towards him. He thought he ought to recognize that smell, and mentally inventoried all the lotions and scents that Maude had used. He still had some of the bottles and, although he wouldn't have admitted it under torture, he sometimes uncapped one or another and took a long, deep smell, just reminding himself of her while he pictured her. Sometimes it made him smile, sometimes it made him so horny it hurt, and sometimes it brought tears to his eyes.

This perfume, though, wasn't one that Maude had ever used. And it wasn't any kind of flower that grew here – the island smelt mainly of pine or swamp or sea and most of the

81

flora was odourless. It was a man-made perfume, that was for sure . . .

And it's one I know from somewhere, Davey added, as the scent grew stronger. He sniffed again, his ankle forgotten as he searched his mind for the perfume's identity. It was a heavy one which he didn't associate with Straker's Island. And then he knew.

It was a smell he had only ever experienced in Jim's house, a perfume that lingered faintly in all the rooms but Jim's office. It was the smell he associated with Sooty. That rich, musky perfume was some expensive stuff that Sooty had made especially for her, if he remembered correctly, by someone up in Seattle, of all places.

Sooty? he thought, suddenly confused. *Here?* He glanced round, half expecting to see her. The forest was empty. There was no movement behind him back at the Straker house.

'I'm going senile,' Davey told himself, remembering that people developing brain tumours were said to smell things that didn't exist. Perhaps his fall and the accompanying pain had blown something in his brain – a little vein or artery – and he'd suffered a stroke. Maybe that was why he'd picked up Sooty's scent.

He shook his head. He wasn't paralysed, anyway. He was thinking clearly and his heart-rate was steady and, barring his ankle, nothing else hurt or was numb.

And anyway, he thought, *we all have to go sooner or later and if now happens to be my time, there's nothing I can do about it. It'd sure be good to see Maude and old Charlie again.*

His ankle protested when he forced his foot back into his boot, but it didn't shoot bolts of agony up his leg. When he got back on his feet he found he was able to walk, too, and it wasn't particularly painful.

4

It wasn't until Davey had followed his route to its furthest point from the Straker house – all the way up to the edge of the swamp – that he snapped back into focus. He'd been daydreaming as he walked, picking his way over his trip-wires and traps on auto-pilot while he thought about Sooty.

He'd started out by comparing her to Maude, trying to figure out how the two women differed. It wasn't just a matter of age: he could picture Maude vividly when she'd been Sooty's age and in her prime, and it wasn't just a matter of build. Sooty was lighter than Maude had ever been and had better legs and a smaller butt – which was either good, or not so good, depending on a man's preference, he guessed. Personally, he liked a woman who had something you could grab a hold of.

Sooty was sexy, there was no doubt about that. He'd seen the way young Peety's mouth dropped whenever Sooty brought her car into the workshop; he'd seen the way his grease-monkeys ran around after her like she was queen bee and, truth be told, he'd entertained a few off-peak fantasies about her himself, although he'd have traded her body for Maude's in a moment.

But it wasn't her sexiness, either. She might well fuck like a rattlesnake rattled (Jim was certainly still under her spell!), but there was more to life than sex, especially when you had passed the point in your life when you thought exclusively with your dick.

The truth was, Sooty had something about her that Maude had never had. Pinning down exactly what that thing was, however, was tricky. To Davey it seemed like she carried an atmosphere around with her; an invisible force-field or something. Whatever it was, it enveloped you when she drew close and you became enchanted. If you weren't careful you might start thinking she was the most wonderful person you'd ever met and were ever *likely* to meet. And when she went away again, she left a part of her force-field behind to entrance you still. Everyone who came in contact with her seemed to end up loving her, at least just a little, and Davey couldn't understand why.

And now, snapping out of his reverie, he gave up the attempt.

'Jesus!' he said, peering in astonishment at the muddy edge of the swamp. He had no memory of the walk. A flat patch of black mud ran down to the water from here, like a nasty beach. If he hadn't caught himself, he might have walked right into it and become stuck. Dragged under, perhaps, and drowned. Instead of turning with the path, he'd pushed through the bushes and gone straight ahead.

The good thing was that his ankle didn't hurt any more. Better still, wherever the tree had fallen, it wasn't on this half of the track. And the other half – the route he'd take back to the house – wasn't so important. If the way was blocked, it would be only a matter of minutes to re-route the path.

The bad thing was, time was running short. And worse, Davey suddenly remembered not having seen the grill-stand for the camp-fire. His heart sank. If he'd left it in *Canary* he was going to be in trouble. Jim and his gang would almost certainly arrive before he could fetch it, and if he couldn't fetch it, they were going to be unable to cook over the camp-fire. And if they saw him, the walk through the woods would be a disaster because they'd know he was there causing all the mayhem.

'Shit!' Davey said, turning away from the swamp and quickly heading for the nearby bushes he'd come through.

Then he stopped.

Did I see what I thought I just saw? he asked himself, and a huge shiver cruised slowly down his back. The fine hairs on the nape of his neck prickled.

For a moment, he was too frightened to glance to his right where he'd seen the dark shadow on the ground. The shadow of a . . .

A person? It was a trick of the light! That's all. The sun shone through a gap in the trees – I saw the sunbeams dappling the water's surface – and one of the bushes cast a shadow. It might have looked like the shadow of a person, but it was just my eyes catching a little glimpse. And that short glimpse fooled my brain.

Davey turned his head to the right and looked at the ground. There was no shadow there now. His heart, which had bunched like a fist in his chest, began to beat again. He turned back to the swamp, smiling at his stupidity.

And was just in time to see Sooty brush past a bush and vanish behind it.

His heart clenched again but his mind insisted, *It wasn't her!* Davey knew he was just trying to fool himself. It *had* been Sooty. The woman he'd seen could have been no one else, even though he'd only caught a passing glance at her back. She was Sooty's height and build with those long legs and small backside and slender waist. Her hair tumbled over her shoulders in exactly the same way that Sooty's did and it was exactly the right dusky tone.

But he'd never seen Sooty dressed in an ankle-length, tight-waisted black dress like the one she'd been wearing. It looked like something from the last century, or earlier.

'Sooty!' he heard himself yell. 'Sooty?'

His paralysis left him and he trotted to the place he'd seen her, half expecting her to jump out at him and shout, 'Boo!' This was evidently Jim's way of evening up the score between them. Each time one of these trips had taken place, Davey had put one over on Jim and now Jim had decided to enrol his wife to turn the tables.

Sooty wasn't hiding behind the bushes, though.

Davey knew the area as well as he knew the lifetime's worth of scars on his hands and took a short cut, hoping to arrive where Sooty would eventually emerge from the undergrowth.

Then he realized that Sooty and Jim were the only other two humans in the world who might have known Straker's Island better than he did. They'd both spent a great deal of time over here from their late teens onward.

He crouched behind a tree, hoping to scare Sooty when she arrived, but after a long, patient wait he resigned himself to the fact that Sooty had known what he'd do and gone somewhere else.

He walked back to the path and followed the remainder of his route, moving quickly and scanning the area constantly for Sooty, who had now, apparently, made herself scarcer than scarce.

'I don't know that the fuck *that* was all about,' he muttered, now heading back towards the Straker house. 'But if she manages to rush about playing the spook all evening without getting herself hurt or drenched in blood, she'll be lucky. If Jim wanted her to come out here and add to the fun, why didn't he just *tell* me?'

But the answer to that was obvious. Jim liked to scare folks. And he didn't much care how or when he did it, Davey knew, which was why he'd had him build that mother bear of a firework to scare the shit out of the fans even *before* they'd started their trip. Add to that the fact that he had old scores to settle with his good buddy Davey Smith and you had something pretty much like this.

'Could have given me a heart-attack,' Davey muttered sourly, remembering the grill-stand again and cursing. He was going to have to get a move on – or 'shake a scaly leg', as Maude would have put it – if he was going to check and maybe fetch that stand before the gang all arrived.

He was less than fifty feet from the patch of the backyard where the blood-bag had burst when he suddenly smelt that distinctive perfume again.

Davey ducked down low in a patch of ferns and waited to see what would happen.

Chapter Seven

The Mystery Woman

1

Jim stood in the galley of the *Mary Celeste* smoking a fresh Virginia Slim and feeling pretty damned pleased with himself. He had a right to, he thought. His story, spontaneously generated, had been well received and – if he did say it himself – well told. Now the pressure was off, his stage-fright had gone and he was beginning to relax. The next spooky story would be told by one of the fans round the camp-fire when night fell.

'How many wanted coffee?' Rosie asked.

Jim had recruited her to help him make it, more to keep her out of the way of the other fans than because he needed help. In his estimation her own tales pushed hard on the limits of people's willingness to believe, and once she got into her stride her capacity for gossip was going to give the game away. He wondered whether he should say anything to her or not. He liked Rosie a lot and didn't want to offend her. 'Frank wanted tea,' Jim said. 'Everyone else is up for coffee. Candy wants hers black with no sugar.'

Rosie didn't appear to have heard him. If she had, she didn't show it. She turned back to him with a thoughtful expression on her face. Her eyes met his, but her mind was elsewhere. Her lips moved silently. Then she shook her head and came back, smiling.

'What?' Jim asked, finding her smile infectious and smiling himself.

'You're good,' Rosie said. 'Very good. *Very* very good.'

'Excellent?' Jim suggested.

Rosie grinned 'And modest, too! Actually, I meant your story-telling.'

'Oh, I *see*! I thought Sooty had been talking,' Jim quipped.

Rosie ignored this. 'I've read the books, of course. All of them. You know that already. And, as I've told you already, I think you *are* a fine writer. One of the finest, in fact. But I've never watched you work before. And today I caught a glimpse of what goes on in that evil little mind of yours. How it works. You *talk* an excellent story too, Jim.'

'You're too kind,' Jim said, with feigned modesty. He breathed on his fingernails and polished them on his shirt.

'That fake history of the island was convincing. You almost had me believing it. That was something to see, believe it or not. My favourite writer working and excelling. I was totally sucked into the story.' She paused, the faintest frown showing on her face and then added, 'It isn't true, is it?'

Jim treated her to his best enigmatic smile.

Rosie blushed. 'Listen to me! What *do* I sound like?' she asked. 'Like an adoring fan!'

'Go right ahead,' Jim said. 'It's what my ego lives for, after all.'

'Then I'll ask a fan-style question,' Rosie replied. 'Where did you get the idea for it?'

'I stole it,' Jim said.

'No, you didn't! I know that tired old reply,' Rosie said. 'I mean *really*. Where did you really get it?'

'Promise you won't tell another living soul?' Jim asked.

'Cross my heart and hope to die. May I drop dead if I tell a lie,' Rosie recited.

'I'd say that but I'd be dead inside ten minutes.' Jim smiled. 'Well, I got the idea where I get all my ideas, I guess. From the island. Or, in this case, close proximity to it. Straker's Island works like magic on my imagination. Or an emetic. In the case of the tale I just told, it came to me in a flash, whole and seamless. There isn't a *real* history of Straker's Island and no one knows who built the house.'

Rosie looked at him, an unspoken question burning in her eyes.

'I'm psychic,' Jim said, butting his cigarette and immediately taking his pack from his shirt pocket and opening it. 'I know what you want to ask.'

'You needn't answer it,' Rosie said kindly. 'I don't like to pry.'

'It's okay.' Jim shrugged. 'It's no big deal. Your question is this: why didn't I come over during my recent block? Am I right?'

She waited.

'Well, by way of an explanation here's a little known fact about your favourite author. In my youth, I stuck a lot of things down my throat. A lot of illegal things. Consciousness-altering things. I enjoyed the mind-bending hallucinations that came with LSD, the crazy god-like, word-spewing feeling of raw energy you get on speed. But a few times, I went as far as sticking a needle in that fat blue vein in my arm and pumping in a shot of nice, pure heroin. And, believe me, that stuff *is* addictive. So frighteningly addictive I had to leave it alone. I got terrible withdrawal symptons and I wasn't even a true addict. But I could have been. I have one of those addictive personalities, I guess. I develop a dependency very easily.'

'And you thought you were in danger of becoming addicted to Straker's Island?' Rosie suggested.

Jim smiled. 'Not only beautiful, but smart, too! Marry me, Rosie!'

'But it's just a piece of land – just an uninhabited island,' Rosie continued. 'What does it matter if you develop a dependency on it? After all, you *bought* it so you can have as much access to it as you like.'

'No one ever *owns* land,' Jim said. 'They just pay to borrow it awhile.'

'So borrow to your heart's content,' Rosie said.

'I have,' Jim said. 'And that's where my problem began. Y'see, it began to feel wrong for me. I've been taking out from that land for years and not replacing anything. Something has to give. You know what happens to arable land when you work it and work it and work it. It stops producing.'

'But you're just being ...' Rosie searched for the word '... *inspired* by the island. You're not taking anything *from* it.'

Jim pulled a face. It was a difficult thing to explain. 'Well,

I feel as if I *am* taking something from it. Taking without replacing. And, worse yet, I feel as if I'm dependent on it. I'm an addict. Christ, Rosie, all I have to do is sit down on the porch of the Straker house and my mind starts *seething* with ideas. And it's a good feeling. A *wonderful* feeling. And when I began to think about my addiction, I wondered, is this ... ?'

Rosie raised an eyebrow. 'Was it you or was it the island, right?'

That was exactly it. If Jim's imagination was as wonderful as it was cracked up to be, it should have been able to produce hot stuff in streams wherever he happened to be. He should have been able to pop out fresh ideas daily whether he was in Seaford or Scotland. So he'd done a little experiment when he'd come to write his new book. He'd jettisoned all the ideas he'd picked up while on Straker's Island and he'd left Sooty and Gloria, slung his laptop in the Porsche and driven right down to Key West where he'd holed himself up in a room in a Howard Johnson's. And *lo!* he became inspired with the idea for *Shimmer*. This time it didn't reveal itself to him whole and crystal clear and seamless, but rather as a shapeless, muddy thing, which needed a lot of careful cleaning and study. But it came.

And he'd started the book right there and then, distantly wondering if this was another of those magical places – after all, Hemingway had liked it there.

But he needn't have worried. *Shimmer* ran out of energy inside three days and he'd packed up and gone back to Seaford, defeated. It had looked pretty much as if the island had been doing the writing for him all along. But Jim refused to go back there. Once his addiction had been broken and cold turkey had been faced, he knew he would start thinking for himself again and writing his own ideas, perhaps for the very first time.

The withdrawal hurt. And people suffering cold turkey weren't nice to be around. He'd yelled and sworn and stomped about like a thundercloud. He'd cried, he'd raged, he'd thrown bottles and glasses. The strain it had put on his relationship with Sooty was terrible. She'd pleaded with him to take the boat out to Straker's Island and be done with it, but Jim had refused. Then had come that hot Sunday night when he'd found himself searching through the drawer for the Colt .45 and a way out of this mess.

Afterwards, when he realized how far he would have gone if Sooty hadn't hidden the bullets, he began to sober up. He still couldn't write for shit, but the withdrawal symptons eased.

'But it *wasn't* the island, after all, was it?' Rosie challenged.

'Jim shook his head, a smile finding its way on to his face. 'Nope!' he said. 'And thank God for that.'

'You began to write again when it was time to write, didn't you?' Rosie reminded him. 'And of your own accord. The island had nothing to do with it.'

'I did.'

'You know what the block was about, don't you?' Rosie asked. 'It was about fatigue. It was about you having worked so hard you'd burned out. That, and the pressure you're under these days. You're aware there's a lot of money riding on whatever you do nowadays and that doesn't make for a carefree mind. And you happen to be someone who doesn't work well under that kind of pressure.'

'But it's back,' Jim said. 'I've beaten the block and I found my talent again.'

'And now you know you can do it without the island, it doesn't matter if you use the island whenever you feel like it, right?'

Jim looked uncomfortable. 'I don't know about *that*,' he said.

'It doesn't matter because you now know you can write without its help. You started on *Shimmer* again and you just told a fine story to our friends out there, who, incidentally, probably think we've died in here. And there's no point in trying to kid me, Jim, that story you just told – and *Shimmer* too – have nothing to do with the island. The talent is *yours* and yours alone. The island is nothing more than a place you find conducive to your thinking. Like Hippocrates and his plane tree. The entire world, as you well know, is dotted with this kind of special place. Sure, they probably possess some kind of power, but it's more of a . . .'

91

'Magnifying-glass for what's inside a person?' Jim suggested. 'That's the conclusion I eventually reached. Straker's is on one of those mystical lines of force.'

Rosie took Jim's hand and squeezed it. 'I'm glad things have resolved themselves,' she said, warmly. 'Truly, I am. Now, let's make that coffee.'

2

Rosie turned to Jim, holding two empty mugs in her hand and wearing a puzzled expression on her face.

'What?' Jim asked. 'Coffee's perked. The teabags are in that cupboard there behind you, for Frank. White coffee for everyone but Candy. We'll take out the box of sugar cubes and let them sort that out for themselves.'

Rosie sighed. 'I'm getting senile in my old age,' she said. 'How many of us are there?'

Jim noticed an odd glint in Rosie's eyes but didn't understand what she was driving at. A moment later it was gone, replaced with that perplexed look again. 'What?' he asked, quizzically. When Rosie merely stared at him, apparently waiting for something, he began to tot up the fans, counting on his fingers,'There's me, you, Candy—'

'Who'd rather you fucked her than frightened her,' Rose said drily.

Jim raised his eyebrows in mock shock. 'My, we *are* learning new things about our prim and proper secretary today, aren't we?'

Rosie laughed. 'I came second in the Seaford Cussing Contest, nineteen ninety-seven,' she chuckled. 'And, besides, you don't know the half of it, O Master of Disaster. If I were a few years younger *I*'d be giving Sooty a run for her money too.'

Jim smiled in surprise. 'I'm flattered. What is it about me, exactly? My whip-lean body? My painfully handsome face? My enormous . . . wealth?'

Rosie's true nature finally got a hold of her and she reddened. 'Actually it's all those steamy sex scenes you put in your books. They make a girl wonder, y'know.' She turned away, presumably to cover her embarrassment. 'How many cups, Jim?'

'Me, you, Candy, Jon, Frank and um, Martha and June. Five of them, two of us. Except that you're *supposed* to be one of them. Six coffees, one tea.'

Rosie turned back. She was shaking her head but that glint was back in her eyes. 'No, *six* of them and two of us, surely.'

'What do you mean?' Jim asked, frowning, and remembered miscounting the fans himself.

'I mean the *other* girl.' Rosie smiled. 'I know what this is all about, Jim.'

'*What* other girl?' Jim asked, genuinely mystified.

'I'm not going mad, Jim. I know I'm not. And do you know *why* I know I'm not going mad?'

'No,' Jim said, suddenly feeling unsettled.

'Because I'm on a boat five miles out at sea with a champion liar,' Rosie said, and nodded for emphasis. 'A skill you've honed close to a perfect edge, I might add.'

'I don't know what you're talking about, Rosie,' Jim said.

'The *girl*,' Rosie explained patiently. 'The one who looks like Sooty, only a few years younger. You're not fooling me, Jim. I know what you're up to. You told the Straker's Island tale and had her float up behind you like the ghost of Majesty Dauphin.'

'How could I?' Jim said. 'I only invented that story on the way here.'

'You're a champion liar, Jim. Everyone falls for them, even me, and *I* know you. You prepared the story earlier and had the girl stashed away down here somewhere so she could waft up behind you at the appropriate moment. Am I right or am I right?'

Jim's discomfort left him the instant he understood what was going on. Rosie was playing his own game. He folded his arms and treated Rosie to a sunny grin. 'You're trying to frighten me, aren't you?' he asked. 'I happen to *know* there were only five fans on the dock – and you, of course. I distinctly remember introducing myself to *all* of them. I didn't miss anyone. And I also happen to know that only five fans boarded the boat. I counted them all again.'

So why did I count seven earlier? his mind cut in. The explanation was simple: he was a writer, not an accountant and he'd counted with only half his mind on the job. Nevertheless, he shivered. Rosie certainly couldn't have known he'd miscounted.

'No, silly,' Rosie said. 'I didn't say she was on the dock. You had her stashed away all the time. Inside the boat. It's no good trying to fool me.'

For a moment, Jim felt as if he were seeing himself and Rosie between a pair of mirrors so that both their reflections went on for miles, diminishing into the distance. She thought he was trying to fool her and he thought she was trying to fool him, and the more either of them said the more mirrors were added. Jim fought off an odd feeling of vertigo, held both his palms in the air and said, 'Wait!'

Rosie smiled her superiority.

'Either one of us is lying,' Jim said, holding up his hand again as Rosie opened her mouth to speak, 'or both of us are lying. Or either or both of us are mistaken. It occurs to me that you're the one telling the fibs here. You said that she looked like Sooty. You should have said she was nondescript. There'd have been a chance I wouldn't have noticed her. I'd certainly have noticed someone who looked like my wife.'

Rosie was no longer smiling. She gazed at Jim, thinking hard while she chewed her thumbnail. She looked as if she was bursting to speak, but Jim continued before she had a chance.

'I can see if from your perspective,' he continued, 'if I choose to believe you're telling the truth and you *did* think you saw someone who looked like Sooty. I did not secrete a Sooty lookalike aboard this vessel. You may not believe me, but it's the truth.' Distantly, Jim realized he didn't much care for the direction this was heading, but it was too late to stop now. 'If I choose to believe you saw someone, there has to be another explanation for you seeing someone I didn't see. I promise you faithfully, I didn't see anyone.'

Rosie held Jim's gaze. 'It's funny. I didn't spot her on the dock, but she's certainly aboard.' If she was lying she was at least as good at it as he was, Jim thought. She continued,

'There is definitely a woman aboard this boat who looks like Sooty. She is wearing a long dark dress.'

'Rosie. It's time to stop! If there *was* a woman, I'd have seen her!'

'Not necessarily. She was sitting to the side of you and slightly behind. Out of your line of vision. She smiled at you a lot. If you're not lying and I'm not lying, which I'm not, and if I'm not imagining it, which I'm not, perhaps she stowed away. She could have known about the contest, done some research locally and hopped on board before you arrived and while we were all in the bar.'

'Oh, shit! *That*'s possible,' Jim said, clinging to the slender strand of hope for all he was worth. His subconscious was trying hard to present him with another solution altogether and he didn't much care to hear it right now. 'Either that or it's another of Davey's little surprises,' he added, wondering if this new nugget of hope had any chance of being right. Either there was someone aboard who shouldn't be or something nasty was happening to Rosie. Or . . .

3

While Rosie walked among the guests distributing tea and coffee, Jim stationed himself half-way up the steps to the wheelhouse where everyone had a clear view of him and he had a clear view of them. If there *was* someone aboard who shouldn't have been, it would be nice to find her. *And if that woman wasn't merely a figment of Rosie's imagination someone else must have seen her.* All the lucky contest winners had been sitting facing him while he told his story, and Rosie had insisted that the mystery woman was to his left and slightly behind him. So he intended to ask.

'Can I have your attention for a few moments, please?' Jim asked. He'd had Candy's attention from the moment he left the bridge, he knew – she had a way of tilting her slender hips a little when she noticed him noticing her – but the others were all spooning sugar into their coffee or talking.

When everyone was looking at him, Jim said, 'Did anyone see what happened to the lady in the long black dress?'

The trouble with being famous for constructing out-of-the-

95

window stories was that it was often difficult to convince people you were telling the truth.

'That'd be Majesty Dauphin, would it?' Frank asked knowingly. 'Nice one, James!'

Jim fought off an urge to run down the steps and plant his fist in Frank's cynical face and said, 'The lady who was sitting behind me when I was talking, I mean.'

Like a schoolboy, Jon Short raised his hand.

'Yes, Jon?' Jim asked.

'D'you mean Sooty? Your wife? It *was* your wife, wasn't it?' he said.

Frank turned on Jon, 'There *was* no one sitting behind him,' he scorned.

'There *was*!' Jon protested. 'Sooty. James's wife. I saw her.'

'I didn't,' June said. There was a general good-natured chorus of, 'Me neither!' through which Jon and Frank could be heard arguing.

It wasn't until Candy reached out, took Jon's arm and said, 'Leave it, Jon,' that Jim realized what was eating Frank: he wanted to get into Candy's pants and Jon was queering his pitch.

Jim walked down to Rosie as the fans began noisily to discuss the mystery woman and her significance. 'I'm lost,' Jim told her. 'I don't know what to believe now. Promise me you're not putting me on because we're going to have to search the boat for this girl. And if we don't find her, we're going to have to look for someone who's fallen overboard and notify the coastguard. And the media will get it and there'll be hell to pay. It'll be bad if there's a body and worse if there isn't.'

For the first time, Rosie looked doubtful. 'Perhaps I imagined it,' she said thoughtfully. 'Or perhaps . . .'

Jim fought off the shivers that wanted to run down his spine. 'You saw a ghost, right? The ghost of Majesty Dauphin, just as Frank said. Just bear this in mind. I invented the history of the island. Most of it while I stood there telling it. As far as I know there never was anyone named Straker or Majesty Dauphin. Christ, I even had to give their daughter

96

my own daughter's name because I couldn't think up a convincing one quickly enough.'

'Jon said he saw something,' Rosie insisted.

'I sincerely hope he was just playing along. I'll talk to him, then I'll have a look round the boat. But, before I do that, I want to ask you a question and I want an honest answer. I don't want you to tell me what you think I want to hear, I want the truth.'

Rosie nodded solemnly.

'Are you feeling okay?'

'I'm fine,' Rosie said. 'As fit as two fiddles.'

'No headache? Racing heart? Anything untoward?'

'I haven't blown a gasket and I'm not drunk,' Rosie said. 'And I'm not using any medication. I get checked over regularly and Sammy James up at the surgery says I have the blood pressure of a fifteen-year-old girl. He didn't say which fifteen-year-old girl, or I'd have gone and got her backside, too. Mine's been affected by gravity.' She smiled.

'One more thing,' Jim said.

'What?'

'You couldn't have seen a ghost. Ghosts can't travel over water. Them's the rules. Same as vampires can't stand garlic and werewolves die if you shoot 'em with silver bullets and zombies hate tanna leaves.'

'And who makes up these rules?' Rosie asked.

'People like me, I guess,' Jim said. 'And you *know* we're never wrong!'

4

During the search of the boat, Jim had time to gather his scattered thoughts and feel a little better about things. Earlier, Davey had made a remark about how Jim himself was going to need clean underwear, so this whole thing was undoubtedly a set-up.

You did well, Davey, Jim thought as he made a cursory, and now unnecessary search of the forward cabin. *You had me fooled. Totally.*

Davey's set-up had worked beautifully. It wasn't until Jim

97

was alone that he'd figured out how it had been done. It was pretty simple really.

Rosie asked to come along, Jim thought, smiling. Those five words explained everything. Rosie had asked to come, not because she really wanted to see Straker's Island but because Davey had enrolled her in his plan to scare Jim.

Evidently when Davey had called earlier, he'd been on the phone for some time before Rosie put him through. During that time he'd outlined his plan and managed to convince Rosie it'd be fun for her to take part. It might have sounded unlikely, but Davey could turn on the charm when he wanted something. Jim knew that for a fact.

Davey knew from past experience that Jim *always* stopped the boat half-way to the island and told a spooky tale about the island to the group of fans. And that since the contest always promoted Straker's Island as a *haunted* island, Jim's tale always involved ghosts.

And this time he thought he'd introduce a ghost of his own, Jim thought.

It was simple enough: Davey had instructed Rosie to wait until a while after Jim's story before she mentioned the mystery woman she'd seen sitting behind and to the side of him. Of course, Jim wouldn't have looked behind him while he was talking: he'd been playing to his audience. Which left, at least, a slim possibility that Rosie *might* be telling the truth. And by the time Jim had arrived on the dock, Rosie had already had an hour or so with the fans. Davey must have asked her to select one who would play along and verify her story. Rosie, clever girl that she was, had made a good choice: another writer, someone familiar with the telling of lies. In order that they might extemporize, they'd settled on an easy description of the mystery woman: she looked like Sooty and she was dressed in a long black dress.

What surprised Jim about all this was the way Rosie had taken to acting: she'd done a fine job. Poor Jon Short, however, was neither old nor wise nor confident enough to keep it up. He'd tried, though. He hadn't cracked under Jim's questioning until Jim had explained that if there was the merest possibility that a passenger had fallen overboard the authorities would have to be notified and the lost passenger would have to be searched for. Then Jon had crumbled and finally admitted that he hadn't seen anything at all. He'd just grabbed hold of Rosie's idea, he had said, in the hope of increasing the spooky atmosphere.

Jim was confident that there were no extra passengers on the boat now and that there hadn't been any to start with. Whether Rosie would admit it or not, the entire thing had been a charade. Now that Jim thought about it, Rosie hadn't seemed very concerned that someone might have gone to a watery grave, which pointed to the fact that she knew there'd been no one who could have fallen overboard.

Feeling pretty pleased with himself, Jim lit a cigarette and went back to the galley. From now on, he'd play along with Rosie and Davey's little game – let Rosie convince herself she had him hooked.

Rosie was in the galley, bent over a sheet of paper that lay on one of the work surfaces. She had her glasses on and was studying the sheet so intently she didn't hear Jim come in.

'*Boo!*' said Jim.

Rosie glanced up, startled, and clapped a hand to her chest. 'Keep beating, heart,' she said. 'Are you trying to *kill* me, Jim?' she asked breathlessly.

Jim grinned. 'I forgot to tell you I got you insured. If I frighten you to death, I pick up about a million bucks. And, God knows, I *need* that money!'

Rosie frowned at him.

'The mystery woman?' Jim asked. 'Can't find her. We've been at anchor since she was last seen, so if she fell overboard we wouldn't have left her behind. And no one heard a splash or a scream or anything, so I guess she didn't fall in the water. I searched the area with my trusty binoculars, but there was no debris or bubbles or floating corpses. And she's not on board, either, I've checked. You know what that means, don't you?'

Rosie just stared at him grim-faced.

'It means you were right and I was wrong. Ghosts *can* travel over water. Either that or you and Jon imagined it.'

Rosie picked the sheet of paper up from the work top and held it out to him. 'I'm not imagining *this*, though, am I?' she said, actually managing to convey fear.

Pretty good, Rosie, Jim thought, keeping his face blank. *You should move to Los Angeles and get an agent.* He took the paper from her and read it. The words were typed and centred. It looked as if whoever had done it ... *Rosie, for example* ... hadn't had much time because there was a typing error.

And she hadn't had much time, because she'd been in Jim's office doing it while Jim had gone to the bathroom. The sheet of paper had come from his workroom, he guessed. It was the weight of the photocopier paper he used and looked the same shade of white as his current batch. The typeface certainly belonged to the old Smith Corona in his office in which he'd found a similar sheet of paper because the dot over each 'i' was faint and the tail of each 'e' was distorted. The words said:

You won't go backNot without me
I'm taking you for my own.

Jim looked up at Rosie, trying to ignore the worm of fear that was growing again, deep in his bowels. 'Where did you get this?' he asked.

'It was here when I came back down,' Rosie said. 'Don't keep doing this, Jim, I really *am* getting frightened now.'

It was frightening him too, and he knew Rosie had done it. She was just a tad *too* convincing for his liking. There was absolutely no way you could tell she was acting.

Perhaps she did it without even realizing she'd done it, he thought, and then dismissed it because it was way too scary to contemplate. There had to be an easier explanation.

Look at me getting frightened of my own shadow! he admonished. *There's a way round this. A way in which Rosie could look like she does and not be acting.*

But Jim wasn't certain he wanted to address this thought, either. He'd been down in the abyss recently. So deep down that at one time it had seemed the only way out was to suck on the barrel of the Colt .45 and plaster the wall with his brains. Maybe while he'd been there something had happened. Something that was now making him type up threatening notes he didn't recall typing and place them where he could find them later.

Now *that* was scary.

'I didn't do it!' Jim heard himself say. The note of clear desperation in his voice shook him to the core.

And then everything stopped. The fear and the frustration stopped. The breath in his lungs stopped moving and the blood in his veins stood still.

And his muse shat on his head. It felt as if a gush of warm, sweet honey was rolling down over and *through* him.

It lasted only a moment but afterwards his fear was gone and he *knew*.

'As far as I know, no one else has been down here but you and me,' Rosie was saying. 'And it's written on the grade of paper you favour. Same watermark, everything.'

Davey was far cleverer than Jim had given him credit for. He was plotting and orchestrating this trip like a master – presumably because he wanted to leave Jim with special memories of the last ever event like this on Straker's Island. And he must have started months ago. He'd got to everyone he needed and had persuaded them to play their little parts, without allowing them to know about the parts the others were playing.

The reason Rosie looked so scared was because she hadn't typed that paragraph on that paper. And neither had he, come to that.

Evidently Sooty had done it for Davey, some time ago. And Davey was resourceful: he'd even got Henry Skate up in Miami to rig up something in Jim's computer so that on the day of the trip warning words would automatically appear on the screen.

Sooty could easily have inserted that sheet of paper he'd found this afternoon into the Smith Corona. Davey could have arranged for Aaron Spreadbury – whoever he was – to make the warning phone calls that had frightened Sooty so badly. And the reason she'd been so worried about today's trip was because she knew something that Davey *didn't* know – that her husband had recently been depressed enough to think about suicide and was still a little delicate.

Jim felt deep admiration for Davey: it had been his ambition to out do the Master of Disaster and he'd worked a minor miracle this time.

Jim held up his hands. 'I didn't type this. Honestly. Unless . . .'

'It was Majesty Dauphin's ghost?' Rosie said, disbelievingly.

He shook his head. He would have liked to have kept up the pretence, but Rosie looked badly shaken. 'It was a fix,' he said. 'Davey's. He somehow got this typed on my typewriter and coerced someone to leave it here. It wasn't me, it wasn't you, so Davey must have approached one of the fans. How he did it, I don't know.'

'But no one else has been down here,' Rosie said.

Jim thought about it. 'Are you sure Candy didn't slip down here while we were on deck? I don't remember her leering at me when I was up there. That'd fit.'

Rosie nodded. 'Yes, it would. Now I come to think of it, Candy did sashay off while I was on deck. I thought she'd just gone for a pee or something. God knows where she'd hidden the piece of paper, though. She's hardly wearing anything.'

'She has a purse,' Jim said. 'Women *always* take their purse to the bathroom with them. Everyone knows that. It was Candy. I'll have to keep an eye on her.'

Rosie looked relieved. She found a smile for Jim and said, 'Keep an eye on her, by all means, but keep your hands off or Sooty will have your balls on a plate.'

Jim grinned. He felt as if a large weight had been lifted from his mind. 'She's cute!' he said.

'And so are you, but you'll end up looking worse than the guy who called the Dallas Cowboys a bunch of prancing queens if Sooty finds out you've so much as laid a finger on her. Anyway, Sooty's cuter, I think.'

Jim thought about it. 'Maybe she is, maybe she isn't.' He grinned. 'Maybe she'll tear my face off, maybe she'll never know! I'll risk it,' he finished, giggling, and dodged when the blow he anticipated headed his way.

'Well, if I'm gonna get in Candy's pants – what there is of them – I'd better get this boat on the move again,' he said, heading for the steps. 'And then, when we're all on the island, perhaps Candy and I will just slip quietly inside the old house. If you should hear screams, it's because I'm scaring her! That's all!'

'Get outa here, Captain Bullshit!' Rosie said, good-naturedly, searching frantically for something to help him on his way.

The used teabag she threw missed his retreating form by less than an inch.

Chapter Eight

The Suggestibility Wall

1

In every classroom in every school in every town and city in the world, they said, there was always one kid who was thought by his peers to be the lowest of the low. This would be the no-hoper they called *geek* or *nerd* or whatever disparaging term was currently in favour.

Jon Short had heard a lot of disparaging terms during his time at high-school and he knew as well as anyone who'd ever lived that the rhyme '*Sticks and stones may break my bones/But names can never harm me*', wasn't entirely true. The name-calling hurt, and hurt badly.

His treatment at the hands of those who called him names was worse, of course, but during his early childhood, Jon had developed a way of handling physical pain. He'd had to because his father liked to express himself with his fists, and sometimes with his feet, too.

But the constant jibes flung at him by his classmates, like stones from catapults, were worst. They didn't just bruise the skin, they sank through it, deep down to Jon's soul.

And the worse of it was, he knew that there was a part of him that was like a big flypaper. Jon called it the Suggestibility Wall. This part of one's psyche was where the important incoming stuff stuck; the events that turned you into what you were.

Which, he guessed, was the reason that he would for ever think of himself as part geek, part coward and as ugly as sin.

Things had lightened up a bit when he'd got to university, but that was probably because he'd blended right in with all the other ugly geeks and nerds on his English course. It had been more like a two-year-long outcasts' convention than a degree course. It had been reasonably comfortable there and Jon had been reasonably happy. Escaping Kansas had been the best thing he'd ever done. Even if it had been difficult to get out.

Before he left, his dad, talking through a belly full of beer as usual, had assured him that he'd turn into 'a sandal-wearing, bearded faggot pinko' if he 'mixed with all those drug-taking queens' and Jon had finally cracked. For the first time in his life he understood what it was like to feel truly murderous. Jon had smiled and said quietly, 'Bobby, compared to turning out like you, it'd seem like I'd been transcended.'

2

Bobby Jackson, an uneducated horny-handed farm labourer from outside of Topeka, was a proud man. When his wife had wounded his pride one time too many he'd disposed of her by beating her so badly one night behind Smitty's Bar and Grill that she'd later died of a brain haemorrhage. He was proud that to the very end Betty had claimed, 'I just fell downstairs and messed myself up a little.' He was proud of his strength, his ability to control those around him through fear. And he was proud of his ability to drink all night and *still* show a whore a good time. Bobby, in his own opinion, was *salt of the earth*. What he was not proud of was having squired this useless long streak of piss, his son, who spoke those clever-clever words because he thought his old dad wouldn't know what he was getting at.

Bobby didn't *need* to know what 'transcended' meant to understand that his son was putting him down – it was all in the kid's sneering tone. And it was high time that length of damp string was put in his place. He rose from his ancient, stained Lay-Z-Boy, like a volcano erupting. He could feel the adrenaline suddenly coursing through his veins, feel that stroke of white lightning approaching: the fury; the mist from beneath which he would do what was necessary.

'I should have done this years ago,' he seethed, clenching his fists into rocks.

'You did, you drunk,' his son said, looking strangely unconcerned. 'You just can't remember.'

Apparently of its own volition, Bobby's arm pistoned out. And hit nothing.

A moment later, Jon's face swam into view. Then his body. He hadn't even dropped the small suitcase he'd been holding in his left hand.

Left hand, Bobby thought, knowing that it was significant in some way, but not knowing how.

'You've hit me for the last time, Dad,' his son said, evenly.

Oh, no, I haven't, Bobby thought, and said, 'You're not walking out on me now. Your mother's gone, your sister ran away and now you want out, too. You're not leaving.'

'Why not?'

'I'm not gonna let you, you dumb fuck,' Bobby said, suddenly realizing that, for the first time in his life, he'd thrown a blow that hadn't connected. This increased his level of irritation to a point that made him feel like he might explode. 'You're gonna learn a hard lesson. A very hard lesson.'

And his nose exploded.

Bobby sat down hard in his Lay-Z-Boy, white-hot agony searing through his sinuses and tears springing to his eyes. The long streak of piss had *hit* him, for God's sake. His rage increased to a point where he knew this was going to be no ordinary beating he would mete out to Betty's stupid fuck of a son. Betty was gone and that was a good thing and now her child would follow her to whatever backwater of hell she'd vanished to. A moment after that, Bobby's rage reached white-out and he ceased thinking and let his instincts take the driver's seat.

He wiped the moisture from his eyes with the back of his hand, spat out the blood that had trickled from his nose into his open mouth and leaped up from his chair.

Half-way to his son he distantly registered that the big blurry brown thing arcing horizontally towards him was the suitcase Jon was carrying. It hit him square in the face, cancelled out his momentum and knocked him off his feet, backwards.

Fucking case must be full of those half-wit books, Bobby

106

thought, as the ceiling spun above him. And then his brain shut up shop and drew the curtains.

When he woke up, the long streak of piss was long gone.

Bobby never saw him again.

3

The *really* weird thing, Jon thought, was how things never turned out the way you expected them to. Or how you'd planned them. Sometimes life seemed to take enjoyment from seeing how perverse it could get; occasionally it got so damned *personal* you began to think that someone up there was playing games with you, like the Greek gods had fooled around with their subjects.

Jon stood with the others at the bow of the *Mary Celeste* watching the hazy smudge of land ahead grow larger, and thought about one of the odd things life had thrown at him.

His father hadn't come after him. Even though Bobby knew full well where his son was going and had a score to settle, he hadn't come. Jon had lived those first few weeks in fear, expecting the man to walk out of the shadows around the edge of the dorms late one night, or imagining he could see him outlined at a distance in broad daylight, too far away to make out his features.

But Bobby hadn't come and the fear had subsided. Even more surprisingly, he began to forget, as if he'd cast aside his past. In the recesses he'd gone down to Austin with his new friend Peter Mandelton, or had hung around on campus with Iris, a frail waif from Mississippi to whom he lost his virginity.

And then, one day in January, he got a letter from a law firm back in Topeka. It took him two days to work up the courage to open it because the buff envelope reeked of trouble. He suspected that he was going to have to go home and care for his dad, who'd taken a fall and broken his back, or something similar. Life had been going too well for it to be good news.

But good news it was. Bobby had died in a farming accident. But along with that news there was something even more surprising. His dad had left him fifty thousand dollars.

107

Enough to pay for the rest of his education, buy him a car and, if he was careful, give him a couple of year's freedom in which he could develop his career as a writer.

Four years later, the money was gone, the house and its bit of land sold and the proceeds split between Jon and his sister Kathy. Jon couldn't hold out too much longer, but he wouldn't *need* much longer, he knew. His writing was *good*. Very good. He knew this in spite of the stack of rejection letters he'd collected.

What I really need, Jon had thought, less than three months ago, *is a champion. Someone with authority, someone respected, a person who would talk to the right people, convince them they should take my work seriously.*

He remembered thinking this because, in its perverse way, life smiled on him again. Perhaps it had been trying to make up for his lousy childhood. Jon didn't know. What he did know was that he appreciated the stroke of luck, even if it had come via the worst toothache he had ever known, and, indirectly, from Bobby again.

Jon did not have good teeth. When you had a father who smacked a hard fist into your mouth for no good reason, other than that you'd brought in mud on your boots or left a mark on a plate you'd washed, the result could be seen in the amount of dentistry you needed. Jon was a martyr to toothache. And out of nowhere, a fresh one sprang up on the day he'd decided he needed a champion.

The next day he called Jack Brooking's office and got in on an emergency appointment. Apart from Kathy, Jack Brooking was the only other person on the planet who knew what Bobby had done to his son's teeth and Jack was sympathetic: he worked hard and cheap on Jon's behalf.

While he was in the waiting room, feeling just as sick as he always did on visits to Jack's surgery, Jon had picked up a copy of *Cinemaxima* and browsed listlessly through it. Until he'd found the page bearing the advertisement for the trip to the haunted island with James Green.

Serendipity! he'd thought. *I'm going to win this!*

And he had. And all it had cost him was his lower right eight and fifty bucks.

'Can I squeeze in here?' Candy asked Jon, breaking into

his thoughts. Without waiting for a reply, she pushed in between him and Martha. She'd changed from her bikini back into the cut-off Levi's and halter top. She grabbed the guard rail with her left hand and took Jon's arm with her right, pressing his forearm against the hot bare flesh of her waist.

The *Mary Celeste* was surging forward at speed now, and Candy's lithe, barely covered body swayed softly against him.

What do you want with me? Jon asked silently. *I'm a geek.*

The question wasn't easy to answer. You could practically *see* Candy aching for Jim whenever he was around, but between times she clung to Jon like a limpet. He stole a glimpse down at her. She had a quite *phenomenal* body and she was totally at ease with it. Jon had never met a woman so confident in her skin before, had never known anyone who seemed to exist on such a purely physical level.

Candy grinned up at him and Jon looked away, suddenly as embarrassed as he would have been if he'd drilled a hole through a wall to spy on her.

'It's the cool breeze,' she said, hugging his forearm to her waist. 'It's windy now we're going real fast.'

Jon glanced down again, certain he was blushing to the roots of his hair. 'What?' he asked.

'You were looking at my nipples.' She giggled. 'You needn't be shy,' she added when he turned his head away. 'I *like* to be admired. It turns me on. And I like *you*, Jon.'

'Sure,' he mumbled.

'It's true!' she said. 'I have a feeling there's something in store for both of us over there.' She let go of the rail and pointed at the smudge of land ahead on the horizon. 'Something good.'

Jon nodded. Usually when things like this happened, he was being set up as the butt of some joke or other. But Candy didn't look as if she possessed the guile for anything like that. Her clear blue eyes were honest.

And besides, he thought, *it's Jim she wants.*

Personally, Jon would have swapped Candy, her aura of raw uncomplicated sex, her wonderful body and everything, for Jim's wife in a moment. Sooty had something that Candy

109

did not – you could tell that just by looking. Jon thought about it for a moment, wondering what it was he found so achingly attractive about Jim's wife. She was tall and slender, which was the shape Jon naturally preferred, he supposed, and she was beautiful, too. Not Californian-sun pretty like Candy, but in an almond-eyed *dark* kind of way.

Her shoulder-length hair was jet black, her smooth skin tanned dark olive, as if one or both of her parents had been from South America or Puerto Rico or Cuba perhaps; her bones were delicate; she had shapely hands, and hands were special to Jon. But it wasn't any of this that gave her the extraordinary quality she possessed, he thought. It wasn't even in her grace of movement.

Mostly it lay in her eyes, which were a colour of brown almost dark enough to qualify as black. A world of promise sparkled in those eyes. Jon was sure that Sooty – a name that seemed apt now he had seen her – would understand pleasures and experiences darker and deeper than Candy would ever think of. And who would bestow love and kindnesses that would bind you to her for ever.

She was the kind of woman whose affection Jon would have gladly sawn off his right arm to win.

He briefly wondered what the game was with Sooty. It was a construction of Jim's, no doubt, something he hoped would add to the general atmosphere of unease among the contest winners. The most unsettling thing about Jim's having her waft up behind him and smile at Jon while he told the history of the Dauphin family wasn't that Jon had found himself instantly falling hopelessly in love with her, but that the others refused to admit having seen her at all.

Even more strange, Jim had come to him afterwards, looking agitated, and asked if he was *sure* he'd seen the 'mystery woman'. He seemed to want an answer in the negative – presumably to enhance the 'ghost' theme of the trip – so Jon pretended he hadn't seen Sooty. He wondered if he'd missed anything back on the dock; if Elaine, the publicity woman, had instructed the others to play along and pretend they hadn't seen Sooty and everyone had heard but him. The terrible thing was that Jim seemed to have open and easy access to his Suggestibility Wall: the more he

110

thought about it, the less certain he was that he really *had* seen Sooty. That was scary. He'd seen many pictures of her, of course, so he knew what she looked like. Was it *possible* that he'd imagined her there?

'What are you frowning at?' Candy asked, breaking into his thoughts again.

'Nothing,' Jon said. 'Just thinking.'

'I want to read your stories,' Candy said. 'You're a writer, too, I know. I heard you and Jim talking. I *like* clever men. Are you as good as Jim?'

'Better,' Jon said. It was his stock reply, but there was a part of him that was certain he could write prose that at least matched Jim's. But writing well wasn't the be-all and end-all that most people thought it was. It was catching the imagination of the public at large that counted. And in that area, Jim really *was* the Master of Disaster.

'Great!' Candy said. 'I can't wait to read some!'

Jon spent a few moments wondering how the words 'I can't wait to read some' could possibly convey the message 'I can't wait to fuck you', then gave up. Something else had caught his attention.

4

A few minutes ago, Jon had been busily telling himself that things never turned out the way you expected them – and as far as Candy was concerned, the theory was holding up nicely – but here in front of him was an exception: he wasn't yet sure whether or not this was the exception that proved the rule but it was certainly a stunning one.

The *Mary Celeste* was now close enough to the island for them to be able to see the bay that lay ahead. The stunning thing was that what could be seen of Straker's Island and the bay was *exactly* how Jon had pictured it. It looked so damned familiar that, like Jim and Sooty, he might have spent his youth going back and forth to the island in a small motor-boat.

As the island grew larger an odd feeling of excitement built in the pit of his stomach. Every detail he'd imagined was here, made real. The *déjà vu* sensation wasn't just an

111

epileptic flicker like the ones he'd had before: this one felt as if his entire reality had been very slightly, but very distinctly, rearranged.

I know *this place*! he thought, and found himself smiling ruefully. Here was a kid who had been looking for a home – a spiritual home – for the past twenty-two years or so, and now he'd found it, he was certain. And it belonged to the man he considered his closest professional rival. The man to whose achievements he aspired.

5

Jim anchored the *Mary Celeste* about a hundred yards out in the bay, which, he said, was as close as he could get because of the depth of draught of the boat. He explained that the water nearer the beach was that pretty Caribbean blue because it was so shallow. 'We'll have to go ashore in relays,' he said. 'I'll lower the dinghy from the stern and take you in two at a time.'

Jon and Candy were the first to make the short crossing. When the front of the rubber dinghy nudged the sea bed and Jim tilted up the outboard, Jon leaped nimbly out into warm, clear ankle-deep water and gave his hand to Candy to steady her as she stepped out. On Jim's instruction, he yanked the dinghy round so it faced back towards the *Mary Celeste* and pushed hard, sending it back into water deep enough for Jim to lower the outboard again. Jim started the engine and when the dinghy was racing back towards the cruiser, Jon turned to Candy and said, 'What do you think?'

Candy shook her head. 'He *owns* this island,' she said, in a small, wondering voice. 'It's gorgeous, it's deserted and it's ... *his*.'

Jon nodded. 'There but for the grace of God – and being born in the wrong place at the wrong time, to different parents and having an entirely different life – go I,' he said resignedly.

'I know what you mean,' Candy said.

'You do?' Jon asked in surprise.

Candy shot him a rueful glance. 'I was thinking,' she said, 'what's Jim's wife got that I haven't got? She's got Jim, right?' She held Jon's gaze, her clear blue eyes searching his face for a sign that he could see the profundity in her words.

'You'd like to take her place?' Jon smiled.

Candy grinned. 'You betcha!' she said. 'Wouldn't you like to take Jim's place?'

He sighed. 'It sure sounds appealing,' he said. 'The boat and the island and the fame and the money and everything.' He left out the fact that a major bonus of stepping into Jim's shoes would be getting Sooty into the bargain – but there was no sense in destroying his chances with Candy this early on.

Candy's face fell. 'I mean, look at me,' she said. 'What have I got? Okay, so I have a nice body. And . . . er, I have a nice body. Unfortunately that's it.'

'You have a stunningly gorgeous face,' Jon said.

Candy shrugged. 'Well, I'm popular with photographers, but I don't really think my face is why I'm in demand, do you? And besides *me*, as in my body and face, I don't have much of anything else. I don't have a talent. I can't act or sing or anything like that. And I'm not exactly an intellectual. Sometimes I don't even understand jokes. I was useless at school.' She pouted.

'You have a sweet, uncomplicated personality,' Jon said, staring at his feet.

Candy brightened. 'You really think so?' she asked.

'I do.' He was certain he was blushing.

'You're sweet, too,' she said. 'And I already know you're clever. Maybe you'll be another James Green. You have a chance. I don't have any chance. Jim and his wife have everything. And you know why?'

Jon shook his head. 'Raw talent, I guess,' he said.

'Nope,' Candy said. 'Breaks.' She spat out the word as if it tasted awful. 'Talent isn't worth shit if you don't get the breaks. Jim has it all because he's been lucky. Fate chose to smile on him. It's not smiling on me or you. Not yet. It probably never will.'

'How do you know that?' Jon asked. 'Something always happens. Life surprises us.'

'It's surprised me, all right,' Candy said. 'It had my mother die of cancer when I was ten and my father of a heart-attack

113

when I was eleven. My twin brother and I moved to be with our grandparents down in Santa Monica, and guess what? Yeah, they both died by the time my brother and I were sixteen. And my brother was killed in a drive-by shooting a year later. I'm an orphan now. I have no family. And I was fired from the only three regular jobs I ever had, and three months ago my modelling agency kicked me out because my best friend told my agent I was sleeping with her husband – which I wasn't. And now, for some reason, I can't get another agency to take me on. Life's full of surprises, right. It's just that none of them are good surprises.'

'I'm sorry,' Jon said.

'Me too,' Candy said, and shrugged. Then she grinned. 'But hey, we don't want to talk about bad stuff today. We're supposed to be having fun. And we're on this gorgeous island and it's still hot and we're gonna have a lovely night! What more could you ask for? Except to be Jim's wife – or, in your case, Jim himself. Come on, let's walk up the beach while we wait for the others.'

6

Out in the bay, the *Mary Celeste* lay silent. In the evening sun her white bulk shone brilliantly against the turquoise sea. Down at the water's edge, almost in the centre of the three-hundred-yard-long crescent of fine white sand, the dinghy lay, its black rubber prow beached and staked in place with rope, its stern bobbing in the shallow water, the anchor-rope taut.

Nearby, perhaps half-way between the water's edge and the tree-line that bordered the beach a hundred feet behind, Jim and Frank were busy snapping and stacking driftwood for what would soon become the camp-fire.

Rosie and Martha and June had settled under a stand of coconut palms a way off to the left. They were talking animatedly while June knitted and Martha ate.

A hundred yards to their right the line of trees broke, revealing the Dauphin house, which Jim had forbidden anyone to approach until he said otherwise. The house front was level with the tree-line. It was long and low, and looked to Jon like something you might find in the old part of Key West or New Orleans. It was built of sun-bleached wooden boards, and a few scraps of ancient paint were peeling from the boards of the pitched roof. There were steps up to the covered porch, which ran the length of the front of the house. It wasn't so much Gothic as nineteenth-century southern Florida practical, and it certainly wasn't brooding or dark. It looked inviting and charming, in a rough-hewn way, Jon thought. The sort of place where you could lie naked on the smooth boards of the porch with Sooty Green in your arms.

The sides of the house were lost behind the branches and greenery of protective trees. Jon wondered what it looked like from the back.

'Don't even think about going up there,' Candy said, from behind him. 'It isn't allowed. And, besides, it's haunted.'

'There's got to be a lot of dead wood up there,' Jon replied. He and Candy had been dispatched to gather fuel for the fire, which was fine by Jon. He was warming to her, even though she wasn't really his type. And, if he were truthful with himself, he was intrigued about what it would be like to make love to Candy. She might have been drooling for Jim, but Jon was available.

Candy looked doubtful. 'Even so, we're not meant to go near the house,' she said, glancing back to where Jim and Frank were busy. Clouds of smoke wafted from Frank's pipe as he explained something to Jim.

'Cowardy custard!' Jon said.

'It's spooky,' Candy replied, staring at the house.

Well, Jim's story has certainly stuck to Candy's Suggestibility Wall, Jon thought. If there was one thing the house *wasn't*, it was spooky.

'It's got blind eyes,' Candy remarked.

'It's got old net curtains over the windows, that's all,' Jon said, turning back to the house.

And one of the curtains twitched as if someone inside had just taken a quick peek at him. For a second Jon went rigid. A rib-rattling shiver fizzled down his back. Then he gave a small, uncertain chuckle. *It was the breeze,* he thought, hating himself for having been taken in by Jim's story too. Christ, he was a *writer* and he knew how these things worked. Jim's tale was taller than the World Trade Center towers – anyone with half a brain could tell that. And yet Jim seemed to have a direct line to that big flypaper part of your brain.

And the curtain twitched again. It didn't *waft*, like it would have done had a breeze touched it, it moved with a jerk as if someone inside was making sure it was shut.

'The curtain moved!' he heard himself announce.

'Stop it!' Candy demanded.

'It moved,' Jon said. 'Honestly.'

'You're scaring me,' Candy said. 'And if you don't quit right now, I'm gonna dump this wood and stuff and go back.'

'I thought I heard you tell Jim you *liked* to be frightened,' Jon teased her. 'Doesn't it make you go *tingly*? Y'know, *right down deep inside*?'

Candy stuck out her little pink tongue. 'Smartass,' she said. 'It depends on who's doing the frightening.' And then she smiled. 'Scare me some more and we'll see what happens,' she said playfully.

7

Inside the lounge of the Dauphin house, Davey Smith risked another glance through the curtain. He thought there was a good chance he'd been spotted already so he wouldn't be risking much. And the girl was worth the risk.

'Jesus H. Christ, will you get a load of that broad!' he whispered to himself for the second time, shaking his head in disbelief. 'What a way to die!'

He fought with himself for a few more moments and then duty got the better of him. He straightened the net curtain, turned back to the bare-boarded lounge and took a quick inventory. It was damned lucky that the grill-stand was here because he'd spent far too long crouched in the undergrowth, waiting for the owner of that perfume to turn up. And while he had been waiting to catch Sooty, Jim and the gang had arrived.

The moment Davey had heard the drone of the approaching outboard, the perfume had vanished. He didn't know why this should be, or if Sooty was really there or he'd just imagined it, and right now he didn't have time to think about it. He'd got up, shaken some life back into his feet and jogged back here, just in time to see the calendar girl and the stocky young guy climb out of Jim's dinghy. Which meant it was too late to collect the grill-stand without giving the game away.

But the stand had been here all the time. The old guy wasn't as forgetful as he'd thought.

'You're a star,' he told himself aloud, and, using one of Jim's pet sayings, added, 'A mon-star.' Then he checked everything for what felt like the millionth time. Once you started remembering you might have forgotten things and then finding you'd merely forgotten you'd remembered them, you tended to lose a little of your confidence. 'Right,' he mumbled, 'we got the beer-cooler full of booze, we got the cool-box containing the steaks and sausages. Fire-lighters. Matches. Band-Aids. Coffee. Bottles of water. And the grill-stand for the fire is just ... well, it *was* there. But now it's not present, my friend. So where the fucking hell did it go? It was here just now. I'm certain of it.'

He turned and saw the stand propped up in the corner of the room. He tilted back his cap and scratched his head, his face etched into an expression of concern by the deep lines that formed when he frowned. 'How'd you get over there, you little mother bear?' he asked the stand, relieved that he'd found it again and concerned that he couldn't remember picking it up. *I never moved it. I put it down with all this shit. I'm sure I did*, he thought.

Davey had welded up the grill-stand from solid steel. Like everything he made, it was substantial enough to withstand any kind of ill-treatment and consequently it was heavy, stable, too. It stood on three eighteen-inch-long steel legs which were welded to a thick steel ring topped with thin steel bars on which you placed the food. It was pretty much like a heavy-duty barbecue grill, except you could stand it over an average-sized camp-fire and, barring an earthquake or tornado, it would stay where you put it.

Which was why Davey was so shocked when, apparently of its own volition, it toppled over. He gazed at it, his mouth open, his heart aching in his chest. Then, when nothing else happened, he began to breathe again and said, 'Sheee*it*!'

8

Outside the house, the sound of the grill-stand falling was heard clearly. Candy gasped, threw down her armful of driftwood and grabbed Jon's arm. 'What was *that*? It sounded like someone in there fell over. There's someone inside!'

'Or some*thing*.' Jon grinned. 'Let's go in and see.'

Candy squeezed herself tight to his side, hugging him around the waist. It was a pleasurable sensation, and Candy not only looked good, she felt good, too. Jon fought off the flush that was undoubtedly rising again to his cheeks and worried about the other rising part of him. In about twenty seconds, the front of his chinos was going to be tented by an erection that was surely going to be harder than drop-forged iron and he had no way of hiding it from Candy. And if she noticed – and she was going to have to be struck blind *not* to notice – he would almost certainly die of embarrassment. Half of him wanted to take advantage of the situation and put his arm around Candy's shoulders and crush her to him, let her feel how hard he was for her and see what developed from there, but the other half, the inexperienced, rejection-fearing half, wasn't going to allow it. He peeled away from her and thrust his hands deep into his pockets. 'Want to go inside?' he asked.

'No way!' she said. 'Let's go back down to the beach. Jim told us not to go anywhere near the house or something would happen.'

Jon wasn't sure if this constituted a rejection or whether Candy really was frightened. He chose the latter. 'Yeah, what'll happen is someone will jump out on us and go BOOGA BOOGA! C'mon, Candy, it's all gonna be tricks. There aren't any such things as ghosts. Let's go in!' Laughing, he grabbed her arm and tried to drag her towards the porch.

9

Davey walked carefully towards the grill-stand. *I've been out in the sun too long,* he told himself. *Or trying to scare people too long. Or both. No one has been in here rigging traps for me to stumble into,* he finished, wondering about Sooty again. Perhaps someone *had* been rigging traps for him. Jim owed him one. Or two or three. The difficult thing to believe was that Jim had managed to enrol Sooty in this kind of prank. He knew full well, because Rosie had told him so, that the main reason this was the last trip to the island was Sooty's bad feelings about these excursions. It could have been a set-up, he knew, with Rosie feeding him a cover story, but it didn't seem likely. Yet Jim was resourceful – it *was* the last trip, after all – and who was to say he hadn't hired a Sooty lookalike?

He didn't notice the sheet of paper pinned to the wall until he'd hefted the grill-stand off the floor and turned away from the side wall. Frowning, he turned back and peered at it. There was stuff written on it, but without his reading glasses Davey couldn't see what. And they were back in his boat. He'd purposely left them there because if there was one thing he'd learned during this life it was that you only wore reading glasses when you were reading; when you were not reading, you were apt to put them in your back pocket and sit on them. And he sure as shit hadn't been intending to do any reading tonight.

Who put this here? he asked himself, but the answer was obvious. Either Sooty or the lookalike Jim had planted to scare him. *Yeah, well, we'll see how scary she feels after she's walked into one of my little trip-wires and got herself all covered in blood,* he thought. He peered a bit closer at the sheet of paper. *If it's for me, they should have wrote it bigger,* he complained. *They know I can't see worth a damn without my specs.* Then he cocked an ear.

And listened to a faint creaking noise that sounded pretty much like the front door being opened. This didn't seem likely – as far as Davey knew the hinges had been rusted shut since Charlie was a pup – but it wasn't impossible.

He hurried back to the window and glanced out. The stocky boy and the stacked blonde were no longer in view.

'Shit in a bucket, they're comin' in!' Davey whispered, panicking. He trotted to the back of the room, pulled up the sash window, climbed out, cursing silently, and ducked down into a growth of tall ferns.

10

Half-way to the porch, Candy broke away from Jon and ran off up the beach, giggling. Jon watched the movement of her buttocks for a few seconds – the cut-off Levi's she'd put on were *extremely* cut-off and a good deal of her was on display. A moment later he gave chase.

Considering how difficult it was to run on the powdery sand, Candy was pretty fast. It took almost fifty yards for Jon to catch her up. Reaching forward with his fingertips he found the waistband of her shorts and dragged her to a standstill.

'Gotcha!' he said, as she swung round.

'I'm not going in that spooky place!' Candy giggled.

'Yellow belly!' Jon taunted. 'There are no ghosts in there.'

'We're supposed to be gathering wood,' Candy said. She pointed back down the beach. 'Look, Jim has the fire lit already.'

Jon glanced back down the beach to where a plume of black smoke was rising. Frank was fanning the stack of wood with his notebook while Jim stood by, gazing in their direction.

'We'd better go back, I guess,' Jon said, not wanting to upset Jim. Jon was a pretty good judge of character and had Jim down as a man of his word. Which meant that he would read the material Jon had brought with him. And when he read it he was going to be impressed. It could just be the break he'd been looking for and he didn't want to foul up his chances.

'Catch me!' Candy said, and sprinted back towards the camp-fire.

Jon followed her, stopping in front of the Dauphin house to gather up the driftwood he and Candy had dropped. He didn't think he was going to be able to carry his own load and hers too, but it didn't matter – it wasn't too far back to the fire.

As he stood up, for no apparent reason he shivered. And his gaze was drawn to his left, back to the window where the curtain had twitched. It felt more like his head was being turned than he was turning it himself.

There was no curtain at the window now. What there was, though, was Sooty Green, still wearing the long black dress he'd seen her in on the boat, except, he now realized with a start, that the dress wasn't buttoned right up to the throat any more. Sooty had slipped the loops from perhaps five of the little pearl buttons so that the dress gaped open to the V of her sternum and quite an expanse of firm cleavage showed.

Jon's mind refused to register any of this for a few seconds, during which he felt as if the inside of his head had been sucked to a vacuum by a huge pump. Then he found his eyes locked to Sooty's dark, searching gaze. He tried to look away and couldn't. Something inside him was melting. A distant part of his mind cranked up: it seemed far enough away from him to be right back in Topeka. And it thought: *She just vaporized your Suggestibility Wall. Things are going to be different from now on. Very different.*

Jon had absolutely no idea what that part of his mind meant because he was falling deeper and deeper into Sooty's inviting eyes. Tasting the fullness of her lips, drinking in her perfumed flesh.

He was dimly aware that not only had he become erect again but he'd become *super*-erect. There was plenty of room inside his shorts and his chinos, but his dick was pushing hard, straining at the material with such vigour he felt as if it might soon burst free and extend itself telescopically across the sand to where Sooty stood. He was so hard it hurt, but it was pleasurable pain that shot little shivering bolts of ecstasy down the length of his dick and into his spinal cord where they pulsated through him, tingling their way to the surface of his skin.

Nothing will ever be the same again, that distant part of his mind promised, from way back in Kansas.

Behind the window, Sooty smiled at him. Her teeth were very white. And then she spoke. Her mouth formed the words, but Jon heard them right inside his head. He'd seen Jim's wife being interviewed on *Oprah* last year and this was definitely her soft, husky voice.

I want you, she said.

If Jon hadn't been in an ecstatic paralysis, he would have nodded. He wanted her, too. Badly. He wanted to lose himself in her tastes and scents and touches for ever.

I want you, too! he tried to think, but the part of his brain that dealt with words had been knocked out by the sheer power of Sooty's gaze. It didn't matter: he was open to her now – had been since their eyes had first met – and anything she wanted from him she could have. She surely knew this. Something inside Jon was smiling so hard it hurt. At last, at long last, he was complete. Dying and going to heaven couldn't have been any better.

And then everything stopped. For ever.

And when the eternity unfroze there was a sensation that felt like a gentle slap – except that it hit him everywhere at once.

The first thing Jon realized was that the horrible wheezing noise was the sound of his lungs heaving in air for the first time in a million years or more. The next thing he realized was that he was sitting down on the sand, his legs out in front of him and a pile of driftwood in his lap.

What happened? he wondered. What *had* happened was breaking up before him the way his dreams did when he awoke and right now it seemed just as unlikely as any of his more outlandish dreams. As he gasped in a fresh breath the remnants of the experience curled up like the ashes of burning paper and blew away in the gentle gust of cool wind that seemed to slip right through him.

I had a hard-on, I'm sure I did, he thought, mystified. *Didn't I just come my brains out or something?* But he was flaccid and dry. *Christ, I'm going crazy*, he told himself. He suddenly had no idea why he'd thought he'd had an orgasm.

He looked up at the Dauphin house suspiciously. The net curtain in the window was still. The front door was closed and the other windows he could see were curtained, too.

'Are you okay, Jon?' Candy asked breathlessly from his right.

He turned. 'Sure,' he replied. Why did she look so concerned?

'What happened?' Candy said. 'I glanced back and you were staring up at the house holding all that wood and suddenly you just sat down on your butt. I thought you'd fainted or something.'

'Got a cramp in my leg,' Jon said, certain that this was all that had happened – he could feel the tightness in his right calf muscle. 'Sometimes I get them and I have to sit down real quick and stretch out my legs.'

'Are you okay now?' Candy asked, biting her thumbnail. 'I mean, do you need a hand to get up or something?'

'I'm okay, I think,' he replied, moving his right foot up and down. The stiffness was easing a little.

Candy gave him a rueful smile. 'You know what?'

'No, what?'

'I thought it had got you,' she said coyly.

'What had?'

'The house, silly! The house and its ghost.'

'Oh, *that*,' Jon said, taking the pile of wood off his lap so he could stand up. 'Yes, it might have been the ghost,' he joked. 'The cramps ghost of Straker's Island.' He got up and began to gather the wood. Candy crouched and picked up her share.

'Nothing will ever be the same again,' Jon heard himself say, as they carried the wood back towards Jim's camp-fire.

'What?' Candy asked, frowning.

Jon grinned. 'I dunno. I just have this feeling that things are going to change for the better. And soon. Real soon.'

'Great,' Candy said. 'Jim's wife's gonna leave him, then?' She turned to Jon and winked.

Sooty? Jon thought, and fleetingly remembered a dream he'd once had in which Jim's wife had told him she wanted him.

'And I'll marry Jim and then kill him,' Candy continued happily. 'I'll put ground up glass in his dinners or something like that. And I'll inherit all his money and then you can

123

come and live with me and we'll take their places. And I bet your books are even better than his.'

'Oh, they *are*!' Jon agreed.

'We'll make even *more* money,' Candy said, 'and live happily ever after.'

Jon chuckled. 'You know what else?'

'I don't know nothing,' Candy said, and pouted prettily. 'I'm just a dumb blonde,' she added, then waited for Jon to deny it.

'This is what else,' he said. 'My Suggestibility Wall has gone. There's a big open hole where it used to be.'

Candy looked faintly worried. 'Is that a *good* thing?' she asked.

'I think it's a very good thing,' Jon replied. 'There was a lot of bad stuff stuck on it and now it's all gone.'

'Good.' Candy nodded. She thought for a moment and then said, 'I know this may sound dumb, but do *I* have a whatdoyoucallit wall? And what is it, anyway?'

Jon smiled. 'I'll tell you later,' he said.

Chapter Nine

The Liars' Contest

1

Despite his wealth and fame, Jim Green was a member of that special breed who attracted drunks like a magnet. 'Put me in a crowd,' he'd told endless interviewers, 'and if there's a single drunk there, he'll see me as a big fat blip on his internal radar and he'll lock on. Even if he can barely stand, he'll push past a hundred or more people to get to me.' And if there were no drunks available, Jim knew to his cost that reality would fling the next best thing at him: out of the six he'd brought over on the boat, the guy he least wanted to talk to had attached himself to him like a leech.

Frank wasn't your ordinary bore and he wasn't dull or smelly or even horrendously ugly, but Jim didn't much care for him. It wasn't just that Frank was supercilious, there was something about him that was just plain *nasty*. Frank took pains to hide this part of himself from the world at large, but Jim was an experienced judge of character and could see it as easily as if the man was transparent.

When Frank had volunteered himself to help get the fire going ('Oh, no, we *won't* need fire-lighters, Jim,' he had said smugly) and wouldn't be shaken off, Jim had played a little character-development game to amuse himself while he tried to keep his patience.

The physical details were easy enough – after all, Frank was right in front of him. The first word that flitted into Jim's mind was 'weasel'. Frank was around five nine and fairly thin – perhaps a hundred and forty-seven pounds. He might be an English teacher but with his shirt-sleeves rolled up you could tell that teaching wasn't all he'd done in his time. His forearms were muscled, his hands as hard as a construction worker's, yet his shoulders were too slight for him to have done any weight-training or serious hole-digging. Jim tried to figure out how you'd get a build like that and couldn't come up with anything that satisfied him. He suspected that Frank had been into martial arts of some kind and had stopped, perhaps because of an injury.

Frank, Jim conjectured, was forty-four years old. He'd been married twice. His first wife had left him because he'd hit her one time too many. His second wife had gone because she could no longer stand him putting her down in company, correcting her every time she mispronounced a word and refusing to let her have a hand in the finances. In Jim's mind, Frank wasn't an English teacher at all, but a government employee, perhaps a field worker for the Internal Revenue Service, the kind of guy who mistrusted people on principle and who treated the government's money as if it were his own.

'You married?' Jim asked him, as Frank fanned the tiny flames he'd managed to light at the base of the fire.

Frank looked up at him and grinned. 'Now, why would I want to keep a cow in my house when there's a field full of dairy cattle just a way down the road?'

'Ever been married?'

'Twice,' Frank said, scowling at the fire. 'Everyone's entitled to one mistake. I made two. You know what I did wrong?'

Jim inwardly chalked up a score for a correct guess.

Frank looked at him, his eyes blazing with the past injustices his wives had bestowed upon him. 'I married my mother,' he said. 'They always say you marry someone who reminds you of your mother if you're a man and your father if you're a woman. Unfortunately my mother was a dumb bitch. "Mere reason alone can never explain how the heart behaves." Don Was said that. I second it. You know else? You can't change 'em. Once they're past puberty the book's already written. You can't teach 'em jack shit. You can try, and I did. I tried long and hard, both times. I guess I just set my sights that little bit too high.'

'I'll bet you gave them everything their little hearts desired, too,' Jim said, straight-faced.

126

Frank looked at him long and hard, then evidently decided Jim wasn't taking a dig at him. 'I did,' he said. 'I did *everything* a man can do for a woman and more. All I asked in return was a little consideration. Hot meals when I got home. Shirts pressed when I needed them. The house kept clean and tidy. That kind of thing. That isn't too much to ask for, is it?'

'Did they have jobs?'

Frank shrugged. 'Nooo! They had *careers*. Both wanted to work. I let them, fool that I am. "Just as long as it doesn't interfere with your duties around the house," I told them both. "Just as long as I still get fed and watered." What do you think happened? Yeah, you know what happened. The home stuff stopped. No time or energy to do it. That's women, these days. They all got their little heads filled up with Germaine Greer and Erica Jong and whoever else back in the sixties and seventies and nowadays they want it all ways. Fuck 'em, that's what I say.'

Jim raised his eyebrows and gave a little shake of his head.

'Yeah, that's women, for you,' Frank agreed, assuming Jim was on his side. 'So, how about you?'

'How about me, what?' Jim asked.

'Your lovely wife,' Frank said. 'How's the relationship going? You've been married a long time, I understand. Or you've been *together* a long time, anyway. How does it all pan out for you? Better than it does for me, I'll wager.'

'It's going just fine,' Jim said.

Frank winked knowingly. 'Course, you have the extras, I guess.'

'Extras?'

'Come on, Jim! You know what I mean. They say that seventy per cent of those who buy your books are women. Is that right?'

'Well, I wouldn't know, but I guess they've done their market research,' Jim replied, knowing exactly what Frank was driving at.

'And you do promotional tours, right? You'll be doing another one next month when the book we're here to celebrate hits the official launch date. You'll be on every

127

chat-show they can get you on, you'll do radio, you'll do book signings. There'll be a lot of women around . . .'

'The tour for *Black River* is minimal,' Jim said, wishing someone would come and take Frank away from him. 'I'm busy with a book I'm running late on and I have a tight deadline. I have a film to direct later in the year.'

Frank shrugged. 'Nonetheless,' he said.

Jim shrugged back, playing it dumb.

'The *extras*,' Frank said, and gave a knowing wink. 'It's no good trying to fool me, Jim, I'm a man too and I'm sharp, even if I do say it myself. I've been there, done that, got the T-shirt, worn it out and forgotten about it. Stop me if I'm wrong, but the size of it is about this: sex at the beginning of any relationship is better than it is after five years. Hell, it's better than it is after *two* years, right? Maybe your partner is too tired all the time and the old horizontal dancing just kinda fades out. Maybe you're just bored with the way she does those same old things in the same order every damned time. Maybe you just plain don't get that urge to jump her any more. One of those things *always* happens in time. But you've been with your wife since she was a teenager. Something must be keeping you going and I'd put money on it being the *extras*.'

'The fire's going out,' Jim said, and looked away from Frank.

Rosie, Martha and June were still sitting under the trees. Martha was eating something, but Jim couldn't tell what it was from this distance. Whatever it was, it was sizeable. Candy was trotting back down the beach towards Jim and Frank, and Jon was standing staring at the Dauphin house as if he was fixed there. Jim hoped he hadn't spotted Davey or word would go round and the surprises Davey had laid in would be spoiled.

Frank nudged Jim. 'I know what you're thinking,' he said. 'She's a *very* sexy girl, isn't she?'

Jim had nodded in agreement before he remembered that it was Frank sitting next to him. Candy *was* a sexy girl. And Jim *had* wondered what she'd be like in the sack. He didn't know whether or not he should feel guilty about this. He wouldn't swap Sooty for her, that was for sure. But still, he couldn't help *wondering.*

They can't jail you for that, though, can they? he asked himself. *There's no harm in window shopping, even if your Mastercard has been cut up.*

'What my students would call an exceptional piece of work. Or a horny bitch. Just made to fuck,' Frank said, lasciviously.

Jim glanced at him, but Frank was away in a glassy-eyed little world of his own. One, presumably, in which he was showing Candy a thing or two. As Jim watched, Frank licked his lips, slowly. This struck Jim as the most appalling thing he'd seen for a long time. For that moment Frank looked like some kind of predator, ready to leap on and tear apart its prey. Jim looked back at Candy, wondering if Davey really had recruited her to post the sheet of paper in the boat's galley. Now she'd been up to the house, too. Jim hadn't seen her go inside, but then he hadn't been watching her every second because of good old Frank here.

'God, you're a lucky man, Jim,' Frank said in an odd tone.

'How's that?' Jim asked, losing his train of thought.

Frank turned to him and treated him to a horrible grin. There was envy on his face, and, if Jim wasn't mistaken, a complex kind of hatred. Frank pulled an expression of disgust. 'You don't even know, do you? You haven't even realized. Power, Jim.'

'Power?' he asked, surprised.

'Yeah, power. Your power.'

'Well, I know I have the power to tell a good tale,' Jim said. 'Even though my editor would have a thing or two to say about that. And half the executives at Warner Brothers too, come to that. And that's *all* the power I have. I do what I can to get my own way over things, but I'm usually out-gunned, Frank.'

Frank shook his head. 'No, you're wrong. I was wrong, too. *I* thought your power came from your writing, but it doesn't. There are a hundred writers who turn out clearer prose than you do. There are fifty screenwriters you couldn't hold a candle to. And who's the man holding the biggest pot

129

of gold? It's you. And do you know *where* your power comes from? No, I know you don't. It comes from your *fame*.'

'I don't understand,' Jim said. He felt strangely unsettled. On any other day, he would have been sorely tempted to punch out Frank's lights, but Jim was still a little fragile at having been so close to the edge recently. And there seemed to be something in Frank's words that rang with the crystal clear peal of truth.

Frank rolled his eyes. 'Of course you don't,' he said tiredly. 'Here's an example.' He jerked his head towards Candy. 'She's yours, Jim. You may not understand much, but you understand that, don't you? Candy is yours for the asking. Not because you're such a hot-shit writer. Hell, I bet Candy never got to the end of a book in her life. It's because of your fame. And everyone else here is yours, too. Jon looks up to you like you're a big-time hero. The women go all weak-kneed whenever you speak. And it's not for anything you've ever *done*. It's not for your scintillating personality, either, or your manly good looks. It's because of your *fame* and your *wealth*. Either of those things equals power, together they add a considerable boost to it. These people are here not because they want *you* but they want something *from* you. They're hoping you'll take a shine to them and help them out of their miserable little lives. Or that your power, your fame and wealth will rub off on them in some way. And you play those poor saps for all you're worth. You don't give to them, you take from them as a kind of salve for your ego. And you know what? It makes me sick.'

Jim drew a breath and held it for a count of fifteen. Then he lit a cigarette. He summoned up all the patience he had left in his reserves and said, 'Then why are you here?'

Frank grinned. '*Newsweek* sent me, of course,' he said.

Jim felt as if he'd been slapped round the face. 'You're a *reporter*?' he asked, sounding exactly as astounded as he felt.

Evidently Frank found this gratifying. His grin widened. 'Yeah, I'm a reporter, but not a fan – certainly not a fan. And I'm not a lucky competition winner, either. *Newsweek* wangled the competition to get me on. They knew you'd never countenance a reporter on one of your trips. Not with all the bad tabloid press you get. So they cheated. They got hold of the winners' names early. Contacted Frank Blaine, the English teacher from Boston, and gave him five big ones for his winning ticket.' He chuckled evilly. 'And, boy, is this story gonna be worth it!'

Jim's mind seemed to have emptied itself. The question, 'Why do this to me?' rattled around in his vacant skull, but he couldn't find anything to say. He asked the question, his mouth numb.

'Good copy, that's why,' Frank said. 'We just wanted to catch glimpses into the evil mind of the man who wrote the most violent film script in modern history. See, Jim, your life is always presented in the glossies as being something near to perfect – hell, you are presented as near to perfect. But there's depths to you. Underneath all the nicey-nice Goody Two Shoes stuff there's a bit of a monster, isn't there? We wanted to forget the writing, good or bad, forget all the hassle you've had with the Miami Five Fifteen picture and look at Jim Green's demons.'

'Jesus,' Jim said, shaking his head. 'Jesus.'

Frank's smile expanded. 'So you'd better be nice to me. Otherwise several million Americans are gonna learn the real truth about high and mighty James Green.'

'But—'

'But you've been nice already, right? You are a nice guy? Wrong. I can see the real man beneath the veneer of niceness. And I don't like what I see.'

'Christ, Frank . . .'

Frank broke into laughter. He punched the air and said, 'Yeeeeeessssssss!'

Jim glared at him, uncomprehending.

'Fooled you!' Frank chortled. 'It's a story. I made it all up. Just wanted you to know you're not the only one around here who can make fiction work.'

'Nice one, Frank,' Jim said sourly, wondering if the man's claim to be a reporter was fictional. He certainly came over more like a news-hound wanting to dig the dirt than he did an English teacher. Jim was going to have to be careful around this man. He expected a hot surge of anger to rise in him and wasn't disappointed when it did. Better late than never, I guess, he thought, willing away the delayed adrenaline and drawing hard on his Virginia Slim. He'd always been slow to anger, but never this slow. *Still, you haven't been quite as shocked as that recently,* he reminded himself. *Even the thing with the gun didn't shock you.*

This was true. During his block, Jim had fallen into a state of empty numbness. Apparently it hadn't quite gone yet.

'I guess I take first place in the liars' contest,' Frank said happily. 'I wonder if anyone will top my effort.'

Candy trotted up and stopped in front of Jim and Frank. She was beaded with the kind of perspiration you only ever saw in deodorant advertisements: even little dots of moisture, like water sprayed on oiled skin. It added to her attractiveness, Jim was sorry to note. She hunkered down facing him.

'Got you some wood,' she said, talking to him about something entirely different with those clear blue eyes of hers.

'Good,' Jim replied. 'It's invisible wood, is it?'

Candy giggled and looked back to where Jon was still standing staring at the Dauphin house. 'I dropped it up there where Jon is,' she said, pointing. 'He tried to scare me. He told me he could see the curtain twitching in one of the windows and he tried to drag me inside to look for ghosts. I dropped the wood and ran for it when he loosened his grip.' She turned back and gazed deep into Jim's eyes again.

Frank snorted. 'You sure he was going to drag you in to look for ghosts and not for your G-spot?' he asked.

Candy didn't seem to hear. She was too busy talking to Jim with her eyes. She held his gaze for so long that Jim felt embarrassed.

'So why don't you go back and fetch your wood?' Jim said, tearing his eyes away from hers. 'We're gonna need loads.'

'What time does it get dark around here?' Candy asked, trying to lock on to him again.

'Late,' Jim said, studying the base of the fire. He was aware of Frank looking from him to Candy and back again as each of them spoke. He was undoubtedly memorizing this conversation to note down later. 'Gone nine this time of year,' Jim continued. 'Plenty of time to find some food and cook it before we can't see one another.'

Either Candy wasn't aware of Frank's leer, or she didn't care about it, or she was trying to taunt him. Jim didn't know. What he did know was that the girl was laying it on with a trowel. She just wouldn't leave him alone.

She gave him a coquettish look and said, 'Then what?'

Jim did his best to match her. 'Wait and see,' he replied.

Candy dropped her eyes and smiled secretively. Then she glanced back towards the house and gave a little cry.

'What?' Jim asked.

'Jon just fell down,' she said, already starting to sprint down the beach.

Jon was now sitting down on the sand, his legs out straight and a pile of wood in his lap. There was something about his odd position that unsettled Jim. He looked as if he'd been picked up, bent into shape by an unseen hand and placed where he sat – as if he'd become the human equivalent of an Action Man doll. Even more strange was that he wasn't moving, apparently he was stuck in position.

Jon stayed right where he was until Candy approached him. Then he turned to face her.

'He wasn't dead then,' Frank observed. 'That was lucky,' he added, sounding disappointed.

Jim watched Jon get to his feet. He didn't look very steady. It was possible that the sun had got to him, Jim supposed. It was still pretty damned hot, and humid, too.

You won't come back this time! part of his mind whispered, as Jon and Candy began to gather up their wood.

Everything will be fine, Jim told himself. *Jon won't get sick with sunstroke, Frank isn't a reporter, Davey's recruited Candy to stick up the notes everywhere. It's all dead simple when you think about it.*

But he tried *not* to think about it. This trip was like a jigsaw puzzle in which none of the pieces would fit. And a part of Jim thought that if and when he found the key section and began to see the pictures the pieces made he wasn't going to care for it.

133

Candy dumped a fresh armload of wood beside Frank and Jim, stood up straight and mopped the sweat from her brow with the back of her hand. 'Phew, I'm hot,' she said, glancing up at the line of trees where the women had been joined by Jon.

Jon looked a little too pale for Jim's liking. He'd done enough sweating to plaster his hair down to his scalp and forehead, and his hands trembled. When Jim had questioned him he'd admitted he'd felt a little dizzy and thought he'd fainted, so he'd been ordered to rest and drink lots of water while Jim, Frank and Candy built the fire.

'I think that's about enough wood,' Jim said. 'It'll last us.'

'I'm going for a swim to cool down,' Candy said, looking directly at Jim. 'Coming?'

Jim smiled up at her. 'No swimwear,' he said.

'Me either,' Candy said provocatively. 'I left my bikini back on your ship. We'll just have to skinny-dip.'

Holding Jim's gaze, she crossed her arms, took the hem of her tiny top and whipped it off. She cast it aside in the sand then stretched taut running both her hands through her hair on the pretext, Jim supposed, of getting it back into place. But whatever way you looked at it, it was a photographer's model's pose, designed to show off flat belly, slender waist and breasts to best effect.

'Wow!' Frank whispered softly.

Jim knew exactly what he meant.

Candy held the pose for far too long, then, still holding Jim's gaze, dropped her hands to the waistband of her Levi's and toyed with the button. A second later she had popped it undone then the zip.

The shorts were tight and Candy made the most of wriggling out of them. She kicked them away and struck another pose, this one contrived to show her cleanly shaven sex.

Frank made a strangled noise of appreciation in the back of his throat.

Jim glanced at him, and during the second he was looking away, Candy crossed the space between her and him, took his arm and pulled. Taken by surprise, Jim either had to sprawl on his face or find his feet. A moment later, he realized that standing up had been the wrong choice. Candy had dropped to her knees in front of him and had taken hold of the waistband of his trousers. With one deft movement she undid the clasp. Jim tried to wriggle away but she held firm, shuffling up closer to him.

'Come on! Get 'em down and get in the water!' She reached for his zipper.

Jim stepped back a pace, intending to break free of her grasp without having to prise her fingers from his trousers, but the movement drew her off balance and Candy was pulled forward so that her face fell against the wide-open V of his trousers.

From the right of him, Jim heard a familiar noise that made his heart sink. It was the sound of a stills camera being driven at the rate of four or five frames a second by a motor-drive.

As Candy finally let go of him – presumably to see what the noise was – Jim turned to Frank just in time to see the man lower a huge Nikon camera that he'd produced from nowhere.

Candy glanced at Frank, shrugged then got up. 'I'll be waiting for you, Jim,' she said, winked at him and ran down the beach and into the water, shrieking as the cool sea splashed up around her.

Jim glared at Frank.

Frank smiled up at him happily. ''S okay. Really. Just a few snaps for my photo album. Nothing else. Honest!'

Zipping up his trousers, Jim scowled at him.

'Boy,' Frank went on, impressed, 'is that ever gonna look like you were copping a blow-job from our dear Candy!'

'Who's in the house?' a voice demanded, breaking into Jim's vision of his thumbs pressing hard into Frank's Adam's apple.

Jon Short stood there. He looked quite a lot better than he had ten minutes ago.

'I think you should try to stay out of the sun, Jon,' Jim said.

'Fair-skinned people *always* have trouble with heat and

sun,' Frank observed, scratching in his notebook. 'It's because they all originate from cold countries. Sweden. Norway. Places like that.'

'I remembered,' Jon said, ignoring Frank. 'It just popped back into my mind. I saw someone.'

'That's pretty unlikely,' Jim said, hoping like hell that Davey hadn't let himself be spotted. 'You fainted. Are you sure you're not just remembering something you dreamed while you were out of it?'

The certainty left Jon's face. 'That can happen?' he asked.

'I've heard it can,' Jim lied. 'Same thing happens when you've been put under nitrous oxide and stuff like that. When you come round, you hallucinate.'

'I've been knocked out plenty of times,' Jon said, 'but I never had that happen to me. A bit of confusion when I've woken up, perhaps, but no solid, real memories or anything.'

'It can happen,' Jim assured him.

'I've never heard of it,' Frank said, glancing up from his notes.

Jim shot him a look he hoped would kill. He was sorely disappointed. He turned back to Jon. 'What did you remember having seen?' he asked, certain that Jon was going to describe Davey in minute detail.

'Someone at the window,' Jon said, creasing up his face in an apparent effort to clarify the memory.

'A man?' Jim prompted, ready to claim that it had been, undoubtedly, the ghost of Straker Dauphin.

Jon Short shook his head. 'A woman,' he said.

You won't come back this time.

'She looked just like your wife,' Jon continued, then waited for Jim to confess.

Jim remembered how Jon had looked as if he'd been picked up by an unseen hand, bent into shape, then set down again. *You've got a vivid imagination*, he reminded himself, but this didn't make him feel any more comfortable. Jon hadn't seen a man, he'd seen a woman. The same woman that he'd said he'd seen on the *Mary Celeste*.

His mind conjured up a picture to order back on the boat, Jim told himself. *And when he fainted, his mind replayed that image to him, that's all.*

136

'She's here, isn't she?' Jon asked.

'No, she's at home,' Jim replied, briefly entertaining a notion that Davey might have recruited her, then dismissing it as ridiculous. Sooty didn't approve of the trips here and never had. Even Davey couldn't have convinced her she should take part in trying to scare her husband. She'd been too worried about him lately to do something like that.

Jon smiled slowly. 'Well, I think you've got a few surprises set up for us here. And I also think that Sooty's part of whatever it is you're gonna try scaring us with. That's why you engineered the panic on the boat about having seen her.'

Suddenly Frank looked interested. 'Is that right, Jim?' he asked. 'If she were here it'd explain why you chose not to go skinny-dipping with Candy, I guess.'

'Guess again,' Jim said. 'Sooty isn't here. She wasn't on the boat.'

'Then who did I see in the house?' Jon asked.

Jim studied him, looking for any tell-tale sign that Jon might have entered the lying contest that seemed to be going on here. There weren't any signs. At least, not ones Jim could read. Jon looked pretty much as if he were telling the truth. He looked *genuinely* puzzled. 'I don't know who you saw,' Jim said, wondering. No one could possibly mistake Davey for a woman who looked like Sooty. Therefore Jon had hallucinated it or he'd made up a story.

Which means there's nothing whatsoever to worry about, Jim told himself. 'It was the heat, Jon,' he said. 'That's all. You're remembering something that your mind played to you while you were out cold.'

Jon sighed. 'Maybe,' he said, staring out to sea where Candy was frolicking. 'I think I'll go take a swim. Cool down a little.'

'I think I'll join you,' Frank said, getting up and taking off his shirt.

He had a back so covered in hair that Jim could barely see the skin beneath it. Jim got up and turned away before Frank took off his trousers, but was able to judge the moment it happened from the shrieks of June, Martha and Rosie.

He trudged up the beach, refusing to look back in case the sight of Frank's butt showing above his underwear turned him into a pillar of salt.

3

'He seemed certain,' Jim said, standing at the window where Jon claimed he'd seen Sooty and examining the ancient net curtain. The dust on it had recently been disturbed. 'It was a woman and she looked like Sooty.'

'He was just having you on, Jim,' Rosie said, from behind him. 'God, Davey brought enough food to feed a platoon of foot-soldiers. It's gonna take for ever to lug all this down the beach.'

'He must have hallucinated it. Sooty can't be here and I can't believe Davey would have hired a damned lookalike just to spook me.'

'There are no female-sized footprints in here,' Rosie said. 'There's plenty of dust and plenty of prints of Davey's boots – some of which lead right up to the window where you're standing – but there aren't any ladylike ones anywhere. Either Jon's kidding about or he imagined what he says he saw. Why's it making you so uncomfortable?'

Jim turned back from the window and grinned sheepishly. He gave a shrug. 'I don't know,' he said. 'It's just that everything feels a bit funny this time. It's like I've slipped from my normal reality into another.'

'Stress,' Rosie said. 'Under normal circumstances, you'd think it was way cool if Davey went to all that trouble to try to spook you. But this time you've just come out from under a big pile of nasty stuff. Of course you're gonna feel a little odd. I blame that damned Frank. And *I* think he's putting you on, too.'

'He certainly appears to hate me,' Jim said.

'There's nothing to worry about,' Rosie assured him.

'I hope so. If he really *is* from *Newsweek*, I've got a fresh dumpster-load of shit coming at me. I can imagine the cover now. There'll be a picture of a nude Candy hanging on to me. The headline will be taken from last year's interview: "Jim Green: 'I'm a family man'." And under the shot they'll quote the shout line from *Miami Five Fifteen*: "Nothing is Ever as It Seems". They'll save the really dreadful pictures for the feature in which they trash me. You should have heard what Frank had to say about me.'

'Don't worry about it. Think of the increase in sales,' Rosie said.

'I'm thinking more of the way Sooty will tear off my balls with her fingernails,' he replied.

'I'll put her straight as soon as we get back,' Rosie said. She smiled and winked, and glanced at her watch. And said, 'You won't come back *this* time!'

Jim felt as if he'd been submerged in icy water. His mouth worked but no sound came out. He could feel the cool weight of the Colt .45 in his hand again. The oily taste of lubricant filled his mouth.

'What's up, Doc?' Rosie asked.

'What did you say?' Jim gasped. *'What?'*

Rosie frowned. 'When?'

'After you said "I'll put her straight,"' Jim said.

'I said "We'd better get back. Look at the time,"' she repeated.

'You're *sure*?'

Rosie sounded concerned. 'Are you okay, Jim?'

'Yeah.' He sighed. 'I'm just a bit jumpy. There's a recurring motif in *Shimmer*. The line that opens the book. It goes: "You won't come back *this* time." I thought that was what you said.' He pulled out his pack and lit a cigarette and drew hard on it. 'I'm being stupid,' he said.

'You're doing just fine,' Rosie said. 'Let's get this stuff back. People will be talking!'

Jim found a smile. 'May as well be hung for a sheep as for a lamb,' he said.

'Or both!' Rosie said, and watched the smile fade from Jim's face. 'What now?' she asked.

Jim smiled again, with difficulty this time. 'Probably just imagining this, Rosie, but turn to your left and look at the wall. Tell me what you see there.'

Rosie turned. A grubby sheet of plain foolscap was pinned to the wall. There were words written on it in a neat

139

copperplate hand, but she couldn't see what they said. 'I see a piece of paper,' she said.

'Did you notice it earlier?' Jim asked.

'No, but my attention was fixed on all these cool-boxes of food and beer,' Rosie replied. 'I wasn't looking for messages.'

'Me neither,' Jim said. 'It was here all along, right?'

'Of course,' Rosie said. 'What else . . . oh *Jim*! There's no ghost, is there? Tell me there's no *real* ghost. There's no such thing, right?'

'There are no ghosts,' Jim said mechanically. 'And that sheet of paper has been pinned up there all the while we've been in here.'

'Then why am I getting the shivers?' Rosie asked.

'Because all of us, deep down, are afraid of ghosts,' Jim said. 'It's inbuilt. But there *are* no ghosts.'

He strode across to the wall and snatched the sheet of paper from where it was pinned and read, '"He stole our dreams. He stole our nightmares. He stole everything we were. Now the thief is ours."' He looked up at Rosie. 'Now what d'you suppose *that* means? And who do you suppose stuck it up there?'

Rosie shuddered. 'I don't like it, Jim. It sounds threatening.'

'It's supposed to,' Jim said, brightening. 'Who's the only person who's been in here? Candy wouldn't come in and I saw what happened to Jon. Frank has been on the beach all the time. I don't know if he's a teacher or a reporter and I do know he's got a chip on his shoulder where I'm concerned, but he didn't pin this here because he's been irritating the shit out of me since we landed. Which means my initial theory was correct. All of this weirdness is Davey's doing. Davey is the only person who has been inside this house. And if you didn't pin it up and I didn't pin it up, it must have been him. Easy-peasy, lemon squeezy!' He balled the piece of paper, threw it into a corner and turned back to Rosie, looking relieved and happy. 'We'd better get some of this food and drink down on the beach. It'll be starting to get dark soon. And then the fun *really* begins.'

Rosie picked up a heavy cool-box and headed for the back

140

door with Jim behind her. She heard him stop and turned. His head was cocked slightly to one side and there was a puzzled expression on his face. She wished he'd stop doing this because it frightened her half to death. 'What *now*?' she asked.

'Shh!' Jim said. 'Listen!'

Rosie listened. She could hear the sound of gentle waves lapping at the seashore. Nothing more.

'There!' Jim said. 'Hear it?'

Rosie shook her head.

'And again!' Jim said. 'Hear it *that* time?'

'What am I supposed to be able to hear?' she asked.

Jim sighed. 'Don't mind me, I'm just cracking up. I heard a phone ring. On an island where there isn't any electricity, let alone any phones.'

'I have the mobile,' Rosie said, 'but it's back up the beach and I turned it off to save the battery. Maybe someone else has one too.'

Jim gave her a wry grin. 'Cellphones don't work over here,' he said. 'Anyway this wasn't a cellphone blitter. It was a bell. Like the one we have at home in the kitchen. There! I heard it again!'

Rosie raised an eyebrow.

Jim rolled his eyes. 'Don't worry about me,' he said. 'I'll be just fine. Come on, let's get this stuff outside. It's starting to get heavy.'

Chapter Ten

Sooty and the Word Factory

1

When the phone rang in the Green household – the place Jim had named the Word Factory – it didn't go ignored for long because of the godawful racket it made. The phone in the kitchen rang, the switchboard buzzed, the extension in Jim and Sooty's bedroom bleated and there was a bell up under the eaves on the back of the house so that calls wouldn't be missed when everyone was out in the garden. It might have been overkill, Jim had occasionally admitted, and it might have irritated the shit out of everyone, but it *worked*.

This time, the phone was also ringing in Jim's empty study. Where the blank screen of the shut-down computer flickered twice and lit up, white and empty. And where, letter by letter, three words slowly appeared in the centre of the screen:

WON'T COME BACK

In the kitchen, Sooty Green was cursing Thomas Edison and his infernal works while she held her daughter in her arms and tried to calm her sobbing.

'Daddy!' Gloria cried. 'Daddyyy! I want *Daddyyyyyyy*!'

Sooty hugged her and rocked her and whispered, 'It's all right! Everything's going to be fine.' She hefted the little girl up in her arms and added, 'Gosh, you're getting heavy.'

'Make him come home,' Gloria moaned, into her mother's shoulder.

Sooty glared at the telephone, just knowing she'd turned into one of Pavlov's dogs. The need to answer that damned thing, if only to stop it ringing, was an imperative.

142

'Daddy's going to be fine,' she whispered, moving towards the phone against her wishes. *Why don't they just realize no one's home and ring off?* she asked herself, not wanting to pick up the phone in case it turned out to be Spreadbury.

Whoever it was at the other end didn't give up easily. It must have been ringing for more than two minutes by now. Which meant, she assumed, that the caller had urgent information to pass on. The trouble was, the word 'urgent' meant something entirely different for some people.

It's probably just a publisher from Japan or somewhere it's early morning and the office has just opened, she thought hopefully. *They're probably trying to fax through a review of* Black River *in the original Japanese or something that's equally important. Ha, ha!*

That would certainly be better than the alternative. *Don't let it be Spreadbury,* she silently prayed.

The phone rang and, in her arms, her daughter shuddered and sobbed. For what must have been the thousandth time, Sooty wished Jim hadn't made that quip about Candy wanting his body; for the thousandth time, she wished she'd taken that damned Game Gear away from Gloria before she'd immersed herself in its imaginary world so deeply.

There was something nasty about that *Razor Gang* game, she thought. She was sure it'd had an adverse effect on Jim when he'd become so obsessed with it a while back. She tried to remember if he had complained of nightmares, then rephrased her mental query. Jim didn't complain about nightmares at all. He didn't get enough of them, in his opinion. Nightmares were his stock-in-trade. Unlike Gloria, whose subconscious – opened for the computer game – had sucked in Jim's words about body-snatching and had stored them for now.

It was odd, really. Gloria slept well unless she was ill and she'd never been like this in her life. Not long after six she'd said she felt sleepy, so Sooty had bathed her and put her to bed. *That should have alerted you that something was amiss,* Sooty told herself. *She* never *wants to go to bed!* But within minutes, her daughter had been fast asleep.

Then, ten minutes ago, she'd woken up screaming. Except that she hadn't really woken up at all. She seemed to have been caught in a weird state where she was half awake and half dreaming. Her eyes were blank, her speech mostly unintelligible. And, since then, nothing Sooty could say seemed to reach her. Gloria wouldn't go back to sleep and she wouldn't wake up properly either. Sooty would have suspected a high fever and delirium if Gloria's temperature hadn't been a rock-solid 98.6°.

'His *body*!' Gloria moaned over the incessant ringing of the telephone. 'Taking his *body*!'

'Shh!' Sooty whispered, unable to prevent herself answering the phone any longer. If it turned out to be Spreadbury, she'd just hang up. 'No one is going to take Daddy's body! Be good while Mommy gets the phone.' She carried her daughter over to where the phone was mounted on the wall and snatched up the handset with her free hand.

'Hello?' she said, into the wave of static she could hear. It sounded like a thousand distant fire-hoses aimed at a burning building. There was no reply. Sooty waited for the tone that would signify an incoming fax message but when nothing had happened for a count of fifteen she slammed the handset back into its cradle.

The phone began to ring again with no pause at all. She snatched it up. The moment she put it to her ear, it emitted a shriek loud enough to cause pain. 'Shit!' she yelled, whipping it away from her ear.

Gloria lifted her head and looked at her mother through dazed eyes. Her chest still hitched, but her tears had stopped and she looked as if she'd finally woken up.

Welcome back to the land of the living, honey, Sooty thought, relieved. In her other hand the phone screeched.

'Daddy?' Gloria said, trying to grab the phone.

Swiftly Sooty moved it out of her reach. 'It isn't Daddy,' she said. 'It doesn't seem to be anyone at all.'

The shrieking ceased. Sooty moved the phone close enough to her ear to hear if anyone spoke and far enough away to prevent her eardrum suffering any more pain if the noise came back.

A female voice that she thought she should recognize, but didn't, cut through the static that still hissed in the earpiece.

144

'He won't come back,' it said, and was instantly swallowed in the following wave of static.

'Who won't come back from where? Who's calling?' Sooty demanded, suddenly sure that the mystery voice was referring to Jim. There was no other 'he' in her life. 'Who *is* this?' she asked again, her muscles turning to steel while a freezing jet of panic shot down her spine and wound through her intestines.

The line cleared again. 'He stole our dreams. He stole our nightmares. He stole everything we were.' The voice was clinical and cold, its tone flat. And yet it was so familiar it might have belonged to her mother or her best friend Sophie. Sooty knew that voice, knew it as well as she knew her own. In her arms, Gloria began to sob again quietly.

Sooty fought against the fear that was threatening to paralyse her and tried to replace it with anger and outrage. 'Are you sure you have the right number?' she heard herself ask mildly and cursed. She was shaking now: her neck muscles had turned into vibrating steel hawsers that made her head wiggle and twitch of its own accord.

'There *is* only one number,' the voice said. 'The number is three minus three.'

'What in God's name are you talking about?' Sooty demanded, now unable to keep the fear from her voice. *'Who is this?'*

'We are the three. The thief stole it all.'

'Fuck you!' Sooty sputtered in a tight, high voice and slammed the phone back into its cradle.

'Dadddddyyyyy,' Gloria whimpered.

'That's who I'm afraid for, honey,' Sooty murmured, still staring at the phone.

2

Jim Green might have been the Master of Disaster for millions, and he might have been *millions* dressed in jeans and a T-shirt to the suits out in Hollywood but to Mrs James Green, Sooty Alexander, he was simply Jim, the gentle, intelligent and sensitive man she'd fallen in love with all those years ago.

Sometimes – like now, for example, as she sat in the lounge with a stiff shot of Glenmorangie in one hand and her other arm round her daughter, who'd now settled back into an uneasy sleep – she half wished that whatever had happened *hadn't* happened.

Sooty still didn't know what that miraculous thing was. Jim had merely written another book, just like all the other books he'd written, this one called *Deathless*. The only difference Sooty could see between *Deathless* and the previous five that had been consigned to the top shelf, unwanted by the publishing world, was that Jim had started out with a screenplay and made a novel from that. This made it shorter than his others, although why that should have made a difference, Sooty didn't know.

But something *had* made a difference. Magic had happened. Sooty still wasn't sure whether this magic had been of the good, bad, or benign variety – at times it seemed to be each of those in turn. Where the previous books had been turned down by all and sundry, this one had led to a weird kind of happening called a 'bidding war'.

Jim had sent the book to an agent in New York. The agent hadn't replied for months. This was normal. Then, what usually happened was that the manuscript would return, all dog-eared and ringed with the marks of coffee mugs. This time, there was an excited phone call from the agent, a weird woman named Ruth. Hollywood wanted the screen rights and one studio had offered a million and a half. Five major houses were interested in an auction for the publishing rights, and Ruth was setting the floor at half a million dollars.

Sooty remembered the day vividly. They'd been living in a tiny shack way outside Seaford, supported only by her income from teaching at the school at Cutler Ridge. Which meant she was up very early each morning, back home late and exhausted all the time. They were desperate days. Back then it had looked as if things were never going to get better. Jim had been on the verge of giving up his dream and hauling Sooty and himself up to Miami to work at a *real* job.

She'd watched Jim take that call from her place at the kitchen table. It had been a hot day and there hadn't been

146

air-conditioning in the shack. She'd had a glass of cold orange juice in her hand and she'd been sweating her hair into rats' tails and her dress into the washing basket. At first it hadn't seemed any different from any other call, then she'd noticed that Jim's voice had begun to sound a little shocked and suspected that one of his distant relatives back in Scotland had suffered an accident or, perhaps, had died.

Then Jim said, 'Really? Are you *sure*?' and 'I can't believe it,' and 'You're kidding. Promise me you're not kidding.' And he'd glanced at her, shocked and perplexed, but not unhappy.

Then he had gently placed the phone back in its cradle, dragged her into his arms and cried into her neck for the next ten minutes, unable to explain what had happened.

Life had changed, quickly and radically. The following week Jim flew to New York and Los Angeles for meetings. The week after that, Sooty had quit her job and started planning her ideal home, which would be built entirely to her design.

And then the money had started rolling in. Sooty hadn't been sure exactly how much money until she picked up a copy of *Time* a year later when the film of *Deathless* was released and read that it was estimated that Jim was now making almost two dollars every single *second* of every day. A hundred and twenty dollars for every minute of his life, waking or sleeping. In the four minutes it took Jim to smoke a Virginia Slim 100, he'd earned four hundred and eighty dollars. When she'd mentioned this to him, Jim had grinned and asked if he'd make nine hundred and sixty if he smoked them two at a time.

The money had never seemed real. It hadn't then and it didn't now. Jim's accountant occasionally complained about how much tax the government was taking, but none of it made sense because no matter how much the taxes were, there was always too much left. Even after Jim had set up substantial regular donations to half a dozen charities – something which apparently frightened his financial advisers half to death – there was so much money it just couldn't be spent as fast as it was coming in.

Through it all, Jim had stayed the same as he'd always

been, and Sooty was thankful for that. They'd built the big house and Jim had his cars and the *Mary Celeste* and he'd bought Straker's Island and somewhere along the line he wanted to learn to fly, but that was about as far as the change in their lifestyle went: they could afford what they wanted. What they *most* wanted, it had turned out, wasn't fabulous wealth and rich folks' toys and fame, but *one another*, just as they always had.

Life, Sooty supposed, had been good to them. But everything had its price and there was a downside to Jim's fame and fortune. There were times when he'd been away in Hollywood, working on the films, and she'd missed him so much she'd *ached* for him to be there. She'd tried going on the set with him, but hadn't felt comfortable: images of Yoko Ono following John Lennon everywhere had lit up in her mind and people had treated her with undue reverence. She'd felt like a spare part, and while she was there, there were things at home she should and could have been doing.

Then there were the fans who turned up out of the blue. She clearly remembered following Jim downstairs, wrapped in nothing but a tiny hand-towel and yelling that she was pretty sure their sex life was over for ever because each time they got hot and horny the doorbell would ring and there'd be some poor sap there who'd travelled all the way from Australia or England in the hope of getting to shake the hand of the Master of Disaster.

And Jim wasn't the type to ignore his fans. Each tired traveller was invited in and made a fuss of. A couple of them had been invited to stay overnight.

Good for the fans, bad for the sex life, Sooty thought, sipping her Glenmorangie. She and Jim had recently given a kind of his 'n' hers interview to *Rolling Stone*, because they had both thought it might be fun. They'd been interviewed separately and had been asked the same questions by two different interviewers. One of those questions had been: *How is your partner in bed?* Sooty had giggled and said, 'Asleep, usually, and pulling all the covers over to his side,' only to find that Jim had made exactly the same reply, although he'd added, 'But as far as the sex is concerned – and I guess that is what you *really* want to hear about here –

148

it's excellent. Either no-holds barred stuff, yowling and screaming and scratching like a couple of cats on heat, which, incidentally, is partially where she got her nickname, or slow and tender and loving and gentle. She laps like a cat, too.'

'Jim isn't just the Master of Disaster, he's a master lover, too,' Sooty had said and, for some strange reason, hadn't even been embarrassed. 'He's an SLSG – we have this diploma on the wall over our bed. An SLSG? That's an acronym for Shao-Lin Sex God. You remember David Carradine in *Kung Fu*? He was a Shao-Lin priest. Jim's a Shao-Lin lover. He has total control over himself. He'll last just as long as you want him to last, do exactly what you want him to do, exactly when you want him to do it. I guess we have a kind of telepathy or something. Course, it's taken years of practice.'

Just get back home soon, you big dummy, she thought. I love you. And I'm missing you and worrying about you!

'I'm a happy man now,' Jim had said, in the same interview. 'But it's not just about money or success, although the money is useful. I'd have been as happy even if I'd never made it. And you know why? Sooty. Sooty and my daughter Gloria.

'If it came to a choice between the money and the fame and my wife and child,' he'd continued, 'there wouldn't be any contest. I'd give it all up for them in a moment.'

Remembering, Sooty was still amazed, even after all these years, that he could say such a sweet thing. And, even more amazing, he *meant* it.

She'd cried when she'd read that bit and had clung to Jim, never wanting to let him go.

'But no one's asked me to give up anything yet,' he'd continued. 'The world chooses to smile on me and just keeps on giving. And, more often than not, I smile back.'

That was true, too, but not the whole truth. That interview had been just after Jim had run into trouble with *Shimmer*. The block had been new, and back then he hadn't been worrying about it. But it had gone on. And on. And both Sooty and Jim had found out the real price of his fame and fortune.

Back then, at the beginning of things falling apart for Jim,

Sooty had told *Rolling Stone* that she wasn't the worrying kind. She'd eaten those words now. She'd eaten them a hundred times over while she'd watched her husband and lover sink deeper and deeper into the mire and found herself powerless to do anything about it. She'd talked sense to him, joked with him, made light of things. She'd loved him, held him, cussed him out, but he'd turned into an unthinking, uncaring block of ice.

Until then she hadn't realized how much his work meant to him. And when she found it meant enough to him to bring him to the brink of suicide she had been forced to do a great deal of mental recalculation.

She wasn't the most important thing in his life, after all: his work was.

For a couple of weeks back there she was sure they'd lost it. Certain that this love story wouldn't have a happy ending. It looked as if she was suddenly going to be free, single and rapidly approaching middle age.

But the crisis had passed. In a way.

Even though Jim's dam seemed to have broken now, Sooty wasn't at all sure that either of them was entirely out of the woods. It wasn't quite as simple as that. His confidence was still low, hers had taken a severe knock, and there was more.

'It's all like a dream!' she'd told Jim, when he'd hugged her off her feet and whirled her round in the brand new home she'd designed. It had been an empty shell then, smelling of damp cement and echoing like a warehouse and this had been the first time they'd been in it together so near completion. 'I keep thinking that one day I'm going to wake up and it'll all have been taken away from me,' she'd added.

'Never!' Jim replied happily. 'Nothing and no one can take it away. And if they do, we'll still have each other.' And he'd punctuated the end of this sentence by dotting a kiss on the tip of her nose. Whenever she thought about it now, she could still feel that kiss, lingering.

Sooty sipped her single malt and thought about it all. In retrospect a lot of the things they'd said, either recorded or just remembered, seemed like tempting Providence. She had a distinct feeling that something was going to happen that

150

would take everything away from her. And not just the wealth and fame, but Jim too.

Because of Spreadbury.

And because of Straker's Island.

You didn't have to be in possession of anything more than common sense to know that Straker's Island wasn't just any old lump of land floating in a cobalt blue sea. The island was *special*. Once it had simply been a peaceful place to where two hopelessly romantic teenagers could escape from the world at large into a world of their own. A place where the young Sooty and Jim could lie naked in one another's arms on the porch of the crumbling old Dauphin house. But even back then, Sooty had sensed the island's *difference*. It was a kind of magical place where no animals lived; where the feeling of peace and tranquillity increased the longer you stayed. Where your inhibitions vanished. Where you felt *at home*.

Now, it was *their* property, which made it even more special. Add to that that their daughter had been conceived on that porch *and* that the island was the place where Jim's muse handed him gifts of gold, and you had a place you wanted to keep for yourselves.

Taking boatloads of fans over there for camp-fire food and romps through the woods had always felt to Sooty a little like profaning sacred soil. Not as bad as holding a black mass in a church, perhaps, but she'd always been uneasy about the trips. Just before the first one, Jim had asked her if she felt that the fans would 'break' Straker's Island, and she'd nodded. She had always thought that there was something delicate about the place; a balance there that might easily be disturbed.

This year, that feeling had been worse. So bad, in fact, that Sooty had made Jim promise her that this year's trip would be the last time he ever took fans over there. To her surprise, Jim had not only agreed but confessed that he felt exactly the same as she did about the trips and the island. Tonight was the last ever trip.

But Sooty was acutely aware that the party wouldn't be over until the fireworks went off at midnight. And midnight was still a good long way away. Which left plenty of time . . .

151

For things to go wrong? she asked herself, taking another sip of her whisky and remembering Spreadbury again.

Another downside to Jim's fame was that some of the people who knew who he was (and some of them were most certainly *not* his fans) were lunatics. Throughout his entire life, Jim had attracted drunks like a magnet attracts iron filings, but since he'd become a household name he'd begun to attract weirdos, too. Mostly they sent abusive, barely legible letters claiming that Jim was responsible for their pregnancies, giving them syphilis, unleashing the devil on them and so on. Only two had been death threats and they'd both contained the senders' return addresses which made it easy for the authorities to deal with them.

Jim had been attacked by a woman on a television chat-show in New York and had been stalked briefly by a strange – and harmless – Swedish kid, who turned out to have been under the misapprehension that he was Robert de Niro. Which wouldn't have been so bad if Jim had looked even vaguely similar to Bobby, but he hadn't and never would.

What they'd never had, until recently, was weird telephone calls. The house had an unlisted number, which had helped, Sooty supposed, but weirdos, for some odd reason, seemed to like to write rather than call. They'd had one or two calls, but only from genuine fans who'd somehow got hold of the number. Telephone-wise, things had been fine.

Until the day Spreadbury had first called.

It had been still a few weeks ahead of the arrival of Jim's block, but Sooty had been aware of the upcoming trip to Straker's Island and she'd already been uneasy about it – in much the same way as she could wake up on a normal morning and know that she would finish the day with a blinding headache even though there were no symptoms.

It had been a Tuesday – Rosie's day off – and Sooty had taken the call herself. The terrible thing about Spreadbury was the way he managed to sound absolutely sane. His voice was smooth and deep and relaxed, his tone confident. And yet . . .

'Good afternoon,' he'd said. 'Do I have the residence of Mr James Green?'

'You do,' Sooty replied, smiling. 'Who's calling?' The man

might have been a new partner at the law firm Jim used, for all she knew. He had that official-but-friendly tone. She'd been deep in thought when the phone rang and didn't think to wonder if it was a stranger at the other end of the line.

'My name is Aaron Spreadbury,' he'd replied – which was exactly the kind of name Sooty expected lawyers to have. 'I'd like to speak with Mr Green, if it's possible.'

'Mr Green isn't available right now,' Sooty had said, still not suspecting anything untoward. 'I'm afraid he's working. This is Mrs Green. Can I help you?'

'It's rather important that I speak to *Mr* Green,' Spreadbury had said, his voice still full of professional warmth. 'Would you be so kind as to tell me when he will be available?'

Sooty had sighed. 'Not unless I know the nature of your call,' she said. 'I'm acting as Mr Green's personal assistant and he's deeply involved in a project from which he doesn't want to be distracted. If you'd like to state the nature of your business, I'll decide whether or not he needs to be informed of your call. And whether or not he'll call you back. I'm sorry to sound so rude, but he's working to a tight deadline.'

The pause that followed was long enough for Sooty suddenly to wonder if Spreadbury was a doctor calling with the results of some test or other that Jim had sneaked off and had done without telling her. A tiny flame of concern lit in her while her mind dashed off a selection of what-ifs? What if Jim had been unfaithful and had gone to be tested for HIV? What if he'd found a lump he hadn't told her about to save her the worry and it'd been biopsied? What if . . .?

'He'll want to be informed of my call, I'm certain,' Spreadbury said smoothly, and Sooty got the distinct impression that he was smiling at her stupidity. She was suddenly a little angry.

'He won't be informed of *anything* if you're not prepared to disclose the nature of your business,' she snapped. 'And how did you get this number anyway?'

'If I told you how I got your number, you'd instantly dismiss me as a crank and a liar,' Spreadbury said, unaffected by her anger. 'Which, I suppose, you may well do in any case. I understand that you're not very happy with me so far, but I beg you to hear me out before you ring off. You see, I have important information for you and Mr Green. Vital information.'

'Just tell me what you're selling,' Sooty said, already itching to hang up on the supercilious idiot. He was rapidly turning into the kind that Jim called Know-Betters on account of the fact they always thought they knew better than you.

'What I have is information. Momentous information. And I do not require payment for it. My information is a gift to you. You see, Mrs Green, your husband is in terrible danger.'

Which was when Sooty hung up.

Against her better judgement, she lifted the receiver when the phone rang again.

'Please hear me out,' Spreadbury said, in a pained voice. 'I know this is difficult for you to hear, but you *must* listen.'

'Who are you, *Mr* Aaron Spreadbury?' Sooty fumed. 'And what the hell do you want? What are you after? You're not going to get any money out of this, you know. We won't be blackmailed. And I'll be reporting this call to the police.'

'Feel free,' Spreadbury said mildly. 'I have nothing to hide and I have no evil intentions. I am a respected member of the community in Miami Beach. My only wish is to help. You may take my telephone number and address whenever you wish. Let me give you my telephone number.'

'Okay, I'm listening,' Sooty said, when she'd finished jotting down his number. 'Start by telling me how you got this number.'

'I dialled it at random,' Spreadbury said, and Sooty could *hear* his lips curl into a smug smile.

'Do you want to tell me the truth now, or should I hang up?' Sooty asked grimly. 'I'm already very tired of this conversation, my patience is being tested beyond the limits of its endurance and you've made a threat. My husband is in terrible danger, you said. Now, if you're not telling me the truth in ten seconds, I'm hanging up and calling the police. I have detective friends up in Miami. Ten. Nine. Eight.'

'Please believe me,' Spreadbury said. 'It would be a mistake not to.'

Sooty slammed down the phone. When it rang again, she lifted it off the hook and put it straight down. Then dialled the number for Ruth, Jim's agent in New York.

An hour later, she hung up, having finished talking business and chewing the fat with Ruth. Business was good, but Ruth's faithful beagle Raffles had torn the cruciate ligament in his hind leg and he'd gone in for an operation today. Ruth was beside herself with worry and Sooty had spent most of the hour listening and sympathizing. When the phone rang immediately after Sooty had replaced it, the last thing on her mind was Aaron Spreadbury, the idiot from Miami Beach. She simply assumed that Ruth had forgotten to tell her something important and had rung straight back.

'I divined your telephone number,' a deep, confident voice said.

'Leave me alone!' Sooty yelled angrily. Then she frowned. 'Divined?' she said, mystified.

'I am a psychic,' Spreadbury oozed. 'And I trust my unconscious implicitly. I needed to call you so I merely let my fingers press the buttons they wanted to press. My unconscious knew your telephone number. Now, don't ring off. I know you're hardly likely to believe me. But I understand your husband deals with psychic matters in his writing so you may well be familiar with divination, portents, omens and other psychic phenomena. You may not believe in any of this, of course. You may think that it's merely the stuff of fantasy fiction, but the fact is, I'm talking to you having dialled a random number which turns out to be the unlisted number I wanted to be connected to. Strange, as they say, but *true*.'

'And you want to deliver a warning,' Sooty said.

'I want to help.'

'And you'll want paying, no doubt.'

'Of course not. People who seek me out pay me for my services, but you have not sought me. I have contacted you. I have contacted you to warn of the danger that lies ahead for your husband and to offer to help, free of any charge.'

155

'And if people pay for your services, whatever they might be, why would you want to help us for free?' Sooty asked.

'Because Mr Green's case is an interesting one. I've never felt anything as powerful as the thing that approaches your husband, Mrs Green. Its psychic force is awesome. And destructive.'

'And what can you do about it?' Sooty demanded.

'I don't know,' Spreadbury said, apparently surprised at the question.

'Can you stop this thing?' Sooty said.

'Perhaps. Perhaps not.'

'Then goodbye,' Sooty said. 'Don't waste my time calling again.'

And Sooty had tried to put Aaron Spreadbury out of her mind. The man must have read too many of Jim's books and believed what he read. She was so certain she'd seen the phrase 'Its psychic force is awesome' in one of Jim's books that the following day she leafed through three looking for it. She hadn't found it, or anyone named Spreadbury in the books she'd checked, but it didn't mean that neither the sentence nor the character wasn't in *something* Jim had written.

She should have told Jim, she supposed, but the love of her life was deep into *Shimmer* and battling to meet the deadline, and she thought he'd make more of Aaron Spreadbury than she had. What made Jim's books so good, in Sooty's opinion, was that in spite of his protestations to the contrary, a part of him really *did* believe in the things he wrote about. The little boy under the wise-cracking pragmatist believed in ghosties and ghoulies and long-legged beasties and things that go bump in the night.

And Sooty didn't for a moment believe Spreadbury was the real thing. She was sure some people *were* genuinely psychic, but she was equally sure that Spreadbury wasn't one of them. He might have thought he was, of course, but it was easy to delude oneself in such matters. Practically all the Hollywood stars who believed in channelling and reincarnation were certain they'd been someone amazingly important in a previous life. As far as Sooty knew, there wasn't a stable lad or a milkmaid among their previous incarnations. It was all ego and self-delusion.

Aaron Spreadbury might have been a crank, but he was undoubtedly of the harmless variety. A mad killer might have made a similar phone call, she supposed, but he would have been unlikely to leave his telephone number. And Spreadbury really *had* left his telephone number. Sooty had called Sophie up in Virginia and asked her to check out the number. Sophie had reported back that she'd been connected to Aaron Spreadbury's answering service.

During the following week, Sooty forgot about the supercilious psychic. Until he called again, insisting that the trouble was growing ever closer and that he should be recruited to help. This time Sooty merely said, 'Fuck off!' and hung up.

But Spreadbury was nothing if not persistent. He rang at the same time on the same day each week. It became so regular that at one fifteen each Tuesday Sooty would wait by the phone, snatch it up on its first ring, yell her obscene greeting into it and slam it down.

And then Jim got writer's block.

And Sooty felt uncomfortable. Perhaps Spreadbury really was psychic. Maybe the big bad thing he'd intuited was here and not a massive evil force at all, but a great big wall through which Jim was unable to pass.

And then she'd thought of the forthcoming trip to the island. Perhaps the psychic had foreseen something that would happen over there. Something that would upset the delicate balance of the place and ruin it for ever.

And the calls had gone on, reminding her every Tuesday at one fifteen that someone knew that something big and bad was headed this way and wanted to help.

If things get much worse, I'll talk to him, Sooty had decided during the third week of Jim's block. *That wouldn't hurt, would it? Just to see if he has anything to say. Perhaps he just might be able to help.*

But she hadn't given in. Her rational mind knew that Spreadbury was nothing but a charlatan hoping to worm his way into her life and towards Jim's money.

And then they'd had the switchboard installed, and each Tuesday lunch-time Sooty had set it to divert calls to the answering service. And each Tuesday at two, she wiped the messages without listening to them.

And each Tuesday at two minutes after two, her uneasiness increased.

Chapter Eleven

The Power of Love

1

Jim sat on a fold-out stool close to the fire with Rosie beside him while he watched Candy, Frank and Jon romp in the shallows. There was a lot of giggling and squealing as Candy splashed after Jon trying to get a grip on the waistband of his shorts. Evidently she didn't intend to rest until all three of them were naked.

'At least Frank's had the decency to turn his back on us,' Rosie said. 'Even if he does have a huge hairy behind.'

Candy hadn't so much had to tear off Frank's underwear as to work up the courage to take it off him. 'I'm gonna getcha nekkid!' she had called, as he'd waded into the water, and she'd made comically threatening claws of her hands.

'Go right ahead,' Frank had invited, and had held up his hands in submission.

Candy had made a last swipe at Jon, who darted away, then turned back to Frank, who was now facing her and standing sideways on to the beach. Jim and Rosie could plainly see his erection through the front of his shorts. This didn't stop Candy, however. She splashed across to him, yanked at his shorts – which got entangled with his erect penis – and finally put her hand inside them to clear the obstruction. A moment later Frank was standing there naked for all to see, his dick pointing upwards at an angle of sixty degrees or so off the vertical. Candy frowned at it for a moment, then dashed off after Jon again.

'I don't have much experience of naked, priapic men,' Rosie said thoughtfully, as Frank, grinning, turned back to wave at those on the beach, 'so tell me this. Is it common for their dicks to curve to one side like that? Like a banana?'

'It's not unheard of,' Jim said, not knowing whether to be disgusted at Frank, embarrassed at discussing the man's penis with Rosie or whether the whole thing was as hilariously funny as it seemed. No one had ever stripped naked on the previous trips he'd made. 'Evidently it's the first time Candy's run across anything quite as bent,' he added, taking a cold bottle of Mexican beer from the cooler and searching for the bottle opener.

'I'll tell you something else,' Rosie said, grunting as she tried to loosen the cork from a bottle of champagne. 'Damn, I can't shift this. Will you do it, Jim?'

He pushed his bottle of Sol into the sand and took the bottle of Bollinger from Rosie. 'What else?' he asked.

'I've never seen an uncircumcised man before,' she said. 'Frank is my first. Including the bend, that's two firsts in one day. How about you?'

Jim twisted the cork a little and when it began to move aimed the bottle out to sea and helped the cork along with his thumb. It slowly rose from the bottleneck. 'How about me, what? Yeah, I've seen uncircumcised men before. I *am* one. That's what you wanted to know, wasn't it?'

The cork left the bottle with a tremendous *pop!*, arced through the air and landed at the water's edge. Frothy champagne fizzed out and Jim filled Rosie's glass. 'They've stopped circumcising male American babies as a matter of course these days,' he added. 'I know that because someone wrote to me complaining about the age of the character in a short story I wrote called "Sacrifice".'

Rosie sipped her champagne and gave a ladylike belch. 'I know the one.' She nodded. 'The guy who kept cutting bits off himself with a pair of heavy-duty scissors. It's in the *Strange Landmarks* collection, right?'

Jim nodded. 'Trouble was, I'd made the guy an American. And as you know, the first bit of himself he cut off was his foreskin. Well, I got this really snotty letter from someone over in Houston explaining that at the age my character was he wouldn't have had a foreskin to chop off. They'd have done it shortly after his birth. It seems the Surgeon General, or whoever it is looks after the health of the country, was under the impression that circumcision prevented penile cancer and all sorts of other things. I wrote back apologizing to the guy that I was a Scotsman and couldn't be expected to know stuff like that.'

'Yesssss!' Candy cried.

Jim and Rosie both looked up just in time to catch Jon pulling his shorts back up and making a bid for freedom.

'I wish I had half her energy,' Rosie said ruefully. 'Frank isn't much, but little Jon over there has a good body.'

Jim laughed. 'All this sun and champagne is going to your head,' he said. 'First you tell me that if you were a few years younger you'd be giving Sooty a run for her money and now you're after Jon!'

Rosie gave him an exaggerated wink. 'If it came to a choice between Jon and you, it wouldn't take me long to make up my mind,' she whispered. Then she chuckled and said, 'Have you caught the sun today, or are you blushing, young man?' Before he could reply she turned to where Martha and June were still sitting in the shade and called, 'Champagne is being served! Come and get it! Hurry before the drunken writer slurps it all down!'

She turned back to Jim and raised her glass. 'Cheers!' she said.

Jim waved his bottle towards her glass. 'Nosferatu!' he said. 'What are we drinking to?'

A huge grin stole across Rosie's face – to Jim she ended up looking exactly how he'd always pictured the Cheshire Cat, except, of course, she had blue-rinsed hair and no whiskers. 'We're drinking to a good trip. And . . .'

'And what?' Jim asked.

Rosie's grin broadened.

'You smile any harder and your mouth will meet round the back and the top of your head will fall off,' Jim said. 'And what? What else are we drinking to? Hurry up, my beer's getting warm.'

'To *Newsweek*'s photos,' she said.

'That's not nice,' Jim said, feeling a little hurt.

Rosie's smile didn't falter. 'Funny you should say that,' she said, 'because it's exactly what Frank's going to say when he gets his shots processed.'

She held Jim's gaze, reached down beside her, lifted

something from the bundle beside her own seat and brought it up into view.

It was Frank's Nikon camera.

Jim's mouth dropped open in astonishment.

'Well, it's like this,' Rosie said. 'When Frank went swimming, he took off his clothes and piled them neatly on the beach. And I just happened by, see. It hadn't occurred to me that he would have left his nice expensive camera behind since it isn't waterproof. *That* wasn't the reason I wandered over to where he'd left his bag and his clothes. Honestly!' She chuckled. 'But when I got there, I noticed his bag was open and the sun was shining right inside it and making his camera all hot and I thought: We don't want anything to happen to Frank's nice shots of Jim with Candy kneeling in front of him looking as if she's giving him a blow-job, now, do we? We'd better do something about this. I mean, it wouldn't be fair on him to leave his camera out in the sun where it might get damaged. So I did what any thoughtful grandmother would do. I picked up the bag and brought it over here and set it down in the shade beside me.'

Jim snapped his mouth shut and drew a breath to speak, but Rosie leaped in before him.

'Now I don't know a lot about cameras, but I reckon I know how to take a photograph with this one because I've seen Frank taking them. You just fiddle with the lens at the front till everything is in focus and press this here button on the top. And I think I should take a shot of Frank out there in the sea with a bent hard-on. Y' know, so he remembers the trip. So he's got something he can take home as a memento, something he can treasure for ever.'

'Rosie . . .' Jim started.

'Shh, I'm concentrating,' Rosie said, and put the camera up to her eye, holding it as if she was about to take a shot.

'The lens cap is on,' Jim said, frowning.

'Strange.' Rosie chortled from behind the big Nikon. 'I can see exactly what *I* want to see. I think we just press this little button here.' She fiddled with the lens, then with the shutter button, then adjusted one of her hands. Something clicked and Rosie said, 'Oh dear! Oh *deary* deary me!'

It wasn't until she moved the camera from her face that

162

Jim finally understood what her intentions had been all along. Half of him had thought she really did want to take a photo of Frank in the nude. As she brought the camera down, he realized that Rosie hadn't tried to take a picture at all. She'd pressed the button that opened the back of the camera.

And the back now swung open. Rosie turned the camera so that Jim could see the film stretched from one side to the other. 'Damn!' She giggled. 'I'm such an old fool. I seem to have pressed the wrong button. I didn't mean to do *that*. Do you think the film will be damaged?'

'I'm sure it'll be just fine,' Jim said, glancing out to where Frank stood. He was still facing out to sea. Jon was swimming for his life towards the *Mary Celeste* and Candy, using a surprisingly neat and powerful freestyle stroke, was gaining on him like a shark.

'Maybe we should just wind the film back a few frames, just to be sure what's gone by isn't damaged,' Rosie said, fiddling with the motor winder. The Nikon burst into life and the film withdrew back into the film canister leaving a four-inch tongue poking out. 'I'd say the sun shone on all those frames, wouldn't you?' Rosie asked. 'Oh, and it's a fast film, too. Good!' She deftly attached the tongue of film to the winding spindle and, leaving the back of the camera open, used the motor-drive to take sixteen shots. Then she closed the camera and put it back in Frank's bag.

'Like I said'—she smiled—'when Frank gets his pictures back, he's gonna say, "That's not nice!"'

Jim chuckled. 'It's about time I gave you a pay rise, Rosie.'

'I'll hold you to that, too,' she said picking up her glass and holding it out towards Jim. 'To *Newsweek*!'

2

Martha and June were half-way between the shade of the trees and the camp-fire when Jim felt a trembling under him. He'd been in Los Angeles shortly after the last earthquake and before the aftershocks had died out. The locals, sensitized to the tiniest twitch of the ground, had felt motion that Jim hadn't, but he had felt some of the larger aftershocks.

And this felt rather like one of those. Which would be something new for this area. Florida had hurricanes and tornadoes, but no earthquakes.

The tremor lasted only a second or two.

'What was that?' he asked Rosie.

'What was what?' Rosie replied, indicating that she had felt nothing.

A wave rolled up the beach and crashed apart. It wasn't a big wave by anyone's standards – probably only knee-height at best – but it came in further than any preceding wave had done that day and there had been no sudden wind to power it.

It probably rolled all the way across from Seaford, Jim told himself. *And what I thought was a tremor was probably my seat settling in the sand.*

'I thought I felt a tremor.'

Rosie grinned. 'That'd be Martha, Queen of the Cream Cake, rising to her feet, I guess,' she said. 'Have you noticed how the fat around her ankles drapes down over her feet? Yuck!'

'She's sweet, though,' Jim said. 'I like her. And she has good taste in writers. She is my *greatest* fan, after all.'

'You'll be fine just as long as she doesn't decide to sit on your lap!' Rosie said.

And Jim felt the tremor again.

'Woah, *I* felt that!' Rosie said uncomfortably. 'What the hell was it? Look, there's a real big wave coming in.'

But Jim wasn't looking at the sea, he was looking back up the beach towards the tree-line. Something up there was making an odd noise. He heard the big wave break behind him, but the ground had steadied now.

'Jeez, do you know what?' Rosie said.

'What?' Jim asked, still scanning the tree-tops. Something up there was rustling.

'Candy and Jon. They're *at it*,' Rosie said distantly. She sounded a little shocked, but there was something else in her tone, too. Jim didn't quite know what it was.

'At it?' he said, glancing from the tree-tops to Martha and June, who were half-way between him and the tree-line.

164

They'd stopped and were both looking out to sea, shading their eyes from the sun with their hands.

'Having sex,' Rosie said, in a tremulous voice. 'Fucking. In the sea. Standing up.'

Frowning, Jim tore his eyes from the tree-tops and twisted round on his seat. Rosie was right. Out in the sea – maybe fifty yards offshore where the water was almost hip-height, Candy had apparently caught up with Jon, got his shorts off him and made him an offer he'd been unable to refuse. Now she was wound round him, her back to the shore, her legs wrapped around his hips, her arms around his neck. His hands supported her buttocks as he heaved into her, hard and fast; his shorts trailed from the fingers of his left hand.

Rosie glanced at him, white-faced. 'When the swell drops you can see *everything* he has. And there's a lot of it,' she said, and Jim realized that the odd edge to her voice was excitement.

Frank stood out in the sea, watching them just as everyone else was. Jim glanced back to Martha and June, who might have been turned to stone for all the movements they made.

'Oh, Jeez, just *look* at them,' Rosie said, in a small voice.

Jim glanced at Rosie and from Rosie to Frank, then to Martha and June. All of them seemed transfixed by what Jon and Candy were doing. There may as well have been nothing else in existence for them but two people fucking.

This is a first, he thought. *This can't be happening.*

But when he looked back, it *was* happening. Except that Candy was now lying back, her head on the surface of the water, her hair fanning out around her and water sparkling on her taut smooth skin as her hips rose and fell against each powerful thrust Jon made.

And then Candy rose, pulling her body up from the water, and she screamed and shuddered as her hands clawed for purchase on Jon's shoulders.

And in the woods behind the tree-line, Jim heard that odd noise again. Heard it above the sobbing yelps that Candy was now making. It was a rustling noise as if someone had hold of the trunk of one of the big trees in there and was

165

shaking it like crazy, making the leaves dance at the ends of the branches.

'Shit, what's that?' Rosie asked, tearing her eyes away from the couple in the water.

Jim pointed. 'That tree. Right over there. About thirty feet in from where the beach ends. Behind the Dauphin house.'

'Jeez, it's *moving*,' Rosie whispered. 'What's doing that?'

Jim had a moment of extreme clarity during which he knew *exactly* what was making the tree shake like that and why it was shaking and why shy Jon Short was down there in the sea fucking Candy like there was no tomorrow. It all dovetailed perfectly. But the thought was so stupid he put it right out of his head.

'I don't know,' he said, looking at the tree and suddenly feeling cold. The tree wasn't a sapling, it was a large, fully matured tree and, if Jim was right, it stood at the bottom of the backyard of the house. It stood maybe forty or fifty feet tall and its trunk, Jim knew because he and Sooty had once carved their names in it, was bigger than you could reach around at full stretch. It was a big tree. It *couldn't* be being shaken like that. Unless there was a very localized earth tremor. Local to one tree only. Jim didn't much care for the sound of that.

'If there's someone at the bottom shaking the trunk, they must be pretty damned strong to make the top move like that,' Rosie said. 'Is it something Davey's doing?'

Behind him, Candy yowled a long slow moan that sounded as if it was all over for her now. Jon didn't seem to have made any noise at all throughout the exhibition they'd put on.

'She's done,' Rosie said, glancing back over her shoulder. 'If she can even stand after that she'll be lucky, let alone *walk*.'

It's Davey, of course, Jim told himself, still looking at the shuddering tree. *What else would make a tree move like that? He's got a chain round the top and he's winching it taut. Maybe he's gonna use it to drag something heavy out of the undergrowth.* Jim liked this idea a lot better than his previous one.

166

The motion of the tree lessened now and, as Jim watched, it ceased entirely. Behind him, Candy had fallen silent, too. Jim tried not to associate the two things. They were *not* connected. Certainly not.

'I saw someone!' Rosie said, stabbing a finger towards the house. 'Over there, by the corner! He pushed through the bushes! There he is again! Look! To the right, Jim. Just gone behind that tree. He's coming out again. Nope. Gone.'

'That'll be Davey,' Jim said, frowning. 'God only knows what he's up to. We'll find out soon enough, I s'pose.'

He turned back and watched Candy and Jon walking back towards the shore. Jon had his shorts on and was listening intently to something Candy was explaining to him. Whatever it was, it was serious, Jim judged from the hand gestures she was making. He wondered what they would say when they got back up here. Would they apologize? Or would they just carry on as if nothing had happened? Jim put his money on the second option. Evidently they had nothing to apologize for. There wasn't a person among the group who hadn't been transfixed.

Except me, he thought. *And that was only because I was so damned shocked.*

But what had shocked him hadn't been watching the sex – he'd found it just as arousing as everyone else evidently had – but the memories that lived in his head.

Jon and Candy had just walked out into the sea and mimicked, in every tiny detail, move for move, thrust for thrust and yelp for yelp, something that had happened here before, less than ten weeks ago. Unlike everyone else here – including Candy and Jon – Jim knew this because he'd taken part in it.

Christ, they even stood in the same spot that Sooty and I stood in, he thought.

As yet, he didn't know what any of it meant.

But it'll be bad, I'm sure, he thought, remembering the words he'd opened *Shimmer* with; the words that had appeared on the screen of his computer.

You won't come back this time!

'We'll see about that,' he muttered.

'Sorry?' Rosie said.

167

'Nothing,' Jim said. 'Let's get some food going here. Our happy trippers are all going to be hungry after watching the floor-show.'

He pulled the lid from a cool-box and began to take out the food for the barbecue.

Chapter Twelve

Calls

1

Sooty yelped when the phone rang and jolted her out of her reverie. She'd been on the cusp of sleep, she realized; in that state where her mind was wandering off on its own, down pathways it never walked when she was awake. A string of words had been scrolling across the cinema screen of her mind; words that seemed to make some kind of sense, but once the phone rang the *knowledge* they imparted dissolved, leaving only a vague recollection of their progress.

Gloria moaned but didn't wake. Still not quite conscious, Sooty moved her gently aside and settled her down in the corner of the sofa.

Sooty stood up: her mouth felt like the bottom of a bird-cage, as if she'd been drugged. She glared at the bottle of single malt and suddenly remembered seeing a bottle just like it a couple of weeks ago. The image lit in her mind: standing in the doorway of Jim's workroom at twenty after four and seeing what used to be her devil-may-care husband sitting there lost in the depths of despair, an almost empty bottle of Glenmorangie hanging from his left hand and the stub of a Virginia Slim smouldering in his right. And the way his eyes had looked. Alien was the only word she could think of to describe it. Alien. As if they belonged to someone else. A total stranger. Or, perhaps, the demon that had been driving Jim these past few weeks.

Jim's in trouble! she thought, remembering the words that she'd been viewing as she drifted off to sleep. They'd read: *He stole our dreams. He stole our nightmares. He stole everything we were. Now the thief is ours.* Sooty could clearly recall that she'd understood the entire message these words

169

had conveyed, but now she had no idea what they meant. Except that the news wasn't going to be good. At the other end of the line there was going to be someone from the local emergency services with bad news to impart, she was certain. Maybe Eileen Kaelen, the local police sergeant, or Andy Petersen, the doctor.

'Tomorrow it'll all be over,' she rasped, dry-mouthed as she reached for the telephone. 'It'll be over. For ever.' And the moment she'd finished saying this, she saw it could be interpreted in another way entirely from the way she'd meant it.

She took a breath, snatched up the receiver, said, 'Yes?' and found herself listening to that old familiar static chorus. She waited for a count of five while her blood cooled in her veins, then put down the phone.

I can't take this any more, she thought, close to tears. *I don't know who the hell this is, but I just can't take it! Why can't they just leave me alone?*

She tore a tissue from the box, dabbed the corners of her eyes and blew her nose. Suddenly, and for the first time in two years, she wanted a cigarette. Not one of those suck-so-hard-your-head-caves-in low-tar no-nicotine things Jim smoked so many of, but one of the old-fashioned honest-to-God, unfiltered, brown-lips-guaranteed coffin nails she'd smoked till she gave up.

There were no Camels in the house but Jim kept a huge supply of Virginia Slims in the kitchen cupboard. Like all dedicated smokers, his worst nightmare wasn't of dying a long, slow death from lung cancer, but of having nothing to smoke on his death-bed. She tore open a pack, broke off the filter, lit the ragged end from the gas stove and took a huge inhalation. Which was when she remembered that non-smokers couldn't do this sort of thing. It felt as if someone had suddenly stuffed barbed-wire deep into her lungs.

The coughing fit that followed brought fresh tears to her eyes. But the nicotine hit felt good. She drew on the cigarette again. This time it wasn't so painful. A moment later she felt dizzy. A moment after that, she felt sick. Then, with the third inhalation, everything levelled off. *There you go!* she told herself, finding a small smile at the edges of her mouth. *Once a smoker, always a smoker.*

As far as this woman was concerned, the research that had proven that nicotine really *did* aid concentration was right on the button. The more of the cigarette she smoked, the clearer everything became.

It was obvious, really, now she thought about it. It should have been obvious what was going to happen from the first moment Aaron Spreadbury began to talk to her. Extortion. First he put the frighteners on, then he enrolled help to turn up the tension all the way to maximum.

Bastards! Sooty thought, as righteous anger replaced her fear and uncertainty.

The telephone rang. She snatched it up again and yelled, 'Go *away*! Just fuck off and leave me alone! I know *exactly* what you're up to, now get the hell off this line and don't call back. *Ever!*'

And a surprised voice said mildly, 'Oh . . . sorry if I caught you at the wrong time, Sooty. Is everything all right?'

'What the hell do you *mean* "Is everything all right?"' Sooty half screamed, realizing only distantly that the voice on the other end of the line wasn't Spreadbury or his female accomplice. 'Of course everything's not *all right*.' Then she stopped and started to feel very stupid indeed. This was someone she knew. Someone she'd been expecting to call. 'Hello?' she said, wishing the ground would open up and swallow her.

'Sooty? You know who this is, right? It's Elaine. Elaine Palmer. Y'know, Collis and Anstey's publicity whiz and your good friend. *That* Elaine. We'd arranged to meet when I'd done with the fans. Well, I'm done, so I'm calling you. But it looks as if I've called at a bad time. Are you sure you're okay? You sound a little upset.'

'Oh, Elaine, I'm so embarrassed. I've just had a couple of crank calls and I thought you were her calling back again. I'm sorry I yelled like that.' Sooty brightened a little.

'You give 'em hell, sister,' Elaine said.

'I try,' Sooty replied. 'Anyway, in all the trauma, I forgot you were coming. I've been so worried recently my mind's been a bit of a butterfly.'

171

'You forgot *I* was coming?' Elaine chuckled. 'I'm mortified!'

'Shit, it's great to hear you,' Sooty said. 'I wish you'd hurry up and come over. You didn't need to call.'

'Lucky I did,' Elaine said. 'In the state you're in you'd probably have bludgeoned me to death on the doorstep. If I'd got past all the security devices, that is. So, this caller of yours. Police job?'

'Not yet, but it's getting close,' Sooty said. 'I've been keeping it from Jim. It's a long story and I'll fill you in on the details when you get here. Lots of stuff has been happening recently.'

'Same here,' Elaine said. 'We have a lot to catch up on. So, when's it convenient to come?'

'The sooner the better,' Sooty said. 'I could use some company. This is getting to me.'

'The phone calls? What did they say?' Elaine asked.

'Not just the phone calls. Everything's suddenly gone weird. Well, maybe it hasn't. I could use a disinterested observer to tell me if I'm just getting all antsy over nothing at all. I can't tell any more. Remember that Candy you mentioned? The sexy one who's gone on the trip?'

'How could I forget?' Elaine said, sounding as if she knew a lot more about Candy than she was prepared to say. 'Body like Venus, mind like a mollusc. She's no problem.'

'Well, she *is* a problem over here,' Sooty said. 'We were all out in the garden and Jim made the mistake of saying she wanted his body. And when Gloria asked why, he said she was going to take it over. Gloria's been acting strangely ever since and wanted to go to bed early. A while back she kind of half woke up. She was terrified. Convinced that Daddy isn't coming home because Candy's going to get his body.'

'I see,' Elaine said.

Sooty couldn't read the tone of Elaine's reply, or the subtext. The two words she spoke weren't enough, but something was there. 'Are you keeping anything from me about Candy?' she asked.

'Nothing to worry about,' Elaine said. 'I'll tell all when I get there. How does half an hour sound?'

'Like twenty-five minutes too long,' Sooty said. 'I got a

172

daughter with night terrors, an extortion plot being worked against me, a husband who recently decided to blow out his brains with his Colt .45 and my nerves are so frazzled I've just taken up smoking again. Ain't life sweet?' Sooty smiled bitterly.

There was a brief pause, presumably while Elaine fought not to ask any more questions. 'Okay, honey. Hang on and I'll be there as quickly as I can,' she said, and rang off.

Sooty replaced the receiver, tore the filter off another cigarette, lit it and inhaled, wondering if she was neurotic. She had the distinct feeling that, somewhere along the line in the past few weeks, something fundamental had changed. And it wasn't due to Jim's trouble with his block and ensuing depression, or Spreadbury's calls, or her worries about desecrating the island with fans. It felt as if somewhere back there – unnoticed until now – reality had bifurcated and she'd found herself on a different track.

You've been reading too many of Jim's books! she admonished herself, but that certainly wasn't the case. Once upon a time she'd read everything he wrote on a daily basis: as soon as he'd printed out the day's work, she'd eagerly snatched it away from him and read it and she'd drooled for more. Nowadays there didn't seem to be the time. Jim was already well into *Shimmer* and as yet she still hadn't read a single word of it but for the title. She hadn't even finished *Black River*, she realized with a small shock. And unless she forced herself, she wouldn't have read it before it was published.

It was frightening how quickly you got used to things; how soon those marvellous happenings became commonplace. Not so long ago she and Jim had celebrated each time he finished a book: champagne, caviar – or tuna on one notable penniless occasion – and lovemaking on the very same night that he'd written the two traditional words 'the end' at the bottom of the last manuscript page. Nowadays they were lucky if they got to celebrate publication day together. On the US launch day for *Miami Five Fifteen* Jim had been in Kyoto, Japan, on the set of *Switchers*. And she had been here, heavily pregnant with Gloria and as lonely as hell.

And when you don't watch reality – when you don't keep

173

*driving it along with a whip, the way you want it to go – it'll
change on you. Luck, like an untended flower will either dry
up and die or turn rotten.*

Maybe that was what had happened. Things had turned
because she and Jim had taken too much for granted. Reality
had bifurcated and led them both down the Bad Luck lane.
You didn't have to have a vast imagination or a huge store
of ideas to reach that kind of conclusion. All you needed
was a little intuition of the type that women were supposed
to be so good at having. And, Sooty thought, she possessed
intuition in a good measure. After all, she'd known Jim was
a diamond in the coal-face the first time she'd met him,
hadn't she? And whose idea had it been to take the slugs
away from the .45 and hide them in the bottom of the flour
tin?

*So, what are you intuiting now, O mighty and infallible
woman?* she asked herself. And then wished she hadn't.
Because she was indeed picking up something from the ether
and that thing was *Loss.* With a capital L. Something was
going to happen and she was pretty damned sure it was
going to happen tonight.

*If we can just get through to tomorrow morning, we'll have
diverted whatever it is heading at us both,* she thought. *We'll
have won. And afterwards we'll be safe for ever.*

Of course, the problem of dealing with whatever was
heading at them wasn't made any easier by its refusal to
identify itself. It could merely be the extortion attempt by
Spreadbury and his helper or helpers, but Sooty was sure
this was only the tenth of the iceberg that showed above the
water-line. The rest of it was down there in the icy sea,
lurking, huge and threatening.

The telephone rang. Sooty jumped then snatched it up,
knowing it was safe: it would be Elaine calling back. She
intuited this. 'What's wrong, Lainey?' she asked, through the
wave of interference.

A man's voice replied, 'Something seems to be jamming
your telephone, Mrs Green. I've been having trouble getting
through.'

Sooty's heart sank. The telephone reception might have
been terrible – maybe the exchange was suffering from

overheating, it had happened before – but she would have recognized that self-satisfied tone if it had been coming at her from under water.

'For Christ's sake, Spreadbury, *leave me alone!*' she snapped. 'Just quit bothering us! I'm not interested and neither is my husband!'

'I've been leaving messages,' Spreadbury said calmly. 'Every week. Each one urging you or Mr Green to contact me. I've been watching this bad weather approaching for quite some time now and it's close. Very close. A large storm is coming your way, Mrs Green. Bad weather on an unimaginable scale.'

'Then I'll crawl down into the storm-cellar and sit it out,' Sooty replied.

'You know what I mean,' Spreadbury said amiably. 'This is inner weather. The weather of the soul.'

'The ass-soul?' Sooty seethed.

Spreadbury ignored her. 'Your husband is on the island belonging to Straker Dauphin right now, isn't he?'

'For your information Straker's Island belongs to my husband and me. Who Straker Dauphin is, or was, I've no idea,' Sooty said, violently ripping the filter from a fresh cigarette.

'Dauphin was the island's original owner,' Spreadbury said smoothly. 'I am rather taken aback that you don't know the history of your property.'

'It doesn't *have* a history,' Sooty said. 'I should know. I tried hard enough to find out who built the house out there. There *is* no record.'

'Ah, I imagine you bought the island from the administrators of Biscayne National Park. I understand it was previously an unwanted part of the sea park.'

'So what?'

'You researched through their records, no doubt. And found nothing. You should look closer to home, Mrs Green. Perhaps in the archives of the *Seaford Gazette*. Trust me, the previous owner of the island was Straker Dauphin. Hence its current name. It did indeed belong to Mr Dauphin.'

'Then why isn't it called Dauphin Island?' Sooty challenged, more to cover her embarrassment than anything

175

else. A sick feeling had crept into the pit of her stomach. She suddenly had the distinct feeling that she and Jim had made a fatal error back when they'd bought the island. She was barely able to believe that neither she nor Jim had thought of tracking back through the local papers to find out more about the island.

None of the townsfolk knew a damned thing about the place – she knew that because she'd grown up here. She wasn't even aware that the *Gazette* kept an archive. The paper was staffed only by old Mitch Langton and his even older girlfriend, Cecile Brite, and most of the news was either sent in by part-timers dotted around the area between here and Miami and Key Largo or culled from the wire services.

'I've no idea why it isn't called Dauphin Island,' Spreadbury said. 'And it's not my chief concern right now. My concern is that Mr Green is currently over on the island. Now don't hang up on me. I implore you not to! Would you please confirm whether or not I'm right about this?'

'What if he is?' Sooty demanded.

'That's confirmation enough,' Spreadbury said. '*If* he's over there, he's in terrible trouble. And I can help him. You need me, Mrs Green. I beseech you – let me help. To put it bluntly, without me you're both sunk.'

'I've had quite enough of you pair,' Sooty raged. 'First she calls and tells me Jim and I are thieves, then *you* call and say we're under threat and you can help. Look, *Buster*, I can detect the distinct odour of rat here. I don't know what you're trying to pull, but if you don't quit now, I'm calling the police. Now *go get fucked!*' She slammed the phone down.

Without pause, it began to ring again. Sooty looked at it for a few moments then picked it up. There was a slim possibility it might be Elaine, stuck at the gate. She had the keypad code, but like everything else in this house that depended on electronics, it had developed a fault and only worked about sixty per cent of the time.

'Yes?' she said, her heartbeat banging in her ears.

'The stealer is ours. Now we have him just where we want him,' said the female voice Sooty knew so well.

176

And with a cold, sick shock, Sooty knew exactly why the voice was so familiar. It was her own. Through the shock a powerful sensation of *déjà vu* hit her. She *knew* these words.

'Who *is* this?' she tried to demand. The words left her mouth sounding like the plea of a terrified woman.

At the other end of the line Sooty's own voice chuckled and Sooty remembered where she'd last heard that sound externally, rather than from inside her head where it sounded slightly different. They'd bought a video camera shortly after she'd become pregnant with Gloria. It was the only device in the house that had entirely escaped the Silicone Curse – it had never even been cleaned, let alone fixed. They said that the second most popular use for a video camera was to make pornographic movies with one's partner and after Gloria was born and Sooty rediscovered her libido (now twice as powerful, for some unfathomable reason, and interested in experimentation) she and Jim had made plenty of use of the JVC for exactly this purpose.

In the last video they'd made, maybe ten weeks ago, she'd been playing dominatrix. She clearly remembered watching the recording the following day and getting turned on all over again. She'd had the Master of Disaster naked, blind-folded and spreadeagled on their huge bed, his wrists and ankles roped to its four corners, his body oiled and shining in the soft light, his erection as huge and hard as she'd ever seen it. And she'd turned and winked at the camera, then turned back to Jim and given her best evil chuckle and said, 'Now I have you just where I want you!'

The words the mystery caller had just paraphrased.

She knows, Sooty thought, her mind reeling. In spite of all the security cameras and alarms and gate-locks, someone had broken in and found and stolen the cache of erotic movies she and Jim had starred in.

'I am you,' her own voice said, from the other end of the telephone line. 'You are me. Soon we will be together.'

Sooty slammed down the receiver. 'It's answering-machine time from now on, I think,' she said, in a small, shaky voice. She hurried into Rosie's office and punched in the code to set all incoming calls silent and to the answering-machine. Then she went back into the lounge, where, thank

177

God, Gloria was still sleeping. She took a hefty swig from the bottle of Glenmorangie, went back to the kitchen, tore the filter from another cigarette, lit it and hurried upstairs to her bedroom.

The videos, all still on the little Hi8 tapes, should have been in the small fire-proof safe in the back of Jim's walk-in closet. She fought her way through the junk that was strewn around in the closet, knelt before the safe and punched in the code. The door clicked, she turned the handle and pulled it open. Computer disks and back-up tapes and a dozen working-copy manuscripts crowded the small safe. She lifted an early copy of the *Miami Five Fifteen* screenplay and there they were. All six ninety-minute tapes. All present and correct. All safe and sound.

She breathed a sigh of relief. *Coincidence!* she told herself. *Those won't be showing up on the Playboy channel after all!* She butted the cigarette in the ashtray Jim had left on top of the safe, closed the door and locked it again, wondering what Spreadbury and his impersonator and accomplice would do next.

Spreadbury said he wanted to help save Jim from something terrible, although he hadn't mentioned the name of that thing. It was a possibility that he and his female helper were intending to kidnap Jim and hold him to ransom and extort money from Sooty for his release. If that was so, she couldn't understand why they would pick tonight when Jim would be surrounded by people. Unless they were going to snatch him from the island during the tour of terror that Davey had lined up.

It didn't seem likely. For one thing they'd have to know the island as well as Jim did – and he knew the place very well indeed. For another, they were going to have to get there and they would be noticed on their way in – the bay where Straker's house stood was the only good landing place – unless you wanted to moor your vessel at sea, swim in through the rocks on the east side of the island and then scale what amounted to a cliff-face.

It was possible, she supposed, that Spreadbury had deposited more accomplices on the island earlier. But, according to what Rosie had said, Davey had made several trips back and forth during the day and he would surely have noticed anything untoward. And since Spreadbury was able to use a phone to call her, he wasn't within half a mile of the island because from there on in it was a dead zone as far as cellular phones were concerned.

But he says he's a psychic, Sooty thought. *He probably wants to help me and Jim using his powers. Which means that he'll probably want to divert whatever it is from wherever he happens to be at the time, physically. So I pay him and he goes away for half an hour, then calls back to say he's fixed the problem.*

This didn't sound likely either. Maybe he wanted to get her out of the house to kidnap Gloria. She and Jim had talked about kidnap threats.

'Shit, I just don't know,' she said aloud.

What she *did* know, deep down, was that it was make or break time. Spreadbury was right about one thing: bad weather *had* been approaching for quite some time, and now it was very close. Bad weather on an unimaginable scale.

But, dammit, I can't do anything until I know what's going on! she complained inwardly.

We have him just where we want him, the voice of the mystery woman whispered in her mind. *I am you. You are me. Soon we will be together.*

'And only one of us will leave with her eyes scratched out,' Sooty promised. 'And it won't be me!'

But that feeling of impending loss wouldn't go away.

2

The thing that Sooty tripped over as she made her way out of the closet turned out to be a Yamaha electronic keyboard that Jim had bought way back when he and some pals of his up in Miami had decided to finance and make their own movie. The movie had never happened, but for a time it had looked as if it would. Jim had bought the Yamaha intending to 'do a John Carpenter and score the damned thing myself'. What Carpenter had that Jim hadn't was a little musical talent. But Jim had kept the keyboard. One of his life's ambitions, he'd said, was to be able to 'knock out a recognizable

179

tune on a Joanna'. Maybe one day he would, but Sooty had privately thought that it would be the self-same day that hell froze over.

The keyboard, which had been stood up on its end against the wall, became entangled in Sooty's legs and she knew she would fall from the moment the plastic barked her shin and her other foot kicked into the end where the high notes lived.

She went down hard on her face and banged her forehead just above her right eye on the corner of one of the discarded mobile phones the house had killed off. This one was a brick-sized Motorola. It was in a leather case, but that didn't afford much protection from the hard plastic underneath. Sooty's vision flashed white, then dulled to black as purple stars swarmed around the periphery of her vision.

She might have been out cold for a few moments – or a few minutes – Sooty didn't know which. What she did know was the pain didn't really start until her vision cleared again, and even then it didn't hurt very much. What was worse than the dull ache, the area around which would surely swell to a cartoon-sized bump, and worse than the indignity a grown-up will always feel at finding themselves prostrate, was the uncomfortable feeling that she'd somehow twisted around inside her body so she was askew and looking out of her eyes from a new angle.

Her right shin and her left foot hurt. She disentangled herself from the keyboard and drew herself up into a sitting position. The top of her foot would bruise, she thought, and she'd lost a little skin from her shin, but other than that and the bump that was already forming on her head, she was okay. She touched the bump gingerly. It didn't hurt unless she put pressure on it and her eyesight seemed fine now. She didn't have a headache or anything that might suggest she needed checking out by a doctor, which was good news.

She twisted round to see if she'd broken the keyboard and realized how she'd come to fall. Jim had left the mains adaptor connected to it. Her foot must have hit the cable and dragged the keyboard away from the wall. Frowning, she pulled it across her lap. It felt good there, which was odd: she'd lost any interest she'd had in playing the piano at the age of seven when her dad had sent her for her first ever lesson and she'd discovered that it wasn't as easy as it looked. You had to do one thing with your left hand and another with your right.

But now, sitting here looking at the keyboard, she found she *did* have an interest, after all. And not only did she have an interest, she knew without having to count that there were eighty-eight keys on this particular model. Which meant it was a full-sized keyboard. She'd never before had the slightest interest in the number of keys on a piano, or any other instrument come to that.

Sooty smiled, feeling good about things again. She found the power switch and flicked it. The little red light came on, winked and faded and went out again and she felt a pang of disappointment. *Batteries are flat,* she told herself. *They've probably been in it for ten years, so you can't really blame them, can you?*

She got up, picked up the keyboard and took it out into the bedroom and placed it on the bed. She plugged the mains adaptor into the wall socket then sat down, put the keyboard across her knees and switched it on again. This time the light stayed lit.

C, she thought, looking at a key. Then counted, C sharp, D, E flat, E, F, G flat, G, A flat, A. Then she realized that wherever she looked, she knew which keys were which notes. Then, with a small shock, that her fingers were itching to contact the cool ivory of the keys.

Except these keys were not ivory or ebony, they were white and black plastic.

Weird, she thought. *These keys should be discoloured. The white ones yellowing. They were the last time I played. And the middle C is a tiny bit flat. One of the wires is loose on the bottom A, too.*

She shook her head and shrugged. And before she could question the crazy thoughts her fingers had found the keys and were playing her favourite Mozart piano concerto. She stopped at once, shocked, and looked at her hands as if they were alien creatures.

I don't know any Mozart, she thought.

But she *did* know some Mozart. The moment she stopped

181

concentrating on keeping her hands off the keyboard, they fluttered back and began to play a piece from K453 Symphony in E flat. She felt herself being drawn into the music, becoming lost in the piece, while a long way away her mind complained through what seemed like a small hole in a distant box. It was so easy to do. It was good to play. It was wonderful. The spirits *loved* her to play for them!

I could lose myself for ever! she thought, and began to let herself go, let herself fall into the music.

And the tiny voice in the box piped, '*No!*'

Sooty felt as if she'd been slapped. Something inside her head seemed to ping. The sensation was similar to having Jim snap a rubber band at her, except that this happened deep inside her brain. For a moment she was dizzy. Her nerve endings sizzled and she felt herself twist inside again.

Suddenly she stood up, gasping in what must have been her first breath for two minutes or more. The keyboard fell to the carpet, made an angry, discordant noise and fell silent.

Sooty stood still, staring at her treacherous hands. Then tears sprang to her eyes.

What happened? What did I do?

But she knew what she'd done. She'd become able to play the piano. And not just play it, but play a complex piece faultlessly, effortlessly, and from a memory she couldn't possibly have had. She was no longer quite certain of the name of the piece she had been falling into, but she thought it might have been written by Mozart. And she still had the disconcerting memory of an ancient piano with yellowing keys and a flat middle C. And no one in her family had ever played the piano and there'd never been one in her house during her childhood.

I don't even know *anyone who plays*, she thought.

She wiped the tears from her eyes and looked at the fallen Yamaha, which was making a tiny electrical buzzing noise. She was too frightened to touch it again, so she walked round it and using the toe of her shoe, kicked the plug from the wall socket. The buzzing noise ceased instantly. Gathering a little courage, she pushed at the keyboard with her foot. Nothing happened: no urge to pick it up and play it descended upon her and she wasn't suddenly filled again

182

with the knowledge and skill she'd broken contact with when she'd stood up.

I had a brief fugue, she told herself, still shocked and dismayed. She'd read enough about conditions like this at college, where she'd studied psychology. A fugue was a weird mental aberration in which people were apt to forget who they were and assume a new identity.

She felt as if her perception of reality had been raped: as if someone had inserted a two- or three-minute clip of someone else's life into hers. It wasn't a nice feeling.

Stress, she rationalized. *The worry about Jim and the phone calls and everything.*

To prove to herself that the strange occurrence was over and done and that everything was going to be fine from now on, she bent over and picked up the keyboard, her heart in her mouth, her blood singing in her ears.

Nothing happened. Not even when she sat down with the Yamaha across her lap and laid her fingers on the keys. She didn't know which notes were which, how to hold her hands, where her fingers should go and she couldn't even summon up a memory of how *Für Elise* went, let alone anything complex.

Sooty sighed, feeling a tiny amount of relief. She tried to convince herself that everything was going to be all right and failed miserably.

Jim was in peril. Or she and Gloria were. Or nothing untoward was happening at all and she was cracking up.

Choose one and stick with it, she told herself, but she wasn't in possession of enough information to do that.

She took the keyboard back to the closet and stood it where she'd found it, then hurried back downstairs again. She needed a good swig of Glenmorangie and another of Jim's Virginia Slims.

3

She was close to becoming calm again when she heard the noise in another part of the house. She set down her glass of single malt, took a deep draw from the cigarette that had been burning away between her fingers, exhaled, inhaled, held her breath and listened.

'What is it, Mommy?' Gloria asked, waking up.

'Shh!' Sooty said quietly. 'I'm listening.'

Gloria scrambled across to her and clung on, her fingers digging into Sooty's arm. 'What's wrong?' she whispered worriedly. Her eyes were dark and frightened. 'Is she here? Has she come already?'

'Who? Auntie Elaine?' Sooty asked quietly, her head still turned so that her left ear pointed towards the lounge door. The sound had come from Jim's workroom, the Word Factory itself. She was sure of that. What she wasn't sure of was what it was.

Gloria was trembling, Sooty noticed. *In fear?*

'*Her!*' Gloria hissed. 'You know . . . *her!*'

'No one's coming,' Sooty said, as soothingly as she could manage. She hugged Gloria to her. 'Only Elaine. She'll be here soon.'

'Don't let her get me,' Gloria appealed, and buried her head in Sooty's breast.

'No one's going to get anyone,' Sooty assured her. 'Candy isn't after Daddy's body, no one's in trouble and no one's going to get hurt.' *And pigs can fly and the* Titanic *really was unsinkable and there are no such things as serial killers*, her mind added on her behalf.

The noise Sooty had heard sounded rather like a bell. Not a door chime or a hand bell, but rather like the strike of a huge, distant church bell, the tone mellow and penetrative. And yet it seemed to have come from inside Jim's workroom.

She'd first interpreted this as someone trying to break in, which seemed stupid. No burglar, Spreadbury or otherwise, would bother breaking in through the glass window in Jim's workroom when they could have simply walked right in through the huge patio doors of the lounge, not fifteen feet from where Sooty and Gloria were sitting. And no burglar would make a sound like a church bell to announce his or her arrival.

So what was it? she asked herself, still listening. It might have been something Jim had in there; something that had fallen over. For years he'd used a brass propellant casing from an artillery shell as an ashtray and that probably would have made a bell-like sound if it had fallen. The problem was, Jim had given it away in 1996 when someone had asked him for memorabilia for a charity auction. It had fetched $178, too.

And, as far as Sooty knew, there was nothing else in his room that might have made such a sound. What *was* in his room, however, was the Colt .45 and, Sooty decided, now might be a very good time to go and fetch it and fish those bullets out of their hiding place. Whether she liked it nor not, there was a chance that Spreadbury or one of his pals might turn up here wanting to kidnap her or Gloria or both of them. And it was possible they'd get past the security, too.

'We've got to go to Daddy's workroom, honey,' she whispered to Gloria, when there had been no further sound for a count of four minutes.

'We're not allowed,' Gloria said.

'This is an exceptional circumstance,' Sooty said. 'Daddy won't mind just this once.'

'*She*'s not in there, is she?' Gloria asked, and Sooty's skin prickled so violently she was certain her flesh was rippling across her face.

She didn't ask who 'she' was, because suddenly she was frightened of what the reply might be. *I've got the creeps*, she thought, remembering the words the mystery caller had spoken. *I am you. You are me. Soon we will be together*, the woman had said.

I'll feel better once I have that bloody great gun in my hand, she told herself. *It's just a pity I was such a wuss I never wanted to learn to shoot.*

Marty Raddiche, who instructed Jim up at the gun club in Miami, had a bumper sticker on his Mustang, 'Guns don't kill people, people kill people!' and when Sooty had first spotted it she'd read it aloud and then said to Jim, 'All the more reason to stop people having guns, I'd say.'

And Jim had replied, 'All the more reason to be able to handle a gun yourself if you're intending to live in this god-forsaken country, *I*'d say.'

185

Sooty could have mentioned gun disasters that had happened in quiet, peaceful Scotland if she'd cared to, but Jim had a point, she supposed. But for her it wasn't a strong enough point to learn how to handle a weapon herself. No one had *ever* been shot dead in Seaford, or even injured by a gun, to the best of her knowledge. It wasn't that kind of place.

But things, she knew, had a way of changing. Often for the worst.

'Mommy?' Gloria said, pulling her back as she made to get up.

'Honey?'

'Are there such things as ghosts?'

'No, sweetie, there aren't.'

'Say so,' Gloria said.

Sooty's flesh began to creep again. It'd been a long time since she'd had to 'say so' and she was glad about that. It seemed like another of those temptations you held out to Providence. 'There are no such things as ghosts,' she said dutifully. 'No ghosties, no ghoulies, no long-legged beasties, no things that go bump in the night. Okay?'

Gloria didn't look convinced. 'You're sure, right?'

'I'm sure,' Sooty said, remembering hearing her own voice riding a wave of static down the telephone line. 'Now, let's go see what fell down in Daddy's room.'

A few moments later she found herself with her arm around her daughter standing at the door of Jim's workroom, not wanting to go in. She gazed at the small enamel sign that Davey Smith had made a while back and with which Jim had been so pleased he'd screwed it up. DANGER – LUNATIC AT WORK! it said, in red capitals against a white background.

She took a deep breath and opened the door. Nothing happened. She and Gloria entered and from the corner of her eye, she saw Jim's monitor flicker. There were words on the screen, she was sure, she saw them just before they vanished. She gave a mental shrug and looked round for anything that might have fallen over and made a sound like the peal of a bell. There was nothing.

What there was, set on the desk against the back wall in

front of Jim's old manual typewriter, was a small pile of triangular pieces of silver, stacked neatly like a column of coins.

Frowning, Sooty walked over to the desk and looked at the top piece. The things were coins, she was sure of that. They were about the size a silver dollar would have been if you'd cut it into a triangle, but these weren't now, and never had been, silver dollars – their edges were milled, and in the centre of each edge, characters she didn't recognize formed what might have been small words. The upwards face of the top coin had a picture of something that might have been a tree embossed upon it. It was a gnarled and unpleasant-looking piece of vegetation, whatever it was.

She picked up the coin. It was cold. Much too cold to have simply been lying here all day with the air-conditioning on, and the conditioner was on the window side of the room, anyway. The coin was heavy. Too heavy and much too cold. She could feel the chill seeping into her hand when she expected the warmth of her hand to raise the coin's temperature. She turned it over. On the reverse were more words in the odd characters and an image of a naked woman standing before what looked like an inverted cone. It took a few seconds for Sooty to realize that the cone represented a tornado.

Where on earth did these come from? she asked herself, and wished she hadn't, because during her college years, psychology hadn't been the only thing she'd studied. She'd also spent some time researching parapsychology. She had been interested in human skills – divination, telepathy and telekinesis mainly, but she'd also come across that odd breed, the ghost-hunters. Mysterious showers of stones or coins or whatever else that appeared out of nowhere were called *opports*. According to legend, these were often accompanied by the sound of bells and they often arrived freezing cold.

Sooty wasn't an expert on the world's coins or the world's languages, but she was pretty sure there could be only a few cultures, if any, who had used triangular coinage. What this meant, she had no idea. She put the coin back on the stack

187

and turned to where Gloria was standing in front of Jim's computer monitor and keyboard.

The phone rang. Sooty knew this only because the tell-tale on Jim's phone lit green and began to blink. She resisted the urge to answer and watched the flashing light until it steadied, meaning the answering-machine was fielding the call. The light went out immediately after it cut in, which meant that the caller had rung off without leaving a message.

'What does this mean, Mommy?' Gloria asked.

Sooty turned back to the computer screen.

Letters were appearing in the centre, one by one.

WON

'It's one of Daddy's screen-savers, darling,' Sooty said as the next character, an apostrophe appeared. The following letter was a 'T'. 'He sets up silly messages to scroll across the screen,' she said, watching a space appear, followed by a capital C.

As they watched, the words,

WON'T COME BACK

formed in the centre of the screen.

This house is not *haunted!* Sooty screamed inwardly. *It can't be! I won't allow it! There are no such things as ghosts!*

She hit a key, which should have brought up a little box asking for a password but didn't. The line scrolled up, and beneath it, the letters began to appear again, slowly.

'I don't think Daddy meant to leave this running,' she said, trying not to sound as shaken as she felt.

WON'T COME BACK

the second line now said. It moved up the screen to clear the way for the next repetition.

Sooty wasn't the most computer-literate person in the universe, but having acted as Jim's secretary for a couple of years she had a working knowledge of the computer Jim owned. She had one of her own pretty much like it and that one had all the software this one had, barring some of the games Jim liked to play.

The three words had now formed for the third time. 'I think we should turn it off,' she said.

'Why did he write that?' Gloria asked. She sounded frightened.

'It's a joke, honey, that's all,' Sooty replied, not feeling very much like it was a joke at all. It was a statement of fact, she was sure. Maybe her own brainwaves had caused this to happen. Maybe the female voice she'd heard on the phone was a manifestation of her own inner turmoil. Perhaps she wasn't the one at risk here, but the one *causing* the risk. The mere thought that this might be so made her want to throw up.

She hit the 'escape' key and when that didn't work, hit CTRL C, which didn't break into the program either. Finally, she gave the computer the three-finger salute and hit CTRL, ALT, DEL all at the same time. This combination would shut down and reboot the computer from scratch.

Except that it didn't.

It had no effect whatsoever.

'It isn't working,' she heard herself say, in a small, frightened voice. Gloria caught her tone and took a deep shuddering breath. In another moment she'd be crying. Sooty thought she might fall apart when that happened.

She flattened her hands across as many keys as she could manage to touch. On the screen the words kept forming, over and over again.

They stopped when she took her hands away from the keyboard. The screen cleared.

'Fixed it!' she said.

'Good,' Gloria said with obvious relief. 'It was scary.'

And as if some unseen hand was typing them, more letters appeared.

I'M COMING FOR YOU

'I think I've had enough of this,' Sooty said. She left the keyboard, went to the computer tower and hit the 'off' button.

The screen stayed lit and the words stayed exactly where they were.

'Damn you!' Sooty hissed, and bent down over the tower, found the socket and yanked the plug from the wall.

The screen cleared again and this time it darkened.

189

'Did it!' she said.

And in white against the dark background, more words formed.

COMING TO TAKE BACK MY LIFE

Beside her, Gloria began to cry.

On the screen, the words dissolved. This time it stayed empty. Sooty hugged her daughter. 'It's okay, darling. Nothing to worry about,' she said, glancing back at the screen and gritting her teeth. Nothing happened. 'Just wait a moment and we'll both be out of here and everything will be all right. Auntie Elaine will be here soon.'

She let go of Gloria and went to the locked drawer where she knew the Colt .45 lived. She didn't have a key – it was on Jim's key-ring along with his car keys and he'd taken the car to the dock – but a couple of weeks ago when she'd badly needed to get to that gun and unload it, she'd discovered that she could open this drawer by sliding Jim's steel rule into the gap at the top and popping the lock.

It took only five seconds or so to get the drawer open. Another five to unwrap the gun from the rag in which Jim kept it mummified. This time she didn't bother fiddling with the lock so that it popped back into place again, but just left the drawer open.

The weight of the Colt reassured her. She opened it, checked it was empty, snapped it shut again and stuffed it into the waistband of her shorts.

'Come on, honey,' she said to her daughter. 'There are some things I need from the kitchen. They're in the bottom of the flour tin and I may need some help dusting them off.'

Gloria looked up at her with pleading eyes.

'I know, honey, I know,' Sooty said. 'But everything's gonna work out just fine, believe me. There's nothing to worry about. Your mom's just a little jumpy right now.'

As they left the room, the little green tell-tale on Jim's phone indicated that someone was making another call.

Sooty ignored it.

Chapter Thirteen

Tall Tales

1

Twilight had arrived since Jim had begun cooking. He'd lit a couple of small gas lanterns that Davey had left in the house for him and hung them from the same broken branches he'd used on the last trip, setting them up just outside the circle of people gathered around the fire.

The champagne – and almost half the beer – had gone, and everyone was feeding their faces and feeling tickety-boo. There was a lot of laughter and an almost palpable air of companionship seemed to have developed among most of the fans.

In spite of everything, no one seemed to feel any animosity towards Frank, who finally seemed to have relaxed a little, or towards Candy and Jon who had simply carried on as if having sex in the sea in front of a bunch of virtual strangers was the most natural thing to do in the world. For some reason this approach worked beautifully. Jim thought that most of the other fans probably felt a kind of admiration for their boldness and, in some cases, perhaps a little envious, too.

Jim felt fairly mellow himself. One of the surprises Davey had left for him was tucked away at the bottom of a box of food, wrapped in a plain brown bag. This surprise was a good one and it had warmed Jim's heart that Davey could be so thoughtful. It was a bottle of Glenkinchie single malt whisky – one of Jim's favourites and a brand that was hard to find in Florida. God only knew where Davey had come across it, but Jim was glad he had. Even better, Frank and June were the only other members of the trip who liked whisky and June only had a single small shot because, she said, she wanted to keep a clear head.

Jim turned the last batch of burgers, sipped at his latest Scotch, lit a fresh Virginia Slim and sighed happily. Nothing bad had happened, nothing bad *would* happen. A couple of drinks and a full belly had a way of making you see sense.

'I'm gonna take some snaps of us all,' Frank announced, sounding just a little slurred. 'I'll send everyone a copy if I get all the addresses,' he added, getting to his feet.

'Why bother sending them?' Jim asked. 'We'll all go out and buy copies of *Newsweek*.'

'Ha, ha! Nice one, Jim!' Frank said happily. Then he stopped and stared at Jim for a couple of seconds, an odd expression on his face. He looked surprised and shocked. He put his fingers over his eyes and rubbed them as if he were tired and bleary. Then he peered at Jim again and gave a little shake of his head. Now he looked relieved.

'What?' Jim asked.

Frank made a gesture of dismissal and grinned. 'I'm going crazy, that's all,' he said. 'Nothing to worry about. Just that for a moment you looked like someone else. Someone else entirely.' He bent down and took his camera and flash from his bag.

'What do you mean?' Jim asked, as he came up again.

Frank smiled. 'You looked like Straker Dauphin,' he said, and strode from the circle.

'Take no notice,' Rosie whispered from beside Jim. 'You know he doesn't like you. And I don't think that was a threat.'

'A threat?' Jim whispered back. 'What do you mean?'

'Nothing,' Rosie hissed, but Jim knew exactly what she meant: Straker Dauphin was a dead man, hence the threat inherent in Frank's statement.

But it wasn't that at all, was it? Jim asked himself. The answer was, *No, it wasn't.* Frank hadn't made a threat at all. *Because he looked scared*, Jim thought. *He rubbed his eyes as if he couldn't believe them. As if he really* had *seen someone else when he looked at me.*

The question was, *who* had he seen? Not Straker Dauphin, that was for sure. You couldn't see imaginary characters

192

superimposed upon the features of real people, could you? Jim thought about it and decided that it wasn't only possible, it was pretty likely it could happen. *All you'd need is a little psychosis*, he thought.

Jim wished he'd brought the Colt .45 with him.

'I want everyone to face this way and give me a nice big smile!' Frank commanded, fiddling with the huge flash-gun he'd attached to the Nikon. The assembly turned towards him and after a little shuffling around, directed by Frank, he was happy that everyone was in the frame. He fired off about a dozen shots, leaving Jim with blotches and starbursts on his retinas.

'I'm blind!' Martha announced, around a mouthful of the burger she'd stolen from the griddle during the line-up.

'I hope those come out okay, Frank,' Rosie said, elbowing Jim in the ribs.

'They'll be fine,' Frank replied. 'I've never had a failure yet.'

'There's always a first time!' Rosie chuckled.

Frank stared at her as if she were an alien, then rewound the finished film.

'There goes nothing,' Rosie told Jim, and laughed.

'Just make sure he doesn't get anything terrible with the new roll he's loading,' Jim muttered.

'Doesn't matter if he does,' Rosie said. 'The new roll can be fixed. And you never know, Frank might just drop that bag and the Nikon *and* his notebook in the sea on the way home. If I'm feeling clumsy.'

'What are you two scheming?' Martha asked suspiciously. 'I hope you're not putting the make on Jim, Rosie dear. I saw him first and I *am* his greatest fan! He's *mine*!' She chortled and sprayed bits of food.

'Form a line.' Jim smiled. 'And do it in an orderly fashion. There may be a bit of a wait.'

'I read in a magazine that you're some kind of sex god,' Candy said from Jim's right. 'Is that true?'

Jim twisted round. The last time he'd looked Jon had been sitting beside him and Candy had been on the other side of the circle between Frank and June. He suddenly wondered if she'd been slightly behind him and out of his field of view

193

with her top lifted when Frank took the pictures. It wouldn't have surprised him in the least. Rosie was going to have to ruin this roll of film too, by the look of it.

'I heard it was true,' Rosie said. 'I once met his wife in the parking lot behind the radio station on Marathon Key. I've never seen a woman with such a satisfied smile.'

'The proof of the pudding is in the eating, Jim,' Candy said, grinning.

'Well, I'm afraid you've booked the wrong night,' Jim replied. 'Tuesdays are orgy nights. Tonight it's scares.'

'He's no sex god,' Frank said, unsteadily taking his seat. 'Anyone who's ever studied authors can tell you they write to cover their sexual insecurities. The more sex you find in a novel, the less likely the writer is to be any good in the sack. That's a known fact. People who can, do, people who can't, write about it.'

'And people who can't write become journalists, I guess,' Jim said.

'It was a *story*,' Frank said, rolling his eyes. 'I told him I was a journalist from *Newsweek*,' he explained to the gathering. 'And I also told him I was out to get him. That I was intending a hatchet piece on this evening. Unfortunately he believed me a little too well.'

'You're a *journalist*?' Candy asked, astonished.

Frank shook his head. 'It was a *story*, goddammit!' he said. 'I wanted to see if I could scare the Master of Disaster. Seems the only thing he's frightened of is bad press, so I chose to tell him I was a reporter.'

'But you're an English teacher, right?' June said.

'Of course!' Frank nodded. A little too hard for Jim's liking.

'It doesn't matter what he is,' Jim said. 'He's here so let's just forget about what we think he might be and get on with what we're here for. When we've finished eating I'm going to take you guys for a trip through the woods. There's some things in there that have been bothering me and I want to show 'em to you. But first, we're here to swap our night-mares. Does anyone have a scary story they want to tell?'

This was crunch-time usually on one of these trips. If this one was like any of the others, at least half of the cast would have nothing to say, even though they'd known beforehand that the idea was to swap spooky tales.

Jim looked around the fire-lit faces, all of which had fallen silent and none of which looked particularly enthusiastic at having to tell scary stories at all, let alone in front of Jim.

'Frank?' Jim asked. 'You're pretty good with the scares.'

'I'd rather not go first,' Frank said. 'I have a story, but I haven't figured out the ending yet. Let someone else go first. Why don't *you* tell *us* a story?'

'I have one,' June said, raising her hand. 'It's a ghost story *and* it's a true one. I'd be glad to share it.'

'Okay, you go first,' Jim said, lighting a cigarette and looking for his whisky.

2

June's story was a good one and Jim hadn't heard it before. And, despite her initial timidity, she had a great voice and turned out to be an excellent story-teller. Jim found himself spellbound as she told her tale of a man who'd inadvertently picked up a ghost, which attached itself to him like a gas-filled balloon and wouldn't be shaken off, no matter what he did. It ended in tears for the guy when he was driven to kill himself. June got a round of applause when she'd finished.

'Lovely, June,' Jim said. 'And I'll probably be stealing that one to use, if you don't mind. It's a great idea. You'll get a credit if I *do* use it.'

'Will she get any money, though? That's the question,' Frank snorted.

'I wouldn't *want* any money,' June protested. 'Seeing it used by my favourite writer would be payment enough. I could point to the book and say to my friends, "*I* gave that little idea to Jim," and they'd have to believe me because of the credit in the book.'

Frank sneered. 'So, Jim. Are these trips merely to furnish your dried-up mind with free ideas? Do you ever have an original idea of your own, or do you just loot them from writers with an imagination and from your fans?'

Jim's hands clenched into fists and he was about to get up and give vent to his wrath when that odd look came over

Frank's face again. Surprise. Then disbelief. Then fear. But this time Frank didn't put his hands up to his eyes. Instead, his look grew cunning. And then he smiled.

'Just seems very coincidental to me that we're here giving you free stories when you've been suffering from writer's block,' Frank added, that faraway look still in his eyes.

The sideswipe felt like a slap in the face with an icy hand. 'Writer's block?' Jim asked. 'Who says I've been blocked?'

Frank held his gaze. He looked like a madman. 'I have my sources,' he said. 'It's true then, is it?'

'Jim's never been blocked in his life!' Rosie spat.

'And how would *you* know?' Frank asked, raising an eyebrow. 'Is there something you're not telling us?'

'You only have to look at his output!' Rosie fumed. 'Someone with writer's block couldn't turn out as much work as Jim has.'

Jim saw the odd look fade from Frank's face again. It was rather like watching cherry soda being poured from a glass bottle; it didn't fade, but it *drained*. And then Frank shivered and was himself again. Even his tone changed subtly.

Frank shrugged. 'Maybe not. Of course, we don't know how much material he had laid up, do we?' he said. 'I happen to know he collected nearly four hundred rejection slips before he was published. I doubt he got all those for one novel.'

'That's *enough*!' Jim said angrily. 'I don't have writer's block. I've never had writer's block and I do try *not* to steal ideas from people. Now, let's stop bickering and do what we're here for or all go home again. Who wants to quit now?'

No one wanted to quit.

'Frank?' Jim said. 'You'd like to leave?'

Frank smiled. 'Never in a million years! Don't mind me kidding around, I don't mean anything by it. I just have a suspicious mind is all.'

'Try and keep your big trap shut if you don't have anything constructive to say,' Candy said to him. 'You're not being very nice.'

There was a chorus of agreement from the others.

'I'm sorry,' Frank said, looking pleased that he'd managed

196

to throw a spanner in the works. 'Forgive me. If you agree, I'll tell my story next.'

'I'm ready to go,' Jon Short said.

'Well, whenever you want me to try, I'll do my level-headed best,' Frank said. 'Till then I'll just be quiet. I didn't mean any offence.'

Jim took a thoughtful slug of his whisky. 'Okay,' he said, shooting Frank a warning look. 'Go ahead, Jon,' he said.

3

If Newsweek *didn't send Frank, Spreadbury almost certainly did*, Jim thought. He had only spoken to Spreadbury twice and he hadn't told Sooty about it because she'd been about as jumpy as a cat on a hot tin roof already. She'd caught Jim's own jumpiness, of course. The two of them were pretty much like that: their link, he firmly believed, wasn't just one of love and understanding, but of telepathy, too.

He'd tried hard not to give anything away, but Sooty had known he was in trouble as soon as he had, if not before. He wasn't sure if she knew about Spreadbury, but he sure as shit hadn't told her. She'd have gone ballistic. There was a possibility that Rosie had said something to Sooty, but he doubted it. Rosie could be pretty tight-lipped when she thought it was important.

The truth was, Spreadbury had got to him. Had hit him right where it hurt.

'You don't know me, but I know you,' Spreadbury had said, by way of introduction during that first call, back when he'd had a phone number that connected right to the phone in his workroom. Everyone in the business had already known to ring Rosie or Sooty on the other number they had and only to ring Jim's line in an emergency, but this call had come straight through.

'Who the fuck is this?' Jim had asked testily. He'd been sitting at his machine playing computer solitaire. He remembered it clearly. He should have been working on *Shimmer*, and *could* have been working on it, but for this little daily ritual: work couldn't commence until he'd won a game of solitaire. And on this particular day, the computer game was

197

playing hard to get. Which had suited Jim because *Shimmer* was playing hard to get, too. He'd already had problems with it and they'd begun to look pretty much insurmountable.

'My name is Aaron Spreadbury,' the plummy voice had announced. 'And I happen to know you're in trouble.'

'What kind of trouble?' Jim had asked, interested in spite of himself. If he'd been working he would have been severely irritated at having his concentration broken and would have snapped out Rosie's number and instructed the man to leave a message with her. But here was another excuse to goof off.

'More trouble than you can imagine,' Spreadbury said. 'Currently you're experiencing some kind of a wall in your way. I'm afraid I don't know very much about your personal details, my friend. Perhaps if you could tell me your line of work, I would be able to tell you more about the wall I see blocking your way.'

'You don't know who I am?' Jim had asked, surprised. 'You really don't know?'

'I'm afraid not,' the voice said smoothly. 'I don't even know your name.'

'Then how did you get my number?' Jim asked, inspired for once. This was going to make a great scene for a book. He didn't know when he'd be able to use it, but it sounded like good material.

And Spreadbury had said, 'I dialled numbers at random.'

Jim had found the first big smile of the day spreading across his face. *Paydirt!* he'd thought, and his imagination lit like a thousand-watt halogen floodlight. His writing demon grabbed for the reins of his mind and raced away. A thousand possibilities had coursed through his brain; a cascade of ideas, situations, characters.

'Then how do you know you have the right person?' Jim asked, amused.

'I know,' Spreadbury said. 'Trust me.'

'I trust you,' Jim said. 'But how *do* you know?'

'The reason I felt the need to dial random numbers, which aren't in fact random at all, was that I intuited something bad. Something out of order. A kind of psychic thundercloud, wheeling in the sky, the kind of weather that will

198

make towering and deadly tornadoes. Refined, refocused, I could see a tall wall below that huge roiling cloud and cowering at the bottom of that wall, unable to go through it, under it, or round it, was a man.'

'And the man was me, right?' Jim said.

'Yes,' Spreadbury replied.

'And the man is me because I'm the first guy you got through to when you dialled numbers at random? If you'd come up with a table waitress named Marge in Cincinnati, it would have been her?'

'If I'd gotten through to anyone in Cincinnati, I would have failed,' Spreadbury said. 'The source of the disturbance is centred south of Miami. And, as I said, the numbers weren't truly random. I merely dropped into a light trance and trusted my fingers to find the correct telephone number of the source of the disturbance. That source is you. My fingers never fail me. I know that I have the right man because I feel the connection. I feel the turbulence in your soul.'

Jim frowned. There was indeed turbulence in his soul. And the wall this guy was talking about really *did* seem to be looming up. 'You're a psychic,' he said.

Because he wrote about extra-sensory perception he'd had mail from all sorts of wackos who claimed psychic powers. When he was researching *Miriam* he'd actually sought out and met people who claimed to be genuinely psychic and he'd been disappointed. Most were merely sensitive, intelligent people who were also good guessers and, in Jim's opinion, being psychic should have been more than that. Much more.

'Yes,' Spreadbury replied. 'I'm a psychic. And I want to help you.'

'But you don't know who I am,' Jim said.

'Wait!'

'Okay, but I don't have long,' Jim said. 'I'm busy.'

'I'm getting a colour,' the man said. 'Green.'

Jim grinned. 'Nicely done,' he said. 'You *do* know who I am, after all.'

'Your mother and father died in a car crash in Scotland nine years ago.'

'It's documented,' Jim said. 'You could have read it any number of places.'

'You're famous,' Spreadbury said.

'That was a remarkable example of the appliance of logic,' Jim said. 'It wasn't divined using those psychic powers of yours.' This was pretty much the way they all worked: you told them something, they extrapolated and risked a guess.

'Wait!' Spreadbury said.

'I'm getting tired of waiting,' Jim said.

'There's a small house in Scotland. You inherited it from your parents. You don't go there very often but someone keeps the place in order for you. It's in a place called Onich. There's a stone circle nearby. You drew power from it when you were younger.'

'Documented,' Jim said. 'Except the bit about the stone circle. There isn't one.' There was one actually, but it wasn't what Jim would have termed nearby and he certainly didn't recall drawing any power from it. He'd once walked around it and had woken up four hours later in the centre of it in the rain with a splitting headache and no memory of what had happened, but if you called falling down and bashing your head on a rock and becoming unconscious 'drawing power' you were barking up the wrong tree.

And yet . . .

Something did *happen,* he thought. *I was sure of it at the time, even though I had the bump on my head. I was out for four hours, it was midsummer and the place drew a lot of tourists and no one saw me. When I woke up I scared the living shit out of that elderly couple who were standing right in front of me. They were there and they didn't see me till I regained consciousness.*

He'd never told anyone about this, not even Sooty, because at the time he'd been fifteen and dumb and he'd had a number of romantic theories about the ancient sites dotted about the countryside. Looking back on it the following day, what had happened had seemed like a simple accident. The old folks hadn't seen him because they were looking elsewhere. People didn't walk into stone circles and vanish. Not even at Stonehenge down in Salisbury.

'On the east wall of the living room of that small house

something is glittering still,' Spreadbury said. 'Am I right? Is *that* documented?'

Jim felt the blood draining from his face. In his chest, his heart kicked hard. The address of the house just outside Onich wasn't common knowledge. Jim had gone out of his way to keep it private. As far as he knew, not one single fan had ever stumbled across that house and nothing about it had ever been published. Unless Spreadbury had friends in the village, he couldn't possibly know anything about it, let alone what hung glittering still on the east wall of the living room.

'Your surname is Green,' Spreadbury said. 'That's clear now. I think your Christian name may be Jack or Jake. No, that's too long. It's three letters, but I'm sure it begins with a J. Jim. Yes?'

'My name is James Green,' Jim said. 'As you well know. I'm a novelist and screenwriter and film director. Now I don't know how you found out about the locket, but I'm not amused.'

'Locket?' Spreadbury sounded genuinely surprised.

'The glittering thing on the east wall,' Jim said. 'You're not fooling anyone here, Mr Spreadbury, and I'm a busy man. I don't want to know what you want.'

'*Locket* . . .' Spreadbury said. 'I kept getting hair. I've no idea why. Brown hair and black hair. And something red. I couldn't think how it could glitter. Oh, well, now we know.'

'You've been in the house,' Jim said. Not even old Davis McCullough who lived next door and looked after the house knew what was inside the locket. Even Jim hadn't known until after the crash when the undertaker had passed the locket back to him, along with his mother's wedding and engagement rings and her cheap little Timex watch. He'd expected to find tiny photographs of his mother and father inside the tiny heart-shaped locket, when he opened it up. But there were no photos. Instead, in each half of the locket was a tiny lock of hair, neatly trimmed and tied up with a piece of red cotton. Brown hair – his mother's – in the left-hand side, and black hair in the right.

'I've never been to Scotland, I'm afraid,' Spreadbury said. 'What do you want?'

'I want to stop a disaster,' Spreadbury said. 'A disaster that happens to pivot around you.'

'What'll it cost?' Jim sighed. Now they were down on the bottom line. The psychic's charm had worn off quicker than he had anticipated. And since the man had mentioned the locket, all sorts of warning bells were clanging inside Jim's head.

'A great deal,' Spreadbury said.

'I thought it might,' Jim said, and put the phone down.

He'd spent the next hour and a half seething and smoking and wishing he could get his hands around Spreadbury's neck. And then he opened a new document with his word-processor and jotted down notes concerning his odd experience with the stone circle and the psychic's method of tracking down the people he was looking for. There were a lot of opportunities here, Jim thought, now beginning to type at speed as his mind clicked back into fiction mode. He should have been working on *Shimmer*, of course, but working on *anything* was better than not working at all.

As usual, the act of writing worked as a tonic on his emotions. He grew calm as his writing trance deepened and forgot all about what might lie beneath the phone call. It was probably an extortion attempt. It didn't matter.

If a psychic guarantees you he'll avert whatever trouble is heading towards you for a million bucks, he typed, *and then he says he's accomplished what he set out to do, how can you, as a non-psychic, prove if he actually did anything or not?*

Twenty minutes later he had enough ideas for a new novel. Fifteen minutes after that, and he had the bare bones of a story. He saved the document, sat back in his chair mentally congratulating himself and lit a celebratory cigarette. 'Just like every cloud,' he said, 'every crank call has a silver lining.' All Spreadbury had achieved was to help him along his way.

'Towards my dark and monstrous future,' he said, grinning. 'Towards the thundercloud and the big dark wall. Shit, I'll use that, too, if I remember it.'

He automatically snatched up the phone when it rang.

'It won't necessarily be money,' a voice said. 'And it won't be me you'll have to pay.'

'Fuck off, Spreadbury,' Jim said mildly. 'I'm busy.'

'You're also calm enough to listen to me now,' Spreadbury said confidently.

'What do you want if you don't want money?' Jim asked, vaguely remembering an old Adam Faith song of the same name. *That*, he thought, *was* a very *long time ago*.

'I want to help,' Spreadbury said. 'I want to help avert a disaster. That's all.'

'What do you care about what happens to me?' Jim asked, remembering the locket and becoming unsettled all over again. There was just no way Spreadbury could have seen inside the locket. Unless he really *was* psychic. Jim shivered.

'It's not just you,' Spreadbury said. 'I'm talking about a *major* disaster. One you're going to cause. Do you remember the last hurricane?'

'How could I forget?' Jim said.

'The carnage? The destruction?'

'Of course.'

'I'm talking about something that'll be many times as ferocious as Hurricane Andrew. Devastation on a massive scale.'

'And *I'm* going to cause it?' Jim pulled a face.

'Inadvertently, yes. To put it simply, you won't be able to stop it without my help.'

'You said earlier I'd have to pay "a great deal" to avert your disaster. Just a moment ago you said it wouldn't be money and it wouldn't be you I'd have to pay.'

'I did.'

'So what the fuck are you talking about?' Jim asked jovially, refusing to let this get to him. If he treated it like a joke he wasn't going to get angry. He hoped.

'There's more to life than money,' Spreadbury said. 'And fame. Incidentally, I've just been out and bought a copy of *Deathless*. It opens very well.'

'Thanks,' Jim said. 'So, if it isn't going to cost me money to stop whatever it is you have planned, what will it be?'

'I'm not sure yet,' Spreadbury said. 'It's possible that you'll have to pay in blood and money as well. You may lose everything you ever lived for. You may have to make huge sacrifices.'

'Nice,' Jim said. 'So tell me more about the disaster and how we stop it.'

'I can't tell you anything more,' Spreadbury said. 'It's too early. But the first step in the right direction would be for you to allow me to help you. I won't want a red cent of your money. I won't want anything you have.'

'Can I be candid here?' Jim asked.

'Of course!'

'I think you're nuts,' Jim said calmly. 'I think you're planning some kind of extortion. I think you're a crank. I think you have a screw loose. I think you forgot to pay your brain bill. I think what you've just told me is the biggest pile of shit I've ever heard in my life. I think, in short, that you're a fucking idiot. I don't want to speak to you any more. I don't want you calling back here, ever. So, my friend, this is goodbye. It *isn't* see you later, it's goodbye for ever.'

And he put down the phone and pulled the plug. Then he put the plug back in and called Henry Skate and told him to get a modern switchboard down here, *pronto*! And then he pulled the plug again.

And then he wondered what Spreadbury would do next. What Spreadbury did next was call again a week later, while Henry Skate was busy fitting the switchboard. But this time he called on the other number, on Rosie's day off, and spoke to Sooty and frightened her.

But Sooty sent him away with a flea in his ear and he didn't call again.

And as the days and weeks passed and Jim really *did* hit that big dark wall that the man had predicted, he cursed him. Then he sank so deep into his pit of despair that he forgot about Spreadbury.

But he was remembering him now as he looked at Frank, who sometimes didn't seem sure of what or who he was looking at when he looked at Jim. Frank, who had managed to look entirely insane on a couple of occasions.

Maybe Spreadbury had sent him. The two of them might still be playing some game.

Or maybe it's just paranoia, Jim told himself. Whatever it was, he didn't much care for it.

4

It was getting darker now outside the circle of illumination the camp-fire and the two lamps gave. The sky had filled with flat cloud and from here it was difficult to see as far as the tree-line. The Straker house was lost in shadow.

Jon Short took a swig of his beer and smacked his lips. 'Okay,' he said, wriggling himself comfortable. 'Listen up because this is what happened and it's all true.'

'Go for it, Jon!' Martha encouraged him around a mouthful of her latest burger.

'Okay. Imagine the scene. It's dark. And it's raining. We're in a little country lane, miles from nowhere, and there's a small car driving slowly up it, windshield wipers flicking back and forth. The driver is being *very* careful. This is heavy weather indeed.'

June nodded appreciatively. 'Yeah, I can see all that,' she whispered.

'Go on, Jon,' Martha urged.

'Inside the car are two nuns. The one driving is offering up a silent prayer to Saint Christopher for a safe journey. We can see her lips moving. The nuns are travelling through bad lands and they know it. It's dangerous here. It's godless country.

'Up ahead of them, in the distance, the car lights catch a glimpse of something coming out of a hedge to their left. Neither sees what it is, but both of them see it. Both of them try not to tell themselves it's man-shaped. They see it for only a moment and then it's gone.

'Sister Mary, the passenger, is pretty shaken up. In a frightened voice, she asks the driver, Sister Celia, what it was.

'Sister Celia shakes her head. "Nothing," she says. "Just a trick of the light. It was a crow or something." But they both know it wasn't. Neither of them even want to *think* about any of the other things it could be so they drop the subject and plough on through the rain, both of them tense and frightened.

'A minute or two later the car hits something. There's a huge thump and whatever it was they hit rolls up the hood

205

of the car in a black, whirling blur. The thing is heavy and the collision with it makes the car wander towards the steep drop at the side of the road. Sister Celia yelps and corrects the wheel, keeping the car steady.

'And from the black blur, two hands reach up the hood and grab the windshield wipers, stopping them dead. Strong arms pull the thing into view. It's a vampire and it leers in through the window . . .' Jon paused and drank some beer.

'What then?' June asked, wide-eyed.

'Sister Mary says, "It's a vampire, Sister, and it's clinging on to the windshield wipers. What should I do?"

'And quick as a flash, Sister Celia says, "Show it your cross! For God's sake, show it your cross!"

'And Sister Mary does exactly what she's told. She yells, "GET OFF OUR FUCKING WINDSHIELD WIPERS!"'

With the exception of Candy, who didn't get the joke, everyone roared with laughter.

'I've got one!' Martha said. 'Me next!'

Jim looked at Frank, who held out his hands, palms up, inviting Martha to tell a tale.

'Okay,' Martha said breathlessly. 'This isn't a scary story, but you'll like it anyway, I guess. It's about the moon landing. You remember Neil Armstrong when he stepped out of the lunar module on the moon?'

'Yep,' Jim said. 'I was in Scotland back then. I stayed up all night to watch.'

'Well, everyone knows how he screwed up his little speech when he went down the ladder and said, "One small step for man, one giant leap for mankind," but—'

'What do you mean he screwed up?' Candy demanded.

'It doesn't make sense,' Frank said. 'Man and mankind are the same thing. Armstrong *should* have said, "One small step for *a* man, one giant leap for mankind."'

'Everybody knows that,' Martha repeated. 'Anyway, this statement was followed by a bunch of other stuff. Y' know the kind of bleeping hissing messages they do back and forth between there and Houston. The usual stuff. He said things to the other astronauts and so on. But get this. On the way back, just before he went back into the module, he said something else. Something weird.'

206

'About being watched?' Jon asked.

'Nope,' Martha said. 'He just said this weird thing: "Good luck, Mr Gorsky."'

'Now the folks back at NASA thought it was a casual remark, concerning some rival Soviet cosmonaut. But then someone who had nothing better to do checked up and found there *was* no Gorsky in the Russian space program. Or in the American one. So when he got back they asked Neil Armstrong what he'd meant by those words. I guess some of them thought he'd gone nuts, or that he was passing on a code-word or something. But Neil wouldn't say. It was a mystery.

'Well, over the years many people asked Neil what he'd meant by the "Good luck, Mr Gorsky," remark, but no matter who asked him, he wouldn't tell them.'

'Gorsky was a ghost!' Candy said.

'Nope,' Martha said. 'Listen. Neil Armstrong did a speech up in Tampa Bay one time. I forget when it was, but it must have been five years ago or so. And while he was answering questions afterwards, a reporter stuck up his hand and asked Neil about the Mr Gorsky thing. This is like twenty-two or twenty-three years after the event. Course, no one expects Neil to say anything, just like usual, but on this occasion he says, "Okay, I can tell you now, since Mr Gorsky died a while back." He said, "One Sunday afternoon when I was a kid I was playing baseball in my backyard with a pal. I pitched and he hit a fly ball right over the fence into my neighbour's garden. It landed close to the house, right beneath their bedroom window. Now, the neighbours were Mr and Mrs Gorsky and they didn't much care for me climbing into their garden, but I went over there anyway. As I bent down to pick up the ball I heard that Mr and Mrs Gorsky were having an argument up in their bedroom. I heard Mrs Gorsky yelling, "Oral sex! You want *oral* sex? You'll *get* oral sex just as soon as the kid next door walks on the moon!"'

Even Candy got the joke this time. When the laughter had died down she said, 'I want to go next! I want to tell a story!'

'It won't be pornographic, will it?' Martha chortled.

Candy looked genuinely surprised. 'No,' she said, 'it's scary.'

'Go ahead, Candy,' Frank said. 'I'll wait till last.'

'Okay,' Candy said. 'This is a true story, I swear to God. A girlfriend of mine up in Wyoming knew the girl it happened to and afterwards her hair went white overnight. Not just pretty streaks like that woman in *Poltergeist*, but totally, completely *white*.'

'All over?' Frank quipped, smiling.

Candy nodded, her eyes huge. 'All over. Not a hair on her head wasn't white. It's scary how that happens. Anyway, this guy – a kid, really, he was in high-school at the time – has just got his first car. A Plymouth or something. I dunno what it was now, but it was a sedan. Big, roomy car. A Lincoln? I dunno, but he was from a wealthy family so it could have been. His name was Rafe. So, he has this big new car and a hot girlfriend called Helen. She wasn't rich, I don't think. She wouldn't have been at school with my friend if she was, I guess. Rafe went to a different school. They first met in a Burger King, I think. Or a McDonalds. Fast-food place, anyway.'

Jim listened and smiled. One of his favourite occupations was eavesdropping. Sooty often told him off in restaurants because while she was speaking to him he was unconsciously leaning towards another table, having locked on to the conversation the people there were involved in. He'd started doing it when he'd started writing and these days it was so deeply ingrained he couldn't turn it off. You didn't often learn anything of staggering significance from this kind of restaurant and airport lounge eavesdropping, but that didn't matter because the thing Jim was after was the sound of the speech. What Jim loved best of all was the rise and fall of the words, the way they were strung together, the vocabulary and dynamics of the conversation. He collected all this to use in his work. And Candy, bless her, had a lovely, goofy, meandering way of telling a story.

And I bet I know which story she's going to tell, Jim thought, sipping his whisky.

'So, anyway, Rafe has this car and he thinks, Well, I'll go pick up Helen and take her to Lovers' Lane. This is a real

208

place called Lovers' Lane, not just a . . . er . . . metaphysical lovers' lane.'

'Metaphorical,' Frank corrected.

'Right. So, he drives to Helen's house and stops outside and blasts the horn, but Helen doesn't come running out to see his new car like he expected her to. He called her, see, so she knew he had this new car and she knew he was coming and everything. He hits the horn another couple of times, but she still doesn't come out, so he gets out and goes and rings the bell. And the curtain flicks back – they had a window each side of the front door, I guess – and there's Helen, looking worried. She opens the door and peers out past Rafe, up and down the road. He asks her what's wrong. She says she can't come out. He asks why. She says, hasn't he heard? He says, heard what? She says, about the escape. Escape, what escape?

'Okay, so she explains that a couple of hours ago, probably when he was buying the car, there was a jail break. They have this high-security pen up there, see. It's full of murderers and hard cases and stuff. They have everyone back but one guy, who slipped through the net and this guy is deadly. He's a psycho. Like whatsisname in *Silence of the Sheep*, except he's real. So, this guy is out there somewhere and her parents have forbidden her to go out. She tells Rafe he can come in, but he wants to take her to Lovers' Lane and make out. Rafe is disappointed. He says, "Let me talk to your parents. I'll convince them to let you come out. Hell, the guy won't be hanging around here. He'll be miles away, or they'll have caught him already." She says he can't talk to them 'cause they've gone bowling. Or to play bridge. Or to the Rotary Club meeting or something. Anyway, they're out. It doesn't matter where, I guess—'

'Go on!' June said. 'I think I know what's coming and I can't wait to hear if I'm right!'

'So,' Candy said, 'he says, "Well, if it's safe enough for them, it'll be safe enough for us, so come on!" and after a while she goes with him. They cruise around in the big car for a bit and every time they see someone on the sidewalk he goes, *"That's him! That's the lunatic!"* and scares her, so she snuggles up to him. I guess the car had a bench front

209

seat or something. Or she leaned over the shift. So, anyway, they end up exactly where Rafe wants them, down Lovers' Lane. It's a dead-end road and there are trees and bushes either side. It's like being in a tunnel, Shirley says. Shirley's my friend from Wyoming. Usually it's full of couples in cars, making out, but this night there's no one there but Rafe and Helen. She isn't comfortable, 'cause Rafe keeps going "Boo!" and scaring her, but they settle down and start kissing and stuff.

'And they're both getting into it when there's a little tap on the driver's door window. Helen shrieks and even Rafe is scared. They look outside, but there's no one there. She won't let him get out to look, but eventually they see that one of the trees nearby is shedding bits of twig and leaves and stuff in the wind. One of these must have hit the window. Anyway, he locks the doors and they get on with it.

'Then there's another tap at the window. They think it's falling stuff, so they ignore it, but there's another tap and another. Then a big bang, like someone's slapped the roof. They both jump like they've been shot and Rafe looks out and there's this guy standing outside, grinning. He's got his hands behind his back. Rafe reaches out to undo the locks and she yells at him, "*It's him! It's the psycho! Drive away!*"

'But Rafe says, "That isn't the psycho, it's the guy who sold me the car not three hours ago. He must have forgotten something. It must be important if he tracked me down this quickly. Maybe there's something wrong with the car. Maybe it's dangerous."

'Anyway, by this time, the guy is wandering back towards the main road. He's got fed up with waiting. So Rafe gets out of the car and goes after him, trots up the road. It was an unmade road, I think. Anyway, he chases after this guy, who darts into the trees, like he's gone for a piss or something and half-way up the road, Rafe turns his ankle and falls and, since it's dark, Helen loses sight of him. She's still scared, so she locks the doors and waits. If she would have been able to drive, she'd have drove away, I guess, but she can't. All she can do is sit tight. She waits for ages. Then there's this real hard *crash* on the roof of the car like someone's jumped up there. She's scared shitless, but she

210

can't do anything but stay where she is. It goes all quiet then it begins. Thump thump thump on the roof. Whatever it is up there is whacking down on the roof with something hard. On and on it goes. It seems like hours and the poor girl can see stuff like water spraying down across the screen and the hood and the roof is caving in, like whoever is up there is trying to hammer his way through.

'Then, suddenly, everything is floodlit and Helen can see that it's not water on the screen and all down the hood, it's blood. And there are voices booming out at her from loud-hailers, or whatever they call them. Bull-horns or something. It's not fog-horns, is it? Anyway, all these people are shouting, "GET DOWN, GET DOWN!" so she gets down, figuring it's the police, the lunatic is on top of the car and they're gonna shoot him. But she doesn't hear anything. A while later the thumping slows, then stops, and the police yell at her to get out of the car and walk towards the side of the road, but whatever she does, she isn't to look back. So she gets out and half-way across the road she can't help herself any more and looks back.

'And there, in the glare of all the lights, naked on top of the car, not dead, but apparently tranquillized by a dart gun, is her boyfriend Rafe. She knew about the dart gun, which is what that little *thwack* noise she heard was. I forgot to tell you she heard a *thwack* noise before they told her to get out of the car.

'Anyway, he's up there and he's naked and half asleep and he's all covered in blood. And as she turns back he lifts the thing he's been bashing the car's roof with and she sees it's a head. A severed head. He's got a big knife in one hand and a severed head in the other. And his eyes are mad, his face all twisted up, and he looks at her and giggles. "I saved us!" he says, then goes out cold. The head rolls from his hands, bounces on the road and comes to rest at Helen's feet, face up. And it's the guy he said had sold him the car.'

'Oh, my God, that's *horrible*!' Martha said.

'Yeah, but get this,' Candy said. 'Helen later found out, while she was recovering in the hospital, that the guy Rafe had decapitated *was* the escaped psycho. But that's not all. When they found Rafe's clothes, they discovered that he had

211

a bank draft in the back pocket of his jeans made out for ten thousand bucks. It was the draft he was supposed to use to pay for the car. Well, the police couldn't figure out how come the psycho had sold him someone else's car and then let him have it without taking the money, so they went to the address where the car had been sold. And guess what they found?'

'Everyone was dead?' June asked.

'Yep,' Candy said, 'and it wasn't the psycho who'd done it. It was Rafe. The murder weapons and his stained clothing were all in the trunk of the car. How about *that* for a story!'

It was a twist on the story Jim was expecting her to tell, but she'd done well. He began to clap and Candy got a warm round of applause and plenty of hearty congratulations from the others.

Except Frank.

'It's a dead granny,' Frank said, when the excited chatter had died down.

'What is?' Candy asked.

'Your story.'

'No, a dead family and a dead man,' Candy said.

'The *story* is a dead granny,' Frank said. 'It isn't true. It's what's called a "dead granny" after the old tale about the family who went on holiday with their grandmother who died. They were supposed to have tied her corpse to the roof-rack and then lost it. It's what's more formally known as an urban myth. One of those stories that pops up now and again, usually told by high-school kids. I heard a version of the one you just told when I was in college. Years ago.'

'It was a good version, whatever,' Jim said. 'And beauti-fully told, too.'

Candy quit scowling at Frank and treated Jim to a sunny smile. 'Why, thank you, kind sir!' she said. 'But as far as I know it's true. Now you tell us one!'

'Okay,' Jim said. 'Now this one really is true!'

5

As far as James Green was concerned, you could forget 'raindrops on roses and whiskers on kittens': this man's list

212

of favourite things began with reading and writing and telling tall stories. Apart from lounging around playing with Gloria or Sooty, or both, in the sunshine there was nothing he would rather be doing.

This hadn't really struck home for him until his desolate period had broken. Up until the block he'd always said that he could quit telling stories tomorrow if he wanted to. While he was blocked he didn't have many logical thoughts, but afterwards it hit him hard. His work defined him, made him who he was. Writing, whether it was a novel, a screenplay, or a short story – or even a letter to his lawyer or agent – was the thing at which he excelled, especially when he got to tell a story. Not so many months ago, he'd told *Rolling Stone* that if it came to a choice between his wife and daughter and writing, he'd quit writing in a flash. Now, since the block, he wasn't so sure. When he wasn't working – when he was *unable* to work – he felt like only half a man. As if something vital, something necessary for life, had been wrenched right out of his soul. He supposed that until the block he'd taken his gift for granted.

But the gift was back now and while it mightn't have been so powerful when applied to verbal story-telling, he was doing pretty good and feeling wonderful about it. The best salve for a dented ego was to see half a dozen rapt faces hanging on your every word as you told them a story.

'. . . and there wasn't anything left of her,' he said, now at the end of his own little contribution to the evening's story-telling. 'The forensic guys worked over the room for a fortnight, but not a fibre of clothing or a shred of skin was ever detected.'

'*Jeeesus!*' Jon Short said, shaking his head in admiration. 'What a story!'

'It's not true, though, is it?' Martha asked nervously. 'I know you said it was when you started, but it isn't really, is it?'

'Oh, yes, *indeedy!*' Jim said. 'I told it to you exactly as Detective Dan Matthews told it to me. The file's still open on that particular case.'

'That was a good one,' Frank admitted. 'But I think I can top it. After Rosie, of course.'

'I'm fresh out of tales,' Rosie said. 'I'd love to join in and tell one, but my mind is a total blank. You go ahead, Frank. It's getting late anyway. I expect Jim will want to show us around soon.'

'You're sure?' Jim asked, and Rosie shot him a look that plainly stated she wasn't going to tell a story.

'Okay, then. Go ahead, Frank,' Jim said, pouring more whisky into Frank's empty glass. He gave himself another couple of fingers, too, then reached for his cigarettes.

'I have to compose myself,' Frank said. 'I'm not quite certain how this is going to happen. I'm going to have to try to make myself into God. God of this story, at least. It may take a while.'

Jim flicked his lighter and looked at Frank over the flame as he brought it up to his cigarette. An odd, secretive look had stolen across Frank's features and he'd altered his posture to a kind of hunched position. His head was cocked slightly to one side as if he were listening with his left ear.

Then he smiled.

'On the way here,' he said, 'Jim was kind enough to tell us half the story of Straker's Island. He told us some of what happened to Straker Dauphin and his wife Majesty and his daughter Gloria. I'm going to tell you the bits he missed out. I'm going to tell you how he knows the things he's told us already. Now this is going to be uncomfortable for all of us, more uncomfortable for Jim, because his lies will be exposed, but none of us are going to like this.'

'Cool it, man!' Jon warned.

'It's a story,' Frank said, his eyes glittering as red as a demon's in the firelight. 'You want me to tell it, Jim?'

At that precise moment, Jim didn't know. For two reasons.

The first was that underneath all the blather that people had to say about fiction there was a raw truth. The truth was that fiction held power. Deep down at the bottom of it all flowed a raging river of power that could change reality, often for the worse rather than the better. If you wanted an example all you had to do was examine the result of Nazi Germany's fiction that Jews were subhuman. And despite what anyone said, and Jim himself had said it plenty of times, fiction *could* and *did* turn into reality. The old saw

214

'It's only a story!' was a fallacy. Perhaps you couldn't use tall tales to conjure up werewolves and chimera, although Jim was open-minded about even that, but you could certainly manage murder and mayhem.

The second and most important reason for Jim right now was that he'd just seen Frank shimmer, pretty much like poor Walt Creasey had in Jim's own book.

I imagined it! Jim thought, but he wasn't sure he had. Add to that the fact that he certainly hadn't imagined the tree up behind the house vibrating – or *shimmering* – because Rosie had seen it too, and you had one uncomfortable writer.

'Jim?' Jon said. 'You want him to carry on?'

'Why not?' Jim said, managing a smile while he kept his eye on Frank. 'After all, it's only a story.'

Frank gave him a ghoulish grin. 'Okay, folks, here's the news. Here's what Jim left out of his story in case we thought less of him. What no one knows, and what Jim will never tell is this. This island is *not* deserted. It never has been. Straker Dauphin found this out as did Jim. The reason no birds fly over this place, the reason no animals live here, is that there's a god on this island. It's not a spectre, a ghoul, a ghost or anything else. It's nothing less than a god. A hugely powerful immortal being. Now we already know about Dauphin disturbing this entity and perhaps trying to harness it, although for what nefarious purposes we don't yet know. And we know that Jim knows this. Here's something you don't know yet. Jim's been trying to harness that power, too. Of course, he'll be too shy to tell you himself, but he's been thieving from the power source on this island for years. Drawing on it for his skill and his luck. That's how he got where he is today, by sucking power off the island's god like a vampire. So, where did the god come from and how long has it been here? It's like this.

'Once upon a time, aeons ago, before the cavemen, before the dinosaurs, the world spun in the opposite direction and much of the land was connected in one huge lump. You only have to look at a world map to see how South America and Africa still nearly fit snugly if you imagine them put together. We were all joined together, us to what's now Northern Europe, South America to Africa, Africa to the Indian

215

subcontinent and so on. And in those days, before time began, a civilization covered the face of the planet. These old people weren't people like us, but they *were* humanoid. They had dark, almost purple skin, flattish features and three-fingered, one-thumbed hands. They were tall and beautiful. This was the *original* human race. The *uncorrupted* version. The ones that lived before the Biblical garden of Eden was emptied. The Bible story is merely an ancient myth concerning the fall of the original race that lived here.'

'What happened?' Martha asked. 'What happened to make them vanish and the world turn in the other direction?'

'Back in those days, gods walked the earth side by side with the humans, their creation. There *is* no "One True God". What there is, is a usurper: that's who the Christian God is. The other gods are merely temporarily banished, locked in granite and beneath the water and buried deep beneath deserted islands like this one. Back in those days when the world spun the other way and the old race lived on the earth alongside their gods, who protected and provided for them, some of the gods became jealous of the powers of some of the others.'

'They all had different powers, right?' June said.

Frank nodded. 'Think of all those Greek gods who had different talents from one another. The Greek legends are based upon some of what happened when the old race existed. To cut a long story pretty short – or we'll be here all night – there was an almighty war among the gods. A war which literally stopped the world turning, so that on one side it was permanent day with the hot sun blasting down endlessly, and on the other side it was always freezing night. The old race, the original humans, were wiped out. All but a handful who'd seen what was coming and taken steps to protect themselves.'

'The ark,' Jon put in.

'It wasn't a wooden boat, that's for sure,' Frank said. 'I guess it was some kind of a magical field of protection, inside which the few cowered, but even this didn't save them entirely. Many of them died off in there. The war lasted an age, you see. Thousands of years. And inside the ark, the people, exposed to ... I dunno, magic or gamma radiation

216

or whatever, mutated. They grew an extra two fingers. Their skin and their features changed beyond all recognition into diverse shapes and shades. They lost their ability to communicate by thought and to move heavy objects by the power of their minds. Everything they'd had, they lost.

'When the war was over and the land-mass was split and separating as the world began to heave into motion again, those survivors crawled out into the dawn of the new era. An era in which all their happiness had gone. They were no longer protected or cared for. All the gods but one were locked away. Alliances had been made and betrayed until only one god remained and this one was severely damaged. It, or he, or she, now had the secrets of the powers of all the others, but was unable to use them and it was so badly wounded it crept away to recover and left the people to fend for themselves.'

'And that's the god that's on *this* island?' Candy wanted to know.

Frank shook his head. 'Nope. That's our God. The Christian one. The one that's been missing since our times began, barring the little glitch back in the year zero when it slipped into the body of a baby in the hope of becoming master of the people again and found itself swiftly dispatched by folks whose racial memory made them afraid and angry when it came to dealing with gods.

'The god on this island is the god of what this region used to be before the fall. Its powers are vast. It was one of the stronger gods, one of the last to be defeated and trapped. And it's an angry god.'

'Shit, *anyone* would be angry if they'd been locked up for a billion years.' Jon chuckled.

'And over those years, it has been recovering. Slowly. Very slowly indeed. So slowly that to us its progress wouldn't even be noticeable in a generation or two. But trust me, it's been happening. I know.'

He glanced up at Jim, grinning and showing his teeth. In the firelight he looked feral and dangerous. His eyes glittered. And, as Jim watched, he cocked his ear slightly towards the tree-line and gave a big wink.

And then he began to shimmer.

217

It lasted only a moment and no one else seemed to be aware of it happening. In spite of his shock and the cold jet of fear that froze his spine, Jim insisted mentally that he'd imagined it.

'When Straker Dauphin came to this area, he realized there was something special about the island. I'm not sure even Dauphin knew about the god trapped here, but he must have been certain of the place's importance to have bought it and moved here to live when he and his wife and child could just as easily have lived in luxury in Miami, or down on the Keys where there were people, and provisions were readily available.

'And once they'd moved here, Straker found out the truth. And set about awakening the god, perhaps intending to use it like a genie from a bottle, to grant him his wishes for letting it out. Straker Dauphin was a bitter man. He was a man who strongly believed he had literary talent but his stories had been shunned wherever he took them. In his entire life, Dauphin didn't make a single sale. Therefore he had a chip on his shoulder, an axe to grind. All he had to do was release the god.'

Jim's fear increased with each word Frank spoke. His mind had begun to whirl with thoughts and possibilities, scenarios and plots as the story went on. A parade of living-colour dioramas danced across the visual part of his mind: an endless procession of death and disaster and torture and pain.

A distant part of him reported that the air pressure around him had increased, but he wasn't sure if he was imagining this. He'd imagined all sorts of things during the past few weeks and no longer quite trusted himself.

But Frank's entire body told it all. His posture; the way he cocked his head; his distant eyes; the spittle flying into the fire as he spoke; the flatness of his words.

It's all true! Jim's mind informed him. *Everything Frank says is true! It may sound ridiculous, but in spite of that it's all true. And you know why? Because that isn't Frank speaking. Not really. It's his voice, but it isn't Frank saying the words. It's . . .*

Jim shivered. It *wasn't* Straker Dauphin speaking through

218

Frank because Dauphin was an invention Jim himself had made up on the way here.

So? I guessed right. What I thought was a tall tale wasn't fiction at all. I took the truth right out of thin air.

'And boy, did he *try*!' Frank said. 'But he couldn't do it alone and his wife and daughter had to be kept out of it. Straker knew that what he was trying to do was dangerous and he didn't want to put Majesty and Gloria at risk. So he enrolled the help of a friend. A friend who knew a trick or two about the scary stuff. This guy's name was David.'

Jim jumped when a gentle hand was placed on his shoulder, but he managed to stifle the yelp before it left his lips. Rosie was behind him. She bent and whispered, 'How does he know about Davey? "A friend who knew a trick or two about the scary stuff"? He's telling you he knows, Jim.'

'Knows what? And what does it matter if he *does* know about Davey?' he whispered back into her ear.

'He's in on it,' Rosie said. 'The notes. The Sooty thing back on the boat. Which means there's nothing to worry about. It's all a set-up run by Davey. I was getting worried earlier on.'

At least everything seemed clear to Rosie, Jim thought. Everything was getting murkier by the moment as far as this Scots-American was concerned.

'And once he'd started it he couldn't stop it,' Frank was saying. 'The god was awake. Or half awake. It wasn't yet strong enough, but given another hundred years or so . . .'

'Like *now* for example,' Rosie said.

'It would be strong enough to break free of its bonds,' Frank went on. 'Of course, the thing Jim's been keeping quiet about is the fact that *he* also discovered the dormant god. There's a pretty good reason for this. Who knows what Jim's daughter's name is?'

Martha stuck up her hand like an over-eager schoolgirl. 'Gloria!' she said.

'What a coincidence, eh?' Frank smiled. 'Same name as Dauphin's own daughter. *And* Jim owns the same island that Dauphin owned. And what did Dauphin write? Tales of the fantastic, that's what. And what does Jim write? Pretty much the same. Who knows what Jim's wife's name is?'

'Sooty!' Jon called.

'Her *real* name,' Frank said.

'I know it,' Jim said distantly.

Frank gave him that feral grin again. 'Anyone else?' he asked.

'I know it, too,' Rosie said.

'Rosie. Tell us all.'

'It's Reina,' Rosa said.

'She's from South American stock,' Frank said. 'Reina, roughly translated into English is – guess what?'

'Majesty!' a chorus of voices replied.

'Its direct translation is "queen" actually, but that's close enough for me,' Frank said. 'Now, here's what Jim knows and I know, but he's been keeping from you. Jim is Straker Dauphin reincarnated. His wife is Straker's wife reincarnated and his daughter is the original Gloria. All very nicely mirrored, if I say so myself. And, if you'll excuse my language, the other thing Jim doesn't want you to know is that he's been fucking around with the god, too. Making deals. That's why he's so famous and rich. And now it's time for Jim to make his payment to that god. That's why he's brought us all here. What this god needs to raise it is blood. Any kind of blood would do, but Jim chose to give the god quality blood. Our blood. We're here so he can sacrifice us on the altar of his success.'

He looked up and cocked his head again.

'But there's something Jim doesn't know. At this very moment there's a rescue attempt going on. Somewhere out at sea there's a boat and in this boat there's a man called Cheesebury. Cheesebury knows about the island. He knows there's danger here and he knows we all need to be saved, but the poor man doesn't know the nature of the danger. He thinks he's just going to land here and spirit us away before Jim leads us to our doom, but he's wrong. By the time he arrives it'll be too late. He's going to walk up this beach and die before he reaches the tree-line because by then the balance of power will have changed. But there will be survivors. Out of all us, only two will leave this island tonight on the *Mary Celeste*. And those two will walk the earth as

220

gods. Of the others no trace will ever be found. It'll be a mystery to rival that of Straker Dauphin and his family.'

'Sounds good to me!' Jon Short said.

'In a moment Jim is going to lead us into those woods and walk us right into the mouth of the god. And some of us will be consumed. And hell will break loose. Literally.'

'Is that right, Jim?' Jon Short asked.

'Right on the button,' Jim said, sickly. He'd already taken the name Cheesebury and worked it through: Cheesebury, Cheese Spread, Spreadbury. 'I am found out.'

'Great story, Frank!' June said. 'I bet Jim primed you on that one.'

The assembly gave him a round of applause.

I didn't prime you, Jim thought. *But you were primed, nonetheless. Or something or someone else spoke through you. In fact, Frank, I bet if I were to ask you what you've just said when you break out of that trance state you're in, you wouldn't have a goddamned clue.* He didn't know how he felt about this. Everything felt wrong, but that feeling had been going on since his computer had started generating words of its own accord. And, if he were truthful with himself, it had been going on for a couple of months before that, too. And yet he'd never been able to pin down the source of his discomfort. He'd imagined it was mental and physical exhaustion that had worried him and led to his block and, subsequently, his thoughts of suicide. But Spread-bury was all mixed up in it, too, and so was this trip. And Sooty's own anxiety.

Jim thought back and suddenly remembered first having had that leaden feeling in his stomach when he opened the envelope containing this year's competition advertisement. But he couldn't remember if that was before Spreadbury had begun to call or after. He thought it might have been before, but he'd never been a man with a firm grip on time. Most of his writing life he didn't even know what day it was, let alone what had happened when.

Something terrible is going to happen and there's nothing I can do to stop it, he thought. Then he smiled. Having what Sooty called 'an awesome imagination' was a double-edged sword. It had made him rich and famous, but it also gave him nightmares and fears that other people didn't seem to suffer from. And those words he'd just thought were exactly the words that scrolled through his mind each time he was on a plane at the end of a runway and its jets powered up and thrust him back against his seat. *And I've never died in a plane crash, have I?* he asked himself.

'Let's all go meet our destiny!' Jon said. 'What are we waiting for, people?'

The moment the words left his lips, the large tree at the foot of the house's backyard began to tremble again. A little more violently this time, Jim thought. He couldn't see it from here, but the noise was plain. Everyone shut up and turned towards the source of the sound.

'What the fuck was *that*?' Jon said when it was quiet again.

'That'd be the god,' Jim said. 'Just give it a moment to settle down and we'll all go and meet it.'

Chapter Fourteen

Downward Spirals

1

I spiralled, Elaine thought. *Getting off the plane at the airport in Miami, I spiralled. And I did it again when I arrived here and got out of the car to punch in the code for Jim and Sooty's security gates. And now I know what it was all about. Now I know why it happened.*

She glanced from Sooty, who was standing in the middle of the room cradling a glass of whisky and looking as lousy as Elaine had ever seen her looking, to Gloria, who was sleeping on the couch, her eyes flicking back and forth beneath her closed eyelids. What should have seemed a picture of happy domestic ordinariness had canted to the side somehow, making the entire scenario look wrong.

Elaine lit a Camel and waved the big puff of blue smoke away from her face. She hadn't even had time to tell Sooty her news about Mark yet. She'd known something was terribly wrong when Sooty had opened the door to let her in. *Before that, in fact,* she corrected herself. *You knew something was wrong the moment you set foot on Florida soil.*

'Let me get this straight,' she said, frowning. 'You had a bad feeling about this trip from ... When exactly did it start?'

All she knew so far was that Sooty was upset. This was frightening all on its own. Sooty was as happy-go-lucky as they came and, under normal circumstances, as cool as a truckload of cucumbers. But not today. Today she'd blurted out a lot of mixed-up stuff about phone calls and portents and Straker's Island. And she'd been so upset it'd been all out of sequence and chronological order.

'Ages ago,' Sooty said, stifling a sob. 'I can't remember when, but it seems like I've been having these bad feelings for ever. Jim's been blocked. You didn't know that, of course, no one knew but Jim and Rosie and me. He came very close to killing himself over it. Except that now I don't think the block was the real reason he was considering suicide.'

'Jesus,' Elaine said, suddenly off balance again. *Jim blocked and on the brink of suicide!* It was barely believable. The man was a writing machine. Nothing could stop him. He'd never been blocked in his life.

'Jesus has very little to do with it,' Sooty said, dully. 'I should know, I've prayed to him enough. Isn't it funny how in times of crisis even non-believers like me will pray?'

'Hilarious,' Elaine said, scowling. She'd done exactly the same recently. 'Doesn't fucking help a bit, does it, honey?' she added.

Sooty shook her head.

'So, Jim was blocked and thinking of doing away with himself. And you began to feel bad about what was coming up. I can understand that.'

'I left the gun in his desk drawer, but I broke in and took the bullets,' Sooty said, a kind of challenge in her eyes that Elaine didn't understand.

'That was a neat idea,' she said carefully.

'You may not think so after tonight,' Sooty said, that odd look still in her eyes.

Those few words were about as shocking as anything Elaine had ever heard in her life. She held up a hand. 'Be calm,' she said. 'Relax and tell me all of it.'

'It might have been better,' Sooty said, 'if I'd left those slugs in that Colt. I don't know why I feel that, I really don't, but I have this horrible sense of foreboding.'

'Honey, nothing could be worse than what you're suggesting,' Elaine said. That corkscrew feeling was trying to start again. She fought it off this time. She was already suffering a weird kind of reality fracture from standing in a room with someone you regarded as your good friend – someone whose life was perfect and perfectly happy – and listening to them

224

say they wished they'd let the love of their life shoot himself, and she didn't think she could take the spiralling feeling too.

Sooty dropped her gaze. 'I think it could. You see, I don't think it was the block. He thought it was, I thought it was, but his unconscious knew better. So did mine.'

Elaine sat down in an easy chair – Jim's favourite, she guessed, since there was an ashtray ready on the arm – and said, 'Sooty, just sit down, sip your drink, try to compose yourself and tell me what you mean. I'm hopelessly lost here. All I can see is that you had a few crank calls.'

Sooty sat down, drained the remains of her drink, then got up and collected the bottle and took it back with her. She filled her glass again and tasted it while she stared at nothing and stroked Gloria's hair with her free hand. After a while, she sighed, looked up at Elaine and said, 'Something's gone terribly wrong. I even know *when* it did it. It was on the day we received the advertising copy for this trip.'

'Honey, are you trying to tell me there's another woman?' Elaine asked, still searching for a rational explanation. 'Is that what all this is about? Jim's having an affair?'

Sooty smiled wanly. 'Yes, there's another woman and I'll tell you about her in a minute, but it isn't what you think. The only affair Jim has other than with me is with his work. Let me start at the beginning.

'I felt a change on the day the advertising material came through from Collis and Anstey – from *you*, I guess. And this was before the calls started.'

'Calls?'

Sooty nodded. 'Tonight isn't the only time I've been called. It's been going on for some time. It began exactly a week after we'd got the contest copy through. But I was going to tell you about that change I felt. I don't know how to explain it. I looked at that ad and I suddenly felt as if a part of me had gone into a downward spiral. I thought I was fainting, but when it finished, I was still standing there and nothing had happened. But something *had* happened. I *felt* it happen. Shit, I wouldn't make it as a writer, would I?'

'You don't have to,' Elaine said, 'because I know exactly what you're talking about. It happened to me, too. Once

225

when I got off the plane and again as I punched in the number for your gates.'

'You're kidding!' There was a hopeful look in Sooty's eyes.

'It's true,' Elaine said. She told Sooty about Mark and her worries that she was going to be killed. And ended with Mark's violent death.

'I'm sorry,' Sooty said, clearly shaken.

Elaine shrugged. 'That's showbiz,' she said. 'You reap what you sow and all that. I guess I should be grieving or something, but hey, the guy was bad and we were done. But I suppose it *is* strange. After all, I've been telling myself I still loved him. I guess I was wrong about that. I have no idea where the grief and shock went. It's like it passed by me entirely. Or like he isn't dead at all.'

'I feel so stupid,' Sooty said. 'Here I am worrying about what's probably nothing, and you've been bereaved.'

'Released, I think,' Elaine said, feeling as if she'd left the real world and walked into one of Jim's stories. *Cancel that*, she thought, *Jim's characters feel grief when someone close to them cops it*. 'So, you had this downward spiral thing and you knew that everything had changed. What changed? Any idea?'

'Straker's Island,' Sooty said. 'The trip. Something bad is going to happen. I've known that from the start, deep down. I've just been ignoring it.'

Elaine jabbed out the butt of her cigarette in the ashtray. 'And then this crank calls you.'

'He said he was a psychic,' Sooty said. 'Gave me a load of bullshit about how Jim was in trouble and he wanted to help. Hey, could I have a Camel?'

She took the cigarette Elaine passed her, lit it and continued, 'He said he could foresee a terrible storm coming our way and that he could help avert it. He meant an emotional storm, he said, but there was more to it than that. Well, I got rid of him in a big hurry. But he kept calling back.'

All of this sounded pretty familiar to Elaine, but the reason *why* had slipped her mind, possibly due to the whisky, which was hitting her harder than it had any right to. It was an odd sensation, this knowing but not knowing.

'And in between times, I had this odd feeling. I thought I was just worrying about Jim – he'd been acting a bit strangely ever since I'd first had that downward spiral thing. A little withdrawn. Then it turned into writer's block and I thought that was what I'd intuited. It occurred to me that he might have been reacting to my odd feeling, which I tried to keep to myself other than making him promise this would be the last trip to the island with fans, but now I think we both intuited the same thing at the same time. You get like that in a long-term relationship. Kinda psychic. Anyway, I was worrying about his block and his suicidal thoughts, even though he didn't know I knew about them. And the calls kept coming in and I kept ignoring them.'

'Your feeling was that if this trip took place, something bad would happen, right?' Elaine asked, thinking, *I know all of this! Did I dream it?*

'Pretty much,' Sooty said. 'Like he would die during it. Or maybe something worse would happen. Everyone would die.'

'The *Mary Celeste* might be lost at sea?'

'On the island.'

'How could that happen?'

Sooty took a long drag on her Camel. 'Someone might kill him,' she said. 'And everyone else. I had this worse idea, too. I don't know if I want to tell you my darkest thoughts.'

Elaine said, 'You don't have to, honey, I think I know what they are.'

Sooty sighed. 'I knew you would,' she said. 'You're sharp.'

'You think *he* might kill everyone, don't you?'

Two big tears trickled from Sooty's eyes. 'Why would I think that?' she asked. 'It's a terrible thing to think. Jim's kind and loving and gentle, so why . . . *how* . . . could I think he could do such a thing?'

2

'You mentioned a woman,' Elaine said, when Sooty had stopped crying. 'It's Candy, isn't it?'

Sooty nodded.

'You really believe Jim would, what ... I don't know ... run off with her?'

'It isn't quite as simple as that,' Sooty said quietly. 'If I thought all he'd do was jump her bones and forget her, I guess I could live with that. It'd be tough, but I think I could handle it. I *love* that guy. Love him to death. If I thought he might run off with her for a few months then come crawling back to me ... I don't know, maybe I'd even have him back then. Maybe not. But neither of those things is the issue.'

'They shouldn't be,' Elaine said. 'Candy is nothing. All body and nothing on the top floor except a pretty face. Not all men are suckers for a Pamela Anderson lookalike. Especially not Jim.'

'The issue is *this*,' Sooty said. 'When the pictures of the contestant winners arrived, I didn't show them to Jim. I kept them away from him. He didn't see them until this morning. Dumb, isn't it?'

'Depends on why you did it,' Elaine said.

'I did it because the people in two of those photographs stuck out to me like they were in 3-D. One of those people was Jon Short, the young writer from Topeka, or wherever it was.'

'And the other was Candy, right?'

'The pictures of the two of them seemed almost alive. I swear to God that when I first leafed through those snapshots, I saw Jon Short's smile grow larger.'

In spite of herself, Elaine shivered. 'Jesus,' she said. 'And Candy?'

'I heard her speak,' Sooty admitted, sadly. 'I'm as crazy as a carload of kids on crack, aren't I? I heard her speak in my mind, and she said, "I'm coming for him. I'm coming to take him away." Anyway, I just told myself it was a momentary glitch, the way you think you see a dog when it's just a bag in shadow, or a man instead of a coat hanging on the back of the bedroom door in the dark. But I kept the photos away from Jim, all the same. I guess that psychic guy got to me.'

'You've been under a lot of pressure, honey,' Elaine said.

'I'm crazy,' Sooty said. 'I must be. Anyway, this afternoon Jim saw the photos. And I tried to make light of Candy, and

Jim was fooling around and made that wisecrack about how Candy wanted his body and Gloria kinda picked it up. Then everything went weird. Gloria went to sleep and had nightmares about Candy being after her daddy. And then the calls started.'

'So, first it was a woman, right?'

'She said, "He won't come back". Of course, I knew exactly who she was talking about. Then she said stuff about "stealing our dreams and our nightmares and everything we were" then some mumbo-jumbo about her being "the three" and the thief stealing it all.'

'That doesn't sound good,' Elaine said. 'And then what happened?'

'Then the psychic guy called and said that if Jim was over on the island he was in terrible trouble and only *he* could help me save Jim.'

'And you think the pair of them are in league and trying something? Some kind of extortion?'

'I just don't know,' Sooty said. 'Rosie reckons this guy is a genuine and well-respected psychic up in Miami. Who the woman is, I don't know. If it was all a little more straightforward I'd suspect a kidnap plot. Maybe they intend to kidnap Jim, but that's unlikely. Maybe they want me and Gloria. More likely, they want to snatch Gloria on her own, which is why this guy wants me to go and meet him. Or go with him to the island or whatever he wants. To get me away from Gloria. But, like I said, it's not that simple.'

'That doesn't exactly sound what I'd call "simple" to start with,' Elaine said. 'And it sounds like there's more to come.'

'There is,' Sooty said. 'The woman caller.'

'What about her?'

'She has my voice. She sounds *exactly* like me.'

Elaine pulled a face. 'I'm having trouble taking all this in,' she said. She wished she could believe Sooty's theory that she'd cracked up, but the longer this went on, the more convinced she became that something nasty was *really* happening. And it was to do with something she'd forgotten. Something obvious. She tried to search her mind for it, but merely kept coming up with her worries that her dead boyfriend had sent a hit-man after her. *And when you think about it,* that's *crazy!* she told herself.

'You'll be having even more trouble in a moment,' Sooty replied.

'Shit, Sooty, there's *more?*'

'You know how this house has always been weird with electronic things?'

'Yep. It broke my last mobile phone,' Elaine said, skating right up to the verge of that disremembered thing that seemed so important and still not quite being able to grasp it.

'I'm not sure if it's the house or someone *in* the house,' Sooty said. 'Jim's always blamed the house, but I think it might be him at the root of all the static.'

'What about it? Where's the significance? Some people are just prone to storing up static and zapping it out again.'

'Jim's computer's been playing up,' Sooty said. Suddenly she sounded angry. 'It's like one of his bloody *stories!*' she hissed. Beside her, Gloria moaned but didn't wake up. Sooty didn't seem to notice. 'It's as if something he's written is coming home to roost,' she finished.

And Elaine's mind switched tracks. When you were in a room with a deluded person, it was easy to take their delusion on board and adopt it and share it with them, bolstering their original belief. *And you should know*, she told herself. *You shared Mark's delusion that you were a worthless two-bit bitch!* The fact of the matter here was that when you put two and two together you came up with a case of someone who was mentally a little fragile doing too much reading.

'Don't tell me,' Elaine said, smiling thinly, 'Jim's computer is typing up cryptic messages of its own accord. Am I right?'

Sooty stared at her in shock.

You had me going there for a minute or three, honey. Elaine thought. *I was suckered and I was right up there with you. Now I know you need help, but it isn't the kind of help you think you need. It's the doctor kind of help.*

And just as soon as that niggling little forgotten thing came back to her and was defused, she intended to get on the phone and get a medic out here. A doctor armed with a syringe full of deep, dreamless sleep preferably.

'How did you know?' Sooty finally asked.

She even looks *half crazy*, Elaine realized with a cold shock. *She really wants this to be happening.* 'It's from "Press: Escape", one of Jim's short stories,' she said, smiling grimly. 'It's in the *Strange Landmarks* collection. Remember?'

Sooty looked embarrassed. 'No, I've never got around to reading that one.'

'Pity. It's good,' Elaine said. 'Anyway, Jim wrote up notes on each story in the back of the book, explaining how they all came into being. He says when he first had the idea, it was of a man writing long-hand and each day, when he came back to his notepad, there was writing present that he hadn't done. Then he updated it to be someone working on a computer.'

Sooty looked as if she believed she was being told a pile of bullshit to calm her down. 'You're saying Jim *wrote* what's happening here?'

'Not just Jim,' Elaine said. 'There isn't a dark fantasy writer in the country who hasn't had a crack at a computer story. People who have computers like to write about them. Sad, but true.'

'But Jim's story . . . the words being added.' Sooty looked at her pleadingly.

'It's close, I'll admit,' Elaine said. 'And I have a very good idea why, too.'

'How could it happen?'

'Okay, listen. Say you were a bad guy or gal working on an extortion plot or a kidnapping. You're gonna snatch the daughter of someone rich, what would you do? You'd find out all you could about them, wouldn't you? And if that someone was Jim, you'd read all his stories, see all his films. Looks like your psychic chose to be a psychic because he knows Jim's on record as saying he's terrified of psychics in case they tell him something bad.'

'Jim said that?' Sooty looked surprised.

'You and Jim may not ever get around to reading all the interviews he does, but I *have* to,' Elaine said. 'It's part of my job. That one, if I recall correctly, was *FHM* in May of 'ninety-five.'

'Shit,' Sooty said thoughtfully.

'And double shit,' Elaine added. 'So we have a psychic calling you. He really wants to throw a scare into you and he's already decided to work something for the day of the contest – you said he didn't start calling till after the contest was advertised – so he gives that day as the date where the shit will happen. It's a day he can easily remember and a day he knows you'll know. But you ignore him. So, on the big day, he's drafted in an accomplice. A woman who sounds as much like you as possible. A good enough mimic to sound just like you over the phone. And he uses her to scare you shitless and then calls back and offers to help. Easy-peasy.'

'But what about the computer?' Sooty asked.

'I've already thought that out,' Elaine replied, now feeling confident. 'And it doesn't involve magic.'

'How's it done?' Sooty asked hopefully.

'Those folks are computer hackers. They've got on-line when Jim's been on-line and hacked into his computer from wherever they happened to be at the time.'

Sooty frowned. 'I don't know much about computers, but I *do* know this. They can't hack into Jim's computer and put words on the screen. No one can.'

'Why's that?'

'Because it's not connected to the telephone line. Never has been.'

'But he e-mails his drafts to New York!'

'We've never managed to get on-line. Henry Skate tried to fix it up for us but every time he plugged in a modem, it blew up. Henry's the guy who supplies our electronics stuff in a never-ending loop. It comes here working and goes back ten minutes later to be fixed. Rosie takes Jim's floppy disks home and e-mails the files to you people from her house. Her modem works. Any other bright ideas?'

Elaine sighed. 'Let's go and have a look at the computer and we'll see what I can come up with.'

Elaine spiralled for the third time as she stood in Jim's workroom gazing at the computer. This time she was forced to re-evaluate her previous notion that Sooty was over-wrought and, perhaps, having a nervous breakdown. And this time she realized that no matter how tightly she closed her eyes and wished to be back in Kansas, she was still going to open them on Oz. Sometimes things couldn't be neatly sorted into logical sequences, she finally understood. Sometimes impossible things *did* happen.

Because you're standing here looking at Jim's computer and the screen is lit and the tell-tale lights on the case are glowing and you can see it with your own two eyes . . .

She shut her eyes again and unimagined what she could see. It didn't work this time, either.

. . . that the plugs have been pulled from the sockets in the wall.

'This is *impossible*,' she heard herself say in a small, shocked voice. Her own tone frightened her even more. She was a woman in danger of stepping on to the slippery slope that Sooty had evidently slid down a little while ago. This couldn't be happening.

But it is *happening*, she thought. *You can see it.*

'There's nothing on the screen,' Sooty said, in a distant voice. She sounded hopeful.

And crazy, Elaine thought. *She sounds like a mad woman.*

But it was impossible *not* to sound like a lunatic when you were gazing on something that wasn't possible.

'You pulled the plugs out yourself?' Elaine asked, tearing her eyes away from the cables she could see lying on the floor like dead black snakes with straight brass fangs.

Sooty's eyes were fixed on the blank white screen, and fresh tears were welling up in her eyes. 'When I left nothing was still plugged in. But nothing's happened. That's good. Isn't it?'

Elaine crouched and picked up the plugs. 'It might be if it wasn't for the fact that I'm holding in my hands the only three plugs in the room that are connected to the computer and yet the screen's still lit and the machine's still running.

And I can't see a UPS that would account for the fact that the machine is still running. Does Jim have one?' She doubted it. She doubted Sooty would even know what one was.

'We *had* an uninterruptible power supply,' Sooty said quietly, 'for when the storms take out the mains, but it interrupted itself after eighteen minutes and Henry Skate took it away.'

'So what's powering it?' Elaine asked. 'No, don't answer that, I don't want to know.' *This house is haunted*, she thought and shuddered. *There's a ghost here. What other explanation is there?*

'Look,' Sooty said, sounding beaten and pointing at the empty screen.

It flickered a few times and settled into a neat grey. And three words began to scroll up the screen from the bottom, one group of three below another, then another.

WON'T COME BACK

Sooty moaned.

Elaine pushed past her to the keyboard and, as Jim's story had suggested in the *Strange Landmarks* collection, she pressed the escape key.

The words continued to scroll up until the screen was full and the top row scrolled off. On and on they marched up the screen like three-legged troopers. Elaine hit the delete key, then the shift, then the space bar, then began to press keys at random.

And suddenly the screen cleared.

Elaine grinned savagely. 'There you go!' she said triumphantly and as she turned to gauge Sooty's reaction, she saw from the corner of her eye that a new line had formed in the centre of the screen. She turned slowly back towards it, her heart hammering, her head pounding and ice in the pit of her stomach.

COMING TO TAKE IT ALL BACK

the words read. They held their position for a moment then slid to the left and off the screen as another line slid on to replace it.

234

COMING TO TAKE BACK MY LIFE AND MY DAUGHTER

The words hung there just long enough for Sooty and Elaine to read them and then, deep inside the bowels of the computer, something gave a small *pop!* and the computer shut down.

Elaine and Sooty stood side by side watching the dead machine. Elaine caught a whiff of overheated electronics, which was swiftly overcome by a waft of a heavy, gorgeous-smelling perfume that she knew was the stuff Sooty had specially made for her.

Sooty read her mind. 'I'm not wearing any perfume,' she said mechanically, her eyes still fixed on the screen. 'She has my voice and she has my perfume. And she wants my life and my daughter.'

Elaine felt as if she were about to faint. 'I don't know how this is being done, but whoever is doing it is out of their tree. And I'm talking dangerously psychotic,' she heard herself say from a distance. A part of her was spiralling downwards, deep into the ground.

Then she snapped back to herself. It felt as if an enchantment had been broken. Instead of the silence and awe, the air was filled with urgency and fear and motion, even though neither she nor Sooty had moved.

'They're coming!' Sooty said, having broken out of it, too. 'We should ring the police!'

Elaine put her arm around Sooty's shoulders, as much for her own comfort as Sooty's. She suddenly felt protective towards her friend, and very angry that some jerk or jerkess or both had the nerve to threaten her. She smiled grimly. 'And what's our story going to sound like? Nuts, that's what. A couple of crank calls and a computer that delivers threatening messages when it isn't plugged in? They may not tell you that you've been reading too many of your husband's books, but they'll certainly *think* it.'

'Then what do we do?' Sooty asked.

'There's only one thing we *can* do,' Elaine replied, wondering about that forgotten important thing again. If she could only drag it up from where it was wedged deep in the folds and crevices of her brain she would know *exactly* what to do and it wasn't going to be what she was about to propose. 'We wait here and see what develops,' she said. 'If we're lucky, probably nothing will.'

Sooty frowned. 'And if a mad man or woman, or both, show up?'

'They'll wish they hadn't,' Elaine said, hefting her handbag from Jim's desk and snapping open the catch. She put her hand in, found the cold, comforting weight of what she was looking for, hooked her forefinger through the guard and carefully lifted it free. She dangled the huge shiny revolver in front of Sooty. It hung upside down from her finger.

'This is a point three five seven Magnum. The most powerful handgun in the world,' she said, and made a quick, deft movement with her hand. The gun, as she knew it would – the damned thing acted like a trained dog in her hand, which still surprised her – spun the right way up and slapped into her palm. Her fingers automatically found their grip in the correct position for firing and to complete the fluid movement her thumb snapped back the hammer. All of this happened inside a second.

'Fuck,' Sooty said, in a small, impressed voice, as she stared at the gun.

'Fuck, indeed.' Elaine marvelled at the unwavering barrel of the gun. The .357 just sat there comfortably, feeling like an extension of her hand, ready to act at her slightest command.

Elaine had turned out to be a natural, something that had come as a total revelation for her (and for poor dead and not sorely missed Mark) the first time she'd been taken to the range. She distantly wondered if Mark had taken his other lover to the range, too, and had sown the seeds of his own demise. Guns liked her, the instructor, a big man called Danvers, had told her. And he was right. She was a dead shot.

Elaine grinned evilly. 'They call me Annie Eastwood down at the range. Or Clint Oakley. We're safe. Trust me. "God help the mister who comes between me and my sister!"' she said, waving the gun.

'Are you sure we're doing the right thing?' Sooty asked.

'Sure I'm sure,' Elaine said, confidently. But the truth of it was that she wasn't sure. All this had hit her like a whirlwind: her leaving Mark, Mark being killed, the psychic caller, the mystery woman, the computer messages. She didn't know what it all meant or where it was all leading. She wasn't at all sure that sitting tight was the right thing to do.

Because you forgot something, she reminded herself. *Something to do with that spiralling feeling. Something to do with all this. There's a right thing to do and you're not aware of it. Won't be aware of it until you remember. Until that niggling doubt is resolved.*

'We'll be fine,' she assured Sooty. 'Let's have a little drink and another cigarette and sit tight and wait.'

Chapter Fifteen

Tricks and Traps 2

The hissing, swishing noise and the trembling of the earth beneath him woke Davey Smith from a deep sleep in which he'd been having one of those dreams of clarity and understanding. The kind in which one is apt to perceive the true meaning of life.

It wasn't a pleasant awakening.

'Ohmigod!' Davey yelped in surprise and shock. 'Earthquake!'

His mind had switched from the dream to fully-awake-and-panicking with no transition at all. For a moment he couldn't understand why all he could see above him was green. Then he realized that he'd been lying down in the middle of a patch of tall ferns where, presumably, he'd fallen asleep.

Davey had been in Los Angeles in the last big quake – had landed there about three hours before it began, in fact – and he'd never forgotten that feeling of solid ground becoming flexible, almost liquid, beneath him. It had been the most terrifying experience he'd ever had. And now it was happening again.

Except it wasn't, he realized, as he sat up and peered around. The ground beneath him was shuddering, true, but this wasn't a quake – Florida simply didn't *get* earthquakes – but a reaction to something that was being done to a nearby tree.

'What the Sam Hill is *that*?' he asked himself, peering at the big tree that stood at the foot of the Straker house's backyard. Something appeared to be shaking it. Hard. The branches swished back and forth as if they were being subjected to blasts of a high wind. The leaves hissed through the air as they moved. It sure as shit wasn't a sharp wind doing it though, because this was the only tree that was being affected. And wind didn't generally make the trunk of a tree you couldn't even reach around at full stretch *vibrate*.

Davey got to his feet and remembered he'd hurt his ankle. It felt fat and painful, but only distantly. His entire attention was fixed on the shuddering tree.

I didn't rig that one, did I? he thought, wondering if the motion was being caused by one of his trip-wires. 'Nope, I sure didn't, did I, boy?' he said aloud, and automatically reached down to pat old Charlie, who should have been at his side, grinning up at him. But, of course, Charlie wasn't there because he'd gone to join Maude on the other side of the great divide.

'Shit,' Davey muttered, sighing and feeling a stab of that old loss-pain in his stomach and heart. Sometimes he wished he'd lived his entire life on his own. It would have been easier for him now. They were right when they said you didn't miss what you'd never had. He rubbed his bleary eyes and was relieved to discover that this time they'd stayed dry.

Twenty yards away from where he stood, the tree trunk stopped vibrating and the movement of the branches and leaves died down with what sounded like an amplified echo of the sigh he'd just heaved.

He tilted back his Caterpillar cap and scratched his head. 'That's fucking odd,' he said, still staring at the tree. 'I don't understand that one tiny little bit.'

Then he began to smell that heavy, pleasant perfume again. It seemed to have drifted to his nostrils from behind him. He turned and scanned the deep ferns and undergrowth but saw nothing.

I have a brain tumour, he thought. Maude would have told him you had to have a brain before you could have a brain tumour.

Something cracked, off in the undergrowth to his left, and the heavy odour of perfume increased. Davey spun round to face the direction from which the noise had come and found himself looking at a large bush with big green leaves. He was

239

half certain he'd never seen this particular bush before. The leaves looked wrong: they were shaped like sycamore leaves, but they were dark green and shiny and looked fleshy and thick.

This must be the kind of bush that the woman up in Seattle uses to make the perfume Sooty wears, he thought, inhaling the odour that drifted across to him. *It's some kind of aromatic herb or something.*

But that wasn't the point at all. The point was, he realized, that the bush hadn't been there a moment ago.

Or I just didn't notice it.

It was possible, but unlikely. He was damned certain he would have noticed a bush like this if he'd ever seen it before on this island. Most of the greenery was commonplace, but a bush with perfume, and a perfume that smelt like Sooty's wouldn't have gone unnoticed.

The leaves on the bush began to move. Slowly at first. Almost imperceptibly. And as the motion built from a gentle wave, to a fierce wiggling, the soft, loamy ground beneath Davey's feet began to shudder again. The movement built in a shuddering crescendo and then stopped.

'Christ,' Davey muttered, 'I don't much care for this.' And then he smiled. He was frightened and that was exactly how Jim wanted him to feel. Jim was still peeved about the last trip, when his old pal Davey had outdone his pissy stories with the disembowelment he'd laid on for the guests. And Jim wanted to even up the balance. And he'd gone to great lengths to achieve it. It wasn't the bush – which now looked too much like a *fake* bush to have ever fooled him – giving off that perfume at all. It was Sooty herself, who was evidently hiding nearby. And Jim was behind the bush, rattling it. It was easy when you thought about it, although Davey would have given his right arm to discover just how Jim worked that ground-shaking trick. That was a real professional job.

'Nice try, Jim!' he called in a low voice towards the bush. 'You had me going there for a moment! It is you, isn't it?'

'No, it's me,' a soft, familiar female voice said from behind him.

Davey gave a tiny gasp of shock and whirled round.

And there was Sooty, about ten feet away, standing in the deep ferns.

Davey gaped. For a moment his mind quit working.

Sooty was wearing the long dark dress he'd seen her in earlier, when she'd vanished into the bushes. It had a button-through front. Normally this wasn't the first thing Davey would have noticed, but there was no missing it here because the dress hung open, from top to bottom. And beneath it Sooty was as naked as the day she was born.

'Wha—' Davey heard himself try to say.

Sooty's dark hair was in tangled rat's tails and there were streaks of mud on her dress, face, body and hands. Her fingernails were ten crescents of filth.

She looks, he thought, *as if she's just* dug *her way here.*

But in spite of this, there was something astonishingly attractive about her. She seemed to shine, somehow, as if her life-force was too great for her surroundings, which made her appear more real than the forest. And she was radiating pure animal desire.

Davey gazed upon her lean curves, the swell of her breasts, her dark erect nipples, the little patch of clipped and downy pubic hair, shaped into a heart which pointed to the smooth lips of her sex and felt a *need* for her that was greater than anything he'd ever felt for Maude, greater than those hot, lonely nights of his teens when he'd almost burst with desire.

And this sixty-five-year-old man found that not only could he still attain an erection, but an erection so hard that you could probably bend iron bars over it. An erection that threatened to rend the denim of his pants and burst out of its own accord.

She smiled at him and the ache in his crotch was magnified. She wanted him as badly as he wanted her. She wanted him deep inside her, slamming hard into her, again and again; she wanted to swallow him up, consume him. She managed to convey all that and more with the expression he saw in those dark seductive eyes, the curve of her lips.

'Sooty?' he heard himself say in a small voice.

Sooty's smile became beatific. 'Not yet,' she said in an earthy voice, 'but soon.'

241

Davey's mind reeled. He had no idea what she meant; all he knew was that she intended to take him. And that in spite of himself he was going to let her take him without a protest, even though he knew it was wrong.

'But what are you *doing* here?' his voice asked on its own behalf, and Davey realized that he was no longer one whole person. Sooty had split him in two: she wasn't addressing the part of him that thought, she was addressing a deep, primal part of his brain; the part where instinct reigned. The logical, higher part of him was split off entirely. But it was still functioning, in spite of his body's desire to go to her and force himself into her as deeply as he could get. It was functioning and talking, just like normal.

'I've come to take you home,' Sooty said, holding him with those liquid eyes.

It's her eyes! The thought ricocheted around inside his head like a pea in a bucket. Earlier, he'd been wondering what it was about Sooty that set her apart, that made her something special. Now he knew. It was those dark, seductive eyes.

'What's happened to you?' Davey heard his rational side ask. His dick was aching for her, his heart was hammering hard with desire and this time there were no complaints being registered about how old he was getting and how his arteries might be furred up. It was a good feeling. A feeling he'd forgotten somewhere way back when.

Sooty reached out a hand towards him. 'Come with me, Davey. Come!' she said.

She didn't answer the question! This thought conveyed exactly no meaning at all for Davey. Nothing mattered. Nothing mattered except this raging inferno of desire, except losing himself in Sooty. And her eyes . . .

His eyes were blurred. Davey blinked hard and felt moisture trickle down his cheeks. They were tears of happiness, he was sure. He was crying because he'd found his home at long last; found what he'd lived his whole life for. Sooty was going to take him there.

'I'll take you there,' she promised quietly. 'I'll show you heaven.'

'What happened to you?' his voice asked again, as his eyes

242

clouded with tears. He bent his head and wiped his moist eyes with his fingers. When he moved his hands away he found he could no longer focus on them. They swam in and out, sharp then blurred. It didn't matter, he was sure. Nothing mattered now that his life-long quest was at an end.

Except that you're fooling yourself, his darling dead Maude announced in his mind, her voice so crisp and acerbic she might have been standing right next to him. *If you had a brain that worked, you'd know that. If I'd only married a man with some grey matter!*

When he looked back at Sooty, he felt giddy. She was closer now. Much closer. She'd moved soundlessly towards him while he'd wiped his eyes. He smiled up at her. She was taller now, a fractured part of his mind registered as he opened his arms to accept her.

Sooty stepped into his arms and kissed him passionately. Her mouth was moist and sweet, her tongue inquisitive. The kiss went on and on and Davey became lost in it, hopelessly entangled in Sooty, merging with her until he no longer knew where she ended and he began.

When she finally pulled away, Davey found himself crying like a baby.

'It's *wrong*,' his voice announced. It sounded confused and upset. 'It's all wrong. Everything's *wrong*!'

He wished he could find that part of his mind and strangle it to death. It was no longer needed. All he now existed for was to fuck like an animal. To lose himself for ever in a sea of boiling passion.

'Nothing is wrong,' Sooty told him, in a voice that shook with desire. 'I want you to pleasure me, Davey. I want you to take me. To have me, totally and utterly. Come with me.'

She took his hand in hers and gently led him towards the bush.

'What's happening? Where are we going?' Davey heard himself ask, but the larger part of him realized it didn't matter any more. He would go wherever she took him, do whatever she asked of him. She had him in her power.

You're thinking with that thing between your legs again, Maude's voice rasped in his mind. *I'd have thought you were past that stage of your life now.*

But Davey wasn't past that stage, judging from the solidity of his manhood and the sweetly agonizing ache for relief that burned there.

Sooty led him around the outside of the bush and into what appeared to be another world. Beyond the bush there was light and space and the air was cool and fresh. Davey found himself in a small grassy clearing through which a crystal clear stream ran, tinkling with what sounded like joyous laughter as it passed over stones and rocks.

'This isn't right,' Davey said, bemused. 'None of this was here before. I was round here setting a trap two minutes ago. It was all different then. What's happened?' His heart kicked and a brief flare of pain crossed his chest and ran down his arm.

'This is your heaven,' Sooty said, turning to face him. 'This is the place you've dreamed of since you were here before.'

'I was here just now and it wasn't like this,' Davey said.

'The last time,' Sooty said, smiling serenely. 'You don't remember yet, but you will. This is what you used to ache for. Search back for it, Davey. Think back.'

And Davey found himself remembering. Layers peeled away from his mind in their thousands until he clearly recalled this place, although he didn't know how or why. All he knew was that he'd ached for Sooty. Long ago. So long ago it wasn't even in this life, but a past existence. And *how* he'd ached for her. How deeply, how badly!

'You had to wait a long time,' Sooty said, smiling. 'It'll be worth it!'

And she shrugged off her dress and stood naked before him.

'Sooty . . .' Davey said. 'It's wrong!'

'It's *right*!' Sooty whispered. 'And it's *time*! Fuck me, Davey, like you always wanted to. Fuck me hard. Harder than you've ever fucked anyone before. Use me. Ruin me. Take me until there's nothing left but my spirit. Just like you always wanted to.'

And Davey's memory lit with a dark image of something huge and menacing crashing in circles through the trees and roaring like a thousand angry lions, while he and Jim looked

244

on, grinning like fools. *We did it!* he'd thought as the thing strained at the bonds they'd placed upon it. *We woke it up!*

The moment before Davey grasped the memory with total clarity, it was driven from his head by Sooty's fingers as they began to tear at the front of his shirt, not unbuttoning it, but ripping it apart. Davey felt the memory tear away from him as he was stripped of his shirt.

It doesn't matter, he thought crazily, as Sooty's hands began their feverish work on his belt. *That was before and this is now!*

Sooty ripped the belt out of the waistband of Davey's trousers, cracked it like a whip and dropped it. Then she undid the button and her deft fingers took the tab of his zip and began to yank it down.

In the back of his mind Maude was jabbering about not making the same mistake twice in two lifetimes, but Davey didn't know what she meant. He was lost. All that existed was him and Sooty and the soft green grass and the stream.

The zip jammed half-way down. Sooty hissed like a snake and yanked at it hard enough to make Davey stagger sideways. His foot turned and the hurt ankle complained bitterly. His brain distantly noted that if it hadn't been broken before, it certainly was now, but it didn't seem important. It didn't even hurt much.

'Oh, my, it's jammed!' he heard himself say.

What happened next was surely impossible, surely proof that he'd fallen asleep and was dreaming all this, even if it *was* the most vivid dream he'd ever had.

Sooty buried her hands in the waistband of his jeans, one hand at each of his hips, and lifted him clear of the ground. He could see the muscles bulging in her arms as he rose. And then she yanked her hands apart tearing off his jeans and his shorts in one movement. It hurt. A great deal.

Davey found himself on his back on the grass, naked, his heart kicking so hard that he was sure it would burst out of his chest. The pain was tremendous. He was pretty sure his other leg had been broken when the denim of his jeans had been pulled against it. Skin had been torn from his hips and he was bleeding from a number of other abrasions on his legs and belly and the swift removal of his shorts had given him rope-burns high on the insides of his thighs, right up close to his crotch.

But in spite of everything he still had the hard-on. If anything, his desire had increased.

Sooty reached down, took one of his hands and pulled him to his feet. Davey cried out in agony: bones were grinding together in his bad ankle and the thigh of the other leg and now there was a heavy, dull pain spread right across the left side of his chest and down his left arm.

She pulled him to her and her cool fingers closed around his hot, hard dick and nothing seemed to matter any more when she bent down and kissed him, long and deep and slowly.

She tasted of earth.

When she broke away from him, he gazed up at her through the tears in his eyes and moaned. 'You're *dead*!' he heard himself say in a tiny, lost voice.

The thing that held him in its arms, that held his aching cock and worked at it so gently, was a rotting, maggot-ridden corpse. Davey looked into her empty eye sockets. In one of them something small and white squirmed. The scent of Sooty's perfume left his nostrils and was replaced with the stench of long-dead flesh.

'Let me go,' Davey pleaded, still wanting to fuck her and wishing he could die right here and right now for even *having* that terrible thought. 'It isn't right,' he whispered, as Sooty's gentle fingers caressed his aching erection.

And Sooty let go, turning him away from her as she moved. The ground spun before his eyes.

'You don't change much,' an accented voice said. 'Still wanting to fuck my wife after all these years.'

Through the pain and the tears Davey looked up. And there was Jim standing before him, smiling sadly. Except it *wasn't* Jim, just as Sooty wasn't Sooty. Jim looked like he'd been dead and buried for a hundred years. His rotten, filthy clothes hung from him in ribbons, as did a good deal of his flesh. Jim was corrupt and damp and oozing black stuff that looked like swamp mud and stank like a gutted deer's innards. Just below his chin, his throat gaped darkly, the

246

gash running from ear to ear. He raised his head in a nod of greeting and Davey saw the ancient gash widen.

'How are you *doing* this, Jim?' he heard his voice ask, but it was just a weird autonomous reaction: he already knew this wasn't Jim and the woman behind him wasn't Sooty. He knew exactly who they were because he remembered them from *before*. The French accent had brought everything into sharp focus.

The pain in his chest increased and Davey prayed that he would die now before it was too late.

'You remember me, *mon ami*!' Straker Dauphin said, in a voice like grinding gravel, and came closer.

Davey backed away a step and felt Straker's wife's arms clamp his own arms to his sides, felt the power in her rotting body as she pulled him tightly to her. His erection was gone now, forgotten about. All he wanted to do was die and be with his darling Maude. The thought of an eternity without her was suddenly terrifying.

'So you like to frighten people, do you?' Straker Dauphin grated. 'How does Jim put it?' He frowned, and black liquid oozed from his forehead. 'You like *to throw a scare* into them? Now *you* know exactly what it means to feel fear. Don't you, Davey? Real fear is not half so pleasant as the fictional variety, wouldn't you agree?'

'Hurts,' Davey whispered. 'Let me die.'

Straker shook his head. 'No, we won't let you die. Ever.' He looked down towards his own right hand and turned back the cuff of a blue dress coat that had been splendid and expensive perhaps a hundred years ago. Davey realized that Straker still had the skin and nails on his fingers, but that his flesh ended at his wrist. He could see Straker's ulna and radius bones moving as he moved his hand.

'What do you want?' Davey asked breathlessly. He was one huge mass of pain, fear and disgust now and someone had apparently stacked concrete blocks on his chest. He hoped he would die soon and on his own terms. He wanted to see Charlie, his old muttley, again. At that moment he would have cut off his own right arm and given it to Straker just to see the dog.

'Justice,' Straker grated. 'I want what is duly mine.'

247

Davey struggled feebly against Majesty's grip. 'Nuthin' . . . I got nothing of yours,' he moaned.

Straker's eye sockets weren't empty. The whites of his eyes were the colour of old tobacco and the texture of sponge, but the irises were bright blue, the pupils pin-pricks. His eyes swam in a dark, filmy substance but they were bright and lively, quick and piercing. He looked Davey up and down and grimaced what Davey guessed was a smile.

'I woke the god that slumbers upon this forsaken land. It is a god of favour and fortune, but it is also a cruel god. Its price is pain and sacrifice. And I paid that price. I want my reward. My creativity. My fame. My wealth. My life. And the lives of my family. All these things were promised. All were stolen,' Straker said, moving closer to Davey.

'*It wasn't me!*' Davey cried desperately, but he knew this wasn't the full truth even as he spoke the words.

'Do you believe in reincarnation, Davey Smith? I do. Only sometimes a reincarnation can take place before the previous life has ceased. James Green has the body that should have been mine. And I will have it back.'

'*But it's nothing to do with me!*' Davey heard himself shriek. The pain in his legs was phenomenal now, each beat of his heart was agonizing. But he couldn't lose consciousness, couldn't die.

Straker leered at him. 'I once had a friend called Davey. He was full of tricks and traps. Davey turned bad, but once he was my friend. He was here, on this island with me, a long time ago. Davey was good with his hands. And he knew how to work magic – of a kind. He told me things, things I would never have guessed at on my own. Davey told me about the god that slept on this island. Told me that wealth and power and fame could be mine, were we to wake that god. He was the snake of temptation and I was tempted. I didn't realize then that Davey intended treachery. His intention was to sacrifice me to the god, keep the power himself and have what was mine. He wanted my wife.' Straker smiled. 'Can you imagine that? My best friend wanting my wife?'

Davey moaned.

'He helped me wake this island's sleeping god but it ran

out of control. Things didn't go according to Davey's plan and he fled, leaving me to appease that god. Do you remember doing that, Davey?'

Davey *did* remember. He remembered aching for Majesty, the power, the riches. He remembered it from deep in his soul. *But not in this life*, he pleaded. *Please, God, I've been good in this life. I've atoned! I've made up for it!*

Straker nodded. 'I swore I'd kill him if I ever saw him again. But later, during the long years while I wasn't quite dead and wasn't quite alive, I decided that killing him was too good for him. I decided I wanted to cause him ten times the pain he caused me. And that I'd do it if I ever saw him again. I'm seeing him now. Welcome back, Davey.'

'Don't do it, for Christ's sake!' Davey pleaded.

'Oh, I won't be doing it for Christ's sake. I'll be doing it for the sake of the devil you woke for me. Last time, *I* gave it what it needed to put it back to sleep and paid with more than a hundred years of pain. Pain so great you could never imagine it. I could not die and return to earth. I was locked here in this place with my wife while my daughter went free. At least I managed to save Gloria.'

'Your god,' Davey moaned. 'I remember. You called it up. You woke it. You wanted the power. You tricked me into helping you. With the blood.'

Straker grinned. His teeth waggled in their dry sockets. 'But you wanted my wife.'

'I wanted to *save* her,' Davey said. The greater the pain in his legs and chest became, the clearer the memory was. He assumed this was because he was rapidly approaching death and that the veils of previous lives were lifted upon death. 'You'd gone crazy!'

'A part of you remembered the blood,' Straker said. 'A deeply implanted memory of a previous existence. You wanted to see it happen again and you brought blood here in a sack, spilled it on the garden at the back of the house, in exactly the same place as you spilled blood the last time. It's *your* sin. You woke the god both times.'

The blood-bags? Davey thought, his heart sinking. He'd fallen and hurt his leg and burst his last bag – the spare – in the backyard of the house. And he remembered doing it

249

before, too. Emptying blood from a barrel into a hole Straker had dug in the yard.

'And now you've woken it a second time with your tricks. And this time *you*'re going to give it what it needs. You and your friends. What it needs is pain and blood. And death. So I'm not going to kill you. I'm merely going to settle my old score. Your body will die, but the god will have your soul. For all eternity.'

Davey could no longer speak. His chest was a band of iron and his eardrums felt as if they were about to explode. *Let me die. Just let me die now and quickly*, he thought.

'Do you have any idea, dear Davey, of how much we suffered? No, you don't. Like the coward you are, you ran away and never came back when you saw the immensity of the thing I had woken. I tapped the power of the god, Davey, and it cost me dearly. It takes a long time to wake fully. I underestimated its full strength. It's not merely a minor god, a god of a small island. It is tremendous and ferocious and it ran out of control before it was even half awake.

'And I was forced to appease it, to put it back to sleep with a blood sacrifice, while I used the power I siphoned off from it to get innocent little Gloria away and hide and protect *us*, here on the island. It worked, after a fashion. It wasn't perfect. The power of the god reached us, but in a minor way. Its emanations, even while it slept, kept us trapped for longer than I'd anticipated. And meanwhile two new spirits took our place in the scheme of things. James Green and Reina Green.

'They came here and worked sex-magic, which enabled them to siphon off power and us to siphon off their power. And on their last trip here, they reached such heights of ecstasy that we were able to gain almost enough energy to break free. They fucked in the sea, on a fault in the rock mass that lies beneath. The fault that was caused the last time the god began to wake; the crack its power made in the bedrock. After that we were able to extend our minds beyond our prison. And today two others fucked in exactly the same spot and gave us what we needed to break free.'

'I don't care,' Davey moaned. 'Just kill me and get it over with. I *hurt*.'

'You will die, but remain alive and naked and unprotected from its wrath,' Straker said. 'And that will be a price a thousand times greater than the one we paid.'

Davey closed his eyes and willed himself to die. He was close now, he knew that. He was going to pay for his previous sins in agony – was paying for them right now, in fact – and that was all. No one and nothing could keep his spirit trapped, he was certain. He'd made no deal with anyone for his soul and no one could take it.

He was close to Maude now, he could *feel* that. To Maude and Charlie and all the other dogs he'd loved and lost. And to peace. Eternal peace. It was merely a matter of passing through the membrane that kept this life apart from the other life, the *real* life. The place where *everyone* went whether they were good, bad or indifferent while they were on this hard planet. *Home.*

If you can hear me, Maude, he thought, through the blanket of pain, *get the coffee on. I'll be there right away.*

As he opened his eyes again, Straker Dauphin, a walking impossibility from another time, another life, reached out his right arm and placed his fingers against Davey's forehead. Davey barely felt the pressure of the man's fingers at first. It was nothing more than four cold points on the left side of his temple and one in the hollow on the right side.

Go ahead, he thought. *Do your worst!*

And the pressure of Straker's grip increased.

Davey didn't see the nails fall from the dead man's fingers as he squeezed, he didn't see rotting flesh slide back so that only bone pressed at him, but he felt the nails pop off, one by one, felt flesh become naked bone.

And the pain became agonizing. Davey felt warm blood begin to flow as the sharp fingers pierced his skin and his skull crackled and complained under the enormous pressure. His heart seemed to have seized solid in his chest now and his breath was locked in his lungs. A rebellious part of him refused to let the dead man have the satisfaction of hearing him scream.

And Davey kept this last promise to himself as he felt first one finger, then the next break right through his skull. But when the thumb burst through into his brain and Straker yanked downwards, tearing off the flesh and bone that composed his face and the front of his head, he died with a long, blood-curdling scream.

His last thought was that the noise he was making must have been loud enough to have been heard back on the mainland.

Chapter Sixteen

Searching for Spreadbury

1

Deep inside Sooty something snapped. 'Damn that man,' she muttered, glowering at nothing. She was tense and frightened and now had the distinct feeling that Elaine's plan of sitting here and waiting to see what happened was fatally flawed. *We should be* doing *something*! she thought, tearing the filter from another Virginia Slim and dropping it in the ashtray. *Jim's in trouble and we're sitting here waiting for a kidnap attempt that isn't coming. We should be . . .*

'What man?' Elaine said, looking up as if she'd just woken.

Sooty looked at her and felt a wave of compassion. Elaine had been in a world of her own, probably thinking about Mark and her life up till now and wondering what the hell she was going to do next.

'That damned Aaron Spreadbury,' Sooty said. 'If only he hadn't called, everything . . .' She stopped in mid-sentence. At the mention of the so-called psychic's name Elaine had shot to her feet as if someone had zapped her up the backside with a cattle prod.

Her ashtray and glass of whisky fell to the floor, the glass bouncing, the ashtray shattering. Elaine didn't seem to notice. Her face was distraught, her body seemed to want to run in several different directions at once. She began to hammer her forehead with the heel of her hand. 'Oh, shit shit *shit*!' she wailed. 'I'm *so* stupid! I should have known! I should have *realized*!'

'What?' Sooty asked, trying not to let her panic grow any more than it had so far. 'What's wrong? Elaine! What *is* it?'

'Oh, I'm so sorry!' Elaine moaned. 'I was all caught up in some dumb fantasy that Mark had sent a hit-man after me.

So caught up that I didn't realize. I couldn't put two and two together and make four. I *knew* I'd forgotten something of the utmost importance and it was bothering the hell out of me, but I didn't know what it was until now. We have to *do* something. Where's my damned jacket? My jacket, where did I put it? Quick!'

'Slow down!' Sooty said. 'Take it easy! What did you remember?'

'Spreadbury!' Elaine said, looking as if she might burst if she didn't act soon. 'He *called* me. I was in the hotel lobby and I was thinking – you'll think I'm crazy, but I know . . . *knew* . . . Mark pretty well. What he was capable of. And I thought he was sending someone to kill me for dumping him. He said he would.'

'Oh, God, Elaine, no! No wonder you look so stressed.'

'I was a fool for believing him, I guess,' Elaine said. 'But that's neither here nor there. I was in the lobby and I was *sure* something bad was about to happen. The spirals? Yeah, you got it! And my cellular rang and I thought it was the hit-man out in the street making a positive ID on me. That he'd shoot the woman who answered the phone. And I lifted it and a voice said, "It's okay. Everything's okay. You're safe. No one's going to hurt you," and I just *knew* this man was trouble. I rang off. Turned off the phone in my pocket when it rang again. And when I decided to call Mark's office and turned it back on again, there was a message on my answering service. I think you should hear it. Now.' She half ran from the room.

Half a minute later she came back, ashen-faced, and carrying her cellular phone. Sooty watched her hands shake as she turned it on and entered her PIN number. She pushed a few buttons then handed the phone to Sooty.

Frowning, Sooty held the mobile up to her ear. 'This is your personal recall service,' a bland female voice announced. 'You have . . . one . . . message.'

'Listen up!' Elaine urged.

The phone clicked and Spreadbury's supercilious voice filled Sooty's ear once again. 'I know you've turned off the phone because I frightened you on my first call and I know why you're frightened,' Spreadbury said. 'But you have no need to be scared of me. I'm on your side. My name is Aaron and I badly need to get in contact with James Green. I called his publishing house in New York and they gave me your number. I understand Mr Green is going on a trip this evening and is out of contact because of this. I'm told you may be able to get in touch with him. I know this is going to sound very odd, but I need to speak to him because it's possible something very bad is going to happen tonight. I have information which I need to pass on. Please call me back on the following number . . .'

'Is that him? That's Spreadbury?' Elaine said, already nodding on Sooty's behalf. 'Tell me the number. Let me write it down.'

Sooty told her the number Spreadbury had left then handed back the phone.

'We have to call him,' Elaine said. 'That's what I forgot. God help me.'

'What difference will it make?' Sooty asked, already feeling that calling the man was the right thing to do. If nothing else, it was action of some kind. Anything was better than sitting here.

'Jim's in trouble,' Elaine said.

Sooty frowned. 'You don't think it's a kidnap attempt any more?'

'Nope,' Elaine said. 'Not on you or Gloria, anyway. I've had this horrible feeling since I spiralled and now I think I know why.'

'Why?' Sooty asked.

Elaine shook her head. 'I can't tell you right now. But I do think we should call Spreadbury.' She took the piece of paper from Sooty and dialled the number on it on her cellphone. 'It's ringing,' she said. Then she swore. 'It's an answering service! Hello? This is Elaine Palmer of Collis and Anstey. You called me earlier. Please call again.' She turned the phone off. 'Fuck it, he's not there,' she said. 'What are we going to do? We have to get hold of him!'

'Why?' Sooty asked, wondering what had come over her friend to make her so frenetic. It wasn't like Elaine at all. And yet Sooty felt the same urgency.

'Because you and Jim are the best people I know and I

won't let anyone or any*thing* harm you or him or Gloria while I can still stand. No matter how much it costs!' Elaine snarled. 'And that's final!'

'But why Spreadbury?' Sooty insisted. 'After all, we suspect him of being behind this, don't we?'

Elaine's eyes blazed. 'You're darn fuckin' tootin' we do,' she said. 'And now I think it's time we started fighting back. We should have done something an hour ago. I bet we could have got him on the phone if I hadn't forgotten. It's like . . .'

'Like something stopped you remembering he'd called?' Sooty asked.

Elaine looked astonished.

'You're not the only person who has the feeling we've been delayed on purpose. I've been thinking that there's a good deal more to this than meets the eye. And I'll tell you something else. I mean to put a stop to whatever it is. I've had too much of being scared and worried just recently and back there a few minutes ago I had the distinct impression that someone I cared about – not Jim, but someone – was about to get badly hurt. And I became even more scared. And then I snapped. I don't know what it was. Something snapped inside me. And I wanted to move, to do something. Anything. Like get hold of our friend Spreadbury by the throat, for instance. You know what else?'

'What?' Elaine said.

'I think we'd better go back into Rosie's office and check the answering-machine tape. The last time I was in Jim's workroom another call came in and it switched over to the machine. I'd imagine it was Spreadbury or one of his merry men or women.' She turned to Gloria who was still asleep on the couch beside her. 'Won't be ,long, honey,' she whispered.

In Rosie's office the answering-machine registered that there was one outstanding message. Sooty rewound the tape and hit the play button.

'I'm sure you're still there, Mrs Green,' Spreadbury's voice said. 'And it's getting very urgent now. That terrible storm I told you about is brewing. We need to move. I'll be on the docking in Seaford in ten minutes or so. If you want to help save your husband, you'll find me there. I can't do it

256

without you, so I'll wait and hope that you decide to come. My boat is called *Majesty*. Please come.'

'What do you make of *that*?' Elaine said.

'He sounds sincere,' Sooty observed.

'They all do,' Elaine said. 'Mark did when he told me he was hiring someone to kill me. Let's go get him!'

'What about Gloria?' Sooty asked. 'We can't leave her!'

'Shit!' Elaine said. 'I clean forgot about poor Gloria.'

Which was when Gloria screamed.

2

Gloria was on her feet in the centre of the lounge, her arms spread as if she were ready to catch a ball. Her body was rigid and trembling, her mouth twisted into a frozen grimace and her eyes were wide open, but Gloria wasn't behind them.

'Nnnnnnn,' she said, from deep in her throat as Sooty and Elaine rushed into the room.

Sooty ran to her, took her in her arms. The child was rigid and unyielding. She took a step back, shocked. Elaine grabbed her arm. 'What's wrong?' she asked. 'Is she having a fit or something?'

'She isn't awake,' Sooty said. 'She's sleepwalking or something.'

'Don't!' Gloria said. 'Mommy, don't!'

'I'm not doing anything, honey!' Sooty protested.

Gloria gave a little yelp and flinched. 'Please don't help him any more, Mommy,' she said. 'Uncle Davey! Uncle Davey! Run!'

'Davey?' Elaine said, puzzled. '*The* Davey? Davey Smith?'

'Ohhhh,' Gloria moaned. 'Mommy's going to kill Uncle Davey. Please, Mommy. Please don't do it again. Don't hurt any more people, Mommy!' Tears began to roll down her cheeks, but her breathing remained deep and even, as if she were still sleeping peacefully.

'I'm scared,' Elaine said, from behind Sooty.

'Me too,' Sooty said. 'It's like she's – shit, I don't know, like she's having a—'

'Nightmare?' Elaine asked hopefully.

'You know what I mean,' Sooty said.

'A vision,' Elaine said. 'Yep, I know what you mean. And I wish I didn't.'

'Mommy, *no!*' Gloria squealed. '*Pleeeeeeease!*'

'Davey's on the island,' Sooty said.

'And you're killing him,' Elaine said.

Sooty shook her head. 'No, I'm not killing him. I'm not the mommy she's talking about.'

'What do you mean?' Elaine asked now, sounding close to hysteria as Sooty grew more calm. 'You're her *mother*. Her *biological* mother.'

Sooty looked at Elaine and said, 'This time around I am.'

'Oh, my God!' Elaine said. 'You can't be *serious*?'

Gloria gasped and went limp. Sooty caught her before she fell and guided her back to the sofa, where she laid her down. She gently touched Gloria's face. 'Honey?' she whispered. 'Honey? Can you hear me?' There was no response. She gently prodded her daughter's ribs, then shook her a little. 'She isn't going to wake up,' she said.

She looked up at Elaine. 'Have you ever had the feeling that you got something you didn't deserve?' she asked.

Elaine gave a bitter smile. 'Only Mark,' she replied.

'I mean something good,' Sooty said. 'Something good that happened to you, that you didn't really deserve to have and you were frightened that whoever or whatever it is that hands out the luck would realize they'd made a mistake and take it back again? I've had that feeling for a long time,' Sooty said, gently smoothing back Gloria's hair. 'I've been too lucky in my life and I think someone will take it all away. Jim. Gloria. The island. This house.'

'I guess everyone fate chooses to smile on has those feelings now and again,' Elaine agreed. 'Like sooner or later they'll be found out.'

'Jim and I have this little theory. I've never told anyone before. We think we're "Old Souls". That we've met before. In previous lives, maybe. Previous existences. We think our paths are intertwined. That we've known one another down through the ages. That our souls knew and loved one another back before there were any human beings.'

Elaine smiled. 'That's sweet,' she said. 'So you like the idea of reincarnation, right?'

Sooty nodded.

'And it follows that Gloria's soul may well have once been born to a woman who wasn't, or isn't, you?'

'Yes,' Sooty said. 'It's like she chose to join us this time. And it's a wonderful thing. We feel kind of honoured to have her.'

'And scared of losing her?'

'Of course.'

'And all this ties in with your feeling that you've had undue good luck?'

'It sometimes feels like there's been a celestial mistake,' Sooty said. 'Like Jim and I are going to have to give it all back. I have a feeling that the time to pay up has come.'

'Not if I have anything to do with it,' Elaine said. 'You got what you deserve and I'm gonna see that you get to keep it.'

Sooty smiled. 'Thanks,' she said.

'*Noooooooooooo!*' Gloria screamed.

Sooty held her. 'It's okay honey,' she said. 'I'm here. I'm here!'

3

'It's something else sent to hold us up,' Sooty said. 'I'm certain of it. We're frightened to leave her and we can't take her with us so we just don't go.'

Over the past fifteen minutes, she'd tried to rouse Gloria, but the child seemed unconscious, or in a trance, or, perhaps, in shock, and wouldn't wake up. Her temperature was normal, her breathing was regular and she looked as if she were just sleeping peacefully now. She hadn't made a sound since screaming, 'No!'

'So, what do we do?' Elaine asked.

'We leave her,' Sooty said. 'I'm gonna call in a favour from Hettie Baker, Rosie's cousin. She owes me one. She can baby-sit while we're away. She's okay.'

'And what if our original suspicions were right? That this guy Spreadbury and his cohorts intend to kidnap Gloria? What if they see us go out and come in here?'

259

'I don't think there's a kidnap plot, not now,' Sooty said. 'But if anyone comes in here, they aren't going to find anything. Here's what we do. Jim has an old-style Chrysler Le Baron out in the garage. Neither of us ever drives it, but it's in perfect working order. It's the car Jim drove before he had any money and it holds special memories for us both, so he's kept it. It was a wreck when he first bought it, but it's in better condition now. So, we put Gloria in the Le Baron, out of sight. No one who isn't local knows about that car. You drive away and deliver Gloria to Hettie. I'll follow you out in the Merc so if anyone's waiting they'll follow me. I'll drive down to the dock and park in the lot behind the bar. When you've made sure Gloria's okay, you join me there and we'll go see Mr Spreadbury and see what he has to say. Okay?'

'If you're sure,' Elaine said.

'I'm sure,' Sooty said, relieved to be able to move at last. She strode to the phone, lifted the handset and punched in Hettie Baker's number.

4

Elaine didn't know how the hell it had happened, but whoever was in the lounge of the huge power-cruiser *Majesty*, which was moored on its own, right on the very end of the dock, knew she was out there. Either they had binoculars or second sight.

Maybe the boat moved when I crept up the walkway, she told herself, but the boat was bobbing and rolling gently under her anyway. And she hadn't made a sound as she'd come aboard. She'd left Sooty a way behind her, concealed behind a row of oil-drums. Sooty had the Colt .45, but Elaine doubted she'd manage to get off a shot without the gun's recoil whipping it from her hand. Sooty was barely used to shooting small-bore weapons. But the threat of the gun might be enough if anyone went after her. Elaine didn't think anyone *would* go after her, though. Whoever was the source of all her problems was on this boat, waiting.

And they know I'm here, Elaine thought, now so tense she could barely move another step closer to the steps that led down to the cabin. It wasn't much like being a heroine in a Jean Claude Van Damme movie, that was for sure. The heroines in action-adventure pictures seldom wanted to upchuck or run away whinnying. They just breezed right in, full of confidence and witty one-liners. Elaine doubted she could even cough out a single word right now, if it was anything more complicated than '*Eek!*'

Out in front of her, her hand remained rock steady; the barrel of the Magnum didn't even waver. While this didn't do much to boost her confidence, Elaine was certain that if it came to gunplay this woman was going to come off best. If someone so much as batted an eyelash at her when she went in, that person was going to lose a leg.

She crept down the stairway and stood before the brown varnished doorway, looking at its brass handle and listening. Inside the room – which she was pretty sure would turn out to be a large living area – someone turned down the sound on the television. She had no idea what channel they were watching, but judging from the noisy audience, the show had sounded pretty much like *Jenny Jones*. Elaine wasn't sure what that said about the tastes of the room's occupants.

She waited, taking deep breaths and trying to think up an opening line. Her mind was a desert. The only thing she could come up with was the line that Honey Bunny had yelled during the opening scene of *Pulp Fiction*: 'Any one of you fuckin' pricks move and I'll execute every motherfuckin' last one of you!'

Inside the room the sound of the television came back up again. Elaine guessed that she must have made a noise. They'd turned down the sound to listen, heard nothing, then turned it back up again.

Good, Elaine thought. *Very good.*

She moved back, took a deep breath, thanked the gods that she'd put on a pair of sensible shoes this morning, lifted her right leg and, in a perfect karate move, kicked the door in and shouted her opening line.

'*Any one of you fu*—' was all she had time to yell before the door hit the wall behind it with a great deal of force and a loud crash, bounced back and closed in her face.

The door was open exactly enough time for her mind to take a snapshot of what lay beyond. A surprising snapshot.

Part of her had expected a gathering of tough-looking swarthy guys, dressed in black fatigues, a couple sprawled on easy chairs watching the television and maybe another four at a card table, smoking and playing poker. Somewhere off to one side Mr Big would be sitting: a fat, balding, perspiring man dressed in a stained white suit and mopping his brow with a polka-dot handkerchief.

What her mind told her she'd seen was entirely different. The lounge was plush, carpeted and had oil paintings on the walls. The only person inside was a portly, bespectacled, innocuous-looking man in his fifties. He was balding and dressed in shirt sleeves and slacks and he sat in a comfy chair in front of a small television. He was holding a glass of what looked like Pepsi in one hand and a gone-out pipe in the other. There had been a bemused expression on his face as he looked up at her.

Elaine kicked the door open again and strode through into the lounge, her Magnum held out in front of her. When she'd cleared the door, she assumed the shooter's position: legs spread, gun held in both hands.

'Okay, Buster, *freeze!*' she snapped. 'One move and your brains take the easy way home – through the fucking great hole you're gonna have in the back of your head!'

The portly man stayed exactly where he was. The only movement he made was with his eyebrows, which arched questioningly.

Elaine moved carefully into the room, checking out the corners and places where someone else might be hiding. She already knew this man was alone. Already knew who he was. But it paid to take care. She came to a standstill in front of him, holding the gun about an inch away from his nose. She was pleased to note that the barrel was still rock steady.

'Where is she?' Elaine demanded.

'I assume you mean Mrs Green,' Spreadbury said, his voice proving she'd got the right man. 'I don't know where she is. She certainly isn't here. Are you a policewoman?'

'Nope, I'm not a policewoman, I'm a homicidal maniac. So don't fuck me around. Just tell me where your partner is,' Elaine said, letting the tip of the gun's barrel come into contact with the tip of Spreadbury's nose.

Spreadbury didn't tense. 'If when you say my partner you mean my wife,' he said mildly, 'she crossed over six months ago.'

Elaine pushed the barrel a little harder against the man's nose: it flattened a little and now Spreadbury moved his head back. Elaine followed his movement, keeping the gun where it was until Spreadbury's head was trapped against the back of his chair.

'I'm sorry to hear that,' Elaine growled. 'It must be tough for you. But I don't mean your wife. I mean the woman you set up this scam with.'

Spreadbury was either an excellent actor or genuinely surprised. 'Scam?' he asked. 'What scam?'

'Don't fuck me around, I'm an angry woman. And, as I'm sure you know, hell hath no fury like a scorned woman.'

'I'm not sure what you mean,' Spreadbury said.

'You'd better be,' Elaine replied. 'Because there are two people here and one of them is a psycho with a gun who is pissed off on two counts. Count one: her ex-lover threatened to send a hit-man after her, hence the bad attitude and weaponry. Count two, which is more pertinent here, is that you and your ladyfriend have been working a scam on a pair of very good friends of mine. Any idea who they might be?'

'I've no idea,' Spreadbury said, now looking concerned. 'Are you sure you have the right person?'

'You're Aaron Spreadbury, famed psychic, are you?'

Spreadbury nodded. 'But I've never worked a ... *scam*,' he said the word as if the taste of it disgusted him, 'in my entire life. I am a genuine psychic.'

Elaine spat out a gobbet of disdainful laughter. 'Some psychic. You didn't even know I was coming. But that's neither here nor there. I want to know where the woman is. The woman who accused my friend and her husband of being thieves. Her calls alternate with yours.'

A look of relief passed over Spreadbury's face. 'Ahh, of course!' he said. 'Your friends must be Mr and Mrs Green.' He reached up slowly and pushed the barrel of the gun from his nose. 'The woman is not an accomplice of mine –

263

although I know which woman you mean. And I am trying to work no scam. I am trying to save the lives of both Mr and Mrs Green. I imagine you came with Mrs Green, so now might be an opportune moment to invite her in.'

'Not till I've searched the boat,' Elaine said, 'and I'm sure there's no one else here.'

'No one but me is here. If you wish, I'd be glad to show you around. But time is short. I would suggest you take my word that we're alone. I badly need to see Mrs Green.'

'Tell me about the kidnap plot,' Elaine said.

Again Spreadbury looked surprised. 'Kidnap?' he said.

'Forget it,' Elaine said. 'Show me round the boat and, if it's safe, I'll get Sooty.'

5

Sooty crouched behind the row of oil-drums for what seemed like an interminably long time. Her legs began to ache after five minutes, her back after ten. And all she heard was silence. She didn't know if this was good or bad. The plan was that she stay here for ten minutes and that Elaine would call her when it was safe to go aboard the boat. If she heard any odd noises – from gunshots to a struggle – she was to flee and fetch the police. If she'd heard nothing after ten minutes she should do likewise. Under no circumstances, Elaine had warned her, was she to go aboard the boat without Elaine's personal say-so.

And I've been here ten minutes at least, Sooty thought, glancing at her wrist again and cursing herself for not having worn her watch. She'd counted off sixties for a few minutes, but when you were scared half to death – so scared your teeth chattered and you wanted to throw up – you had a job remembering whether you'd counted four minutes or five and you were apt to count some minutes twice.

Whatever it was, it seemed like a long time.

And during that long, lonely time, while she'd crouched and clutched the oily-smelling gun to her, she'd realized several things. The first was that there was no kidnap plot. Gloria was safe and Spreadbury was telling the truth. She

264

intuited this and, for the first time in months, she had begun to trust her intuition.

The second thing was that she really *did* feel like a thief, as if she'd stolen everything she had. The third was that she expected to die tonight – as, apparently, Elaine also did, judging from some of the things she'd said earlier. The fourth and final thing was that even if the woman who spoke in her voice turned out to be telling the truth and she and Jim *were* thieves, even if only psychically and unwittingly, this was one woman who was going to fight tooth and nail to keep her ill-gotten gains.

And if Elaine doesn't come out of that boat and yell at me in the next twenty seconds, I'm going to get up and stride over there and cause some mayhem of my own, she thought angrily. *And I'm counting now. One. Two. Three.*

She'd got to eighteen when someone nearby did an ear-shattering wolf-whistle.

'You can come over now,' Elaine called from the distance. 'It's safe.'

Sooty waited for the code words. And waited.

'Press Escape!' Elaine called finally. 'Sorry. I forgot!'

6

Two minutes later she followed Elaine and Spreadbury (who looked exactly as she'd imagined he would, but who sounded a good deal less condescending in the flesh) into the lounge of *Majesty*.

Elaine had said it was safe, but she still had her gun trained on Spreadbury. Sooty kept hers held loosely in her hand, her finger outside the trigger guard. She still wasn't sure she would be able to hit anything that wasn't less than six feet away from her and she was also worried that she might shoot by mistake and perhaps kill herself or Elaine. The Colt didn't have a hair-trigger, but it didn't take much to fire it.

Elaine and Sooty sat down on a sofa and Spreadbury, looking agitated and pale, turned his easy chair to face them.

He's frightened, Sooty realized, a feeling of dread

gathering in her own stomach. *But not of us. He's frightened about what's going to happen.*

Without lowering the gun, Elaine got out her Camels, lit one and passed the pack to Sooty, who lit up too. Inwardly she felt as if she were made of jelly.

'Okay, Buster,' Elaine said, around her cigarette, 'tell us your story. And it'd better be good.'

Spreadbury raised his hands. '*Please*,' he said. 'We don't have *time*! If we're to avert disaster we must leave *now* to get to the island in time!' He sighed. 'I know you're worried and I know you don't understand and I haven't helped much so far, but I can explain on the way. It's vital that we leave now.'

'No one goes anywhere until we know what's going on,' Elaine said calmly.

'You're sceptics,' Spreadbury said. 'I could explain all I know over and over again and you'd still pick holes in my story. We could stay here for ever, arguing about it.'

Elaine waved the gun at him. 'Just spill, or I'll blow your head off your shoulders,' she said.

Spreadbury sighed.

'Mr Spreadbury. Aaron,' Sooty said. 'I know it's urgent, but we can't let you take us anywhere until you've told us at least a little of what your concerns are. Look at it from our point of view. We have no idea where you might take us or what you might do. We really don't know what you have in mind. All we know is that you've warned me about something that you think may happen on Straker's Island tonight. We need more. That's a reasonable request.'

'Your husband is on Straker's Island right now and he's in terrible trouble,' Spreadbury said. 'We may be able to help him. I told you this earlier.'

'You *think* he may be in terrible trouble,' Sooty said, already acutely aware of her own urge to move. The man was genuine and he was right. She couldn't believe she'd doubted him.

'I *know*,' Spreadbury replied.

'Because you're psychic,' Elaine sneered.

'I am. And I hear a voice. A voice I trust. A voice that has never been known to be wrong.'

266

'And whose voice might this be?' Elaine asked. 'A native American tribal shaman? A chief?' she added sarcastically. 'I've heard all this claptrap before. Jim writes better stuff in his books.'

'It's a voice that sounds exactly like my own voice sounds,' Spreadbury said angrily. 'I believe it's the voice of my higher consciousness. But that's not what's important right now. We can argue about it later if you wish. Either we go and try to help or we leave Jim to his fate. And I, for one, don't want to do that. It will lead to devastation on a terrible scale. There is a massive force at work on the island – something with power akin to that of a god. It may *be* a god. And your husband's presence is going to set it free if we don't act. It may be too late already, but it may not. We need to *move* and move now!'

Sooty looked at Elaine, who glanced back and gave a little shake of her head.

Elaine turned back to Spreadbury and sniffed. 'It's a complete load of hogwash, of course,' she said. She held Spreadbury's plaintive gaze and said, 'C'mon, Sooty, let's go. I've never heard such a lot of sour crap.'

'Please don't go!' Spreadbury said.

'Look, big guy, if you're so concerned, go ahead and see what you can do. We're not going, but nothing's stopping *you* from making the trip,' Elaine said.

'I can't go alone,' Spreadbury said. 'Well, I *could* go alone, but I'd be wasting my time. There's nothing I can do without having Mrs Green there too.'

'How do you know?' Sooty asked. 'The voices?'

Spreadbury nodded. 'I can't supply proof,' he said. 'I need your faith in me.'

'Did you really dial my phone number at random, knowing you'd get through to me?' Sooty asked.

'I don't expect you to believe me, but yes, I did,' he replied.

'Hogwash,' Elaine said, but she didn't sound quite as angry now to Sooty. There was interest in her voice.

Sooty took a thoughtful pull on her cigarette. 'These voices you hear . . .'

'Voice,' Spreadbury cut in. 'There's only one. It's been

267

with me since childhood. I'm not schizoid. I'm genuinely psychic.'

'They ... *it* definitely told you *specifically* that Jim and I were in danger. It's not something that's open to interpretation, like the predictions of Nostradamus?'

'No. The voice was quite specific. None of what I have told you is lie or construction. And now I can *feel* the power of the force on the island, even without the voice telling me it's there. And I know that you can, too, Mrs Green. Even if you're not feeling it as clearly as I am. You know. You know it's there, stretching its bonds.'

'Did the voice mention anyone else?' Sooty asked. 'Like the fans, for instance?'

'Fans?'

'Jim's readers. Half a dozen of them are over there with him right now.'

'Oh, my God!' Spreadbury said paling visibly. 'That must have been occluded.'

'I take it this is bad news?' Elaine said. 'Just tell us what you want from us, will you?'

'I want your help. Nothing more,' Spreadbury said. 'But there's something more I should tell you. The island is populated by two rogue disincarnated spirits. The ghosts of a man and a woman. Straker and Majesty Dauphin. It is my belief that these entities intend to take over the bodies of you and your husband. This is the main danger to you and James.'

'Oh, *come on*!' Elaine said. 'You're *kidding*. That crap wouldn't fool a nine-year-old!'

Spreadbury suddenly frowned and cocked his head as if listening. His eyes focused on a point above and beyond him.

Elaine glanced at Sooty and rolled her eyes.

Spreadbury said, 'I am told that Mrs Green has witnessed manifestations of the female spirit. Writings on a window? *Moving* words? How can words move?'

'Computer screen,' Sooty said, fighting off the huge shiver that ran up her back.

'And a voice,' Spreadbury said, still with his head cocked

to one side. 'A voice she heard. A familiar voice. Does that mean anything?'

'The phone,' Sooty said.

'It's fixed,' Elaine said. 'He knows because he fixed it.'

'Wait,' Sooty said to her. She turned to Spreadbury. 'Let me get this straight. There's a god on the island, but it's not the god that wants to kill us – although it will if it has a chance. It's Straker Dauphin and his wife. Right? Or their ghosts, anyway. Or whatever they're supposed to be.'

'I don't know what form any of the spirits take,' Spreadbury said. 'That is also occluded. Otherwise, yes, you're right.'

Elaine gestured with her gun. 'Okay, you're the bright spark with the link to beyond so answer me this: what's made it happen? Jim and Sooty have been on the island many times before. Why now?'

Spreadbury looked beaten. 'I don't know.' He sighed. 'I only know what the voice tells me.'

'Some voice.' Elaine snorted. 'Trade it in for a new one.'

'What I *do* know is that it's started and time is running out,' Spreadbury said, his desperation plain. 'We need to act now!'

'And what are we supposed to do when we get there?' asked Elaine. 'How do you fend off two ghosts and a god? Say your prayers?' She made a show of slapping her pockets. 'Oh dear, I seem to be fresh out of holy water.'

'We can, perhaps, get Jim and the others off the island before it's too late,' Spreadbury said.

Sooty turned to Elaine. She was convinced that Spreadbury was right now. He hadn't claimed to know all the answers and he seemed desperate to do something. Sooty had always thought herself a pretty good judge of character and Spreadbury came across like a man who was aching to try to fix something he thought he could handle; something in which he specialized. Of course, there was a chance that he was fooling her because he was fooling himself, but she no longer suspected he was working a confidence trick.

Which is what he wants you to think, her rational mind protested. But Sooty's intuitive part was now in the ascendancy. It felt *right*.

269

'I want to go,' Sooty said to Elaine.

Elaine scowled. 'Bad idea, Sooty. It's *got* to be some kind of a con. If there *was* any trouble, well, Jim's got the boat. They could leave. But there *isn't* any trouble. Which is why they're not back here already.'

'What if it's the kind of trouble that prevents them leaving?' Spreadbury asked.

Both women ignored him.

Sooty said to Elaine, 'I believe him. Up to a point at least. There's something I haven't told you. Something that happened to me earlier. I know it's going to sound stupid when I tell you and I know you're going to blame it on something else, just like I did, but listen till I'm finished, okay?'

Elaine was silent. Spreadbury watched, frowning and anxious.

'Something got hold of me,' Sooty said. 'I was in the closet and I fell over an old electronic keyboard that Jim's had in there for ever. I picked it up, took it into the bedroom, plugged it in, and guess what . . .'

'You played it?' Elaine said.

'Yes – but I *can't* play. I've never been *able* to play. And yet I played a piece by Mozart. I even knew what it was called, although I've forgotten again. And while I was playing I had a sense that I was someone else. Someone who knew that piece inside out. Worse, I felt that there were a couple of keys that should have been slightly out of tune. On the piano I knew so well. I made it stop, but it could have gone on, I think. Like I say, something got hold of me.'

'They're almost free,' Spreadbury said.

'Shut up, you!' Elaine commanded. To Sooty she said, 'You're not kidding? You're sure?'

Sooty nodded.

Elaine sighed. 'This is all too weird for me.'

'It doesn't matter either way,' Sooty said. 'If there *isn't* any psychic-type trouble going on over on the island, it'll be safe to go. I'm not entirely comfortable with this possession business – it could have been any one of a number of mental glitches that caused it. But I'd rather go, just to be sure. And Aaron can't exactly kidnap us while you're pointing that gun at him, can he?'

270

'Unless he has accomplices. On the island or waiting at sea.'

'I don't,' Spreadbury said. 'I came alone because . . .'

Both women turned to face him. 'Because?' Elaine demanded.

Spreadbury looked as if he wished he could rewind a couple of seconds and do them again in a different way. He'd said something he hadn't intended to say. He looked crestfallen.

'Because of the danger,' he admitted. 'Some of us, or all of us, are going to die.'

'Fuck,' Elaine said.

'Your voice told you this?' Sooty asked.

Spreadbury nodded.

Sooty sighed and turned back to Elaine. 'I'm convinced. We're going. And that's that. Jim's in trouble. I don't know what kind, or whether there are body-snatching ghosts or gods or whatever, but I *do* know he's in trouble. I can feel that right down to my bones. We're going. Unless you'd rather stay here, Elaine. In which case I'll go alone with Aaron.'

Elaine grinned. 'Sweetheart, do you think I'd let you go *anywhere* alone tonight? I'm coming right along with the two of you. Christ, he's even got me half believing in this load of old donkey-do.'

Spreadbury looked relieved. 'Let's go,' he said.

'Not so fast, Buster,' Elaine said, aiming the gun at him as he made to get up. 'Sit tight. Sooty?'

'You keep the gun on Aaron, I'll drive the boat. I know what I'm doing and I can navigate too. If there's anything I need to know Aaron will be right alongside to help me out. Let's go to the bridge.'

'You heard the woman,' Elaine said, waving the gun at Spreadbury. 'Like James Brown says, take us to the bridge! And there'd better not be any funny business because if we run into some pals of yours out there in the water, I'm gonna start shooting and when that red veil drops down before my eyes, I tend not to quit shooting until nothing is moving any more. Got it?'

Chapter Seventeen

Tricks and Traps 3:
A Walk on the Wild Side

1

The party on the beach were getting themselves together for their trip through the woods when the long, agonized scream split the island's air of quiet. Several of the party, including Jim, whose back prickled with fear, yelped in surprise.

'Jesus H. Christ, what the fuck was *that*?' Jon Short asked, spinning round to face the woods.

'That'd be the god,' Rosie muttered, taking Jim's elbow and tugging at it.

Martha giggled nervously. 'Sounds like someone just stuck a pig. It'll be bleeding a bit now,' she said.

'It sounded serious,' June said, worriedly. 'Who's out there in the woods, Jim? Only he or she must've hurt themselves.'

'*Hurt* themselves?' Jon said. 'Sounded more like they'd torn themselves in half!'

'No one's out there,' Jim lied, feeling as if someone had put a thick pane of glass between him and the rest of the gang. 'Except the ghosts of Majesty and Straker Dauphin and their little girl.' He shivered again.

The gathering broke into an excited babble as everyone argued about what, or who, had made the terrible noise.

'What happened, Jim?' Rosie whispered. 'Davey's hurt.'

Jim shrugged off his shivers. 'Nothing happened,' he whispered back. 'Except exactly what Davey wanted to happen. He's here to be scary and he's good at it.'

'How would you know if he really *had* hurt himself?' Rosie wanted to know.

'He *won't* hurt himself. He *hasn't* hurt himself,' Jim replied. 'He's been doing this kind of thing for years.'

'But—'

'I'll go and check,' he whispered. 'I'm meant to run off alone anyway. That's the way we do things on these trips. I crash into the woods and you guys come and look for me. I lead you into the traps.'

'Jim?' Jon asked. 'What shall we do? What *was* that?'

'I don't know. Stay here and I'll go and investigate.'

Frank nodded wisely. 'Okay, Jim, you do that. We'll pretend we don't know you have an accomplice up in the woods. Someone who can scream real good.'

Jim turned to face Frank, his mind in half a dozen places at once. In spite of what he'd told Rosie, Davey had never screamed before. It could have meant any number of things. Davey could be dangling from a tree right now, his leg snared in one of his trip-wires, his own body-weight threatening to pull the wire right through and lop off that leg. 'There's no one on this island but us,' he told Frank. 'It was probably animals fighting.' He turned and ran up the beach towards the path that ran alongside the Dauphin house.

'You need a better editor, Jim,' Frank called after him. 'There *are* no wild animals on this island. Remember?'

2

Jim ran past the corner of the Dauphin house and into the deep gloom of the woods, a cold dagger of panic in his guts and his brain throwing out a series of nasty images. He stopped at the bottom of the house's backyard, in front of the tree that had been shaking earlier. Davey did not appear to be in it, or dangling from it.

'Davey?' he called, in a low voice. And listened.

There was no reply. Jim called again, a little louder this time, but not loud enough for the fans to hear. He held his breath and listened.

And heard a *swishing* noise.

What the hell is that? he asked himself. And, of its own accord and against his wishes, his mind began to fictionalize the answer.

273

Scene 32. Exterior. The Clearing in the Woods. Twilight.
The camera dollies into the clearing through the undergrowth.
As we approach we can hear a gigantic swishing noise –
rather like the sound the descending blade makes in The Pit
and the Pendulum.

The camera enters the clearing and we see Davey – or,
rather, what's left of him. He's kneeling on the ground in the
centre of the clearing. His face is gone, his right leg is missing
from the knee down and he's waving an arm in the air that no
longer has a hand. The area around him is stained with blood
and chunks of his flesh. The ghosts of Straker and Majesty
Dauphin cannot be seen, but they are obviously there, because
as they pass between him and the camera, he disappears.

Davey is not dead yet, but it's only a matter of moments.
We hear the huge swishing sound again and half the waving
arm drops from Davey's body. He turns under the force of
the blow, but doesn't fall. As he turns back, there is another
swish and a hand-sized chunk of flesh flies from his side.
Then it stops. There is no noise whatsoever – except the sound
of Davey's agonized breathing and the spatter of the blood
jetting from his arteries. He tries to say something. The word
sounds a little like 'Jim'. We finally hear another huge swish
and Davey is split open from throat to pubic bone.

The odd swishing sound stopped and Jim shook his head
to clear the unpleasant vision. He still had that terrible
feeling of dislocation; the big sheet of glass between him and
reality hadn't shifted an inch.

You worked a good one this time, Davey, he thought. *I'm
scared. More scared than I've ever been in my entire life.*

This thought was followed by another: *There wasn't any
Straker Dauphin, or Majesty, or Gloria. There is no god on
this island. I'm just too susceptible to fiction. Either that of
my own making, or that of other people. I've been close to
the edge and I'm not all the way back yet and I have a fecund
mind which sometimes runs out of control and imagines the
worst. Or worse than the worst. Nothing is happening here
other than what is supposed to be happening. Davey generated the noise to scare us, that's all.*

This didn't aid his sense of dislocation and it didn't
convince him that Frank's story of gods at war, and his own

of Straker and Majesty, were nothing more than fiction, but it was enough to get him moving again, forward and away from the madness in which he'd been entangled over the past couple of months.

He ran deeper into the woods and smiled with relief when he spotted Davey hidden just a few feet from the track in the tall ferns. Davey was badly camouflaged as a grassy hummock in the centre of the ferns. One of his work-boots protruded from the far side.

Jim trotted past the hump and said, 'Nice scream, big guy! You sure had me going there for a couple of minutes. Thought you were hurt.' Then he looked back over his shoulder, paused, said, 'Pull your foot in, they'll see it!' and carried on until he spotted the first trip-wire across the track. It was where it should have been – in exactly the same place as it always was. This was Jim's prearranged starting point.

The glass partition was gone. Jim noticed this when he stopped and hunkered down beside the tree trunk to which the wire was attached. A hatchet was embedded in the bark of the tree as a marker. He grinned. Everything was going to pan out just fine, he was sure of that now. All his doubts and fears had retreated.

He yanked the hatchet from the tree trunk, dropped it out of harm's way off the path beside the base of the tree, then crouched and felt around in the undergrowth. Davey was supposed to have left him a flashlight here. It was pretty dark now in twilight, but in twenty or thirty minutes it would be pitch black – something he knew to his cost. On the last trip, the flashlight the big guy had hidden for him had had flat batteries and Jim had blundered around the woods trying to find the fans, rather than scare them. There should be kerosene-soaked torches beside the path a little deeper in the woods for when the gang eventually got together, but the flashlight would allow Jim to skip about being scary while the fans took the brunt of the special effects Davey had set up.

His fingers closed around the big four-cell Maglite and he tugged it out and turned it on, half expecting the same dim red glow as last year.

Wrong again, my man, he told himself, as the beam

275

powered out across the woods like a Star Wars light sabre. Davey had everything well under control this year. Jim turned off the flashlight, got to his feet, stepped carefully over the trip-wire, trotted another fifty yards along the path to his designated hiding place and hid himself in the tall ferns behind a tree.

He set down the torch, cupped his hands to his mouth and yelled, 'It's okay, folks! There's no problem! Come on in here and see what I've got!'

'Jim? Where are you?' the distant voice of Jon Short replied.

'I'm right down here with the dead men!' Jim yelled back. Grinning, feeling good about things for a change, he settled down in the ferns to wait.

Overhead a tree began to shake angrily.

Jim shone the light up at it, puzzled. *How the hell did you manage that effect?*

'He's up here somewhere,' Jon said, from what Jim estimated was the vicinity of the Dauphin house's backyard.

Jim snapped off the flashlight. *Now you're in trouble!* he mentally told his fans.

3

Something had happened to Candy and she wasn't entirely sure what it was. It had begun the moment she'd set eyes on Jim back at the dock, but it hadn't seemed important then. The best way she could put it was that when her eyes had met Jim's (and, boy, did he have *lovely* eyes – dark and clear and gentle and full of fun) she'd felt a little flash of what she supposed was *recognition*. It wasn't merely that she found him attractive (and what a catch that man would be!), it was something else, something that went deeper. And Jim had felt it too, she knew. It was as if they'd known each other. From . . . *before*.

Candy wasn't certain what that meant. She'd never met Jim before, although she felt she knew a lot about him from reading his books and watching the films he'd written and directed, but in that instant when their eyes had met they'd both kind of *clicked*. It was a lovely *sunny* feeling and it had

276

not only made her feel sexy but, in some way, *worthwhile*, too. Which was a big plus for a girl who spent her life dealing with people who saw her only as a great body on great legs, topped with a pretty face behind which lay an entirely empty head. That didn't do much for anyone's self-esteem.

But Jim had seen right through what lay on the surface to what lay beneath. In some way, she thought, their souls had made a connection.

Which gave her hope for the future. She'd been pretty sure since then that, sooner or later, she would become a part of Jim's life. She didn't know how it would happen, only that it would.

Then later, on the beach, she'd done something so outrageous, even for her, that even now, hours later, she could barely believe it had happened.

Sitting on the beach talking to Jim, she'd found a kind of gravity pulling at her: a strange urge she didn't understand. It was as if being close to Jim had diverted the course of her existence – snatched it up and plonked it down again on a new line. It was like being on a set of railroad tracks with a steam train pushing you along from behind. The thing *had* to happen. There was just no stopping it.

She'd apprehended the nature of that thing in a flash: she had to fuck Jim in a certain way, in a certain spot in the sea. She'd tried to get him in the sea with her and had failed, but the urge, the inexorable need to satisfy what had to be done, just wouldn't quit. So she'd dragged Jon out there and fucked him in Jim's place.

And the act had changed her again. It actually felt as if it had changed *everything*.

It wasn't just that she'd had a multiple orgasm for the second time in her life, but that she'd had a totally mind-blowing orgasm that began when Jon pushed into her and kept right on going, even after he was spent. And it felt as if it would never stop, even as the realization had come to her that Jim had done exactly this in exactly this spot in the sea with his wife – and not so long ago, either. And when, for the last moments of his own orgasm, Jon had seemed to *become* Jim she'd understood.

She was being prepared. And during that orgasm, she'd

changed: she'd been set up for a new life. A life with Jim at her side.

Since then, she'd felt as if she could swallow him up entirely, in every way. As if she could *absorb* him and make him a part of her for ever.

And it was going to happen tonight, too. She didn't know how or why, only that by the time morning came, she and Jim would be together for ever.

It was a wonderful feeling.

Smiling, she followed along behind Jon, who was leading the group, and Frank, who was beside him. Rosie walked beside Candy, and June and Martha were keeping close behind them. There was an air of tension, expectation and a little fear running through them. Jon and Rosie were trading dumb-assed one-liners now and again, but as they got deeper into the woods and tension increased their voices grew quieter and more edgy.

Jim was nearby now. The link they'd forged told her so. 'Where are you, Jim?' she called. 'Are you here? Are you okay?'

Her voice was swallowed up by the woods. It was like calling into a room filled with cotton wool – sound here seemed to become absorbed by the surroundings almost as soon as you made it. Her heart beat a little faster as she waited for his reply. Soon they would be together for ever.

'Help!' Jim called, in a small voice.

'Jeez, where did *that* come from?' Jon asked in exasperation. 'It sounded like it came from about five different directions at once.'

'It came from ahead and to the right,' Frank said, stabbing a finger. 'This way. His voice definitely came from *this* direction.'

'It came from behind us,' Martha protested.

'He's right beside us,' June disagreed, poking in the undergrowth with her foot. 'I bet he's lying down here somewhere ready to pop up and go booga-booga!'

'Over here! It's got me. Help!' Jim called.

Candy grinned. She knew where he was now, knew the exact spot. The link between them told her so. *What are you doing, Jim?* she thought playfully, certain that he would be

278

able to hear her thoughts. Jim was special. He was no ordinary man, she knew that now. *What are you up to?* she asked. She knew she was going to have to break away from the others soon, because she and Jim were meant to meet alone. They weren't going to find Jim, but she *was*. She sensed this strongly. It was written. *Written in the Book of Life*, she thought.

'I told you,' Jon said. 'You just can't tell *where* he is!'

'You're mad,' Frank said. 'Right up here. Just follow me. Rosie? Why are you hanging right back behind us?'

'I ... uhh, don't want to stumble into anything,' Rosie said carefully. 'I'm okay back here. You lead, I'll follow!'

She's going to try to fuck it up for us, Candy suddenly thought. *Rosie doesn't want us to be together and she'll do anything she can to prevent it.*

It didn't matter. Candy knew that she could and would overcome any opposition she met. She wondered how she was going to break away from the group without being noticed.

Up ahead of them a single tree began to shake madly, its leaves hissing. The other members of the group seemed worried, but Candy knew it was another sign. There *was* a god on this island, just like Frank had said. But it was a good god. A god that was going to fix things up for her just like she'd fixed things up for it. She pushed in front of Frank and Jon and strode ahead towards the tree. 'C'mon, you cowardy-custards,' she called back. 'We have to find Jim.'

She didn't see the ankle-height trip-wire gleaming dully across the track close to where the tree was shaking; didn't know it was there until it had dug into her ankle and caused her almost to overbalance and fall on her face. Candy caught herself and stepped backwards into Frank and Jon, still not sure what had happened.

'Shit!' she said, as Jon steadied her. 'What on earth was *that*?' She peered at the thing she'd bounced off. 'It's a *wire*,' she said in surprise.

And as the words left her mouth and Jon Short shouted, 'It's a trap!' the woods came alive with the creaking of trees. Several members of the party screamed and Jon yelled, 'Look out!'

279

Then there was silence.

'Be still my beating heart,' Frank whispered.

And up in the branches of the tree that had been shaking, something went off with a small *pop*.

As one, the group looked up to the source of the sound. A large, dark bag was stuffed between two branches and, dangling across a nearby bough, something that looked very much like a lit fuse was fizzling.

'What the fuck is that?' Frank asked, as the group watched the burning fuse shorten. The loose end fell from the bough and dangled there as the tiny flame climbed it and vanished behind the bag. A tiny *psst!* followed.

And then there was silence.

'It didn't work, whatever it was,' Martha said, and giggled.

Frank tested the trip-wire with the toe of his shoe. He shrugged. 'Let's go find Jim,' he suggested.

The sharp bang that punctuated the end of Frank's sentence made everyone jump. Only two of the fans saw the large dark bag leap from the tree and explode in the air, but everyone except Rosie, who was still hanging back, was showered with a thick rain of rich red blood.

June, Frank, Candy and Martha screamed as the warm liquid hit them, instantly painting them red. Jon made a small sound of shock and staggered sideways. An instant later a firework exploded beside the path.

This device was roughly equivalent in power to the one that Jim had detonated on the jetty. Deafened, blinded and covered in blood, the fans did exactly what Davey had anticipated they would: they split up and ran in all directions screaming and shouting.

Not only had Davey laid traps along the path, he'd also made a spider's web of them, spreading out from this first one so that if the gang *did* split up they'd be caught whichever way they went, unless it was right back down the path.

Candy ran into the undergrowth, her mental link with Jim forgotten, perhaps severed by the sudden shocks. Her ears rang and huge purple shapes reeled and exploded in front of her eyes. Her only urge was to run, to escape. Like the others she was oblivious of the lines and wires over which she stumbled and through which she broke. She wasn't even aware that she was screaming.

4

Jim had hidden, crouched, while he listened to the fans approach. They had paused about ten feet from him and when he had called out, he'd been sure they would be able to tell exactly where he was. In the event, it didn't matter if they had. All he'd expected to happen at that first trip-wire was that a laughing-bag would begin to yammer and giggle. Davey normally liked to work his way up in easy steps from the small stuff in a crescendo. But this time he'd gone for the big one early on.

He'd heard the blood-bag detonate, heard the screams and yells of the fans and he'd giggled a little himself. The flash and bang of the heavy-duty firework, however, had worked on him almost as well as it had worked on the fans.

Jesus fucking wept! he thought, on the heels of the initial shock. *Davey's blown 'em all sky high!*

He stood up, expecting casualties, and was just in time to see the half-dozen blood-soaked fans hammer off in half a dozen different directions.

What followed exceeded Jim's wildest expectations and fears. It all seemed to happen at once, and with such speed that he could barely take it all in. Blood-bags swung from trees and tore open showering people with fresh loads of gore. Laughing-bags yammered and squealed. Convincing dummies swung down from branches – one hit Frank and its head split, spattering him with Davey's idea of rotting brains. Fireworks banged high in trees and low on the ground. Gauzy apparitions flitted along hidden wires screeching with banshee wails.

Candy staggered into a trip-wire and was showered with blood. She gave a short yelp, turned through ninety degrees and took off again. Martha and June, who were slower than the others but just as frightened and disoriented, were running in the direction of the swamp. There was no sign of Rosie, and Jim guessed she'd been prepared for what had happened and had set off back the way she'd come.

Jim saw Frank snag his foot on another trip-wire. What appeared to be a corpse sprang up from the ground right in front of him as if its heels were hinged. Its rotting flesh fell over him. He went rigid, squealed, shot off in a fresh direction and was showered with more goo, this time bright pink. He turned again and ran towards Jim.

Jim bobbed down in the ferns and when Frank was almost on him, stood up quickly and yelled, 'Hi, Frank!'

Frank looked at him with no recognition, screamed out the entire volume of air in his lungs, turned and ran away.

Jim felt a demonic grin find its way onto his face. 'Put *that* in your piece for the paper!' he muttered. A moment ago, he'd had serious doubts about the sanity of Davey's plan – some of these people, Martha, for instance, might well suffer heart-attacks after this level of fear and confusion. *Or during it*, he'd thought. But his joy at seeing Doubting Frank so taken in, suffering so much panic, swept all his worries away.

I'm a baaaaad person, he thought, grinning. He might have been bad but right now he felt wonderful about everything. He was doing what he lived to do – to scare the shit out of people – and those people had come here to be scared shitless. They'd known what they were letting themselves in for long ago. And if the scares turned out to be a little over the top, who cared?

Not me! Jim thought. *I'm having fun!*

All his doubts, worries and fears had left him now, in much the same way they did when he fell into a story. It was a good feeling. Everything that had been weighing him down was gone: he'd finally managed to make the connection with the magic of this island. He'd felt it click into place, like the last piece in a jigsaw puzzle, during the moment of shock when Davey's first firework had blasted into the silence. Suddenly he felt whole again.

'Help me, Jim! *Help me!*'

It was Candy's voice, but it was distant and Jim couldn't see her. He could only just hear her over the noise that the effects and the fans were making as they shot through the woods cannoning from tree to tree like balls in a pinball machine. *She must have run deeper into the forest*, he thought. She sounded stuck. He didn't know why he thought

282

she sounded stuck but, as he'd told countless interviewers over the past few years, Jim was a man who trusted his instincts.

'Jim! Pleeeeease!' she yelled.

He pulled a face. It was probably a ploy to get him alone with her. She was probably hiding behind a tree peeling off her tight little shorts right now so that she would be ready when he arrived.

And would you be able to resist? he asked himself, grinning. Right now he wasn't sure. In fact, right now he felt so horny (and this was another effect of Straker's Island – it would wake up a sleeping libido and goose a tired one into overdrive) he probably wouldn't have been able to turn down an offer from the world's ugliest woman. Except that Sooty would first take out his eyeballs with her fingernails, and then use a blunt knife on his genitals. Jim grinned. He would just have to save it up for her. *Just you wait till I get home, my dusky little beauty!* he thought. He ducked as a nearby apparition whistled over his head.

And Candy yelled again. She really did sound as if she was in trouble.

Jim jogged off in the direction he thought her voice was travelling from. She'd probably twisted her ankle or something.

He didn't realize he'd hit the trip-wire in front of him till the big black thing swooped down at him from the tree at his left. Jim cringed and ducked, but the dark bag suddenly quit moving about two feet above him and to his left where it tore apart, showering him with warm, thick blood that stank like a slaughter-house, stung his eyes and got in his mouth. It was disgusting, and he knew now why the fans had got in such a panic. Davey evidently hadn't been lying when he'd said this was *real* blood. It couldn't be human blood, of course, but it was certainly animal blood and it was half coagulated, too. He wiped his eyes, spat out as much of the disgusting stuff as he could – although it didn't clear the taste – and ran towards the sound of Candy, whose voice was becoming more panicky by the moment. Fireworks and apparitions were set off in his wake, but thankfully there was no more blood.

And there was Candy, right ahead of him, standing knee-deep in ferns in the middle of a clearing.

The sounds of the others running around and screaming were distant now and eventually the forest deadened them.

Candy had stopped screaming. She just stood there, sobbing and panting and looking pretty much as if she couldn't take any more. A distant part of Jim's mind wondered again how the older folks were faring. If Candy had had enough already the others must be in deep shock by now.

'It's okay, I'm here,' Jim called, stopping and checking the area around the clearing for devices. He still had a lot of blood on him and he didn't want any more. 'What's wrong?' he asked, trying to catch his breath. Sooty had been on the case about his cigarette consumption ever since she'd given up smoking. *I'll give up after this*, he thought. *Or cut down, at least.*

'There's a – huh-huh *hand*,' Candy sobbed. She was trembling from head to toe. 'I cuh-an't see where it's gone.'

'Stay there,' Jim said. 'I'm here now. There's nothing to be frightened of. I'll come and get you.'

'Quick, *please!*' Candy said. 'For God's sake. Quick! I shook it off once but it's strong and it keeps following me. It puh-popped up out of the ground and guh-rabbed my ankle.'

When he moved, his legs complained. He'd been desk-bound too long, he knew. Exercise was something else he was short of. *A dog*, he thought stupidly. *I'll get a dog like Davey's old Charlie.*

He broke into a trot and, after only four steps, tripped over something large that lay beneath the ferns and went down face-first. He managed to break his fall with his hands but his right wrist took the brunt of it and something in the joint between wrist and hand snapped. A sharp pain shot up his arm. *It still moves*, he thought, flexing his fingers as he turned back to see what he'd fallen over. *It hurts, but it's not broken because it still moves.*

He carefully pulled the ferns apart and saw a chunky backside encased in a pair of grease-stained jeans. The jeans were low and the crack of their owner's arse was on display.

Davey? How did he get here? What's happened to him? Jim thought.

284

A few yards away from him Candy began to scream, but that weird shield of plate glass had come back and cut Jim off from her. He merely stared at Davey.

'Here it is! It's *here*. Help! *Help meeeeeee!*' Candy screeched.

But Jim's attention was fixed on Davey's body. Out in front of him, his hands, looking like two pink crabs, clawed away the ferns from Davey.

This can't be Davey. I saw him earlier, a way back, Jim's mind insisted.

But it *was* Davey. There was no mistaking him.

'*Jiiiiiimmmmm!*'

Davey was very dead. Huge chunks were missing from his torso and his right arm was gone. Jim's mind refused to process this information. He stared blankly at the bloody shoulder socket; at the deep hole there. His gaze left that gory socket and travelled up his friend's neck. Davey's head was missing. His neck terminated in a nasty stretched tear. It was exactly how Jim would have envisaged someone's neck after their head had been pulled right off their body. For a long, silent moment, Jim had absolutely no idea what any of this meant.

Candy's next scream broke him out of it. Broke him out, *knowing*. He couldn't assimilate the information. Nothing made any sense but the two-word summary that came to him: *deep shit*. And those two words rolled over and over inside his head as he began to act.

He got to his feet, his body charged with a near fatal dose of adrenaline. He gulped in a breath that tasted oily and gasped it out again.

In front of him, Candy was beside herself with fear and doing a spastic backward shuffle that was barely taking her anywhere. Down on the ground at her feet, the ferns had parted and the loamy earth was bulging as if something was trying to force its way up from underneath. With each clumsy step she retreated, the bulge in the ground moved smoothly forward, keeping pace with her.

'Oh, no! Jim! Jim, help me!' she gasped.

As Jim moved towards her not knowing what to do, the top end of the bulge burst open in a shower of dirt and peat and a rotting hand and arm shot out like a snake striking. In one quick movement, the hand clamped itself around Candy's ankle. Candy screamed, long and hard. Jim saw muscles bulge in the corrupt arm and the hand yanked Candy's ankle forward, pulling her off her feet. She crashed down on her back and the impact drove her breath from her, cut off her scream.

The arm – Straker Dauphin's arm, Jim now understood with absolute horror – dragged her towards the break in the bulge of earth. Candy began to scream again and thrash about, but the hand remained clamped around her ankle, its fingers pressed deep into her flesh.

Hissing and swearing, Jim ran round behind her, got his arms under hers and pulled, trying to yank her back. His mind was fractured now, his thoughts bouncing around like balls being dropped on to a spinning roulette wheel.

'My leg! *It's got my leg!*' Candy shrieked as Jim dug in his heels and pushed with his legs. His heels sank into the earth and his hurt wrist shot tiny tracers of molten lead up his arm, but he'd stopped the hand tugging her any further. Candy wouldn't be drawn down into the ground.

Just a little more, Jim thought, pulling harder, thrusting his legs down with all the force he could muster. And Candy slid back towards him an inch. And then another.

I'm winning, he thought, fighting to keep his grip. His arms and hands and Candy's body were all slick with blood from Davey's blood-bags and the struggle was making both him and the girl slippery with sweat. His right wrist hurt like a bastard now, there were stabbing pains in his back and his biceps complained, but he was winning.

'Fight it!' he hissed, and Candy began to kick out at the arm with her free leg.

It worked, to a point. The hand's grip slipped, but it didn't let go. Jim and Candy gained an inch, but the rotting fingers curled around her foot and dug in hard – snapping the little bones in there, Jim thought, judging by the fresh bout of screaming.

And then he lost his footing.

Jim sat down hard and the back of Candy's head crashed down into his crotch. It felt as if one of Davey's fireworks had detonated there, but he clung to Candy, her head in his lap, his arms locked around her chest and his feet either side of her waist.

And the rotting hand and arm tugged, drawing them both closer to the mound of earth.

You don't want to get dragged into that! Jim's mind shrieked over Candy's ear-splitting screams.

Terrified, Jim dug his heels hard into the soft ground and used the traction and the movement of the hand to lever himself up and lean back into a kind of tug-of-war position. No part of Candy was now in contact with the ground – she was stretched taut between Jim and the hand. Candy was strong. Her powerful writhing and bucking threatened to break Jim's grip. The hand, however, seemed firmly attached. Using her free leg, Candy got it with several good kicks, but it didn't budge.

Jim took a deep breath, held it and heaved back, gaining a few inches. The hand immediately tugged hard, losing Jim those precious inches.

'Let go, you fucker!' Jim screamed.

'It's *tearing my leg off*!' Candy shrieked. 'Help me, Jim. *Help!*'

The fingers tightened and dug deeper into Candy's ankle and Jim saw the flesh there tear messily. Blood began to flow freely and Jim's reeling mind reported that the fingers had surely cut through skin, muscle and tendon and were now down as far as the bone. If Candy got out of this alive, she was going to spend the rest of her life limping.

Or walking on a prosthetic foot.

The power of the hand was phenomenal. Even with Jim's heels dug in deeply it was winning. He and Candy moved slowly towards the mound of earth, his heels leaving runnels in the ground.

There was less of the arm on show now and Candy's foot was almost in contact with the mouth of the mound. Jim gave a mighty tug and gained an inch or two. Candy screamed and went limp. When Jim looked down at the hand he realized why. He *hadn't* gained an inch at all. What had happened was that the flesh at Candy's ankle had slipped down the bone like a sock.

During this moment of realization, the hand yanked Candy's foot into the soft, boggy-looking earth. Screaming, Jim heaved back again with all his strength.

Tourniquet, his mind was chanting. *It's okay, I know how to apply a tourniquet.*

Candy's foot didn't snap off, as he'd half expected. It came out of the mound, red with blood, blue with bruise and smeared with oily dirt.

Let go, damn you! Jim screeched inwardly and pulled, muscles bulging, wrist shooting bolts of agony up his arm.

Suddenly his footing was gone again and he was falling backwards. As he toppled he felt his hands lose their slippery grip on Candy.

By the time Jim sat up, she was inside the mound of earth up to her waist. She was conscious again now, gasping in pain and stretching back for Jim's hand as she was dragged deeper.

Jim reached for her, his wrist screaming, and as she was yanked deeper, brushed her fingertips. He lunged forward and clasped her blood-smeared, sweaty hand, but his wrist was agony and she was too slippery. He tried frantically to improve his grip, but she was moving and, for a terrible second or two, he couldn't get a firm enough purchase to be of any use.

But then he managed it. Their hands locked together as if they were made to fit.

He was on his knees, at full stretch, and the next yank pulled him off balance. As Candy was dragged into the mound, he fell on his face and was tugged along after her.

She was up to her shoulders now. And then up to her neck. And finally her screams were silenced as her head went under. All that remained above ground was her arm and hand, locked on to Jim's hand, as powerfully as the rotting hand had locked on to her ankle, and now dragging him in after her.

Candy's gone! She's dead. Finished! Get her off! his mind cried.

Jim found her fingers with his free hand and tried to peel them off, but her grip was like iron and she was slowly dragging him towards the mound.

Straker Dauphin is in there, Jim's mind gibbered. *He's eaten her and now he's going to eat me. He wants me. He got her to get to me. Oh, God! Oh, fuck!*

Jim's left hand found Candy's pinkie and prised at it, levering it away from where it dug painfully into his right hand. He had to use a good deal more force than he'd expected, but finally the bone broke and the finger flopped uselessly. He did the ring and middle fingers simultaneously, cursing himself and Straker Dauphin and Candy and Spreadbury, who'd been right, and all the gods and all the world. By the time he got to her forefinger he was close to the mound of earth. Too close. As he worked on the last piece of her that pinned him, her hand dragged both of his beneath the soil.

It was warm and soft under that mound of earth. Damp and slick and comforting.

Like being back in the womb, Jim thought crazily as he applied pressure to Candy's forefinger. *Maybe it wouldn't be so bad, after all. Just to let go and sink in there in the warmth and peace.*

He felt her finger snap and give, and a moment later he was rolling back, his hands free of the mound.

Look out! It'll be coming at you! his mind yelped, but when he looked the mound had gone. There was no sign of it anywhere.

Jim rolled on his back in the ferns, nursing his painful wrist while he sobbed and tried to catch his breath.

What now? he thought.

Chapter Eighteen

The Shimmering Man

1

Majesty had been powering through the water with Sooty at the helm for almost fifteen minutes when Spreadbury, who was standing beside her alternately chewing the stem of his pipe and puffing out disgusting-smelling smoke, clapped both his hands to his face and made a small sound of pain. His pipe fell from his lips and red-hot embers scattered across the hardwood floor. He staggered sideways as though the boat had listed badly and he was trying to keep his balance.

'Quit it!' Elaine barked, from somewhere behind Sooty.

Spreadbury didn't seem to hear her. He stood by the bulkhead, bent half over, his hands across his face and mewling like a cat in great pain.

Surprised and frightened by the sudden change, Sooty took off the power and let the boat slow. According to the radar there was no nearby shipping. 'What's happening?' she called to Spreadbury. 'What's wrong?'

'Pack it in!' Elaine warned, coming into Sooty's line of sight. She held the big Magnum in both hands and her face was granite hard.

'He can't *hear* you,' Sooty said, fear rising in her. She wondered if the man was having an epileptic fit or something. *Something* worse *you mean?* her mind asked.

'Sure he can,' Elaine said, not taking her eyes off Spreadbury. 'Quit it now or I shoot you! That's a promise!' She glanced at Sooty. 'He can hear me okay,' she said. 'He's up to something, that's all.' She looked back at Spreadbury. 'Stop it, goddamn you!' she yelled angrily.

'You won't come back this time,' Spreadbury moaned, in a voice as thick as treacle.

To Sooty it sounded like someone else speaking those familiar words. A stranger. And yet it sounded a little like Jim himself.

'If anyone isn't coming back, it's you,' Elaine said.

Sooty fought off a deep shudder. 'Those are Jim's words he's saying,' she said, dismayed. 'It's the opening of *Shimmer*. You haven't seen it yet, Elaine, but it's the opening sentence. I've read a little of the book. Jim's confidence was all shot to hell and this time he needed my feedback.'

'Help me,' Spreadbury said, in what sounded like a girl's voice.

Elaine glanced at Sooty. For the first time she looked a little frightened. Her face bore a what-should-I-do? expression. Sooty shrugged.

Spreadbury gasped. His hands fell limply from his face and he suddenly stood up straight like a soldier snapping to attention. His entire head was vibrating.

Shimmering.

Like Walt Creasey in Jim's book, Sooty thought, horrified. She took an involuntary step backwards. Whenever Walt began to shimmer, someone ended up very dead indeed. *It can't be happening*, Sooty complained, but it was happening. Either that or she'd gone mad, which she sincerely doubted. Going mad would have been too simple. Jim's book had come to life. That was all there was to it.

'Jesus Holy Christ on a Harley!' Elaine said, in a small, shocked voice. 'What the fuck is *that*?'

'Help me!' Spreadbury pleaded, in the girl's voice.

'His fucking lips didn't even move,' Elaine said, a distinct tremor now apparent in her voice. She glanced at Sooty, whose face was ashen. 'Tell me this isn't happening, honey,' she said mournfully.

'It isn't happening,' Sooty said, watching Spreadbury carefully.

The motion of the psychic's head seemed to increase. He was now emitting a noise that sounded similar to an electric shaver, but higher in pitch. *A swarm of mosquitoes or something*, Sooty thought, and at that precise moment the

291

largest mosquito she'd ever seen alighted on her wrist. She gasped and slapped it, killing it. Judging from the amount of blood she found smeared across her wrist afterwards the insect had recently fed.

'He's going to explode or something,' Elaine said, backing off.

'That's a distinct possibility,' Sooty replied, also moving away from the man. She glanced at the blood on her wrist. She'd evidently slapped herself a little too hard because now there was a distinct pain buzzing up the outside of her arm. It was centred around her wrist and felt as if tiny tracers of molten lead were shooting up her arm. Her hand felt as if someone was trying to pull it off, but it still moved freely.

'Fuck this for a game of soldiers! Look!' Elaine said.

Spreadbury's face, blurred by the motion, was rippling now. It was the kind of effect you saw on television when the movement of a fan, or a rotating wheel set up an interference wave with the speed of the camera.

'Let's get out of here,' Elaine suggested. 'Good idea?'

But, despite her fear, Sooty knew she had to see this. 'Watch,' she said, biting her lower lip. Pain was the only thing likely to keep her in touch with her sanity now.

The ripples across Spreadbury's face – through his *flesh* – increased in frequency and the pitch of the sound he was emitting rose a couple of tones and got a good deal louder.

Here we go, Sooty thought. *Here we go!*

'What in God's name is happening to him?' Elaine shrieked, over the noise.

'He's having a psychic episode,' Sooty said loudly. Her voice was mashed and broken by the sound Spreadbury was making. 'He's gone into a trance.'

'You hope!' Elaine yelled.

She was keeping the gun trained on Spreadbury and, to Sooty's surprise, it was steady in her hand, despite her apparent terror.

'I do,' Sooty shouted back.

And the noise stopped.

Both Elaine and Sooty staggered. It was like leaning into a gale that had suddenly stopped blowing.

This is it, Elaine, Sooty thought. *This is what we've been waiting for. Either he explodes and kills us, or we get to* know *right now.*

Spreadbury's face was still blurred by the motion, but the frequency seemed to have altered now: the vibration, the shimmering, was more delicate. And while Sooty and Elaine looked on, something began to happen.

'Oh, my *God!*' Elaine hissed.

The skin and bone of Spreadbury's face seemed to have become plastic, pliant. And his features had begun to rearrange themselves in a quick fluid dance. Other faces began to be superimposed upon his own for the tiniest moment before the next one was there. It was all happening so quickly that Sooty couldn't identify any of the faces – especially since they overlaid Spreadbury's own features.

Elaine watched, aghast. 'His face is vanishing,' she said.

She was right. As the new faces flitted across Spreadbury's, his features seemed to lessen, as if each new set of features abraded away his own. Inside a few seconds what was left between the new sets of unformed features was nothing more than a blank oval of pink. The faces continued to meld swiftly from one to another, but as Spreadbury's features had faded the new ones had taken on more definition. Now they were beginning to slow, to stay on the blank slate of Spreadbury's face for a little longer on each rotation.

'I think I *know* these people,' Elaine said, in a voice of utter shock.

2

In Hettie Baker's humble opinion, this child didn't need a baby-sitter, she needed a doctor. Either that, or she needed to be in a hospital where they could wire her up to all those test rigs they had and determine exactly what was wrong with the poor kid.

It just wasn't natural for a girl of this age to be unable to wake up.

But Hettie hadn't complained. She'd known Sooty, or Reina, rather it was only her husband's influence that made everyone call her by her nickname – for a good long time now. Since she was a little girl, in fact. And before that she'd known the parents.

'In fact,' she muttered, as she crept into the darkened bedroom where Gloria lay sleeping in a big frilly single bed, 'I know things about Reina that even Reina doesn't know.'

In the soft light of the single pink-shaded bedside lamp, the sleeping child looked positively angelic. Hettie settled down on a chair beside the bed, feeling that ancient yearning she always did when faced with a child. That tired old *wanting children* ache. Lord knew, she and Artie had tried long and hard enough for children. But she'd been destined not to bear any. She supposed God was to blame for that: He certainly hadn't answered any of her prayers. When she passed through those pearly gates to meet her Maker she intended to stand tall, look Him right in the eye and demand to know why He'd never let her have the thing she desired most in all the world. A child. Just one would have done. Hettie wasn't a greedy woman.

'Here's a secret about your mother,' she whispered to the sleeping Gloria. 'Something even she doesn't know. She's descended from royalty. Oh, I guess you'll find out one day that your grandfather wasn't Spanish like he always said he was. He was Brazilian and had been well connected too, till he had to leave the country, but what you don't know is that your grandma and your mother are of *royal* descent. Which makes you a little princess, I guess. Your grandmother's actually descended from Louis the Fourteenth, an old king, way over there in France. How about that? Isn't that something?'

Hettie didn't know whether it was or not, really. Practically all those old European kings had bastard offspring. There were probably thousands of folks who were descended from royalty. *Tens* of thousands by now.

She stroked Gloria's soft, cool forehead. The little girl looked like royalty, anyway. She took after her mother – although where the blonde hair had come from was anyone's guess: both Jim and Reina were dark.

'They should have taken you to a doctor, darling,' Hettie said, remembering the wild-eyed woman who'd brought Gloria here. Elaine Palmer, her name was. Hettie had

294

memorized that because she hadn't liked the woman on sight and suspected there might be something odd going on over at Reina's house. Reina had sounded panicky on the phone, but had protested that nothing was really wrong, it was just that she and her friend had to go help someone out of a little trouble. They wouldn't be gone more than two hours, she'd said. It sounded like so much flimflam to these old ears. But Reina was a good woman with a good head on her shoulders so Hettie had given her the benefit of the doubt.

'That Elaine, though,' she whispered to Gloria, 'I wouldn't trust her as far as I could throw her. I don't know. I'm sure they should have taken you to a doctor.'

Gloria had been running a bit of fever, they'd told her. It wasn't anything important, just a summer cold, and her temperature had come down now. She was okay and just a little drowsy.

'Drowsy isn't in it!' Hettie scoffed. She'd taken the child's temperature just as soon as Elaine had left and it was 98.6, which was about right, so she didn't have a fever. Probably hadn't ever had a fever. And her pupils and eyes seemed okay, too, so she probably hadn't taken any medication she shouldn't have. Her breath and body both smelt sweet, too.

'It's a mystery, that's what it is,' Hettie said. Mystery was all fine and dandy as far as this woman was concerned – she loved a good mystery programme or book. And real-life mystery was fine, too, but she was uncomfortable with the kind of mystery that left a young girl in an unconscious state.

She leaned over Gloria, peering at her perfect features, her smooth, blemish-free skin. And, to her surprise, Gloria's eyebrows creased into the merest ghost of a frown.

Hettie nodded approval. Perhaps she was just sleeping heavily. Her pulse was fine and her breathing was slow and steady.

Downstairs the cat-flap banged. 'That'll be old Marmaduke,' she said, glancing to the partially open door. The cat would be right up here looking for her to feed it. She listened, knowing she wouldn't hear him until he pushed against the door. 'He's creeping up the stairs,' she told Gloria, glancing back.

And then she gasped and clapped a hand to her mouth, perhaps to stop herself yelling – she could feel the weight of a long, loud, late-night-horror-movie scream brewing in her chest.

I didn't see that! she thought, hanging on to her ribcage. *I imagined it.*

But she wasn't sure she *had* imagined it. What she'd caught the quickest glimpse of, as she looked at Gloria, was movement on her face. Not a change of expression so much as a total change of face. For a moment Gloria had the pasty, slack face of a middle-aged man; a face that seemed too big to fit on her little head. And as she'd taken it in, the child's flesh had rippled and the man's face was gone again.

Gloria gave a small moan and began to writhe as if she were uncomfortable. First she turned on her left side, then spun round to lie on her right, dragging the sheets up to her face. The she sighed and turned on her back again, her arms doing a brief battle as she pushed away the tangle of sheets she'd made. Then she settled again, the sheets pushed half-way down her body.

Hettie shook her head. 'It's a little warm in here, I guess,' she said, still thinking of the man's face she'd imagined overlaying Gloria's. In spite of the warmth of the room, she shivered.

I imagined it, she assured herself, *I'm okay now. I'm calm.* But when she saw movement over by the door, a moment later, she really did scream.

Marmaduke, her tomcat, strolled into the room, looking at her suspiciously. Gloria didn't stir.

'God, you nearly killed me that time,' Hettie told the cat, as she put her hand to her ribs and felt her heart trying to batter its way out of her body.

Marmaduke rubbed himself around her ankles then nimbly leaped up on to the bed and climbed on to Gloria's chest.

'Get down, Marmie!' Hettie commanded, but the cat, as usual, ignored her. It stood on the girl's chest sniffing delicately at her mouth.

'Marmie!' Hettie hissed.

And the cat leaped into the air hissing and snarling, his tail erect, his fur standing up and his claws and fangs on display. A second later he shot out of the room. This time Hettie heard him on the stairs – it sounded like he'd fallen down half of them in his rush to get the hell out of there. Then she heard him hit the cat-flap at high speed. A couple of seconds after that, she could hear him out in the back-yard making that horrible cat-fighting noise that was half moan, half snarl.

Hettie's old heart felt as if it might soon throw up its hands in despair and keel over.

Suddenly she no longer wanted to be in the room with Gloria. Suddenly she felt physically sick and horribly fright-ened. Whatever was afoot here was something worse than a summer cold and a deep sleep, she realized, as every hair on her body rose.

The room had cooled. During the few seconds following Marmaduke's flight the temperature had dropped from an early-evening windows-open eighty to what was probably twenty degrees lower where she was and even colder around the girl. When Hettie looked, she could see the child's breath vaporizing in plumes.

Ghosts, Hettie thought, finding it hard to breathe now. Hettie wasn't the world's most open-minded person when it came to tales of the supernatural, but after her husband had died, things had happened. The flower-pots in the garden – strewn everywhere – had mysteriously tidied themselves up without human intervention. Items belonging to Artie had appeared in places where she knew she'd never put them, and then vanished again. Some had never been found.

There *were* such things as ghosts.

And it now looked as if Gloria was possessed. Or that she was acting like a magnet for spirits.

'Mommy?' Gloria asked in her sleep. 'I'm coming, Mommy.'

Hettie could stand it no longer. She got up, went out onto the landing, pulled the door almost closed behind her and stood at the top of the stairs holding the banister rail while she fought an inner battle. A good eighty per cent of her wanted to run downstairs and get out in the garden with the cat where it was safe, where the warm evening sun shone. But the other twenty per cent – the part that reminded her of the fragility of the small girl she'd been assigned to look after and the part that was evidently her protective maternal instinct – forbade her to move any further away from the child. Gloria needed her help.

'She doesn't need a doctor, she needs an exorcist,' Hettie gasped, as she tried to steady her breathing, to calm her heart before it gave out on her. She stood there in silence for a couple of minutes, fighting off the urge to flee. *Ghosts can't harm you*, she repeated over and over. The ghost of Artie – if that was what it had been – was benign. Helpful, even. But if Gloria was possessed, or if something had found her and was following her around – something dragged up from hell by the power of the awful stuff her father wrote – Hettie was sure it would be a spook of a different colour.

But it can't harm you, whatever it is, she assured herself. *You're a God-fearing woman. You have faith. And devils and demons cannot harm you, let alone ghosts.*

At that moment, however, she wasn't sure of how deep her faith in God ran. They said that if your faith wasn't total you were lost.

Hettie let out a little sob. *Lord forgive me, I can't go back in that room*, she thought. *I just can't. I'm too old and I'm too frightened. I don't want to lose my soul. I want to see Artie again. Please forgive me, Lord!*

In the bedroom where Gloria slept, something made a noise. It was a hard, leathery *thump*! Her heart breaking, her fear almost taking her legs out from beneath her, Hettie looked back over her shoulder at the bedroom door. Her breath caught in her chest. The sound was pretty much what you heard on the *Rocky* films when the bad guy caught Stallone with a haymaker right.

Hettie waited, her eyes filling with tears. *I can't*, she thought.

And in the bedroom all hell seemed to have broken loose. It sounded as if a dozen men armed with baseball bats had materialized in there, and that they had surrounded the bed and were beating the living shit out the child. Gloria made no noise at all. The first blow, Hettie thought, had probably killed her.

But it might not have done, she thought. And suddenly she was filled with a righteous anger and her breathing slowed and her heart turned into a steel piston and her muscles

298

clenched and relaxed and she felt limber and as strong as a platoon of grunts.

'It's too late!' a man's voice yelled from the bedroom. 'It's going to take them all!'

'JUST YOU LEAVE HER ALONE!' Hettie heard herself bellow, and she strode towards the bedroom, ready to take on the devil himself if he was there.

Hettie flung open the bedroom door and stood there, ready to kill if necessary. Ready to die to protect the child. But there was nothing to protect her from except the stench of pipe-tobacco smoke, the chill in the air, the sound of something being beaten somewhere (but not in *this* room) and an odd high-pitched whistle like a faulty fluorescent tube. Gloria lay on the bed thrashing from side to side as if she was trapped in a nightmare. She didn't look hurt.

Frowning, Hettie went to her. The closer she got to the bed, the colder it grew. 'Be *out*, demons!' she commanded, surprised at the power that rang in her voice. 'Leave this child! In the name of God the Father, *leave this child!*'

A disembodied, echoing voice that seemed to come from the air about a foot and a half above Gloria's head and another foot or so to the side gave a very masculine moan of pain.

'Begone!' Hettie shouted.

'Ouch ... hurts ... Gloria. Don't!' the man's voice said, from thin air. 'Leave me some room! You're *hurting* me!'

Hettie frowned. *I know this voice*, she thought, in utter amazement. *It isn't a ghost at all. It's someone I've seen on a television show.*

3

'I *do*! I *know* these people,' Elaine gasped. 'Sooty! Look!'

Sooty was already looking. Her eyes had been fixed on Spreadbury's face since it had begun to change. The fresh faces that swept on and off the blank pink slate his own face had become were now complete and whole. She'd seen Jim's face enter and leave Spreadbury's at least twice already. And she knew why Elaine knew the rest of the people, too. It was the entire company that had set off on the trip to

299

Straker's Island a few hours ago. There was Candy. And Jim again. And the fat woman. Jon the writer. The thin woman. Jim again. Rosie. And . . .

'Jesus, Sooty, that was you!' Elaine cried. 'Oh, my, that one was *me*! What does it mean?'

'I don't know,' Sooty said. But she had a pretty good idea. The god of the island, or the ghosts that existed there, were in direct communication with Spreadbury. What they were witnessing were the faces of those about to die.

'Oh . . . Oh . . . Ouch, Gloria! Leave me some room. You're *hurting* me!' Spreadbury gasped as the line of faces continued to swarm across him. 'Oh, my. It's happening. It's awake and it's got Davey. Davey, *Davey*. The god's *awake*. It's too late. It's going to take them all. Motherfucker. Motherfucker! Elaine!' he boomed, suddenly switching voices from his own to someone else's. Another voice that Sooty remembered and one that caused Elaine to shriek and drop her gun.

The blurred motion of faces suddenly solidified and Spreadbury's stance, his entire stature, seemed to alter. Suddenly Spreadbury no longer stood there at all. He had somehow become Elaine's dead ex-boyfriend, Mark. His right eye and a section of the skull above was missing. Something alive was squirming inside the dark red hole.

'Hi, honey pie!' Mark said, grinning.

'G-g-geddaway!' Elaine hissed, shuffling backwards. She glanced from Mark to the gun she'd dropped and back again.

'I'd love to, but I can't,' Mark said. 'Not till all this is over and done. You see, I made a deal. That much is true. I took out a contract on you just like you thought. But I didn't take it out with a hit-man, I took it out with a god.' He giggled. 'And I didn't take it out until after that bitch shot half my head off. But, hey, don't worry about me! It's better being dead than being alive. It is, if you know the right places to turn off down that long dark tunnel through which we all must pass, anyway. I took the right turn. I heard the god calling to me, offering me a deal. "You want to get even with that emasculating bitch Elaine?" it called out at me. So I went. And guess what, honey pie? You're not just down to die, you're down to suffer the agonies of eternal hell-fire

300

afterwards and I get a free season ticket so's I can come and watch. And taunt you. You'll be sorry you crossed me, you bitch!'

'Go to hell!' Elaine screamed, and dropped to her knees and snatched up the gun.

Sooty watched the way the gun seemed to *want* to mould itself to the shape of Elaine's hand.

'Oh, it's you who'll be going to hell, my poisonous little viper.' Mark grinned. 'I'll just be visiting you there!'

Elaine thumbed the hammer of the Magnum.

'Don't!' Sooty yelled.

'Kill me! Come on, let's see if you have the balls to stand up to me now I'm dead!' Mark taunted. 'You couldn't damned well do it when I was alive, you sloppy little shit-eating cunt! I bet you all the tea in China you can't do it now!'

Elaine growled like a tiger. Her lips drew back from her clenched teeth in a feral grin.

'FOR GOD'S SAKE, DON'T DO IT!' Sooty yelled. 'It's *not* Mark! It's something pretending to be him! It's still Spreadbury under there and this thing wants you to kill him because it knows he can help us!'

Elaine glanced over at her. 'It's not him?' she asked bemusedly.

'It's me, you stupid little cocksucker!' Mark said, amused. 'Who the fuck else could it be? It's me. And I bet you couldn't hit a barn door with that fucking great cannon you're holding. Try me, bitch!'

'Ignore it,' Sooty said. 'It just wants you to shoot Spread-bury. And if it wants that, it must be—'

'Shut the fuck up, Queenie!' Mark said, wheeling towards her. 'Or I'll fuck you so hard you'll never stand again, let alone walk. Dead or not, I can still fuck you harder than that wuss of a pretend writer you're so proud of.'

'Mark!' Elaine yelled. 'Stop that or I'll blow your fucking head off like I should have done two years ago! I mean it!'

'Don't do it, Elaine!' Sooty cried.

'Useless bitch!' Mark snarled. 'Coward!'

And the Magnum roared.

Sooty was momentarily blinded by the muzzle-flash and

301

deafened by the noise. Afterwards she was surprised to see Mark gone and Spreadbury, apparently unhurt, standing where he'd been all along.

'I had to do it!' Elaine apologized shakily. 'I don't know what that fucking thing *was*, whether it was Mark or not, but I knew damned well it wasn't going away until I'd fired this gun at it. And hit it.'

'You missed,' Sooty said.

'No, I nicked his left ear, exactly as I intended,' Elaine said. 'You'll see the blood when he turns his head.'

Spreadbury merely stood where he was, looking pretty much like a machine with its plug pulled out. *His body is empty, right now*, Sooty thought, and wondered what would find its way in there next.

4

Abruptly, the voice stopped speaking and Gloria went limp.

Hettie frowned at her, hanging on to the memory of the man's voice. She knew it very well indeed, but couldn't quite place where she'd heard it, who it belonged to. *It's certainly someone I've seen on the television, and more than once*, she thought. *And recently, too. So how can a television personality – or actor – be possessing the body of a little girl?*

The actor, or presenter, could have died, of course, but Hettie was pretty sure she'd heard that voice earlier this week. Although she wasn't sure whether or not it was on a live show. Most stuff was pre-recorded these days.

It sounds like something from that awful Psychic Week *show they put on*, she thought, still shaken, but no longer scared. She'd found an inner strength she'd never known she possessed. Until now. Discovering this amazing new thing about herself was almost worth the heart-stopping scares she'd been through today.

She stroked Gloria's brow. The chill still hung in the air about the little girl, but she was hot now and her forehead was damp. 'You'll be safe with me,' Hettie promised her. 'Just relax. I won't let anything happen to you. I'll be here

302

for you, sweetheart.' She stroked the hair away from Gloria's cherubic face and found a smile on her own.

And just as she'd begun to relax, Gloria abruptly sat bolt upright and sucked in a harsh breath, the choked sound of which almost curdled Hettie's blood.

'*They're coming to get Daddy!*' Gloria said, in the man's voice, and Hettie remembered where she'd heard the voice before, remembered whose voice it was.

It belonged to the psychic Aaron Spreadbury, the presenter of the popular weekly cable-television show *Strange and Stranger* on which they investigated the unknown. Hettie had seen it once or twice and had actually turned on the television to see it two days ago. Because it had been a live broadcast featuring the fork-bender, Uri Geller. Hettie had dutifully put Artie's broken old wrist-watch on top of the television, as Spreadbury had asked, but it hadn't begun to work again. And all her cutlery had remained intact, too.

'I don't believe it,' she said aloud. She hadn't even *liked* Spreadbury. He was oily and too full of himself. He thought he was a world authority on the paranormal. Hettie suddenly realized, indignantly, that he might well have been right.

'*Oh, my God, they're coming to get Daddy!*' Gloria gasped again, in Spreadbury's deep, resonant voice.

'Who are?' Hettie asked, fighting off the feeling of having entered a strange new world where everything looked the same, but everything was different. 'Who are, and how can I help?'

'I can't hear you,' Gloria said, this time in her own voice. 'He has most of my ears. I can only hear a little bit. He's trying to fix it. Just don't let her get me. Okay?'

'Who?' Hettie said. 'Tell me who and I'll protect you. I'll see they don't get you, honey. Who is it?'

'My mom,' Gloria moaned, and collapsed back on the bed.

5

Spreadbury gasped, gave a quick, scary jerk and stood bolt upright, his eyes open and distant – and, Sooty noticed, the

wrong colour. His watery blue eyes were now a deep mocha
brown, pretty much the colour of her own eyes.

Elaine gave a small cry, but that was all. Her gun was still
clenched in her hand, still pointing steadily at Spreadbury as
if she expected demons to pour from him, but Sooty didn't
think she would fire again. She'd spent the last two or three
minutes explaining to Elaine what she'd intuited about
Spreadbury: that he was the genuine article and that whatever was loose on the island had located him and wanted
him stopped, wanted Elaine to kill him.

They needed Spreadbury. Sooty knew that now and
cursed herself for not listening to the man a good deal
earlier. *Maybe it wouldn't have come to this if I'd listened, if
I hadn't just dismissed him as a crank*, she thought. *We could
have fixed everything way back.* But she had distrusted and
dismissed him and it was no use crying over spilt milk.

Anyone else in my position would have done the same, she
thought, but the fact was, Sooty thought she was a little bit
psychic herself – she depended on her intuition a great deal
in everyday matters. But with this she'd dismissed what she'd
felt was right because logic told her it couldn't be. *Logic and
cynicism and fear*, she added. Those negative things she
normally tried to keep out of her life had screwed it up
royally.

Sooty moaned when Spreadbury's mouth opened and
Gloria's voice came out.

'They're coming to get Daddy!' Spreadbury said.

'Oh, *fuck*, he's got Gloria!' Elaine moaned.

'Gloria? Honey?' Sooty asked.

'They're coming to get Daddy. You have to save Daddy.
They're going to get inside his body so he can bring them
back over the water,' Spreadbury moaned, his new dark eyes
– *Gloria*'s eyes – darting back and forth as if looking for the
approaching attackers.

Sooty was frantic now: she felt as if something inside her
was being torn apart. '*Who?* Who's going to get inside
Daddy's body?'

Gloria/Spreadbury gave a sob. 'My *first* mommy and
daddy,' Gloria's voice said. 'The bad ones.'

Sooty glanced at Elaine, who looked as distraught as she

304

felt. Everything Spreadbury had claimed was true and accurate. 'Honey, can you hear me?' she asked.

In Spreadbury's face Gloria's eyes continued to dart back and forth. She didn't speak.

'Honey?' Sooty said. 'Gloria?'

'I can hardly hear you,' Gloria said. 'Auntie Hettie ... She's ...'

'Hettie? What about Hettie?'

' ... talking ...' Gloria said, through Spreadbury. 'The cat. I can't move, Mommy. I'm stuck. Mr Spreadbury is in here with me. There's no room. It's too small. The cat ... Marmie ... the cat ...'

'Who's going to get your daddy?' Elaine said. 'What do you mean, your first mommy and daddy?'

'Mommy and Daddy Dauphin. The ghosts. I don't want that Mommy and Daddy back again. They're bad. They killed me. Don't let that Mommy and Daddy come back, I don't want to be dead again. Please *hurry*!'

'You're still with Hettie?' Sooty asked.

'I'm in Mr Spreadbury, but I can't see out. He's in me. It's tight. It hurts. We're all tangled up. Hettie. The cat, Mom. Stop the cat. The cat is going to kill Auntie Hettie. I'm in here, but I can see the cat. Marmie. He's outside. I don't know how I can see him, but I can see him. And I can see what happens from here too. The cat comes up the stairs. It makes a horrible noise and Auntie Hettie goes to see what it wants and it's at the top of the stairs and she bends down and it jumps up and claws her face and she falls down the stairs and dies and the cat comes in here and ... Oh, *Mom* ... that cat is *bad*!'

'You're still at your auntie Hettie's?' Elaine asked. 'You're sure?'

'I'm stuck here,' Gloria said. 'That cat wants to kill me so my first mom and dad ... so they ... The monster on the island ate me once, but I escaped and went to heaven. My first mom and dad fed me to the monster. Don't let them do it again.'

'I won't,' Sooty said. 'I promise.'

'And so do I!' Elaine added.

'Just hurry up and get Daddy before Daddy Dauphin or

305

the monster on the island gets him. *Please!* And mind Jon and Candy. I have to tell you that. That's important. Mind Jon and Candy. *They* told me to say that.'

'Who told you, darling?' Sooty asked, but she was pretty sure she already knew.

Spreadbury shook his head. 'I don't know,' Gloria's voice said. 'The angels. The angels on my pillow. I dunno what they are.'

'Honey, I . . .' Sooty tailed off as Spreadbury's face began to swarm and change again. The faces of Jim and all the others flitted across it in quick rotation, but when his flesh settled, Spreadbury had his own face, his own watery blue eyes. He gazed dazedly at nothing. 'My God, that *hurt*,' he said, and collapsed.

Chapter Nineteen

Babes in the Wood: Martha and June

1

Of all the moments Martha Rivers had been on the face of the planet earth – forty-three years, two months and twenty-three day's worth of moments if you were counting – this one had to be the peak, the zenith. She'd never felt anything like this level of fear, exhilaration and, if she was being truthful with herself, raw sexual excitement. Not even her ex-husband, with whom she'd been deeply in love and who had surely been a genuine sex god, had ever brought her this close to heaven itself.

She pressed her back to the tree that she and June had chosen to hide behind and panted in breath after breath of the warm woodland air while her blood coursed through her veins and arteries and her every nerve-ending sang a song of delight.

'Oh, oh oh, my,' she gasped. 'Am I h-h-having the time of my life!' She looked at June and coughed out a chuckle. June was barely recognizable beneath the coating of dirty red blood that had drenched her. She was smeared with dirt all down her dress and somewhere back there she'd been showered in multi-coloured confetti, which dotted her hair, face and shoulders. Martha guessed she looked pretty much that way too – she'd caught more than a dousing of the horrible fake blood and at one point she'd staggered into something that had guts pouring out of it, *real* guts, even if they were from an animal. It was all disgusting, of course, but there was something earthy and sensual about it, too, although she couldn't understand quite why. Perhaps it was a kind of race memory: the joy of the hunt, the feel of the kill beneath your hands.

'You lost your lunch,' June said, finding this statement highly amusing and almost choking herself with a fit of the giggles she couldn't find the breath for.

Martha hadn't thrown up – she hadn't lost a lunch that way for better than twenty years, but she *had* become parted from her bag of food. She wasn't sure when. 'It was dragged out of my hands.' She chortled, not even caring. She had a feeling that from this point on she wouldn't be eating as much as she had. This trip had changed her. The island made her feel different about herself. She was a good-looking woman underneath this big wobbly security blanket she'd begun to build for herself after her ex had run off, and she deserved better from life. 'It doesn't matter,' she told June happily. 'As from now, I'm on a diet. I'm gonna catch me a man!'

'One like Jon?' June giggled, obviously referring to Jon and Candy's earlier escapade in the sea. There had been something primal – and *very* sexy – about that, too. No one had talked about it, but Martha was pretty sure that everyone had felt the same way as she had: that she would very much like to be fucked hard in that way, floating in that warm sea. And with an audience.

'He'd do, for starters,' Martha said.

'It was great the way that corpse popped up out of the ground and how you instantly whammed it in the face with your bag!' June said.

Martha snorted. That was where she'd lost the bag. Its strap had caught around the stiff arm of the shop-window dummy and she'd been running so hard and in such terror that she hadn't paused to untangle it.

'Jeez, I've never seen anything like *this* in my entire life!' June enthused. 'This is . . .'

'Magnificent?' Martha suggested breathlessly.

'Cathartic,' June said. 'Course, if I actually knew what cathartic meant, I might know whether or not I was using the right word. It's kinda . . .'

'Freeing?'

'I feel about a zillion times more alive than I have done since I was a teenager. Last time I felt this good I was tromping up the stairs of the local haunted house on Hill

Street back in my old home town with Joey Navintsky, knowing that when we got upstairs I was going to let him take my virginity,' June said. 'Course, the actual act wasn't so much a climax as an anti-climax, but it was the *anticipation*, the feeling of letting everything go to hell and not caring if it did. That's the way I feel now.'

'Me too,' Martha agreed. 'I'm having the time of my life! If I died right now I wouldn't even care!'

'Me neither! I've never seen *anything* like it in my life, and I've seen a few things, believe me!'

'And it's *still* going on,' Martha said as, deep in the woods, someone shouted in terror. 'I've never *been* as frightened. God only knows how they did all those special effects.'

A nearby firework chose that moment to explode, apparently at random, since no one else was close. Both women jumped and shrieked and then tittered with embarrassment.

'You should have seen your face when that first blood-bag burst over us!' Martha chortled.

'You should have seen yours! I thought you were going to die on the spot,' June replied, pushing her thickly stained hair back from her face. 'Do I look waaaay cool?' she asked, pulling a face.

'Sure. You look like something from a slaughter-house,' Martha told her. 'Hey, did you see the way that Frank took off like a frightened rabbit?'

'What a coward!' June said. 'Mister Macho, I'm-in-control-here, has the heart of a kitten!'

'A wuss in wuss's clothing!' Martha agreed. 'So, what do we do now? Go back to the beach? I suppose that's the general idea.'

June shook her head. 'I don't know if I *can*. Not just yet, anyway. We'll only set off more traps and my heart's still hammering from the last lot.'

'Okay, hon, we'll wait here for a bit. Catch our breath. Let the others take whatever's left. We'll move out when things die down a bit. I can still hear those screeching things going off in the distance.'

'And talking about screeching things,' June said, 'how about the way Candy screamed?'

309

'Anyone would think she was being killed or something,' Martha said.

June sniggered. 'Maybe she and Jon *met up* again . . .'

'Twice? At that intensity? I'd just die!' Martha replied.

Above their heads the branches of the tree they were hiding behind began to swish though the air. Both women looked up.

'I can't feel the trunk moving,' June observed. 'What do you think's doing that? I've seen it several times now. It happened when we were back on the beach. One of the trees behind the house did it. Another did it just before we got splattered by that first blood-bag.'

'It'll be something to do with the effects, I guess,' Martha said, watching the branches. A shower of pine needles was now falling steadily from the upper limbs. 'They've probably got overhead wires rigged up or something.'

Neither woman noticed what had started just to the left of them – both were too busy looking for the movement of hidden wires up in the air.

When the voice spoke to them, both of them shrieked, threw up their hands in terror, then dissolved into a fit of giggling.

Jim stood before them wearing, in Martha's opinion, a pretty damned good make-up job.

'You came as a zombie, I guess.' She chuckled. Whoever had done Jim's transformation must have been a professional – probably a make-up guy or girl he knew through his film work. It was very convincing. His flesh appeared to be blacked and worm-eaten. It hung from his face in tatters. He was dressed in rotted clothing, the style of which had probably been modern a hundred years ago. His feet showed through his ruined leather shoes. His toes were encrusted with dirt and their nails were long and sharp and horny. But it was his face that amazed Martha. She couldn't believe how that hole in his head, *and* the empty eye socket, looked so convincing. Something alive was squirming in that hole, right back where his brain should be. And where was his real eye? The socket looked too deep for his real face to be below it.

'Good evening, ladies,' Jim said.

Martha found herself shivering. It barely seemed possible that this was the same handsome, charming man. His voice was totally different – it sounded like someone grinding stones together. His hair was thick with mud and the wrong colour, too, which suggested it was a wig. But the *voice* . . .

'Oh, Jim! I nearly died of fright! What a day out!' June bleated.

'Brilliant make-up! And that *voice*!' Martha added, with as much enthusiasm as she could muster. Her hilarity had left her now. Jim *smelt*. Surely it hadn't been necessary to make him stink like a rotting corpse, too? A small warning bell was sounding in the back of her mind. There was something different about this, something not quite right.

Jim shuffled closer and stopped right in front of her. He peered at her through his single eye, the iris and pupil of which had somehow been whitened. Martha suspected it was a contact lens, then she suspected it *wasn't*.

'My, you look terrible, Jim,' she said uncertainly. 'What are you going to do now?'

Jim's mouth curled, showing slimy green teeth. 'You've woken the god that slumbers upon this island. Now you must help it go back to sleep,' he grated, with a distinct French accent.

'Uh, so what do we have to do?' Martha asked, as the alarm bells got louder. *This is not Jim at all*, she thought.

'Bleed,' Jim said.

Martha glanced at June, who was grinning inanely at Jim.

'Bleed?' June asked, a hint of humour in her voice. 'Cut ourselves, you mean?'

The man whom Martha no longer believed to be Jim at all but Straker Dauphin, the ghost of the man who had once lived here, according to Jim's tall tale, didn't look at June, but stared deep into Martha and said, 'It scents blood like a shark. And homes in. Blood means life. It feeds on life. When its appetite is sated it will sleep again.'

'I see,' June said, from right beside her, apparently unfazed.

She doesn't know, that's why, Martha thought. She was frightened now. Very frightened.

311

'We have to be sacrificed, right?' June continued happily. 'Okay. How do you propose doing it, Jim?'

'*Don't!*' Martha said, and began to move. She could run. She had her breath back now and adrenaline was pumping into her and she *could* run. This thing, this zombie or ghost or whatever it was, could only shuffle. Half of it was missing. Its feet were rotten. It wouldn't be able to catch her. If she could only break away before it struck, she was home, free. She could get back to the beach and, if it was necessary, she could swim all the way out to the *Mary Celeste*. She was a good swimmer. A strong, fast swimmer. And ghosts couldn't travel across water. Everyone knew that.

Before her, Straker Dauphin was smiling.

As if in slow motion, Martha turned, feeling her muscles tense to spring her away like a sprinter from the starting blocks. There was plenty of time. She was fast. She could make it. Now she had turned far enough and her legs were bent, her muscles were limber and strong and powering her away and Straker Dauphin hadn't moved a muscle.

I'm free! Martha thought, rejoicing inwardly. *I've done it! I'm away!*

2

'We have to be sacrificed, right?' June said happily. It was a neat game and she was enthralled by the face-job someone had done on Jim. She was enthralled by *everything* that had happened so far. She felt exhilarated and strangely elated. 'Okay. How do you propose doing it, Jim?' she added, and was surprised when Martha suddenly spoke.

'*Don't!*' Martha said from beside her, and June glanced at her in surprise. There was an expression of terror on the big woman's face and June didn't know why. Neither did she know why Martha had suddenly become tense as if she meant to dart away.

It's only Jim dressed up as that French man he told us about in his story, June thought. *Jim isn't going to harm us!*

She glanced back at Jim, who was smiling at her. 'I'm going to do it like *this*!' he said. And swiped out a clawed hand.

In the following second June noticed several things as if time had slowed for her. The first was the movement of Jim's arm and hand through the air. Bits were flying off him, scraps of flesh, flecks of dirt, tiny threads of material from his jacket, and spiralled away as if caught in tiny tornadoes. Then there was Martha beside her, seemingly locked in the position of someone starting to sprint away from a standing position. Her face was slack, her eyes wide, her mouth open in a perfect O. The rolls of fat at her ankles had leaped upwards a few inches. She was making a strange keening noise. And last, but by no means least, there were Jim's eyes. They'd changed colour. He now had two perfect eyes rather than one smeared one and an empty socket. The irises seemed to dance with tiny veins of red fire; the pupils were utter darkness – two points of singularity possessing a massive gravity, a sucking power from which nothing could escape.

And the second ended.

The speed of the moment that followed was undoubtedly increased by June's previous sensation of everything happening in slow-motion. The moment came and went before she knew it.

Suddenly, Jim's hand was back where it had started from, now holding something that looked a little like a damp red rag. Martha was no longer poised as if to run. She was on her knees, not falling, not toppling sideways, but merely on her knees, her hands reaching up to her face.

Which was absent.

There was nothing there but a wet red mass.

Martha began to scream, long and loud.

Her face. What happened to her face? June thought stupidly, and her eyes flicked back to the red rag dangling from Jim's hand and she knew. In one awful moment she realized three things. This wasn't Jim in front of her, this was Straker Dauphin incarnate. He'd torn off Martha's face and lastly, and most importantly, June knew she was frozen where she was.

Behind where Straker Dauphin stood, pulling at her with those electric eyes and their black hole pupils, something was approaching. It was invisible, but bushes were crushed

313

beneath it. Trees bent and complained and splintered as its movements cast them aside. The ground was trembling beneath June's feet. Way back there, where the huge *thing* was, tiny fires danced ahead of it, skipping through the undergrowth in bursts of yellow and purple flame before dying away.

Nothing is catching fire, a part of June thought, amazed in spite of the agony of terror that had built to bursting point in her. She was going to die, she knew that. Or, worse, she was going to suffer death and still be alive – perhaps as a facet of the island's god, which was now free of its bonds and up and walking.

The pressure of the air in her eardrums increased as the god grew closer. Her ears whistled and made noises like boiling fat.

I'm going to die, June thought, and relaxed.

Straker Dauphin wheeled around to face the invisible thing, glanced back at June with an expression that was half contempt and half fear, and shuffled to the next closest tree and encircled it with his arms. A moment later he was gone.

And the god was slowly, inexorably, coming towards her.

June took a deep breath to scream what was going to be her last scream, then her body's reflexes took over and she had turned and was running, harder and faster than she'd ever run in her life. She was nimble now, her feet might have belonged to Mercury himself. She flowed through the trees and undergrowth as gracefully as a gazelle, knowing that she was away, knowing that she could keep running, her feet finding their places with utter surety, her sense of balance infallible, for as long as it took to outpace the slow-moving god.

It's not awake, she thought. *Not properly. It's yawning and rubbing its eyes. It's stiff and sluggish after a million years of captivity. I can beat it!*

She glanced back just in time to see the invisible thing whisk Martha from the ground and throw her high into the air. For a second Martha was falling, then she seemed to explode as if someone had put a bomb inside her.

She fell to earth in wet pieces.

314

3

June was barely aware of the fireworks exploding behind her as she passed, or the chittering laughing-bags or the screamers. She had somehow turned from an unfit forty-three-year-old librarian, whose only regular exercise was tottering down to the mail-box in the mornings for the latest letter from her pen-friend in Australia, into a tireless machine that existed only to run.

And yet a tiny nugget of her mind was cool and detached; an ice-cube that refused to melt in the centre of the Sahara. This part deduced that now this had happened she'd very likely never get to meet Sammy, her Australian, the only man with whom she'd ever been truly in love. Sammy was a divorced man of forty-four and June had lived the last four years in daily contact with him by mail and had spoken to him a dozen or so times on the telephone. It had started out as a kind of hobby, this writing to box numbers in the Lonely Hearts section of the paper, but from the moment her first letter from Sammy had arrived she'd *known*. This was her soul-mate, the man with whom she would spend the rest of her life. He was funny, he was handsome, he was strong and he was caring. And in two months June would be going Down Under to meet him. For two months. And after she'd finished humping out at least a year's worth of sexual frustration (his letters, sometimes erotic, sometimes romantic, turned her on so much she could barely function – his voice on the phone made her ache for him) she was going to ask him to marry her. And Sammy would say yes. She just knew he would. He felt exactly the same way she did about their relationship.

Just keep out of its way, that glacial part of her instructed. *For Sammy. Be smart and you'll marry Sammy. Be dumb and you'll die.*

June glanced back. Behind her a spent firework, nailed to the trunk of a tree, dropped red gobbets of flame on to a patch of bare earth. Whoever had set up the pyrotechnics evidently hadn't wanted to set the woods on fire. Nothing appeared to be crashing towards her. June slowed down, suddenly aware of how much her body hurt, how raw her lungs felt.

Be smart! Her mind warned. *It may not be safe. You have to get off the island.*

The trouble with getting off the island was that June didn't have a clue where she was. Her sense of direction had deserted her entirely.

Worse, the light was fading fast.

And now she'd almost caught her breath again, she fancied she could hear that swishing sound of trees shaking back in the distance. The god might still be half asleep, but it was on her track like a bloodhound.

Be smart! If you can get out to sea, it'll lose the scent. Ghosts can't travel over water. I doubt this god can, either. It was put on this island for some reason, so that might be it. All you have to do is find your way back to the boat.

June tried not to think about what would happen if the dinghy was gone when she eventually found her way back to the beach – she couldn't swim. All she would be able to do was wade out into the ocean and hope the ghosts and god couldn't.

It was hope, and hope was almost all June had left. She brought to her mind her favourite photograph of Sammy. In it, he wore only a towel and was posing like a muscle-man and grinning like a fool. That picture was the second one of him he'd sent her and even the thought of it warmed her heart. She just couldn't wait to get her hands on that lean, wiry body of his.

This way, she thought, checking the scar on her hand and turning to her left. She began to trot – surprised there was still strength in her legs, more surprised that, once she began to move, her strained muscles felt good about going back to work.

And a few minutes later she realized she'd made a good choice. Here was a well-worn path. Paths went somewhere and, since no one except Jim and his wife ever came out here, the chances were that the path ran from the Dauphin house to somewhere else they went a lot. All she had to do was choose a direction. She would either get right back to the beach or to the other place, the place where the path went. And if she arrived there, where she didn't want to be, it'd be merely a matter of going the *other* way to get to where she *did* want to be.

She paused for a moment, lowered her head, closed her eyes and asked Sammy for advice, just the way she did every time she had to make a tough choice. In her mind Sammy always answered and always said the right thing. It might have been merely her unconscious she was addressing, she knew that, but she liked to believe she had a psychic link to her man.

Go the way you're facing, love, Sammy said in her mind, in his broad, friendly Australian accent.

June smiled, silently thanked Sammy, opened her eyes and began to run before she'd raised her head to see what was in front of her. This was a fault in her that she hadn't been able to conquer. She *always* dipped her head to ask Sammy questions and she invariably moved off afterwards before she was certain the way ahead was clear. She'd tripped and fallen on numerous occasions in the past year, although she'd never done herself any lasting harm.

Until now, when she ran straight into Straker Dauphin.

A ghost cannot be solid! her mind complained, as the thing took her in its arms and pulled her to it in a lover's caress. The stench was overwhelming. Straker Dauphin dipped his head to her neck as if to kiss her. June fought against his grip then, realizing she wasn't going to break it easily, pulled her head away from his mouth.

It worked. To an extent. If she hadn't moved, Straker's teeth would have torn out the left side of her throat, severing her carotid and jugular. But he didn't miss her entirely. His teeth snapped shut on a good chunk of skin, bit and tore it away. The pain was tremendous. June brought up her knee into the thing's groin, which had no effect, then, feeling her blood moisten her shoulder, struggled frantically and broke free.

'I could eat you all up!' Straker said, as she backed away. His teeth were red with her blood, his lips smeared.

June turned on her heel and ran in the opposite direction, her left hand clamped to the wound on her neck. She didn't know how badly damaged she was and she didn't want to

317

know. All she knew was that it hurt and it was bleeding but that she couldn't possibly stop until she found her way out of this terrible place. She ran.

And suddenly there it was before her. June glanced over her shoulder, wincing at the pain the movement caused her, saw nothing behind her or in the wood on either side of the path.

I did it! she thought. The Dauphin house lay before her to her right. She was standing at the bottom edge of its backyard. There was a patch of something wet and dark on the soil about four feet from her. Beside that lay a sickle. June refused even to consider what that might mean. And it didn't matter because she was less than a minute from open water and safety.

She took a deep breath, glanced around her again and moved on, noticing something happen to that wet smear on the ground as she passed it. It seemed to bloom like a flower. She looked back as she began to run again. The entire clearing where the backyard was was now one massive black hole in the ground.

Oh, my Christ! June thought.

A moment later, knowing now that she would never meet Sammy in the flesh, June exploded.

Chapter Twenty

Babes in the Wood: Jon

Jon didn't have the faintest idea how he'd come to be where he was, or where everyone else was. Some of them were still screaming and the fireworks were still going off in the distance, so he guessed that not everyone had run when it all went haywire back there. Some of the others were still there, still enjoying being frightened.

Jon had run as soon as he'd heard what he'd thought was gunfire from right beside him. There were still demons living inside his head: he had regular nightmares about his father turning up, maddened and armed with a big semi-automatic, and he'd reacted accordingly. Something had exploded and he'd run, just the way he'd wanted to run when Jim had let off the first firework back there on the dock. And he'd kept running until he'd felt safe. There was nothing to be ashamed of in that.

He walked along the small path grinning at his stupidity. He'd come here to be frightened and he'd got his money's worth. He hadn't just been frightened, he'd been scared shitless.

And now he was lost and it was getting darker by the minute and he didn't have a flashlight. If Jim or someone didn't come soon and find him he'd have to sleep here, or wander about until he found his own way back to the beach. At this particular moment he didn't care which.

Because he had the distinct feeling that something magical was going to happen. He was pretty sure he now knew what gave Jim his edge, what made the man so good, and consequently so *rich*. This island was absolutely *stuffed* with magic. You only had to stand still and open your mind and you could feel it flooding in: ideas, sensations, possibilities.

319

The entire place felt like a cross between a gold-mine and a wishing well that actually worked. The very air thrummed with power.

The path led to what appeared to be a dead end in front of a large bush. He peered at the leaves of it for a time, not sure he'd ever seen anything like it before. He wasn't a gardener or a horticulturist, but the bush looked *wrong* as if it belonged in another kind of wood. A rain-forest, perhaps.

While he frowned at the strange leaves, he noticed that the path didn't stop in front of what he was now mentally referring to as *the magic bush* but went past it. It was merely hidden by the growth of those weird-looking big leaves.

Jon pushed past the foliage. What lay beyond was a large dark pool almost large enough to be called a lake, he supposed. The area was completely surrounded – the words 'sealed off' came to mind – from the rest of the wood by thick scrub, bushes and tightly packed trees. Overhead a few stars twinkled in the fading light.

Jon walked a few paces down the gentle slope of mud that seemed to run all round the body of water. It was very soft and sucked at his shoes, but Jon felt a great urge to touch that dark water. There was no smell of stagnant water here, which, he supposed, was because there were no animals and presumably no micro-organisms. The water in the lake might be sterile, he thought.

Better than that, it might possess some of the magic that Jim was able so easily to tap into. Jon intended to crouch beside the water, cup his hands and taste some of that water. And if it tasted good, he would drink some more. He told himself he was pretty damned thirsty anyway, but he knew this was only an excuse. What he wanted was magic. And this looked like a magical place – the kind of lake from which a hand might rise offering up Excalibur. Why else would it be so well guarded against intruders? And the fact that the path existed clearly pointed out that Jim visited this place often. Jon wanted to know why. And intended to find out.

He moved carefully down the bank – at each step the mud threatened to swallow his footwear and eventually let it go with a faintly disgusting slurping noise – and squatted down beside the dark water. Not a breath of air stirred it. It looked like a huge black mirror. Jon stayed hunkered down for a while, wondering if this stuff really was water or a big pool of oil. He tried to peer down into it, but it didn't seem to reflect any light and, as far as he could tell, the fluid was opaque. He entertained a brief notion that there was no water there – or any kind of fluid – but rather that the lake was a gateway into another universe, then forcefully dismissed the notion. It was water. It couldn't be anything else.

When he finally put his fingertips into it the water was warm. It didn't seem to ripple, though, which was stranger than strange. He withdrew his fingers, sniffed them (there was no odour) then tasted his middle finger with the tip of his tongue.

A tiny tingle like an electric current ran through his body.

Jon grinned. Oh, that it had! This fluid tasted just like regular bottled spring water, nothing more, nothing less. In spite of its colour and resistance to rippling, it was just good honest water, darkened by the sky. It had not affected him in any way whatsoever.

Jon cupped his hand, took some water and sucked it into his mouth. It was quite refreshing. 'They'll find me dead here in the morning,' he muttered, as he drank another handful. And another.

'Be careful. One more sip and you'll sleep for a month,' a gentle female voice said, from behind him. Whoever it was sounded amused. 'And when you wake up you'll remember nothing at all. You'll be a child again. An empty tablet.'

If his shoes hadn't sunk down to his ankles in the mud, Jon would have swung round to face the owner of the voice, his heart hammering with shock. As it was, he tried to swing round and fell on his side. True to form, when faced with the slightest shock, even though there was no apparent danger, his heart battered at his ribcage.

And then it began to beat faster and harder for another reason.

Sooty Green stood up there by the bush he'd pushed through not five minutes ago, large as life and twice as good-looking. She was taller than Candy, her figure more elegant, her neck long, her face ... Jon didn't know what it was

321

about her face. Something about her eyes, he thought. The woman wouldn't have made the front cover of *Vogue* or any of the other magazines, but that was because she wasn't pretty in that plastic way that editors and design folk seemed to think was the zenith of gorgeousness. Sooty Green was *truly* beautiful. Her dark eyes looked through your own eyes, right down inside you to where you lived; right down to your very soul. Her smile weakened your knees.

Lying there on his side in the mud, Jon gaped at her, aware that he was gaping but unable to stop himself. He tried to match her, to drink her in the way she was drinking him in, but he was unable to do it. What he could do, he realized, was gain an erection that felt like stainless steel. This wasn't merely a sexy woman, this was a *heavenly* one.

Sooty was wearing the same dress he had seen her in earlier in the house – when he thought he'd imagined her. The memory was confusing. He seemed to have met her in a dream. He wasn't quite sure what had happened back there. Hadn't she made him a promise? Hadn't she wanted him?

Jon couldn't tell and, if he was being honest with himself, he couldn't have cared less. Because being under Sooty's gaze was like being immersed in a bath of warm honey. And because of the aching, super-hard erection in his chinos that just *begged* for relief.

Sooty's black dress with the little pearl buttons and loops was held together only by a single button at the navel. It was wet, Jon noted, as if she'd been bathing in the lake, and it clung to her hips and breasts like a second skin. Her perfect, tawny skin gleamed moistly: Jon knew exactly how it would feel under his fingers, his lips; how it would taste as he ran the tip of his tongue over it in light spirals. Her hair was damp and pushed back from her face, revealing the flawless lines and angles of her achingly lovely face.

When she spoke her voice was soft and low and musical. 'I was hoping you'd find your way here. I've been waiting for you. I've been waiting for you for a very long time.'

Jon moved his mouth to make a reply, something along the lines of 'And I've been waiting for you too,' but nothing happened. It all seemed a little incongruous, as if an ironic joke were being played on him.

322

'You have?' he heard himself ask eventually, in a tone of utter astonishment. He fought to get up. The mud didn't seem to want to let go of him.

'I have.' Sooty smiled, altering her position so that the lower half of her dress gaped. Her legs were long and lean. She put her fingers to her parted lips then ran them over her chin, trailing them down that long, elegant neck to her cleavage where they paused briefly before her hand dropped to her side again. 'You're a handsome man, Jon,' she said. 'Very handsome.'

Nothing will ever be the same again, Jon thought, and wondered where he'd heard those words before. A distant part of his mind – so far away it might have been back in Topeka – reminded him that the last time he'd thought those words his Suggestibility Wall had been torn down. 'Thanks,' he said, still struggling to get up. 'And you're a very lovely woman, too,' he added lamely. Suddenly he was on his feet, squelching his way towards where she stood and wiping black mud from his hands on his chinos.

And Sooty was coming down the strip of mud beach towards him, her dress parting around her legs, almost, but not quite, all the way up to her crotch. Jon stopped where he was, feeling his feet sinking into the mud again. *Why isn't she sinking, too?* the part of his mind back in Topeka asked.

He didn't know. Sooty was barefoot – perhaps that made a difference. Maybe she was just too light to sink in. But the mud didn't seem to have any hold on her at all: she walked across it as if it were solid paving.

Her perfume reached him well in advance of her. It was dizzying. Jon had never smelt anything like it in his life. It was earthy and musky, but had the lightness and freshness of summer blooms. It was a heady concoction, that was for sure – Jon's erection was now so hard it *hurt*.

She stopped so close to him that he could have reached out and taken her into his arms, so close her perfume made him reel. There was another note deep below the musk in that perfume now – a note that was jarring but still sexual somehow. It spoke of corruption; of death and rotting, of old blood. And power.

Sooty smiled. 'Tell me,' she asked in a low voice, 'what do

you most want out of life? Be honest. Be candid. Name it. Anything. I'd like to know.'

Jon gave a rueful smile. 'To write as well as Jim,' he replied, as his shoes sank an inch deeper into the mud.

'You already can,' she replied. 'I've seen the manuscripts you left on the boat.'

Jon felt himself blush. Which was another small irony. His penis was trying to cross the small gap to Sooty's warmth – and they both knew it. 'Thanks, but . . .' he said.

'Is there anything else Jim has that you'd like?' she asked.

The subtext of this question was not lost on Jon. But he thought it wise not to answer directly. 'His money. His boat. His Porsche,' he said.

Sooty affected a crestfallen look. 'Is that all?' she asked. 'There's nothing more of his you'd like to possess? His power, perhaps?'

Jon shrugged. 'Everything, really,' he said. 'I'd like to have it all.'

Sooty smiled knowingly. 'Even me?'

'*Especially* you,' Jon said, feeling his face flare brighter.

'But you want more than that, I know,' Sooty said. 'I can see the hunger burning right down in your soul. You need to *possess*, endlessly and eternally. You want more power than you can imagine. You want immortality, sensual pleasures beyond belief. You want the ecstasy of losing yourself in me and the universe. And I can give it all to you. And I can be beside you for ever. You can have me. Here and now. It's what I want.' Her deft fingers undid the remaining pearl button of her dress and she shrugged it off.

Jon moaned. The Topeka part of his mind began to crow that this was a trick because no one ever gave you something for nothing. No one ever gave without taking. But Jon was lost in Sooty's beauty, her promise.

She reached out her hands towards him. 'I can give you everything Jim has. And more. So much *more*. Come and take it. Take me.'

Jon leaned forward and moved his left leg, intending to take the single pace into her arms. The mud sucked his shoe right off, but Jon didn't care. He now existed just to force himself into Sooty, to lose himself in her, to fill her with him, to *merge*.

Sooty caught hold of his hand in a grip that was surely too powerful for such a slight woman, dragged him to her and kissed him, passionately and violently. Her full lips worked at his, her tongue probed and flicked, searching his mouth eagerly as if seeking some long-lost answer.

And Jon's mind lit with a series of images: Jim and Sooty, fucking in the sea, just as he'd fucked Candy in the sea. A huge, invisible, semi-conscious god stumbling through the woods attracted by the smell of blood, like a fairytale giant. Straker Dauphin in his backyard, babbling insanely as he opened up his young daughter's belly with a sharp knife and tugged out trails of intestine while Majesty held down the still-conscious child, who screamed and kicked and bled. Sooty, looking exactly like Majesty, in her home, slamming down the telephone and looking frightened. Sooty crying, alone in a huge bed. Jim in front of his computer, toying with a Colt .45 while tears ran down his face. A man he didn't recognize at the helm of a power-cruiser, suffering what looked like an epileptic fit while Sooty and Elaine from Collis and Anstey looked terrified. Candy in the arms of Straker Dauphin. Candy on the boat saying: 'I have a feeling there's something in store for both of us over there.' Candy outside the Dauphin house asking, 'Wouldn't you like to take Jim's place?'

I would, he thought. *I'd swap in a second.*

And an image of Jim lit in his mind. Jim smiling on the deck of the *Mary Celeste* as he said, 'Ghosts can't travel over water.'

And Jon suddenly understood. Understood it all, including the rich, rotting smell that lay far beneath Sooty's exotic perfume.

Ghosts can't travel over water, the distant part of his mind thought. *Unless they're incarnate. Unless they have possession of bodies. This isn't Sooty at all! This is Majesty Dauphin!*

And then the Topeka part of his mind was swamped as the kiss broke off and Sooty's delicate, shapely hands went to work on his belt. She didn't so much undress him as *tear his clothes from his body*. And then she was pulling him down on top of her in the mud, the fingernails of one hand scratching gently down the shaft of his penis while the nails of the other dug deep into his wrist. And then he was on top of her, his burning skin against her smooth, cool skin. And then she was bucking him off, rolling him on his back and his huge aching penis was being guided into her as she lowered herself on him and began to fuck him with the ferocity of a wild animal.

It was heaven.

His first orgasm came within seconds, but Sooty didn't cease, just kept on powering down on him, riding him through that after-orgasm period in which his sensitivity increased to the point where pleasure became terrible pain that made him scream. The second time he came, Jon opened his eyes. They were blurred with tears.

For a moment he couldn't see anything at all. Then he realized he couldn't move his head. Or hear anything. He'd sunk deep enough into the mud for his ears to be blocked, for the level of the mud to be at the corners of his eyes. And Sooty was *still* fucking him.

Except that she wasn't Sooty. The thing on top of him was a wizened yellow slack-skinned thing with empty eye sockets and one rotting breast. Its stomach was gashed open exposing its innards. And still it was fucking him. And he was hard for it, thrilling at the sensations. A part of him didn't even want it to stop.

Jon's mind broke.

The thing on top of him cackled out a laugh as he threw up his arms at it. It took his hands in bony fingers, pushed them back down into the mud, fucking him harder. Jon orgasmed again as the corpse's rotting mouth pressed down against his own, sealing off his screams.

Jon fainted. Distantly he heard a voice. Majesty Dauphin's voice. It said, 'I'm going to fuck you right out of your body. Vacate it and prepare it. You wanted everything Jim has. Jim has everything of mine and my Straker's. You'll get what you wanted but it won't be in the way you wanted it. You'll get what Green has, but it won't be you in your body, it'll be my husband.'

It took another five minutes for Jon to become totally submerged in the mud.

Chapter Twenty-One

Babes in the Wood: Frank and Rosie

Rosie didn't quite have a handle on everything that had happened since the explosion on the path and the first batch of blood-bags. After the big bang (and she'd been hanging far enough back to avoid getting covered in the realistic blood) she'd found herself alone on the path while the rest of the gang scattered like frightened rabbits.

Rosie had stayed where she was for a while, watching fireworks and hearing screams and laughter and banshee wails as the fans tripped hidden wires and broke electric-eye beams, or whatever it was Davey had set up. But she hadn't felt good about it; hadn't wanted to be there. Until that first blood-bag had burst she'd been doing fine, but there was something about seeing all those screaming, scared people that chilled her. It all looked too real.

And she had a certain sense that something was going on beneath the veneer of let's-all-have-a-good-time. It was rooted, she guessed, in Jim's odd behaviour. At first she'd thought the thing concerning the appearance of Sooty on the boat and the threatening little notes they kept finding was a put-up job. Something that Jim had arranged, just to make everyone uneasy. And then, back in the Dauphin house, she had half changed her mind. It was something to do with Jim's fake history of the Dauphin family and something to do with Frank's tale of gods at war. When you thought about them in tandem, instead of one at a time, they meshed too perfectly, too seamlessly. She could easily imagine that Jim and Frank had stumbled on something close to the truth.

Hell, when Frank was talking, telling his tale, he went all distant and empty-eyed, like something was talking through

327

him, she thought. It was a pretty good tale for someone who worked as a journalist. Most of the journalists she'd met during her time with Jim didn't have the imagination to tell a seamless lie, let alone a weird and wonderful story about a power struggle between the gods.

She glanced up at Frank, who was hurrying along beside her, wondering whether he really was an English teacher rather than a journalist. He was soaked in blood and covered in dirt where he'd fallen and he was very shaken up. He'd careened into her about five minutes ago, and he'd been on the point of tears. He'd seen Jim dressed up as a corpse, he said, and then he'd seen Sooty dressed as Majesty Dauphin.

Rosie knew the last bit was impossible – unless Frank had seen a mannequin, or an actress that Rosie didn't know about. Or it *should* have been impossible. The alternative didn't bear thinking about too deeply.

What if what Jim and Frank said is all true? she asked herself and shivered.

When Frank had calmed down enough to be able to speak, he had said, 'I don't like this. Let's get the fuck out of here.'

And while Rosie thought Frank deserved all the scares Jim and Davey could put to him, she felt a certain sympathy towards the man. She didn't like it either. And although Frank might have been a slug, he was a *male* slug and younger and stronger than she was. And if she sent him away she would be alone and unprotected in this darkening forest, of which she had suddenly become scared. So she had agreed when he'd said, 'Let's go back down the path and hole up in the Dauphin house till the kids have had their playtime.'

And that was where they were headed now, leaving the sounds of screams (some of them Candy's, Rosie knew) and shouts (the male one was certainly Jon) and the chitter-chatter of laughing-bags and the bursts of distant fireworks behind them.

Rosie was relieved about that. 'It's all a little too convincing for my liking,' she admitted.

Frank stopped and cocked an ear. 'It's all gone quiet now,'

he said. 'I guess everyone's dead.' He glanced down at Rosie and treated her to a sick grin. He looked as if he meant it.

'Don't!' Rosie said, shuddering. *What if Straker Dauphin is back and loose in those woods? And Majesty. And what if the god is waking? What if it was the god making those huge trees shake? What then?*

'It's all trickery,' Frank said, sounding as if he was having trouble believing it himself.

Rosie stopped dead in her tracks and moaned. They were close to the backyard of the Dauphin house now, but there was something on the ground ahead of her and she didn't much care for the look of it. It looked like a head.

Or part of a head.

'What?' Frank said, in a voice pitched a tone and a half above normal.

Rosie pointed in the general direction of the thing without looking there. 'That!' she said. *That thing*, she thought, *with half a face. Half a face that looks very familiar to me.* 'What's that?'

But she already knew what it was. It was the remains of June's head. Someone, or some*thing* had torn her apart and consumed her, leaving only half a skull, which oozed brain, and on the front of which was half of June's face. June, whom she'd last seen yelping and running off like a frightened bunny, with Martha – who was surprisingly spry for such a huge woman – hot on her heels.

'Oh, my good God! It's a mock-up. It *has* to be,' Frank said, from just ahead of her. When Rosie looked, Frank had knelt down in front of the head, shielding it from her. She was thankful for that small mercy. She saw him reach out to touch it and looked away again, closing her eyes this time.

'Oh, sweet *Jesus!*' Frank cried. 'It's June. *How could this have happened?*'

Rosie's world rolled. When it came to rest, reality had altered. Her worst fears were realities. 'I don't know how it happened and I don't want to know. I just want to get out of here,' she said. Her voice surprised her. It was as steady as ever, despite the enormous shock she felt. A god was walking on this island. It was impossible to imagine.

From behind the safety barrier of her closed eyelids, Rosie

heard something moving out there in the place her world had suddenly and irrevocably become. It wasn't Frank, but something pushing through the ferns beside the track. Rosie tried to shout a warning and couldn't. She needed to open her eyes and she couldn't do that either.

Come on! she screamed inwardly.

She summoned up the courage to open her eyes and was surprised to see what she thought was Jim kneeling beside Frank on the track. Except that he was dressed in clothes from another time and he was covered in dirt. She saw Frank look up and turn towards Jim, then yelp and freeze.

'*Jim!*' Rosie screamed, surprising herself. She hadn't intended to make a sound.

Jim looked back over his shoulder, grinning. But it wasn't Jim at all. It was some rotting parody of him. 'Not yet, but I *will* be. Soon!' the thing grated in a French accent as it stood up.

Ohmygod, it's Straker! Rosie's mind screamed. 'Frank, GET AWAY!' she yelled.

And then Straker was slashing at Frank, who was rolling away. The blow was slow and missed by a good six inches. Frank rolled over again and again, then leaped nimbly to his feet. He glanced at Rosie, then at Straker, who was plodding towards him, but between him and Rosie. Then he looked back at Rosie again and Rosie knew he was going to run away and leave her to this shambling monstrous copy of Jim.

True to form, right down to the last detail, Rosie thought, as Frank ran off in a loping curve. Straker glanced back at her, grinned, then set off after Frank.

Less than twenty seconds later, Rosie took back all the assumptions she'd made about Frank as he ran back up the path from behind her, his hair on end, his face a mask of fear and anger.

'Quick!' he gasped, taking Rosie's arm and starting to drag her along towards the Dauphin house. 'The fucking thing isn't far behind. I wanted to leave you to it, believe me,' Frank puffed candidly, 'but I just couldn't do it. I must be getting old or something.'

There was a large steaming crater where the backyard of the Dauphin house had once been, as if a sizeable meteor

330

had just struck it. 'What the hell is *that*?' Rosie said, careful not to look too far into it in case pieces of someone else she knew were strewn about in there.

'Don't know, don't want to know,' Frank said, dragging her past it.

It was a few seconds before Rosie realized that Frank was following the perimeter of the crater towards the back door of the Dauphin house.

'Where are we going?' she said, digging in her heels and drawing Frank to a standstill.

Frank nodded towards the house. 'Where do you think?' he asked, dragging at her arm. 'For fuck's sake, hurry up, woman! That fucking – *zombie* – may come back. Or the thing that made this fucking great hole. Hurry *up*!'

'We *can't* go inside!' Rosie yelled. 'Jim ... *it* ... it'll get us! If we go inside we'll be trapped! Haven't you ever seen a horror film before, you stupid, *stupid* man?'

Frank rounded on her angrily, his fists clenched. For a moment she thought he was going to strike her. 'One: never call me stupid,' he seethed. 'Call me arrogant, call me a snake, but *never* call me stupid, I am *not* stupid. Two: we'll be no more trapped inside than we are out here. And we need something to use as a weapon. There has to be something inside the house I can use. We may even be *safe* in there. Who are you to say?' He grabbed her arm again. It hurt. He leaned forward and dragged her a few paces, his fingers bruising her biceps.

'Frank! Wait! Please!' she yelled. 'Not in the house. We have to get down on the beach. We have to get to the boat. It's a *ghost*, Frank! A *ghost*! *It can't cross water.*'

'Who says ghosts can't cross water? That's what I want to know! Who says?' Frank shrieked in a shrill, cracked voice. 'And, besides, the fucking thing's *incarnate*. It's *solid*. In a *body*. We need to find something to *hit* it with.'

Hissing and pulling against her, he dragged her to the step at the back door. 'We're going *in*!' he spat, yanking her on to the step.

Rosie pulled back, knowing exactly what would happen the moment they entered the house. Straker would appear. And kill them. Once you entered the haunted house, you were doomed. This wasn't just a movie cliché – she could *feel* it, right down in her soul. 'I can't,' she moaned.

'You can!' Frank blazed.

'Just let me go. Leave me here. You go.'

'You're coming too!' Frank said, and pushed open the door.

'Please, Frank! *Please!*'

'I'm trying to fucking *save* you, woman,' Frank said, hefted her up and half threw her through the doorway. The hallway smelt of wood and dust, and Rosie fancied she could also smell Sooty's perfume lingering in the fabric of the house – the expensive stuff she had made for her up in Seattle. It was comforting, somehow.

Frank propelled her down the hall to the first doorway on the left and thrust her into a room that contained a lot of cool-boxes, tools, bags of charcoal, hammers, nails, saws and loads of other junk. It looked like a hardware store, and as Rosie lost her footing, she recognized it was where Davey kept all his stores for these trips.

When her foot went over she was moving quite fast. She staggered across the room, trying to regain her balance, and knowing she wasn't going to do it. She had almost regained control of herself when she hit a big blue toolbox, which tripped her. She sprawled into the room's wood-panelled interior wall and fell in a heap on the floor on her left side, looking back at Frank.

Frank, however, wasn't looking at her. He was searching through the pile of stuff in the centre of the room, presumably looking for a weapon.

Rosie pushed herself to a sitting position and heard something creak above her. She looked up, half expecting the wall to collapse on her, but that wasn't what happened.

Above her, just a bit further up the wall than head-height, one of the panels had swung free of the wall, as if it were hinged.

A secret compartment, Rosie thought. *I must have tripped the catch when I whacked into the wall.*

'Fucking *Band-Aids*!' Frank snarled, throwing aside a small packet. 'What we need is an AK47. Or a flame-thrower or something. Christ, even a little gun would be better than what we have here.'

Rosie got up and turned to the secret compartment, which was too high for her to see into. She dragged an empty crate over and stood on it while Frank continued to search through Davey's kit. *There might be something up here*, Rosie thought, although it wasn't a gun or a knife she had in mind. It was something more along the lines of a talisman, or magical amulet you could use to banish gods and ghosts – or that would at least afford some protection against them. There wasn't going to be any point in shooting at Straker: he was dead already so you couldn't kill him any more.

There was no talisman in the cupboard. What was in there surprised Rosie a good deal more than an ancient magical device would have. There was a stack of bound manuscripts. All were ancient and filthy. She pulled the top one off the pile, dusted the front cover and gasped.

'What are you doing?' Frank said. 'What's that you've got? Notebooks?'

In a daze, and feeling a cold sickness that ran all through her like icy water, Rosie got down from the box and handed the large leather-bound book to Frank. 'Look at the title,' she heard herself say, from a thousand miles away.

'*The Third Coming*,' Frank read. 'By Straker Dauphin. Hey that's one of . . . Uh-oh . . .'

'Uh-oh indeed,' Rosie said, feeling as if she might faint. 'It's one of Jim's novels.'

'Shit!' Frank said, handing the manuscript back to her and getting up on the crate. He pulled the rest down and brushed dust from the uppermost manuscript. 'Damnation,' he said. 'The ink is faint, but it clearly says *Damnation*. That was Jim's second book, wasn't it?'

Rosie nodded. A distant part of her – a part that didn't even seem to matter any more – was pleased to note that rather than sounding smug about this discovery, Frank seemed as horrified as she was.

'And this one is *Deathless*,' Frank said. 'The one below is *Miami Five Fifteen*. They're all Jim's books. But they're ancient. A hundred years old, at least. Maybe older. And they're all . . .'

'Written by Straker Dauphin,' Rosie said. 'They're not *Jim*'s books, they're Straker Dauphin's books. And it's not merely coincidence. It's not just that the titles are the same. Listen.' She picked up the manuscript of *Deathless* and opened it to the first page '"It was the third Thursday in June when William Carter discovered his wife had returned from the dead."'

'Jesus, that's *Deathless*, all right,' Frank said. 'But . . .'

'But nothing,' Rosie replied dully. 'Straker Dauphin wrote them all first. All Jim's books. Every single last fucking one. Jim wrote them second-hand. By telepathy. Or osmosis or something. He can't have copied them. These manuscripts haven't been moved since Straker Dauphin's time.'

Frank shook his head. 'The story he told us on the boat . . .'

'He thinks he made it up. Just as he thinks he made up all Dauphin's novels. Just as you thought *you* made up that story you told round the camp-fire,' Rosie said.

'I don't know where all that stuff came from. I was just . . . *inspired*. For the first time in my life. I thought I'd finally found the story-teller in me, but it wasn't my story at all, was it? It was the island's story. Which means . . .'

Rosie grimaced. 'It's all true. Your story is true. Jim's bogus history of the island is true. And we've just come face to face with the ghost of Straker Dauphin. And he wants to become Jim.'

'But that's not possible! Is it?' Frank looked horrified.

'I don't know,' Rosie said. 'Until ten minutes ago I didn't believe ghosts were possible. But I do know one thing. We have to get to Jim before Straker Dauphin does.'

On the far side of the house something exploded with a huge bang that echoed through the woods and shook the timbers of the house.

'That wasn't a firework,' Frank said.

Rosie followed him out of the room, along the corridor and into the front room, which was also filled with Davey's equipment. Long before she reached the window she knew what the explosion had been. The orange glow in the darkening sky said it all.

Out on the water in the bay the *Mary Celeste* was burning

brightly. On the beach, the dinghy they'd arrived in was aflame.

'Someone doesn't want us to leave this island,' Rosie said.

'*Now* what do we do?' Frank moaned.

'Look for Jim and pray for help,' Rosie said, knowing it was too late now. The cavalry wasn't going to turn up and spirit them away: as far as everyone else knew, the party on the island was going just swimmingly, like they always did. It was too far from the mainland even to think about breast-stroking it all the way back, and now both the dinghy and the power-cruiser were gone. Then she remembered. 'Shit, I just thought of something!' she said, a flame of hope leaping in her heart.

'What?' Frank said, still staring out at the blazing hulk of the *Mary Celeste*. He sounded defeated.

Rosie grinned. 'We *can* get away. All we have to do is gather up the survivors and we can get away.'

'How?' Frank asked, turning back to face her.

'Davey,' Rosie said. 'He has a little speed-boat. It isn't big, but it's here somewhere. Probably hidden nearby. Over in the rocky bits at one end of the beach or the other.'

'Who the hell is Davey?' Frank said. Then he relaxed. 'Ah, I just *knew* you weren't a contest winner. You were in on all this, weren't you? Davey would be the guy who sets up the traps, right?'

'Right,' Rosie said. 'On both counts. I'm Jim's secretary,' she admitted. 'Now you tell me the truth. Are you really an English teacher, or are you a newspaper reporter?'

Frank sighed, then shrugged. 'Hell, what does it matter now?' he asked himself. 'I'm—'

And then the door burst open and Frank shrieked. Rosie spun round.

Straker Dauphin stood in the doorway. A straight razor was clutched in what remained of his left hand. He pointed at them with it. 'Who's been peering into *my* secret places?' he asked, in a voice that sounded like death.

Chapter Twenty-Two

The Thief

1

Jim had never been sure how he stood on the age-old question of *astral travel*. He'd never had an OOBE – an out-of-body-experience – in his life. This didn't mean that he didn't believe it was possible.

'Perhaps,' he had once told an interviewer from *Playboy* – a pretty young girl just out of college who swore she'd met him *intimately* on the astral plane – 'everyone travels in the astral while they're asleep. I know there's a school of thought which claims this happens to us all. And it would explain why I can't remember, er, *meeting* you since most of us wake with fading memories of what happened while we were asleep.'

What Jim was sure of, even if he didn't make his views widely known, was that something special could happen while you were asleep: that on occasion you could contact forces of energy – perhaps, but not necessarily, beings – that were far greater than yourself. Forces that knew a good deal more than you did about the fabric of the waking world and how it worked. Whether this counted as astral travel or not, he didn't know.

In Jim's opinion, anyone who'd ever woken in the morning with a smile on their face thinking, *That's what it's all about!* with the dissolving memory that they'd just been told something of stunning significance (even if they could no longer recall the message) would agree with him about those forces. He'd put this to the young girl reporter from *Playboy* and she'd just looked at him blankly.

This time, Jim knew for sure that beneath the veil of reality lay something else. While he was unconscious he saw things and learned things. And when he finally awoke, he remembered it all.

For almost five minutes.

Lying there unconscious, close to Davey's dead body and hidden from passing fans by the tall ferns, Jim learned the truth about the question most often asked of him: 'Where do you get your ideas from?' And there was more. Much more.

He saw Jon Short – a talented writer who could have made a decent living following his dream – willingly turn himself into a cipher for want of something someone else already had. Jon had made love to what he'd thought was Jim's wife; had desired her not for who she was but what she represented to him. Jon wanted to *be* James Green. Wanted it badly enough to relinquish his own soul, to empty his body willingly, just for the slender chance of becoming someone else.

Candy had also made her choice: if she could be Mrs Green, she *would* be Mrs Green. And she'd paid in the same way Jon had paid. And now they were both lost.

Because what neither Jon nor Candy had known, what they *couldn't* have known under any circumstances, was that Mr and Mrs Green – the *real* Mr and Mrs Green – were Straker and Majesty Dauphin. That those who inhabited the bodies of the current Mr and Mrs Green were interlopers and thieves. Rogue spirits, chosen to represent a greater force in an ongoing game that the gods were playing. Straker and Majesty had the ability to alter the balance of power in the current reality. They could change reality entirely, in fact: they could free an imprisoned god.

In this series of unconscious visions and epiphanies, Jim also understood the reason why Candy and Jon had been tempted. Now that Davey had spilled blood and woken the ghosts, the bodies and souls of Straker and Majesty, the resurrected couple, wanted to take back their rightful bodies from the interlopers, by force. But it wasn't that simple. Because it might not work, Jon and Candy had been tempted and had sold their souls for the chance to be Jim and Sooty. But they'd been tricked. There was no chance of them becoming Jim and Sooty: Majesty and Straker had just needed the empty shells of their living bodies as standbys in case things went wrong.

And things might well go wrong because of Spreadbury, who evidently intended to prevent Majesty and Straker from getting their way. Or to *try* to prevent them getting their way. Because Majesty and Straker were bound to the island's god and once they'd escaped the confines of the island they would free it, whether they wanted to or not. Spreadbury was the only hope.

But what will he do? What can *he do?* Jim asked himself.

The question wasn't answered. Suddenly he was floating above the dark lake at the centre of the island, looking down at Majesty Dauphin's animate corpse. She was kneeling in the mud at the water's edge, naked and smeared with mud. Her hips were working, like a dog's would when you'd just forcefully parted it from your leg. Majesty was whole and young and perfect. Her body, her face and hair all looked exactly as Sooty's looked. She might have *been* Sooty. Which in a way, Jim supposed, she *was*.

As he watched she plunged her hands up to the elbows into the mud and drew up the dead body of Jon Short. The mud didn't want to let him go.

Majesty dragged him to the path beside the bush, laid him on his back and cleared the mud from his nose and mouth. Then, using the heels of her hands, she pushed hard on his chest. Jon drew a shuddering breath and coughed. Majesty smiled and nodded. She got up, took two paces and faded into invisibility.

He can't be alive! Jim complained. *How could that happen?*

And without transition he was in the wheelhouse of a power-cruiser called *Majesty*, standing at the back of the room, while before him Sooty had the wheel. Elaine stood back from her, holding what looked like hand-cannon; a portly, middle-aged man lay on the floor before her, apparently unconscious. Jim knew without doubt that the man was Aaron Spreadbury.

'How far out are we?' Elaine asked, through gritted teeth.

'A couple of miles,' Sooty said, sounding very scared

indeed. She pointed. 'Look, that little smudge right up there is the *Mary Celeste*.'

'I see it,' Elaine said. 'We'd better just hope like hell that the face-changer here wakes up before we arrive. Or we'll be in deep shit.'

'It can't get much deeper,' Sooty replied. Then she said, 'Oh, fuck. Yes, it can.'

Jim saw instantly what she was referring to. Way up ahead the sky had turned red. There was a bright dot of orange where the *Mary Celeste* had been.

'Jesus H. Christ, Sooty! What was *that*?' Elaine gasped.

'Jim's boat going up,' Sooty said, in a small voice. She and Elaine exchanged glances.

'Jim wasn't on it,' Elaine said, with the utmost certainty.

Sooty merely looked at her.

And Jim was back in the woods, watching something huge and invisible as it bore down on June and destroyed her. Then he was whisked backwards to a place where a man who looked uncannily like a long-dead James Green tore the face off Martha's skull in one swift movement.

Then he was back beside his own unconscious body looking at the mound of earth into which Candy had been sucked. There was movement there. Jim had once seen a python regurgitate what was left of a small mammal and the undulations that ran up the mound looked pretty much like the ones the snake had given before coughing out the wrecked rabbit.

The mound of soft earth bulged and rose and at its near end, a dark mouth opened. Jim gazed into its maw and saw a tangle of blonde hair. As he looked on, the throat of the mound contracted and Candy's head appeared, her face blackened by mud; her eye sockets blanked out with it, her parted lips packed with it. It took almost thirty seconds for the mound to spit her out. Candy rolled over to her side, then shuddered, then puked out what seemed to be an endless column of lumpy grey stuff. It reminded Jim of pictures he'd seen of psychics with ectoplasm coming out of their mouths: it looked like a large candle, being ribbed with dripping wax. Except this stuff spiralled out from the central column into the air instead of dripping down it.

Candy coughed and the column of ectoplasm seemed to turn to dust, which flew into the air and vanished. Then she lay still.

I just saw her spirit depart, Jim thought in horror. *I just watched her die.*

And then he woke up.

2

Jim felt as if he'd been dragged from heaven into the deepest depths of hell. His head hurt, his wrist shot bolts of lightning up his arm, he was covered in stinking blood and filth and his mouth tasted oily.

He pushed himself up on his elbows, expecting to see Candy and the mound of earth, but the mound was gone and Candy, if she had ever been there, was gone too. Only Davey's corpse remained.

Now what are you going to do, O Master of Disaster? he asked himself. *Now you know that the messages on your computer were right and that you* are *the thief. That you stole everything you ever wrote, enjoyed the proceeds of someone else's toil, whether you meant to or not. What are you going to do? Give it all back? Say you're sorry, but it was all down to some weird celestial law?*

Jim knew exactly what he was going to do. He was going to arm himself with something heavy and sharp and go after the shambling corpses of Straker and Majesty Dauphin and put them back in the ground where they belonged.

'If you want *this* body, Straker Dauphin,' he growled, as he found his feet, 'you're gonna have to fight me for it. And I'm alive and I'm quick and I'm clever. And it's my intention to send you back where you belong! They don't call me the Master of Disaster for nothing!'

Jim gave a little gasp as something in his mind departed, fluttering away on the wings of an angel. He paused, frowning. He'd just forgotten something important. Something involving Candy and Jon Short. *It'll come back to me in a moment*, he thought, patting his forehead with his left hand as if it would wake up his memory. But the thought was gone.

'Fuck it,' he said, automatically reaching for his shirt pocket. He was surprised to discover that, even after what he'd been through, his pack of Virginia Slims and his lighter were still present, though the pocket flap was unbuttoned. He lit a cigarette, inhaled deeply and put the pack and lighter back in his shirt pocket. He shivered when the little hit of nicotine found his nerves. In Jim's opinion they'd invented cigarettes for times like these.

What I need now is not love, sweet love, but a fucking big axe or something, he thought, realizing suddenly that he felt light and free – unfettered for once in his life. He'd been blocked, he'd been terrorized and now he was going to put things right, once and for all. If he died trying to do it at least he wasn't going to go out like the cowering wimp he'd been through all this. He would die fighting on the side of right.

But I need to be armed and I'm not, he thought, taking another hit on the cigarette and exhaling smoke through his nostrils. And then he remembered where there was a weapon. It wasn't what he'd hoped for but it was better than nothing. All he had to do was find the tree where all this had started – the one where Davey had left him the flashlight. Jim had no idea what had happened to the flashlight but the hatchet Davey had left embedded in the tree would still be where Jim had dropped it.

He glanced around, getting his bearings, and then headed back the way he had come.

The hatchet will do, Jim assured himself as he trudged back towards the path.

3

As he walked something began to work on him. Jim didn't know if it was Straker and Majesty, the island's god, or the island itself, doing it, but his mind became fecund and lit with ideas. He knew now how to get round his problems with *Shimmer*; he had great ideas for a dozen different stories; his confidence as a writer returned and, with it, his confidence as a human being

But every silver lining had a cloud attached and with the

good came the bad. He realized he could only carry on as he was by giving in to the island's god. Not Straker, not Majesty, but the god itself. Whatever happened, he and Sooty would be untouched, would be allowed to carry on as normal. All he had to do was make that bond. And his word, he knew, would serve as that bond. And if he refused he would be signing his death warrant. Without the help of the god he was sunk. He would die and the god would have his soul anyway. So why not just say, 'Yes, I'm yours!' to the god?

Because I'm an old soul. An old soul who belongs to the other side, that's why, Jim thought. *Because the side I'm on allows me free will. I think . . .*

But if it allowed him free will, why had he spent his life writing stories that belonged to someone else? Why had he been a thief?

Jim didn't know. *A job I agreed to do. Before I was here. Before I was born. I can't remember because I'm incarnate. But I must have accepted the task of my own free will.*

The dissenting voice in his head fell silent the moment he stooped and his fingers closed around the hatchet he'd left at the foot of the tree. *I gave you a chance,* the voice seemed to say, as it faded into nothing. *You refused the deal. You're on your own.*

'The fucker is *frightened* of me,' Jim said aloud. He found this astonishing, but he knew his words were true. Whatever had been whispering to him wanted him to defect, had wanted him on its own side. *Which is a sure sign of fear.*

'I'm coming to put things right!' he said softly. 'I know you can hear me! Be afraid!'

He began to walk back down the track towards the beach and the Dauphin house, holding the axe at his shoulder with his good left hand. He hadn't gone far when he found the ruin of Martha's body in front of him, blocking the track. Her face was gone and something with sharp claws had opened up her body from sternum to crotch and had pulled out most of what had been inside. There had been a lot of stuff in there.

Jim found that he was no longer squeamish. He stood in front of Martha, breathing in the rich smell of her blood and fetid stench of her innards and his anger rose and he silently cursed Straker Dauphin and his god before stepping over her and continuing. He felt stronger with every step. Eager to put an end to all this. *Candy's dead*, he thought. *Jon's dead, too. And Martha and Davey. The others?* He strongly suspected everyone on the island but him was dead by now.

And you'll soon be joining them, a voice that bore a distinct French accent said inside his head. *Your soul will survive in the torment of the damned, but I shall have your body, thief!*

'Try and take it, motherfucker,' Jim said aloud. 'Just try!'

In three hours I will be fucking your wife, not your mother, *thief!* Straker whispered.

Jim shrugged. 'It'd take a better man than you to pleasure her,' he said, trudging onwards.

All your power will be turned against you when we stand face to face, the voice whispered. *I am the rightful owner of the body you inhabit. All your power will be mine. You will be as a kitten . . . and talking of kittens . . .*

Jim found himself at the foot of the stairs in Hettie Baker's house. From upstairs came the sound of a cat hissing and squalling and a lot of thudding, as if someone was slamming a door across the animal's body, but it was what was down here that Jim's eyes fixed upon. Hettie lay face up on the stairs, down which she had come head first. She was dead. Her mouth was open and her tongue was swollen and blue, which, Jim thought, meant she'd died of a heart-attack. Before she'd died the cat had evidently attached itself to her face by its claws: Hettie was cut to ribbons. One of her eyes was open, split in two, right through the pupil.

'Jesus,' Jim heard himself say back in the wood.

Guess what the cat's doing now, Straker chuckled in his mind. *Guess who's upstairs in her auntie Hettie's house!*

And Jim was slammed into an upstairs bedroom in the same house. Where Gloria had the cat trapped in the door and was pushing against it with all her might. She was making tiny sobbing sounds in the back of her throat and her little arms were trembling with the effort. Her face was a picture of terror.

And the cat looked as if it was going to win.

You saw what Marmaduke did to Auntie Hettie, Straker's

343

voice whispered. *Just think what he'll do to poor Gloria. She can't hold him out for ever, you know. She's going to lose this little battle, and then she's going to lose the war. All you have to do to save Gloria, your pride and joy, is say, 'Yes! I'm yours!' because, you see, I* am *the god of this island. The god and I are merged now. I am the god's controller and I can stop this happening to Gloria with a snap of my fingers.*

'I'll kill you!' Jim yelled.

Let her die then, Straker said. *And don't think you're any better than me.*

And Jim was back in his body.

A little further along the path he found someone's guts, unravelled along the path like a stinking wet rope. Then he was at the perimeter of the backyard of the Dauphin house. He passed by the deep crater that had formed there in the yard, pushed through the bushes at the side of the house and walked out on to the beach.

Out at sea the *Mary Celeste* was burning brightly. The dinghy that had been tied up on the beach was nothing more than a heap of smouldering ash and melted rubber.

Jim turned back to face the house.

The porch ran the full length of the front, the overhang supported by four oak posts, one on either side of the door and the others at either end. None of the posts was damaged – they had always been as solid as rocks.

And yet somehow Frank and Rosie had been impaled on the posts on either side of the door. Both were naked and their feet dangled about a foot from the porch floor. The uprights had been inserted into their anuses, passed through their bodies and pulled out of their mouths without becoming detached from the porch.

And in spite of the three-inch-square posts through their bodies, they were still alive. Their legs worked frantically, as if trying to seek purchase against the posts and push themselves upwards. Their hands fluttered aimlessly, scratching occasionally at the uprights.

Jim could see Frank's hammering heart, even from this distance. Amazingly neither he nor Rosie appeared to be bleeding. He wasn't sure whether they were really dead and it was Straker making them move, or still alive and aware of

344

his presence. What he *did* know was he was going to kick the shit out of the thing that had done this to them. He hadn't liked Frank, but he wouldn't have wished him harm. And Rosie had been like a mother to him.

Jim was no longer anything but supremely angry and murderous.

'GET OUT HERE, DAUPHIN! NOW!' he bellowed at the top of his voice. His body was seething with wrath that felt like molten metal. There was going to be a finish to this and it was going to be now.

'GET OUT HERE AND FACE ME!' he yelled, distantly aware of something happening behind him, out to sea.

Spreadbury? a disassociated part of his mind asked. *Didn't you see Spreadbury and Elaine and Sooty all on a big plush power-cruiser? Is this them?*

Up on the porch, Frank and Rosie continued to kick feebly. The front door didn't open and Straker Dauphin didn't charge out at him.

Jim glanced back over his shoulder. Way out at sea shone the lights of what looked like an approaching vessel. A fairly large one. Possibly even bigger than the *Mary Celeste*. For some reason the thrum of the distant engines sounded familiar, as if Jim had been on the boat at some point.

A cat! he thought. *Attacking Gloria! Oh, Christ!*

Up on the porch, the door squeaked. Jim turned back.

'Sooty?' he said, his mouth falling open in surprise. 'What the hell are you doing here?'

Chapter Twenty-Three

Tricks and Traps 4: Ghost Hunt

1

'How far in can we take this damned boat?' Elaine asked nervously, glancing from the burning hulk of the *Mary Celeste* to the distant beach, which was now lit with an unearthly pale light. She hoped no one was going to ask her to swim anywhere because she couldn't swim. Add to that the fact that she was scared of the water and you had one Annie Eastwood who wasn't going to be much use unless Sooty could get *Majesty* right up to the beach.

Which just about figures, she thought, glancing down at Spreadbury who still lay on the floor. *We have an unconscious psychic who won't stir no matter what you do to him, a woman scared half out of her wits and a tough-talking gunwoman who can't even face wading through deep water. What a fucking bunch we turned out to be! They'll just blow us out of the water and that'll be that.*

They weren't far from the blazing hulk of *Mary Celeste* now and Sooty was slowing the cruiser. She glanced back, her face pale and sheened with sweat. Her eyes glittered darkly with anger and fear. 'Not much further,' she said. 'This vessel probably has a deeper draught than our boat has ... used to have. We'll have to moor a little way further out than *Mary Celeste*.'

'Then what?' Elaine asked. On the floor at her feet Spreadbury twitched. She glared at him. She'd just spent the last ten minutes trying to wake him and nothing had worked – not slaps or cold water or even the smelling-salts she'd found in the medical chest in the galley. Spreadbury was out of the equation. 'I can't swim,' she admitted.

'You won't have to,' Sooty said. 'There's an outboard-

346

powered launch on the back of this boat. Like the one way up on the shore. The one that's up ahead right now. Burning . . .'

'Honey, we *will* do it,' Elaine said, sounding doubtful even to her own ears. 'We're gonna get away with this.'

Sooty looked away. Then she gasped. Elaine saw her go rigid.

'What?' Elaine said, so tense she thought she might shatter.

'Help us, Jim!' Sooty cried, in a thin voice. 'Please! Set us free!'

'Sooty?' Elaine yelped. 'What is it? What's wrong now?'

Sooty make a little *oof!* noise, as if someone had punched her in the stomach, and staggered away from the wheel, tottering round and bringing her face into Elaine's field of vision.

She wasn't Sooty any more.

That's not strictly true, Elaine thought, horrified. *She is Sooty. But she's someone else, too. There are two of her. Sooty and someone else that* looks *like Sooty.*

Elaine knew without a shadow of a doubt that the other person she'd become, the one imploring Jim to help her, was Majesty Dauphin.

'There's no time! Quick, Jim!' Sooty wailed.

Oh, fuck! Elaine thought, glancing past Sooty and out of the window. She was now alone in charge of a large motor launch, which was slowly heading directly towards the *Mary Celeste* and she had no idea how to stop the damned thing. Either they were going to crash into the burning wreck and sink, in flames, or they were going to bottom out on a rock or something before they reached her and just sink. *And drown.*

'Sooty!' she yelled. 'For Christ's sake!'

But Sooty was elsewhere.

2

'Sooty?' Jim asked, his mouth falling open in surprise. 'What the hell are *you* doing here?'

Sooty was wearing a long black button-through dress he'd

never seen before. She looked a couple of years younger, her hair seemed longer and she was wearing an expression of utter terror.

'Help us, Jim! Please! Set us free!' she cried, staying exactly where she was. Which wasn't the way this writer would have had a terrified wife act. She would have been running down the beach towards him. *Wouldn't she?* Suddenly he didn't know. *Of course! Unless something was preventing her from moving.*

He took two paces towards her, then stopped, hefting the axe from his shoulder. He frowned, no longer sure what he was doing. *You're contemplating chopping up your own wife, that's what!* a tiny voice whispered in his mind. *You already let that damned cat kill your daughter, so you may as well get on with it and kill your wife too. Let's face it, Jim, you've lost the plot here. You're away with the fairies. You cracked and never recovered at all, you just thought you had. So just get on with it and kill the bloody woman, then you can do away with yourself, just like all the other guys who do this sort of thing. Think how good it'd feel just to die and have done with it all.*

'How did you get here?' he heard himself ask.

'There's no time! Quick, Jim!' Sooty replied.

'You're not my Sooty,' Jim said quietly, but right through to his bones he knew he was wrong. She *was* his Sooty.

Because she's not alone. She's not alone.

'Help me, Jim! Quickly!' she called.

And Jim found his eyes locked on hers. And suddenly he *knew* that this was really Sooty. That weird telepathic link they'd always shared had opened again – for the first time since his block. He could *feel* her now, feel that flood of familiar warmth, of love, ancient and true, pass the gap between them. It was like finally being home.

A grin lit Jim's face. It felt good to have it back there again. Everything was over now, everything was done. All he had to do was waltz up to her, snatch her off the porch where they'd made love so many times and drag her away to the safety of Davey's speed-boat and open water.

He'd taken two steps closer to her when the trees around the Dauphin house began to rattle and shake. Somewhere nearby – perhaps on the far side of the island – lightning flashed low in the sky, burning the scene on to his retinas. The roar of the thunder shook the ground beneath his feet and a fresh wind blowing out to sea tousled his hair.

Jim looked up to the sky which had become peculiarly light above the island. Way up there in the thick cloud – which he didn't remember forming, he was pretty sure it had been a clear night up till now – something odd had happened. A hole had formed. A hole that looked roughly the size and shape of the island. A hole through which a pale, flat light shone, brightening the beach and the house and turning dusk into daylight again. The dark cloud was roiling up the inside of the open hole at what seemed an incredible speed.

Jim had seen plenty of weird weather round this part of Florida, including tornadoes and water-spouts, but this just about took first prize.

This can't be happening, he thought, gazing up at it, open-mouthed. *What in God's name is going on?*

'Come to me! Quickly!' Sooty called.

3

Elaine ran to the wheel and yanked it hard to the left, but the boat didn't seem to want to respond and she was now certain it would hit *Mary Celeste*. She glanced at the array of switches and levers before her, wondering how the hell you put one of these things in reverse. She pulled the most likely-looking one – one she was certain she'd seen Sooty handle. The engine note rose and *Majesty* surged forward. To the left.

'We're gonna miss it! *Miss it, you fucker!*' she snarled at the cruiser, pulling the power off again.

'Oh, my *head!*'

Elaine glanced down. Spreadbury was sitting up now, both hands clapped over his eyes. 'Never mind your head, you fuckwit!' she screamed. 'Get up here and stop us crashing!'

Spreadbury jerked as if he'd been slapped. His hands came down from his face and he looked surprised to discover he wasn't alone. 'If you could see what I've just seen,' he

349

said in a tremulous voice. Then he got up. He was unsteady on his feet.

'Get the hell away from me!' Sooty gasped, and Elaine turned to her just in time to see her entire body convulse. Something grey and waxy appeared around her mouth and nostrils and grew out from her in a long, waving, lumpy tentacle, which searched the air around the cabin, then dissolved into dust that vanished long before it hit the floor.

Gasping in what sounded like terror, presumably because he'd realized what was about to happen to his boat, Spreadbury shouldered Elaine aside, took the power off, then applied it again, hard. This time in reverse. Elaine staggered forward into the bulkhead, lost her footing and fell, finding Sooty on the floor beside her. Sooty's temple was bleeding but she was conscious. She gave Elaine a wan smile and said, 'I got rid of the bitch! But my foot's gone. My foot got cut off. It *hurts*. It's gone but it *hurts*.'

At the helm, Spreadbury cursed.

'Your foot is okay,' Elaine said. 'It's still there. Maybe you twisted it.'

Sooty shook her head. 'Jim cut off my foot,' she said. 'But I got rid of the bitch. We have to beware of Candy and Jon. Remember that. She knows about them. They're hers.'

A second later *Majesty* hit the burning hulk of *Mary Celeste*.

The deck stopped being horizontal and became a big hill down which Elaine and Sooty began to slide.

'We're burning,' Spreadbury moaned from way up the hill. 'We have to get the hell out of here. Fast.'

4

Something snapped at the back of Jim's mind. For a few seconds he wasn't sure what it was. Then he heard Sooty's voice inside his head saying, 'I got rid of the bitch!' and then something else, something distorted so badly he couldn't understand it. It sounded like she'd lost her foot. He wasn't sure he knew what any of this meant because something was dragging at his mind, closing it in like parentheses.

He turned when he heard the *crump!* sound behind him.

All he saw was that the ball of fire, which had once been his boat, had grown larger. He gazed at it for a second, thinking of Sooty and wondering why. Wasn't Sooty behind him, waiting for him to rescue her and take her away from all this in Davey's speed-boat?

'Come to me, Jim!' Sooty implored and he turned back.

Behind her, the wood moved and creaked like a living thing. Above him the hole in the sky shone down that pale light. *You don't get out of this one alive*, he thought. *There's no happy ending here. No riding off into the sunset, no living happily ever after.*

The sand beneath his feet was vibrating now, thrumming with the power of . . . *of what, Jim? Gods?* He didn't know and he didn't care. His only hope was to go and get Sooty. Maybe the combination of the two of them would be greater than the sum of their parts. *Like the Beatles*, he thought, grinning stupidly. Maybe together they could find a way out of this mess.

And if they couldn't, it was tough.

'I'm coming,' he said, starting towards her. His feet felt like lead – as if they didn't want to take him to her. Jim found he could barely shift them through the sand. He moved forward slowly, sliding one foot after the other.

Sooty stood there on the top of the three steps that led up to the porch. The bodies of Frank and Rosie still writhed on the posts at either side of her, their hands flapping uselessly, their feet twitching. He could see the blood pooling beneath them now.

From way behind him came the sound of an incoming motor-boat. Jim didn't look back. Whoever it was couldn't do a damned thing to sort out this mess he'd caused. It was *his* mess. He was the thief around here. James Green alone had caused all this and in so doing had sealed his doom. That thing up there pretending to be Sooty wasn't Sooty at all. He knew that now. But there was nothing he could do about it. Nothing anyone could do.

'Quickly, Jim, there's no time!' the Sooty thing urged.

Majesty, that's who you are, Jim thought, as he slid through the sand towards her. *The ghost of Majesty Dauphin. Come to claim me. You were right, if that was you leaving those messages on my computer and typewriter, I* won't *be going back this time.*

He craned round. It was almost dark now, out there on the bay. The weird light ended at the water's edge. A boat was approaching at high speed; its bows were high and water churned around them. A low, sleek speed-boat. He knew it should have meant something to him, but he didn't know what. *You're all too late!* he thought to its occupants, whoever they were. *This is already over and done.*

'Jim! Hurry!'

Jim turned back to Majesty. Her radiant skin had begun to creep. He was close enough now to see that happening. As he watched, a bloated maggot pierced her unblemished cheek and plopped to the boards at her feet.

He grinned. *I couldn't have written it better myself*, he thought bitterly. In his left hand the hatchet felt very heavy. *I wonder*, he thought, as he approached his doom. *I wonder . . .*

5

Ahead of her, as the speed-boat bounced across the rising waves towards the oddly lit island, Sooty could clearly see the bitch who'd reached out from a fault-line deep beneath the ocean and tried to invade her mind. The same bitch whose voice she'd heard on the telephone. The bitch who had found her and her home using another, deeper fault-line – a crack in the rock through which she could exert at least a little influence, even if she couldn't escape. This was the bitch who could play Mozart from memory, the bitch who had helped her murderous husband slaughter her own daughter.

Majesty Dauphin.

Sooty knew that Straker himself was loose somewhere on that island too, but right now, as Spreadbury powered them towards the island, it was Majesty who was the problem on which she had to concentrate. She had to try to forget the weird open hole in the sky through which shone a pale light, forget the waking god that might sweep away most of Florida when it finally escaped, and concentrate on stopping the bitch getting Jim.

And I can do it, too! she told herself. *Because when it comes down to it, I'm a bigger bitch than she is. I'm not giving up anything I have, whether I deserve it or not. It's mine now, not hers, and I'm keeping it. And I'll bring down mayhem and death on anything that stands in my way!*

She stood up on her seat, her footing sure and certain. She could ride the bumpy waves without being thrown off the boat. She found she could anticipate each yaw and pitch, each bounce that the powerful speed-boat made. She cupped her hands to her mouth and, in a voice that seemed loud enough to wake the dead, bellowed, 'JIM! RUN! RUN AWAY. DON'T GO TO HER!'

'Nearly there!' Spreadbury yelled. 'Just a few more seconds!'

'JIM! BACK OFF! IT'S NOT ME!' Sooty yelled.

'He can't hear you!' Elaine said, from the seat beside her. She was hanging on for dear life. She looked sick.

'He can hear me,' Sooty replied. 'Even if it's not with his ears.'

6

I know it's not you, honeybunny, Jim thought, as he walked slowly towards Majesty. *I know it's not you, but I have to do this. I have to go to her. Because of your foot. Because I'm the thief. This is my show.* And then he emptied his mind in case anything he thought could be picked up. He purposely didn't wonder how Sooty had known, how she had come to be here – a part of him knew that anyway: he'd dreamed it at some point, he was sure.

He was close now. Close enough to smell the expensive heady perfume his wife had made up in Seattle – Eau de Skunk, he had always called it, but it was lovely perfume. The woman who made it had called it Sooty G. He was close enough to see how the thing that stood before him mirrored his wife in every detail except one: Sooty was alive. This thing was an animated corpse. The thing driving it was running out of time. Either it got into Sooty's body – or into his, he guessed – or it was going to expire and go back to the hell it had escaped from. This ancient and rotting corpse wasn't going to last much longer.

'Take me!' Majesty urged. 'Pick me up and carry me away. My leg is hurt. I can't walk!'

'Which leg, honey?' Jim asked, keeping his mind blank as he moved closer. His hand tightened around the hatchet. His damaged right wrist pulsed tiny jolts of pain up his arm as he tensed. He was inches from her now, close enough to smell the putrid flesh beneath the powerful perfume.

'This one,' Majesty said, and pushed her left leg forward.

Jim looked up at her, found her dark eyes. He said, 'We're so different, sweetheart. So very different. We're so far apart in time and space that we can't read one another. See, I just can't believe you did that. It's something so unlikely, I wouldn't have even bothered writing it. It's almost a *deus ex machina*.'

'Jim! Carry me! My leg is hurt!' she urged.

Jim clenched his teeth and struck out hard and fast with the hatchet. Something black and cold spattered his face. The sharp edge hit Majesty's ankle with a force so great it cleanly lopped off her foot which bounced a few inches across the boards. Majesty screamed.

'Bet it hurts more now,' he said, raising the hatchet as her clawed hand flashed out towards him. Jim casually swept the hatchet out into the gap between them, accurately estimating where her hand would strike. The keen edge of Davey's hatchet went through Majesty's hand with almost no resistance. It made a tiny metallic *ping!* and three of her fingers fell to the boards.

'THIEF!' Majesty roared, and Jim could see the huge, raging thing behind Sooty's eyes, the thing which she wanted so badly to be free of. Majesty and Straker Dauphin were bound more tightly to the god that had been imprisoned on this island than he'd imagined. Majesty was no longer truly a separate entity. A facet of the god was all mixed up in her, but lost in there: trapped inside and bound to her as she was bound to it.

In that terrible second during which Jim gazed upon the face of the god, he realized it had taken Straker and Majesty, intending to use them as an escape route from its prison here on the island. They had been a gateway for it. It had meant to pass through them and out into this reality but it hadn't understood humans and it had underestimated the strength of the power working against it. And after its brief period of arousal, it had slept and waited, locked to the spirits of its captors until more of what it needed to energize it became available.

Now blood had been spilled and the god was waking; it was no longer in the somnambulant state it had been in when Straker and Majesty had tried to harness its power. And once it was fully awake it would break out.

Jim didn't know if the thing had kept the bodies from rotting away entirely because it needed its captors incarnate, but he could think of no other reason why Straker and Majesty should be walking and talking after all this time. Which presumably meant that if their bodies were destroyed, the god's gateway would be closed.

As this thought tripped through his mind, Jim moved his left hand as far back as he could, tensed his muscles and, yelling wildly, brought the hatchet round in a sweeping blow that with every fibre of his being he knew would decapitate Majesty.

'Fuck you!' he shouted, as the hatchet reached Majesty's neck.

And Majesty winked out of existence.

The hatchet didn't meet the resistance Jim had expected and he threw himself off balance, staggered and went over, putting out his right hand to break his fall. This was a mistake. The struggle to save Candy had probably cracked the ulna in his right arm, Jim knew; now that bone was broken. This was obvious since a jagged and bloody point of it now stuck out through the skin at the bottom of his wrist. Jim lay there, gazing at the bright blood dripping on to the bleached boards of the porch, then got himself up, using the hatchet handle as a stick.

There was no sign of Majesty on the porch.

Down at the water's edge, close to the smouldering dinghy, Sooty and Elaine and Aaron Spreadbury were waist deep in water, wading towards the shore through the rising waves.

Movement to the left of the house caught Jim's eye and he turned. Candy was tottering out on to the beach from the path at the side of the house. She was filthy and the flesh of one of her ankles was mangled, still pulled down like a sock, but she was alive.

The pain in Jim's arm seemed to have cleared his vision until everything seemed so sharply focused it looked unreal. Candy tottered a couple of steps into the sand and then stopped, staring blankly ahead of her. The breeze drew her hair across her face so that Jim couldn't see her expression. On the far side of the island, lightning flickered and thunder racketed through the sky. Above him, the dark clouds still rose into that funnel of pale light.

Jim began to walk towards Candy, not knowing what he intended to do – save her, perhaps. She should have been dead. She'd been sucked beneath the ground and trapped there, so she should have been dead. *But she's alive*, he thought. *In spite of that, she's alive.* He vaguely remembered a dream in which he'd seen Candy ejected from that mound of dark soil. It had puked her up. He didn't know what that meant. That she, too, was possessed by the island's god, probably. The smooth beech haft of the hatchet in his left hand seemed to tremble, as if it was a diviner's hazel twig, trying to point towards the source of water. Except this was trying to point towards Candy.

I knew it would end in tears, Jim thought distantly.

Sooty and Elaine and Spreadbury were closer now – less than twenty feet from the beach. If they came ashore they'd be as lost as Candy was. As lost as *he* was. 'NO!' Jim yelled towards them. 'SOOTY! DON'T COME IN! GO BACK!'

In the trees behind the house, something big and angry was boiling. It was invisible – apparent only by the way it bent the light. The god was wide awake now, trapped only by its connection to Straker and Majesty, who were not incarnate, as Jim had thought, but who were able to generate some kind of body from whatever remained of their corpses.

Behind the house, trees twisted, screamed and fell. The ground shook and the pale light grew in intensity. Tiny wisps of green fire were dancing up the inside of the column of cloud now and fluttering across the branches of nearby trees like living things.

His mind blank and his body filled with pain, Jim strode towards Candy, the beechwood handle of the hatchet seemingly dragging him towards her.

'No! *Leave her, Jim!*' Sooty yelled. She was on the beach now with Elaine and Spreadbury beside her.

I can't, Jim thought, tearing his eyes away from his wife for what might well be the last time in his life, and fixing them on Candy. *I'm the thief. I brought this crock of shit down on us all and I have to fix it if I can. It may cost me my life, but I've got to do what I can.* 'Get back in the water! You're safe in the water!' he yelled, without looking back, then began to run at Candy.

As Jim's foot came down from the first running pace he took, the ground burst open exactly beneath the spot where his foot would have landed. He saw it peripherally, but the thing's timing was perfect and it was too late to avoid it. The putrid arm shot out from beneath the sand with the speed of a harpoon. Fleshless fingers grappled themselves around and into his right ankle and twisted hard.

Jim heard his ankle snap as he fell on his face. The pain was tremendous. There was a moment during which nothing seemed to exist except an ocean of agony, then he heard himself screaming. He was rolling, scrambling and kicking as he tried to shake off the cast-iron grip around his broken ankle.

Candy was up there, just in front of him, taking no notice at all of what was happening at her feet. She stood erect, staring out at nothing. Jim struggled and screamed and swore and kicked at his broken ankle with his good foot. It seemed to go on for ever. Pain, fear and hopelessness threatened to overcome him.

Suddenly he was on his back, his head tilted up to Candy. Jon Short was beside her now. *They're both dead,* a distant part of Jim's mind told him as he fought to sit up. *They've been prepared . . . in case of emergency.*

At his feet, following his arm out of the sand came the head and shoulders of a man. A man who looked pretty much the way Jim thought *he* would look after a good few

357

years in the grave. Straker Dauphin's clothes and skin were rotted and peeling away from his skeleton, but this didn't hinder his quick, powerful movements.

The wooden shaft of the hatchet twitched in Jim's left hand and he sliced it round from his side in a semi-circle, like a man reaping corn. It couldn't possibly miss Dauphin's head.

7

'Don't shoot, you'll hit Jim!' Sooty yelled at Elaine over the sound of the wind. Sand was being lifted from the beach now and thrown into their faces – as if the island itself didn't want them there. Elaine was down on one knee, her left wrist resting on the other and the long barrel of the Magnum on her wrist to keep it steady. Up close to the tree-line, Straker and Jim were struggling: the dead man, still half covered by sand was clinging to Jim's leg while Jim tried to shake him off.

Above the island, cloud boiled up the inside of what seemed to be a huge cylinder. Beyond the house a great, shimmering, almost invisible thing was rising. All across the beach and in the trees, little green flames danced in the air, untouched by the breeze. Each time one snuffed out, another popped up somewhere else.

'I can get a clear shot!' Elaine yelled.

'Don't!' Sooty warned. 'Not till I say. I know what'll happen if the timing isn't right. I'm intuiting this and I'm trusting my intuition. Stay put, aim and wait.'

'I can hit him, Sooty!' Elaine said, but she didn't fire, just stayed exactly where she was, totally still, but for her hair whipping in the breeze. She looked to Sooty as if she'd become stone. 'What the fuck is that thing behind the house?' she added, in a puzzled tone. 'Is it what I think it is? Aaron?'

'It's the god,' Spreadbury said in an awed voice. 'The god of the island. Straker's god.'

'So . . . what do we *do* about it?' Elaine asked.

'*You* do nothing about it,' Spreadbury said grimly. '*I* do what has to be done.' And he started up the beach, leaning

358

forward into the wind, his forearm shielding his eyes from the flying sand.

8

Suddenly the iron fingers were gone from Jim's ankle and the hatchet was gone from his hand. The dead man had moved so fast that Jim hadn't even seen it happen: all he felt was fresh pain, this time in his left wrist. Dauphin slithered out of the sand like a lizard and clambered on to Jim, pushing him down on his back and squatting on his chest. His quick hands found Jim's throat and squeezed.

Stars burst in front of Jim's eyes, clouding his vision. His head felt as if the pressure would make it explode. He clawed at where he thought Dauphin's face was with his left hand and missed by a mile. He tried again and this time hit something hard and unmoving. Then he dropped his hand to the sand and let his fingers search for the hatchet – which wasn't there.

Ignoring the pain, he made one last desperate attempt, bringing his fists together at his sternum, linking his fingers, then punching them up towards his own chin. It worked: the V of his forearms hit Straker's wrists and broke his grip. Jim didn't even try to count of the cost of the extra damage to his compound fracture. He gasped in air and coughed it out again. Then inhaled and screamed, 'It's all over, you moron! You're dead, Dauphin! You're *dead* and your soul belongs to the thing you conjured up! *Go back to it!*'

A moment later Dauphin had him pinned down by the throat again. This time his grip wasn't quite as tight, but the bones of his fingers had already broken the skin and were grating against the raw flesh beneath. Jim guessed that the dead man intended to saw right through his jugular vein and slowly bleed him to death.

Straker pushed his rotting face close to Jim's. 'You stole everything from me. The tales *I* wrote! The success *I* should have enjoyed! You and your wife even stole the bodies intended for the reincarnation of me and *my* wife. It is *your* soul that belongs to the god of the island, not mine. Your

359

soul and the soul of your Sooty. You even have my own daughter! But I will have her back!'

Get fucked! Jim thought, and brought up both his arms as hard and fast as he could, catching Straker's peeling skull in a powerful pincer blow. Jim heard bone crack but that didn't matter. What mattered was that Straker Dauphin's face had narrowed considerably. His remaining eye bulged from its crushed socket. Something black that might have once been brain leaked out from a new gap that had formed beneath it.

Jim snarled inwardly. The pain was a bright hot wire up his right arm; the agony from his ankle extended all the way up to his balls where it curled in like fish-hooks. His arms wouldn't move.

'It's all mine!' Dauphin grated. 'Everything you have is *mine*. And I *will* have it back! I will climb inside this body of mine, drive you out! No longer will you possess my flesh!'

A moment later his hands were gone from Jim's throat and a second after that, a bony fist hit him hard in the side of his head. Jim saw stars. The wind had risen and thunder was rolling and echoing. Trees were creaking and falling and something huge was crashing through the wood, its footsteps making the ground shudder, its angry, wordless voice raking the air.

Straker Dauphin's bony fingers yanked open Jim's mouth and suddenly his whole hand was pushing inside, stretching Jim's lips, making him gag. Sharp fingertips grazed the back of his throat.

'This is how it will be,' the dead man's voice rasped. 'I take back my body in the only way I can. By climbing inside it.' He straightened his arm and leaned his weight on it, driving his hand deep into Jim's throat.

Out there somewhere in the distance, Jim's own hands were fluttering uselessly in the air like injured birds. He'd been ready to take a breath when Straker had thrust in his hand and sealed off his air, and he was still dizzy from the blow to his head. Stars twirled and burst across his field of vision. And as the pressure in his throat increased, so did the starbursts. A moment later Jim felt something inside him let go.

Then he was falling into the darkness on which the stars glittered. Something huge and shimmering, almost invisible, waited there for him behind the endless night.

9

'Oh, Christ, he's got Jim pinned down,' Sooty said, hopping forward a step. She'd felt as if she'd lost her foot back on the boat and then, as they came in on the launch, she'd discovered why – she'd watched Jim chop off Majesty's foot with the hatchet. Her own foot was still there and it was whole, but her body thought it had gone. 'Quick, Elaine! If you can do it, do it now! Shoot him, Lainey!'

'I've got him,' Elaine said, peering down the barrel of her hand-cannon. 'I've got the motherfucker.'

Beyond the house the huge invisible thing crashed madly back and forth through the trees as though it couldn't get out of the forest on to the beach. Spreadbury was at the side of the house now, almost at the end of the path that led into the woods. He brushed past the inert figures of Candy and Jon and disappeared from view.

'Quick!' Sooty urged. 'Fire!'

Elaine didn't appear to move a muscle. She might have been a statue carved from granite. The gun barrel didn't waver at all. But Sooty watched the Magnum's hammer rise as beneath Elaine's finger the trigger pulled smoothly backwards.

The gun roared.

'Got him,' Elaine reported, in a steady voice.

Sooty already knew: she'd seen Straker lose half his head as the bullet hit it. It had simply seemed to vaporize in a dark cloud. The man should have collapsed, dead, but he was dead already and apparently that made a difference. He merely jolted to the side, steadied himself and reached up to touch the open top of his skull.

His hands are off Jim, Sooty thought, *that's the main thing!* She yelled, 'Shoot him again!'

10

Jim heard a meaty *thwack!* then heard himself heave in a breath even before he knew he was still alive. In that instant he was snatched from the mouth of the god that had found him and drawn him all the way across the endless distance towards it and flung forcefully back into his body.

Straker Dauphin was still straddling him, but something had changed. Jim didn't know how it had happened, but the crown of the dead man's head appeared to be gone. Straker's fingers were up there probing it while he cursed and wailed in his torn voice.

Fuck you! Jim thought, and struck up at him with his left hand. The blow never connected; Straker caught his hand, pulled it to his mouth, straightened his little finger and bit on it, hard. Jim yelled.

And down by the sea, Elaine fired again.

A good-sized chunk of Straker's head shattered above Jim. The force of the bullet's impact knocked Straker sideways and caused his jaws to clench. Jim's hand was suddenly free and spouting blood. As his hand passed by his field of vision, Jim realized that he would never again type the letters Q, A, and Z with the tip of this finger: it was gone, down to the first knuckle.

His hand hit something hard and smooth on the sand and, of their own volition, his fingers fastened themselves around it. The smooth beechwood wanted to twitch. And as far as Jim was concerned, it was welcome to do just that.

11

Elaine was setting herself up for a third shot – the first two had removed most of Dauphin's head, but the bastard wouldn't lie down, dead or not – when an unexpected movement to her right disturbed her concentration. She ignored it – it must be Sooty moving – and took aim again.

Which was why she didn't see Majesty Dauphin materializing beside her. She squeezed off another shot at Straker, then cursed herself: she'd been too panicky and this one went wide by a foot.

362

Then something that felt like an anvil hit her in the side of the head and she fell down, the Magnum letting another shot loose in the sand. She didn't lose consciousness, but she might just as well have done because the blow had blurred her vision and it also seemed to have crippled her: she couldn't move a limb. She lay there, gasping like a fish on a riverbank, gaping back at the blurred figure of Majesty, who was now straddling Sooty in much the same way that her husband had been straddling Jim, trying to open Sooty's mouth with one hand while she tried to insert the other into it. Sooty was struggling frantically, writhing and kicking and slapping and scratching.

'Let me in, you *bitch*!' Majesty shouted, in a voice that was a perfect imitation of Sooty's. 'Get out and let me in!'

'It's mine and you won't take it back!' Sooty screamed, in an identical voice. 'You're dead and you're going to stay that way. No one takes away anything of mine!' She slashed out a hand at Majesty's face and Elaine saw a quantity of skin slough away under her nails.

Go get her, honey, Elaine thought. Some feeling was coming back into her extremities: she could tell from the fireworks going off in them. Soon, she was sure, she would be able to move. She didn't know whether it would be in time or not. And then realized it wouldn't have to be. Sooty had always claimed her nickname had been bestowed upon her because of her dusky skin, but now Elaine knew the truth. She'd been called Sooty because she could fight like a maddened tomcat.

Half of Majesty's face was missing now, including her eyes. Elaine didn't know how it was possible for her to carry on fighting blind, but she wasn't far off matching Sooty, blow for blow, scratch for scratch.

And then Sooty screamed long and loud and heaved herself out from beneath Majesty, toppling her adversary. A moment later she had scrambled over to Elaine and had picked up her hand – the one still locked around the Magnum.

Majesty scrambled towards them

Fire, Sooty! Elaine thought, and Sooty squeezed her hand

around Elaine's. The gun fired and kicked. The left half of Majesty's head shattered and she vanished.

'Jim!' Sooty yelled, and tried to peel Elaine's fingers from the gun.

12

Jim heaved up the hatchet, knowing that Straker's quick hands would fly down from his head to deflect it before it struck him. As it came up, he pulled hard to one side at the last moment and instead of having the haft wrenched from his hand, this time the sharp edge hit Straker's wrist and cut half-way through. Straker pulled back the hand – which now hung by a shard of bone and a tendon – and flashed out his other at Jim's face.

Jim was ready. He brought back the hatchet hard and fast. The flat back edge hit Straker's hand, hard enough to snap the ancient bones beneath the skin. Jim hefted the hatchet out to his side and struck again.

The sharp edge took Straker square on the cheekbone and cleaved through his face as if it were nothing more substantial than water.

'Got you, you motherfucker!' Jim croaked, as Straker fell, hit the sand and vanished.

Jim craned round, looking for him, the hatchet ready in case he should reappear.

Back up the beach a little way, Candy and Jon were now moving – going up the steps to the Dauphin house. Jim watched until they'd gone inside, then tried to get up. His right wrist was now a bloody mess with a sharp bit of bone sticking out; his left hand was bleeding heavily and his ankle was broken. Behind the house, the god lumbered, flattening everything it touched. Tiny green fires danced everywhere.

It isn't over yet, Jim thought, knowing he had no more fight left in him.

And Straker appeared before him again.

Down on the beach Sooty yelled something.

A gun fired.

Straker's head exploded and he winked out of existence.

'You got him, Sooty!' Elaine screamed.

Everything stopped as if the frame had suddenly been frozen for everything except Jim, Sooty, Elaine and Spreadbury. The roiling clouds ceased to fly up the inside of the hole in the sky above the island; the massive shimmering shape of the god paused behind the Dauphin house; the wind dropped; the little green licks of flame were as still as glass ornaments. In the distance, either at the other side of the island or out to sea, a bolt of lightning was frozen in the sky.

Jim sat up. From down near the water's edge, where the incoming wave was also frozen, came a series of metallic clicks and snaps as Elaine, now on her feet, feverishly ejected the spent shells from the Magnum and reloaded. Sooty was gazing up past the house, her mouth agape.

And from the back of the Dauphin house Spreadbury bellowed, 'Get thee back to thy hell-hole, spawn of Satan! I banish thee from these places of God. I banish thee from the land of the living!' which, Jim thought through his pain, was about as corny an exorcism line as he'd ever heard.

Jim turned to face the Dauphin house and was amazed to discover that Spreadbury's speech seemed to be working. The massive shimmering form of the god was being sucked down like a cartoon genie dragged back into its bottle. And as it dissipated the hole in the sky above the island began to close, drawn in as if to fill the vacuum in reality that the god was leaving. The flat pale daylight that illuminated the island began to fade and darkness started to gather.

'I think we did it!' Elaine yelled triumphantly. 'We drove 'em away!'

'You'll have to help me,' Jim called to them. 'My ankle's bust and I can't walk!'

Elaine and Sooty hurried up the beach to where he lay.

'Oh, my God, Jim!' Sooty moaned, when she saw the extent of his injuries.

'You don't look so great yourself,' Jim said, spitting blood. He'd lost a tooth or two, his tongue was swollen and torn and his lips were split in several places. He thought his jaw was broken too. But it was the ankle and his finger that *really* hurt. And they didn't hurt as much as looking at Sooty. She was going to need stitches in some of those

365

wounds on her face. A couple of her fingernails were missing, her nose was broken and bleeding and she was badly bruised.

'Cat fight,' Sooty said, glancing from Jim to the house. 'You should have seen the loser. What happened to Candy and Jon?'

'They went inside,' Jim said.

'We're not going in there after them,' Sooty said. 'Aaron said to beware. Something bad has happened to them. Come on, Jim, let's get you up and get the hell out of here. That god, or whatever it is, is almost gone and I don't want to stick around to see what happens afterwards. I've got a bad feeling about it.'

Elaine and Sooty helped him to his feet and wrapped his arms around their shoulders to support him. In a line they started back down the beach towards the launch.

From behind the house came a muffled noise that sounded like something heavy and soft hitting the ground. Everything started moving again. Thunder rocked the island, the wind blew, darkness fell, and low, threatening cloud began to boil in the sky.

'It's gone,' Jim said.

'Aaron did it,' Sooty said. 'Oh, shit! Aaron! Where the hell is he?'

'Fuck Aaron. He can look after himself,' Elaine said. 'We have to get you and Jim to the boat. We have to get you off the island before anything else nasty happens. You need hospital treatment.'

'We have to get Aaron!' Sooty said. 'We can't just leave him!'

Elaine swore. 'We can't handle him now! I'll come back when you're both safe. Come on!'

'Lainey, we can't leave him,' Sooty implored. 'He saved Jim. We can't leave him.'

'Fuck it. Okay, you two go down there and get in that motor-boat. I'll go back for Aaron. If you can't see me coming back by the time you're in the boat, take off. Promise?'

Sooty nodded.

'Okay, then *go*!' Elaine commanded. And stood for a few moments, watching their slow progress down the beach.

366

13

Elaine turned back into the strengthening wind and strode up the beach towards the Dauphin house, her Magnum in her hand and her hair blowing out behind her. Lightning sizzled down into the wood and thunder rolled. Elaine kept her mind blank. She didn't intend to think of the consequences of her stupid decision or of anything else, come to that, until she'd attempted to do what she'd promised and was safe in the boat, heading out of here.

She glanced back to check Jim and Sooty's progress and her heart sank like an express elevator. The idiots were coming back up the beach towards her. *They're half dead!* she thought angrily. *What do the idiots think they can do?* 'GO BACK!' she yelled, and motioned them away, but they just kept trudging towards her. *They couldn't abandon me, just like I couldn't abandon Spreadbury*, she thought. *Are we all fucking crazy or what?*

Sooty stabbed her finger towards the house. Elaine looked round and saw Spreadbury tottering out in front of the house from the path. His fists were clenched and pressed to his cheeks, and he looked as if he were in agony.

Elaine turned and yelled to Sooty and Jim, 'Stay right there! I'll get him!' She began to run towards him.

'No!' Spreadbury called in a high voice. 'Don't come any closer! It's too late! It's too late!'

'It's okay,' Elaine shouted, still running towards him. 'We've done it. We've banished the ghosts. I'll help you down the beach. We've won, Aaron!'

'Stop!' he shrieked.

Elaine slowed to a walking pace. 'What's wrong?' she asked, peering at him. When she saw that he was vibrating again – *shimmering* – like he had on the boat before he'd become possessed, she stopped.

'Get back!' Spreadbury said, in a voice that was now so high it was almost a whistle.

'What's happened?' Elaine asked. 'What, Aaron?'

'The god,' Spreadbury said, jolting as if he were being punched. 'I banished it all right. Oh, yes, I banished it! I stopped it all happening.'

Something else was happening to him now, Elaine realized. He was beginning to *bulge* as if someone were blowing up his body with an air-line. 'I know you banished it,' she said. 'Great work. But we have to leave now.'

Spreadbury's hands fell limply to his sides. His face looked horribly swollen. 'I can't leave,' he said. 'I can't ever leave. But you must go! And tell Jim and Sooty. Oh . . . I can see. I can *see*! Jon and Candy. Tell Jim. Tell Sooty. Jon and Candy are inside the house. I can *see* them. I can see *everything*. I'm seeing with the eyes of the god. I can see it all. The Dauphins. Their bodies are bound to the god. They need to leave the island in *other bodies than theirs*. Their bodies are dead but still bound to the god! They can't leave like that! Tell Jim!'

'You're not making sense, Aaron,' Elaine said. She glanced over her shoulder and was pleased to see that Jim and Sooty had stopped a safe distance away. It was starting to look as if it wasn't over yet. *It's starting to look like Aaron might explode.*

'It hurts, seeing with the eyes of a god,' Spreadbury moaned. 'Straker and Majesty's spirits are alive. They knew. They knew they might fail to take Jim and Sooty here on the island so they planned for it. They emptied Jon and Candy. Drove them from their bodies and fed them to the god. But Jon and Candy's bodies are alive. And Straker and Majesty mean to take them to leave the island. But it'll only be temporary. They have to get into their rightful bodies to survive. The bodies of Jim and Sooty. Warn them! You must warn them!'

'But I can help you!' Elaine said. 'I can get you back to the boat! We can escape. You can tell them all this yourself!'

'No one can save anyone,' Spreadbury gasped. His body was now twice its original size. 'Don't you understand? It's too late. Because the god is *inside* me. I swallowed it. I tried to banish it but I *absorbed* it. A thing as big as an apartment block. It's *inside* me and it's trying to get out. Go. Get off the island before it escapes. Quickly! I can't hold it much longer. GET AWAY!'

Elaine glanced back at Jim and Sooty, then at Spreadbury again, not knowing what to do. Spreadbury was bulging like the Michelin man now, his skin stretched taut across his face.

Even his hands were bulging. His shirt split and his trousers tore apart.

'GO!' he wailed.

Elaine turned and ran, faster than she'd ever moved in her life.

14

Sooty saw Elaine turn and sprint away from Aaron Spreadbury and had a flash of intuition as to the final resting place of the god. Spreadbury had somehow sucked it up and contained it. And now it was trying to escape: the increase in his size was plain to see, even from this distance in the flickering light from the angry clouds. As Elaine ran, Spreadbury inflated like an aeroplane life-jacket and his head became a huge round balloon with a tiny stretched face painted upon it.

'Get down!' she yelled at Jim, and tugged him down as she dived for the ground.

'*Looooook oooooout!*' Elaine screamed.

A moment later Aaron Spreadbury turned into something akin to an atomic blast. Sooty saw a white flash, which blinded her, and the air was filled with a huge noise she thought would never end. A wave of heat washed over her, then she was showered with sand and earth and detritus from the house.

When her retinas cleared and she sat up to look, Spreadbury and Elaine were gone. And so was the Dauphin house, the backyard and a good section of the wood beyond.

Debris – most in tiny pieces – was raining down from the sky.

'Fuck,' Jim said, in a small, shocked voice. He gave a bitter laugh. 'Just like a Jim Green book. It all blows up in the end.'

The steaming thing that thunked down in the sand close to Sooty turned out to be Elaine's .357 Magnum, coated in a rind of frost, but carrying a full load and undamaged. Sooty picked it up, the warmth of her hand melting the ice. 'Come on, Jim, let's get out of here before anything else happens,' she said, scrambling to her feet. 'We've only got Aaron's little speed-boat and the sea's getting up. It's a long way back to Seaford. Here, take my hand.'

369

Chapter Twenty-Four

After Straker's Island: Day One

1

Jim watched it all from his normal writing vantage point: he began by hanging in the air in a corner of the room, looking down at the action, then, as the action developed, he saw it from all angles, all points of view, switching from one to the other with no more effort than a simple movement of his eyes.

He didn't much care for what he saw.

Jon and Candy walked into the lounge of the Dauphin house like two automatons. Their movements were unsteady and stiff, their eyes didn't blink and their heads didn't turn. Their mouths hung open and were muddy inside. And yet they were alive: Jim could tell this, not from their breathing because it wasn't perceptible, but from the steady slow pulse in the left side of their throats.

They walked to the centre of the room then lay down on the bare floorboards, side by side, close enough for their hands to touch, although Jim thought the touching was mere coincidence.

A few moments later, Majesty and Straker appeared. Jim didn't know where they'd come from. One moment they weren't there, the next they were. He guessed they'd materialized. After all, they were ghosts. It seemed odd that they were ghosts who were able to materialize incarnate, whose ancient and rotting bodies took damage just like real bodies, but Jim knew there was a reason for this. The flesh belonged to the god and although it was beyond the god's capability to regenerate it except by illusion the thing wouldn't let it die. Because it owned the spirits through the flesh and the flesh bound them to it.

But the god was no longer here. It had vanished like a genie would vanish after granting its customary three wishes. For a while, at least, these living dead were about as free as they'd been since raising the god from its slumber.

Majesty and Straker Dauphin exchanged glances. Or they would have been exchanging glances if they'd had the physical equipment to do it. As it was, they turned what was left of their heads to one another.

This flesh will serve, Straker Dauphin said. *Temporarily.*

Until . . . Majesty replied.

Soon! Straker assured her. *Soon we will have all we are owed and more!*

'This isn't fair!' Jim cried, knowing he wouldn't be heard. He wasn't even here as far as they were concerned. 'This isn't fair! You lost and we won! You were blown up in the explosion! The god's gone. Banished!'

Straker and Majesty approached the supine bodies of Jon and Candy. Straker straddled Jon, sitting on his hips, and Majesty did the same with Candy. Both took the jaws of their respective hosts and prised them open, then, using both hands and what must have been immense strength, tore the bottom jaw down towards the throat.

Jim could hear the pops and crackles as the sinew, muscle and cartilage tore away. Straker leaned forward, nipped the corners of Jon's mouth and pulled hard, splitting his cheeks all the way back to the bottoms of his ears. A second later Majesty did the same to Candy.

Then both of them began to push what was left of their heads into their captives' extended mouths, working the ripped, but stretched-tight skin of the cheeks around their skulls.

'*You cannot be fucking serious!*' Jim shouted. 'It's *imposs-ible*! It can't happen!'

But it could.

Majesty and Straker wriggled up to a half-standing position. In unison they pushed forward, forcing their heads down their captives' throats. It wasn't easy. Jim watched the bodies bulge as the Dauphins scrambled and heaved their way right in. Now Candy's throat was bulging like a snake that had swallowed something two sizes too large for it. Jim

371

expected her skin to rupture, but it stretched to accommodate the stress being put upon it.

Straker's shoulders seemed to dislocate so that he was narrower. He was still too wide, Jim knew. It wouldn't work.

But, somehow, it *did* work. Candy and Jon's stomachs bulged unbelievably as Majesty and Straker burrowed into them, sloughing off foul flesh. Inside them the invaders turned. Through their ripped mouths Jim could see Straker and Majesty's heads come back up their throats and force their way up through the back of the nasal passages and into the heads.

It was disgusting to watch.

'It can't happen!' Jim shouted, and his eyes blinked open on daylight. Daylight in a clean, sparse, white-painted room that smelt faintly of disinfectant.

2

'Shh! Stop screaming! It's okay!' Sooty's voice said.

But when Jim looked over at her, it wasn't Sooty. The woman in the bed next to his didn't look anything like Sooty. This woman's face was fat and round and blackened and scratched. There were stitches over the right of her brow and her hair was clipped short – shaven in places where her scalp had been stitched.

'We're in hospital,' the woman said.

It took a few moments for Jim to understand that this *was* Sooty. You could tell by her eyes – or, at least, by the one that wasn't swollen shut. The white of the one he could see was red with blood.

'What happened?' he asked, realizing that he felt about as bad as she looked. One of his fingers felt as if someone was applying a blowtorch to it, his ankle hurt like hell and his right wrist screamed for mercy beneath the layer of plaster-of-paris that protected it. 'No, don't answer that. I remember,' he added.

'You were shouting in your sleep,' Sooty said. She climbed slowly out of her bed and came across to his. She brushed her dry, cracked lips to his cheek and took his left hand in hers.

'Nightmare,' Jim said.

Sooty tried to smile. 'We've had enough of those to last for ever,' she said. 'They're all over now. We made it.'

'I don't remember getting back,' Jim said. 'How long have I been out?'

'Not long. It's tomorrow afternoon now. The day after. They picked us up about three thirty in the morning down on the jetty. Hester Williams and Charlie Farris found us and rescued us just before the tornado that was following us hit. I couldn't get you out of the boat. You were unconscious. I thought you were going to . . .'

'I didn't, though,' Jim said, squeezing her hand. 'I'm here. By the way, where *is* here?'

'Mount Cedars, Miami,' she said. 'We're top security. Floor nine. The press are having a field day, the nurse told me. They're swarming around like flies out there.'

'The others?' Jim asked. He already knew the answer to the question.

Sooty shook her head. She was still too shocked to cry, Jim guessed. It was going to be a long hard road back to normality. If they could ever find the road in the first place.

'Gloria? Is she okay?' he asked.

'With Hester,' Sooty said. 'She's fine, they said.'

'Who said?' Jim could almost remember something about a cat attacking her.

'The nurses. Relax.'

Jim frowned. 'There's something wrong. Still. Something to do with the dream I just had.'

'What did you dream?'

Jim sighed. It had dissolved when he woke. 'Can't remember shit,' he admitted.

'Want the television on?' Sooty asked. 'Or a drink or anything?'

'Water,' Jim said. 'And a pack of Virginia Slims.'

'Water you can have,' Sooty said, and poured him a cup. 'Ciggies are off the menu.'

Jim tried to pull a face, but it hurt too much. *You'd only cough up your lungs anyway*, he thought, almost remembering the dream. *Didn't someone crawl into someone's lungs?* he wondered. It was no good, he couldn't bring it back. He sipped the water, which was almost impossible to swallow: his throat felt crushed. *Not so surprising for someone who got half strangled*, he thought.

Something still felt badly wrong. Not just that everyone he'd taken on the trip – and Elaine – was dead. There was more. 'Tornado?' he said. 'A tornado chased us?'

Sooty nodded. 'Yeah, and that was just the first of them. We got out just in time. I saw Spider Murphy's bar get sucked to bits as Hester drove us out. Southern Florida got hit real bad during the night – worst weather in years, from tornadoes to killer lightning storms to grapefruit-sized hailstones. You name it. Not as much damage as Hurricane Andrew did, but it was a close-run thing, the nurses told me. This hospital was jumping when we got in.' She looked at him, questioningly.

Jim frowned. 'It didn't get free,' he said. 'If the god had got free we'd all be dead. There wouldn't be anything left. But it woke and for a while there, it walked and talked.' He shrugged. 'Put the TV on,' he said. 'We may as well see what they're saying.'

They may well have been saying something about him, he knew: the shit storm that was going to follow this débâcle might run for years, but that wasn't the reason he wanted to see a news broadcast. The fact was he thought that, from watching, he might pick up a clue or two about what felt *wrong* about everything. About why the tornado that had chased them seemed so significant.

'Sooty?' he said, when she didn't respond.

Sooty snapped out of her reverie. 'You know I said all the nightmares were over now?'

Jim nodded.

'Did you believe me?'

Jim shook his head. 'You can feel it too,' he said.

'Yes,' she admitted, and sighed. 'Jim, I don't want any more of this shit, but it isn't over. We both know that. There's something I want to tell you and I want you to listen to me. If you think I'm being stupid, just tell me so and I'll think again, but in my opinion you'll agree with me. I turned into Queen Bitch yesterday, over on the island and it kinda super-sensitized me to danger. I can sniff it in the air, like a

374

dog. And I'm sniffing it now. Listen, because there's something I want you to do. It may sound stupid, but please listen
and do as I say. And when I'm done I'll turn on the television
and we'll see if we get a mention.'

3

'. . . says the damage to property in this area of Dade County
alone is estimated at running close to two billion dollars,'
the female ABC reporter said. She was standing in front of
what had once been a mobile-home site and which was now
a sprawl of tangled wood and metal. 'What's most amazing
about all this is that, despite the devastation the weather
caused last night, there doesn't appear to have been one
single death as a direct result of it. God must have been
smiling on Florida in the early hours of this morning. Back
to you, Dan.'

The picture cut to Dan Anstey, the studio anchor. 'God
wasn't smiling on everyone in Florida yesterday,' Anstey
said grimly. 'Last night, eight people were thought to have
been murdered when yesterday's trip to spend the evening
on a haunted island with the world's most popular horror
writer, James Green, went badly wrong.

'The trip was apparently ambushed by unidentified assail-
ants who slaughtered most of the party. But, as ever where
Green is involved, the plot isn't quite as simple as you first
thought. Richard Amis reports from Seaford.'

The broadcast cut to a young blond man standing on the
concrete apron of the harbour in Seaford with a wild grey
sea crashing angrily behind him and rain teeming down on
him.

'The small town of Seaford, south of Miami,' Amis said,
as the wind buffeted him, 'is a sleepy seaside town which
still makes most of its living from fishing. Yesterday, however, terror came to Seaford.

'This is the hometown of world-famous writer and film
director James Green, who yesterday afternoon loaded up
his motor launch *Mary Celeste*, with his secretary, his wife,
Reina, a publicist and five people who had won a competition run by Green's publishers. The prize they had competed

for was an evening on the reputedly haunted Straker's Island in the company of their hero.

'But on Straker's Island last night, the fun turned to terror as the gathering, including local mechanic David Smith who was on the island alone working as a special-effects technician, were attacked and slaughtered by a gang who had apparently lain in wait for them. Last night, a total of eight people were suspected dead. That's everyone except Green himself and his wife who escaped in a friend's speed-boat.

'However, in a dramatic new twist, two of the fans thought to be slain have turned up alive. In spite of having been severely beaten and having had their mouths slashed open and their jaws broken, Candy Hoenikker and Jon Short apparently *swam* the nine miles back to the mainland. They were found, dazed and exhausted, on the beach at Seaford late this morning. Along with Mr and Mrs Green they are now being treated at Mount Cedars hospital in Miami.

'Another strange twist to the tale involves the Greens' daughter Gloria, who was left in the care of local woman Hettie Baker, a relative of James Green's secretary. During the evening Mrs Baker's cat, Marmaduke, attacked her, causing her grievous harm, which resulted in her death from a fall down the stairs of her house. The maddened cat then went after the Greens' daughter, who was sleeping in an upstairs bedroom. The little girl, alerted by Mrs Baker's cries, managed to trap the cat against the door-jamb using the bedroom door and despite being scratched, squeezed it to death. Her heroic efforts saved her from harm. The cat was examined later and found not to be rabid. As James Green himself would say, "If you can imagine it, it *can* happen." Back to you, Dan.'

Neither Jim nor Sooty had heard the last section of the report. They were looking at one another in utter dismay. Jim now knew what had been worrying him. He'd remembered his dream, too. 'It isn't possible,' he said.

'No, but that didn't stop it happening. They did it,' Sooty said. 'I knew they had. I could *feel* it. I could *smell* it in the air. Remember what I told you just now?'

'But they were *blown up!*' Jim complained. 'Jon and

376

Candy were inside the house and they were blown up! They *can't* have escaped that.'

'We don't know they were in the explosion, Jim. They could have left before the house went up. They might have gone out of the back door. We wouldn't have seen them.' She adjusted the blanket she'd laid across her lap, put her hands beneath it and wound her fingers into the material.

'The tornado,' Jim said, shaking his head in disbelief. 'Talk about following the fucking yellow brick road. They're here.'

'We both knew that,' Sooty said, dropping her hands into her lap. 'Just remember what I told you.'

'They're in this *hospital*,' Jim said.

'In this room, in fact,' said a voice bearing a distinct French accent.

4

Sooty yelped. Jim twisted back to face the door. Where Candy and Jon stood, grinning all the way back to their ears where their cheeks had been split. Jim's mind threw up an image from his dream for him to consider: Straker Dauphin nipping the corners of Jon's mouth and tearing the flesh. Their wounds had been beautifully stitched. The scars would barely be discernible, a spinning part of Jim's mind noted.

'It became a little more complex than we had hoped for,' Jon said, in Straker Dauphin's voice. 'But we were prepared. We've had a long time to plan.'

'Get out of here!' Jim yelled.

Jon smiled. 'We will. Soon. But first you have to die. We didn't want that. It would have been better, simpler, if Majesty and I were able to force you two into these bodies when we take back our own. Our rightful bodies. But I'm afraid it is impossible to do. Which means that when this is all over we're going to have to explain the two corpses. Jon and Candy will be dead. How would *you* explain the dead bodies of Jon and Candy, Jim?' His grin widened. The wounds on his cheeks stretched and blood began to weep from the left side. 'You're supposed to be a writer, after all.

Show me how clever you are when you're not able to suck up *my* talent!'

Jim glanced at Sooty, whose face was impassive. There were a million things he ached to tell her. Like how he loved her more than he'd ever thought possible; how his love for her grew with each passing moment; how damned *clever* she was for knowing this would happen. But he kept his mind blank, just as she was doing.

Jim took a deep breath and turned back to Jon and Candy. The door behind them was closed now; Candy flicked the lock catch, sealing them in.

'So, Jim ... any bright ideas?' Jon said. 'Didn't think so. You never had even an ounce of your own talent. Let's face it, your passing won't deprive the world of anything.'

'I'd do this,' Jim said carefully. There was a distinct tremor in his voice, but he didn't work on keeping it away. There was no point in trying to hide his fear. 'I'd say you two came in and threatened us with a gun. You said you intended to kill us because you held us responsible for what happened on the island. Any cop would go for that story. Any member of the public would swallow it. Because you've seen things and suffered things that would unhinge you, at least for a while. You'd be in deep shock.'

Beside him, Sooty slowly withdrew one of her hands from beneath the blanket and laid it limply on top, palm up.

'So, you told us you were going to shoot us,' Jim said. 'There was a struggle. We took the gun from you. *Tried* to take the gun from you. In the pandemonium you, Jon ... Straker ... whoever you're supposed to be, got shot and killed. And I got the gun and Candy launched herself at me and in panic I fired. Even better, Candy got the gun and I fought her for it and she got shot. It'd work. Self-defence. It wouldn't even go to court.'

Jon nodded. 'Some of me rubbed off on you, Mr Thief,' he said. 'It is a fair attempt. Not excellent, but fair. However, the major flaw is that there *is* no gun. Unfortunately the only thing causing the death of these two bodies will be the departure of the souls.'

Jim pushed back his sheets, swung his legs out of the bed and stood up. The pain from his ankle was agonizing and he felt dizzy. 'You're still going to need signs of a struggle if you're going to come up with a convincing tale,' he said. He grabbed the night-stand and yanked it over, hopped over to the television on one leg and heaved it to the ground. It imploded with a fairly loud bang and shot glass across the room. He hopped over to Sooty's bed, pulled the bedclothes and mattress off it, threw her cabinet aside and overturned the chair that stood there.

Jon and Candy watched him impassively as he wrecked the room.

'If you're doing this to attract attention,' Jon said in a lull, 'you're out of luck. This is the high-security floor. The top floor of the building. There's no one above us. The floor below is empty. And there's no one else on this floor but the four of us. You can make as much noise as you wish, but no one will come to your aid.'

Sooty said, 'He's not doing it to attract attention. He's doing it to provide an alibi.'

'There's no need,' Jon said, now sounding exactly like Jim. The French accent had vanished, replaced with Jim's own peculiar American accent with a hint of the Scottish lilt. 'We'll simply carry these bodies back into their room and place them in their beds. No one will know why they've died. We don't need an alibi.'

At the back of the room, Jim picked up the water-cooler and dropped it on the floor. Then he stopped and faced Straker and Majesty, grinning through gritted teeth.

'You've got it wrong. It isn't you two who need the alibi. It's *us*.'

'Because just before you came in, Jim and I had a little chat,' Sooty said. 'We knew you were coming, you see. So we made a plan. Provided ourselves with a workable alibi. *We* need an alibi.'

'Because there *is* a gun,' Jim said, finishing with a friendly smile.

With her left hand Sooty whipped away the blanket from her lap and raised her right hand, in which Elaine's .357 Magnum was clutched, as steady as a rock. ''Bye,' she said, and fired two shots in quick succession.

Jon Short's head exploded and Candy took the hit in the

centre of her sternum. The bodies fell to the floor and stayed there, pools of blood and gore gathering.

'Guns don't kill people,' Sooty said, in the ringing silence. 'People kill people.'

Chapter Twenty-Five

Karpathos, Greece

For the third time in the last ten minutes, Sooty sat up and peered, across the heat-haze of the crescent of shingle beach on which she was lying, towards the track that wound down through the rocky hills.

Jim should have been up there in the distance by now, carefully making his way down the treacherous track on the trail bike he'd bought just after they'd moved here. She knew from experience that she would be able to see him a long time before she heard the growl of the motorcycle: the afternoon wind whipped the sound away from her and up into the dry Greek mountain spine of the island.

But he wasn't there yet and it made her uncomfortable. He'd been gone too long.

You have to get used to it sooner or later, she thought, glancing at Gloria, who sat at the water's edge, her feet in the flat, cobalt-blue Mediterranean and her head in a book. *We can't stay in one another's sight for ever.*

But they had stayed in one another's sight, almost, for the first six months. They'd stayed close because they could not bring themselves to believe it really was all over. There had been no god to keep the souls of Majesty and Straker alive, when she'd shot the bodies they were using back at the hospital, so the ghosts were gone. They'd hoped.

So they'd travelled. Over water. And here, on the quiet, sparsely populated island of Karpathos, in the Dodecanese chain, they'd found peace and comfort. There wasn't much here except a mountain range, a few little beaches, some of which were only accessible by boat, and a tiny town, but the moment they'd stepped off the tiny plane from the nearby island of Rhodes, they'd fallen in love with the place.

Arriving here had felt like coming home. And they'd stayed. And made plans to build a house here, up on the empty plane of rock above this very beach.

Jim had a new cruiser on the way – a slightly larger and more expensive version of *Mary Celeste* – except that this one would be named *Sooty G.*

Everything was fine. Or it would have been, if the feeling ever went away that something dreadful would happen soon.

What if he fell off? she thought, feeling that all-too-familiar tightening in the pit of her stomach. *What if he swerved to avoid a goat and drove over one of those steep drops?*

But the real question, the one she refused to verbalize, hung over her like a dark cloud. *What if Straker and Majesty found him?*

Way down the beach, so far away she couldn't pick out any of their features, the only other people on the beach – a couple who had been here already when she and Gloria had arrived – got up and ran splashing into the sea. They were naked and tanned almost mahogany. Sooty was getting used to seeing people around here sunbathing and swimming nude, and Jim stripped off the moment he got here, but so far Sooty hadn't been able to let herself do likewise. Being naked in the sun not only reminded her of Straker's Island but left her feeling horribly vulnerable. That was another thing she would have to work on.

She lay back and closed her eyes and waited. She dreamed of dolphins.

The moment she woke up, she sat up and looked down the beach towards the path. And there was Jim, in shorts and sandals and a baggy T-shirt, strolling down the beach towards her. Her heart leaped and relief swept through her. He still had a slight limp and his right wrist sometimes hurt him, but he was otherwise fitter and healthier than she'd seen him in years. He swam a lot, which was probably why his writer's stoop had gone and his muscles had filled out a little. He was carrying a newspaper in one hand and his snorkelling gear in the other and he was smiling.

He sat down beside her, grinning, kissed her and handed her the paper. While she unfolded it, he lit up a Pallas – a

382

Greek cigarette. He'd complained bitterly when he'd discovered that Virginia Slims weren't available on this island, then he'd discovered he was rather partial to the Greek ones anyway.

'There it is,' he said. 'Front-page news!'

The paper was a copy of *Publisher's Weekly*. It was two weeks out of date, which was pretty well par for the course around here. It didn't matter: life was lived at a snail's pace on this island and Sooty loved it. The banner headline read:

MASTER OF DISASTER JAMES GREEN QUITS WRITING

'It's official!' Jim said happily. 'I'm no longer a writer. I'm just going to do what I should have started to do two years ago. Spend the money I have and enjoy spending it. Spend my entire time thinking about good things rather than bad things – thinking about those I love. You and Gloria.' He took Sooty's chin, tilted her head towards him and gently kissed her mouth. 'Hey, why the tears?' he asked. Then kissed them away from her cheeks and eyes.

'Happy tears,' Sooty said. 'They're happy, hopeful tears.'

Neither of them saw the two people approaching them until they were close enough for their shadows to block out the sun.

Jim looked up and gasped. He couldn't see the faces because the sun was right behind them but he recognized the size and shape of the bodies: one voluptuous female with blonde hair, one stocky young man. His heart almost burst through his chest. *It can't be! Jon and Candy are gone! It can't be them!*

Everything froze.

Who else could it be? he asked himself, in the silence.

Beside him, he heard movement as he stared up, trying to see the faces – which seemed blurred, as if they were ... *shimmering*. He knew what the movement was, because he'd heard it before. Would probably hear it for the rest of his life, if his life got past this moment. It was Sooty dragging her already-open bag towards her and putting her hand into it. A moment later he heard the metallic *click!* as Sooty cocked the hammer of Elaine's .357 Magnum.

383

'James Green?' the man asked, in Jon Short's voice. '*The* James Green?'

For a moment Jim couldn't speak. His head felt like it might explode and the bones in his wrist and ankle ached with the memory. Then he heard himself say. 'What if I am?'

'If you *are*,' the man said, reaching into the bag that dangled from his shoulder and whipping out what Jim first saw as a gun, 'I'd be really, *really* pleased if you'd sign this copy of *Shimmer* for me! It's the best book I've *ever* read!'

Beside him, he heard Sooty gently make the gun safe again.

With shaking hands, Jim took the book and waited for someone to hand him a pen.